MW01259172

UNTIL WE SHATTER

Also by Kate Dylan

Mindwalker
Mindbreaker

An Illumicrate exclusive signed edition of

UNTIL WE SHATTER

Signed by the author

KATE DYLAN

Published by Hodderscape in association with
Illumicrate, October 2024

UNTIL WE SHATTER

KATE DYLAN

HODDERSCAPE

This one was to prove to myself I could.

First published in Great Britain in 2024 by Hodderscape
An imprint of Hodder & Stoughton Limited
An Hachette UK company

1

Copyright © Kate Dylan 2024

The right of Kate Dylan to be identified as the Author of the Work has been asserted by her in accordance with the Copyright, Designs and Patents Act 1988.

All rights reserved. No part of this publication may be reproduced, stored in a retrieval system, or transmitted, in any form or by any means without the prior written permission of the publisher, nor be otherwise circulated in any form of binding or cover other than that in which it is published and without a similar condition being imposed on the subsequent purchaser.

All characters in this publication are fictitious and any resemblance to real persons, living or dead, is purely coincidental.

A CIP catalogue record for this title is available from the British Library

Hardback ISBN 978 1 399 72873 7
Trade Paperback ISBN 978 1 399 72874 4
ebook ISBN 978 1 399 72876 8

Typeset in Baskerville MT Std by Manipal Technologies Limited

Printed and bound in Great Britain by Clays Ltd, Elcograf S.p.A.

Hodder & Stoughton policy is to use papers that are natural, renewable and recyclable products and made from wood grown in sustainable forests. The logging and manufacturing processes are expected to conform to the environmental regulations of the country of origin.

Hodder & Stoughton Limited
Carmelite House
50 Victoria Embankment
London EC4Y 0DZ

www.hodderscape.co.uk

Dear reader,

Let me tell you a story about a terrible idea that so desperately wanted to be good.

Back in 2018, this book started life as a manuscript called The In-Betweens, *and it was about the tooth fairy. Yes, you read that right:* Until We Shatter *was originally conceptualized as a portal fantasy about the tooth fairy—and yes, the concept was so bad that when I showed the first chapter to my (then) agent, she promptly urged me to write something else.*

So I did.

I wrote Mindwalker, *and then* Mindbreaker, *and they went on to become my debut and sophomore novels. But as much as I loved writing those sci-fi books, I always knew I would return to writing fantasy eventually, and the central concept of that tooth fairy book—which, hilariously enough, had nothing to do with the tooth fairy—kept niggling at me.*

A girl who could only survive our world by staying in between things.

By 2020, when I was ready to tackle this idea again, I had been firmly informed that nobody—and I mean nobody—was looking for this kind of fae (wings were in, teeth were out), and so my tooth fairy became a witch and my misguided portal fantasy became a contemporary fantasy set in New York.

Which still didn't feel right.

But it wasn't until the end of 2022, when it came time for me to pitch my editor a new book, that I finally realized the reason this story wasn't working: it was too big for our world. The idea was crying out for a world of its own—two worlds, in fact—and that meant it was time to leave my comfort zone and make it a full-blown second-world fantasy.

And so my witch became a Shade, New York became the walled city of Isitar, and instead of heisting teeth, my girl found herself at the heart of a deadly heist across two realms—one of which could shatter her to pieces. The only part of this book that never changed was the concept of the In-Betweens; everything else reformed around that central premise until, finally, after almost five years of trying, I had the right version of the story. An older, darker, more complex version, but every bit as full of action and fun.

I'd like to say that it was easy going from that point on, but that would be a lie. Pure creation is terrifying for me, and there was a lot I wanted to do with this book. I wanted messy bi girls, and pretty lying boys, and a dysfunctional found family who always makes the worst decisions. Then I wanted to give them a bunch of rainbow magics and see what happens when they're backed into a corner.

Until We Shatter *is my most ambitious book to date, and the one I'm most excited—and nervous!—about sharing. As with all my books, it's designed to be a fun (if stressful) read first and foremost, though if you choose to look deeper, you might find that it's actually a book about the dangers of misinformation.*

I hope I've done it justice. I hope you fall in love with Cemmy and the gang as much as I did. But most of all, I hope that once you get to the end, you'll forgive me ;)

Love,
Kate

THE SEVEN SHADES OF MAGIC

Red
to control

Orange
to strengthen

Yellow
to alter

Green
to heal

Blue
to hasten

Indigo
to foresee

Violet
to know

CHAPTER

One

The problem with only being half a Shade is that you only have half the magic.

And half the magic equals half the power.

Which, by some cruel twist of luck, equals twice the problems.

Hells, it downright triples them on a bad night. I retreat into the depths of my hood, appraising the Governor's manse with a growing unease. The house looms large before me, an intimidating construction of ash-colored bricks, white accent windows, and steeply pitched slate tiles, with a manicured lawn that yawns too wide and too deep.

Too dangerous.

Sweat beads at my temples, the urge to turn tail and flee nipping at my insides. Though Vargas had promised to clear my way of guards and leave the two doors I'll need to navigate unlocked, now that I'm actually here, staring up at this Church-blessed goliath, it suddenly feels as though I'm facing an impossible task—especially since I don't trust him enough to traverse the grounds in the real world: I mean to do it in the Gray, where I'll only have sixty seconds in which to reach the study.

Half a Shade, double the problems, remember? I don't get to dip in and out of the shadow realm whenever I please like Mom could; I need a bridge. An In-Between. And midnight is the king of all In-Betweens. A full minute between night and day where I can move freely through the world that exists in tandem to our own, like an overlaid echo. Where I don't have to be so afraid.

Then stop hesitating like a coward and start acting like a thief. The moment the twelfth bell rings out across the city, I set the time-keeper cuff at my wrist ticking, phasing into the Gray right as the temporal In-Between seizes hold. Night turns to smoke and color to black ink, affording me the freedom to dispense with discretion. Since typics can't see into the shadow realm, speed trumps stealth in the Gray, so I need not waste precious time creeping between corners or quieting my steps.

Ten long strides and I'm across the yard.

Fifteen short seconds and I'm safely through the front door.

Five more and I'm barreling towards the study marked on Vargas's map.

Around me, the rooms are rendered in a rainbow of ash and charcoal, the antique furniture stripped of its honeyed luster, as though viewed through a monochromatic lens. That's just what things look like in the Gray . . . gray and hazy, a smoke-clad replica of their counterparts in the real world. Or at least that's what they look like to *me*. The way we experience the shadows differs based on the shade of our magic; the distinct manner in which our typical parent diluted the color flowing through our veins. Our hue, if you like. That's why we're often referred to as Hues. Since Mom is an Orange, Mom plus a typic equals a Bronze. And since Orange Shades specialize in strength-based magics—spells that serve to fortify, affect, or weaken—my power translates to a physical gift in the Gray. It's not a direct translation—our gifts don't tend to manifest in entirely linear ways; they're more like an offshoot of our base color's specialization, a sideward twist on the magical feats that they perform. In my case, the ability to feel, and move, and touch objects—and take them. And if I take something in the Gray, I take it outside the Gray, too, all while remaining invisible to prying eyes.

It really is the perfect crime.

Or it *would* be.

If my accomplice had remembered to leave *both* doors unlocked.

By my colors, Vargas, you had one job. I curse as the latch to the study squeals in denial, the metal clanging hard beneath my fingers. *I'm going to flay you alive, you pompous, pious, unreliable piece of—*

Breathe, Cemmy. I try the handle again, and again, and again, drowning out the rhythmic tick of my cuff. *Panic won't get you through this door. Neither will anger.* Which is a shame since I've always been quick to both, with a bark that's infinitely worse than my bite—or my follow-through. I am the fist that stops an inch shy of your nose. And if I don't keep my head, I'll wind up losing it entirely.

So think more, curse less. I force in another breath as I assess the lock. With enough time, I could pick it, but time is the one thing I don't have, and the only reason I agreed to rob the godsdamned *Governor of Isitar* in the first place is because it was supposed to be easy. Despite what my friends might tell you, I don't have a death wish, and even if I did, the death inflicted upon those who seek to steal from power wouldn't be my first choice—I wouldn't trust the blood-hungry sadist wielding the blade to finish me off clean. That's why, as a rule, I leave the ruling class alone. They might all be pinch-faced misers who'll spend more coin on their caskets than the average citizen will make in several lifetimes, but the city's merchants are plenty gold-flush too and robbing *them* isn't a capital crime.

Which is why you should have said no. Everything about Vargas's offer was strange, especially since he doesn't know I'm a half Shade; if he knew that, I'd be dead, not attempting to fleece his master. When he caught me flirting with his pockets, he should have dragged me straight from the tavern to the law—if for no other reason than I was careless enough to try and rob the Governor's personal aide in the first place, a man whose face I'd have easily recognized had I not been so distracted by the contents of his purse. Instead, he'd leaned closer and whispered, *how would you like to stop scrounging for scraps?* And when a member of Isitar's hard-nosed elite inexplicably offers to trade your prison sentence for a bigger score, the only questions you ask are: where, when, and what's my cut of the job?

Vargas promised me enough coin to keep my head above water for *years*.

And I was desperate enough to believe him.

Ever since Mom got sick, desperation is pretty much where I live.

Make a decision here, Cemmy. My foot taps a nervous staccato against the varnished floorboards. My cuff is thirty-eight clicks into its rotation, which means I only have twenty-two seconds left until my typical half is no longer welcome in the Gray. So now my choices are—in ascending order of stupidity: abort the lift and try again another night; phase back into the real world and hope the Governor's staff don't catch me in the act; or attempt to make my own In-Between once the midnight one elapses.

It's a risky bit of magic. A spell that requires both mental strength and control. Using only my words and my will, I'd have to physically *repel* the shadows, anchor my power to my surroundings in order to prevent the Gray from collapsing back in.

Which might be hard but it's not impossible . . . The voice in my head takes a valiant stab at feigning mettle. This indulgence of a manse certainly boasts enough junk to support the spell. Right now, I'm standing at the neck of a narrow, wood-paneled corridor, in between two mammoth portraits of the ghosts of Governors past. Their size and proximity should make it easy enough to sustain the magic—the bigger and closer my anchor objects are, the more likely it is the In-Between will hold firm—then once I'm safely sequestered in the study, I could slip out of the Gray and deal with the safe in peace, just as I'd originally planned. Even fleeing the crime wouldn't pose that big of a risk, seeing how there's an embarrassment of overpriced furniture stationed between here and the door. Plenty of metaphorical scaffolding on which to anchor my In-Betweens.

It's definitely not impossible.

Up until last year, I'd have done it without hesitating one bit.

Thirteen seconds left, Cemmy. You in or out?

Habit has me twisting Dad's ring around my finger for strength, the familiar slide of metal working to conquer my nerves. *In.* I fish my picks out of my back pocket, where they've lived since the day I learned to crack a lock. It shouldn't take me long to break through this one; the Governor's zero-tolerance policy towards magic means it's not protected by any spell—few things are on the *reformed* side of Isitar, where religion's overtaken logic in the war against Shades.

There's no reason I can't tease it open and keep an In-Between around me at the same time. No reason except fear.

"I am in between the two portraits and the door." I start chanting the words aloud, lacing each syllable with conviction. Technically speaking, I'm in between a lot of things—the floor and the ceiling, the study and the hall, the porch at the front of the manse and the garden at its rear . . . or if you want to get esoteric about it, I'm in between typic and Shade, my nineteenth and twentieth name day, birth and death. In theory, I could turn any one of those fanciful states into an In-Between—beat back the Gray by holding the idea of them in my mind and speaking my magic around their edges—but in practice, that would be like trying to tie a rope around the ocean. Corporeal anchors trump figurative ones; stationary ones trump moving; and the more solid they are, the better. Which is why I'm staking my life on the nearest, most tangible objects in the room.

"I am in between the two portraits and the door."

Around me, the air ripples, solidifying as my magic trickles out to form a shield, an impenetrable barrier between me and the Gray.

"The two portraits and the door."

Thing is, the Gray doesn't much care for tricksy little half Shades who abuse their visitation rights. Push the shadows too far and they'll happily start pushing *back*.

"I am in between the two portraits and the door."

I brace for the way my task will harden once my cuff emits its final *click*. For the way the darkness will suck back in around me and try to pulverize my bones.

"The two portraits and the—*fuck*."

The moment the midnight In-Between collapses, I lose my nerve and phase back into the physical realm, my bounty forgotten, my mind buzzing with the memory of what befell the last half Shade to overstay their welcome in the Gray. The sound Magdalena made when the shadows shattered her to pieces.

Crack, clink, crunch, shatter.

No amount of coin is worth splintering like glass.

No matter how much I need it.

What you need is to move. *Now.* I press my body flat against the wall, praying to all three Gods that the guards will stay gone another fractured minute. That they won't deign to investigate the urgent squeak of boots on varnish or notice the hooded figure inching its way towards the door. Which is—thankfully—still unlocked. I wince as the wood creaks open, the cold night air stinging the relief in my throat.

Out. You made it out. I will my cards to stay lucky as I slink away from the manse, keeping low and quiet until I'm safely back on the street. Only then do I notice the sweat soaking through my doublet and the rush of blood pounding in my ears. The violent shake trembling my fingers.

That escape was far too close for comfort.

Far too reckless and too rash.

An act of theft against the Governor would have already spelled my death, but if even a single guard had witnessed me phasing out of the shadows, then I'd have really been done for. As a half Shade, my very existence makes me illegal—on both sides of the magical divide—and getting caught *existing* by the reformists, well . . . that would have taken a quick death off the table. The Church's tastes run far crueler.

Damn it to the deepest of hells. My nails gouge bloody half-moons into my palms. I had one shot at landing this score and I blew it—all because Vargas couldn't keep his promise and I'm too much of a coward to take an actual risk. I could have held that In-Between long enough to pick one measly lock; I've done it before, on more than one occasion. Half Shade or not, my magic is capable of that much. There are even tales of Hues anchoring their shields across continents, traversing entire mountain ranges through the Gray without fear. But now that the sickness has reached Mom's lungs, my fear has me by the marrow. The expensive cocktail of tinctures she needs to keep her blood from thickening is near impossible to steal, and paying for it has me running way more jobs than a year's worth of midnights could cover. If I'm reckless enough to get caught or shatter, I won't just be killing me.

Since the Governor's manse sits to the west of the holy quarter—a stone's throw away from the parliament chambers, the military barracks, and the city's eminent holy plaza—it takes me an hour to snake back to the faithless—sorry, the *east*—side of Isitar, where the Church's reach turns brittle and the shadows grow teeth. There's no *official* divide, of course. No wall or gate or line inked across the concentric maze of stone-cobbled streets. Why would there be, when, as far as the Conclave's concerned, there's no *official* problem. There's only those who have been reformed, and those still in need of some . . . persuasion. And since all but one of our elected officials are now religiously inclined, vote by vote, quarter by quarter, the zealots are starting to win.

First, they tore down the hex-lights, replaced them with a magic born of science and coal. Then they came for the spells, the charm houses, the potion halls, all the tiny ways a Shade can improve on the ordinary—for a price. And when that only served to anger the faithless, the fragile truce that kept tensions at a low simmer slowly bubbled to the boil. Then came the riots. The negotiations. Another delicate truce. The Council of Shades lays claim to the east, while the Church devoured the west, but with mountains to the north and an ocean grinning around us, there are few places left for the seething anger to go. So now the great walled city of Isitar teeters on the brink of a reckoning. Safe from everything except the war brewing within itself.

Like the rings of an aging oak tree, the city's streets spiral down from a central crest towards the cliffs that line the water, the buildings growing smaller in size as they near the encompassing wall. But though my strides lose their haste once I've returned to the faithless quarter, by the time I hit the densely packed crush that marks Isitar's outermost ring, my anger has given way to a dark, twisting dread, the kind that chews through your skin and burrows deep into your bones. I just traded a night picking pockets in chase of a fantasy. Right when I most needed a big score. Maybe that's why instead of heading home to face the music, I reach for the trio of scrys hanging around my neck. My direct link to Novi, Ezzo, and Eve.

Show me. I clasp the crystals in my hand, willing the Shade-forged bonds to find my friends awake and at our usual haunt. Though the damn things cost me a small fortune—Indigo magic is expensive, and no pre-spelled talisman has ever come cheap—I've never regretted spending the coin. There's a comfort in being able to check up on the people who matter to me most. A convenience in being able to pass them messages at will and having a facility with which to glean their location, ensure that they haven't fallen foul of a Church enforcer, or lost their life to a Council tracker's blade. In knowing they're safe.

The scrys warm against my skin, rewarding me with a vision of the three of them together, exactly where I hoped they would be. *Well, at least one thing's gone right tonight.* I'm already carving a path towards the abandoned monastery we've claimed for our own. From the outside, it still looks every bit as ruined as the riots left it: all burned stone, soot-covered windows, and an explosive fury towards the Church. But on the inside, it's a whole different story. Novi's a Cobalt, which makes speed her gift in the Gray, but in the real world, she excels at compelling favors. With little more than a smile, she sweet-talked an Orange Shade into magically augmenting our den. No matter how cold the nights get, the nave remains the perfect temperature, the crumbling roof repels the rain, and a handy twist on a warding spell keeps the roaches and rats—and the trackers—at bay.

It's the kind of magic I *should* get to enjoy at home, but even if the Council hadn't bound Mom's magic, she would have probably found a way to bind it herself. *Actions deserve consequences, Cemilla,* she used to tell me, back before I learned the futility of raising that point. *I made my choice when I knowingly broke their rules.*

That choice was me, by the way, since the Council's rules basically amount to: no magic for the typics without payment, no typics in the Gray, and for the sweet love of blood color, do not procreate with them. Because the inevitable halves won't exist in balance with the Gray; they'll drain it. Siphon power from the shadows instead of nourishing the haze. And contrary to what the laws of logic would lead you to believe, two half Shades don't make a whole, they just make a load more half Shades—albeit with a little less power and a weaker command of their gifts. A further dilution of a dilution. A drain that would only grow more egregious if *those* half Shades saw fit to breed with the typics as well.

Allow too many of us to exist and the shadow world begins to dim.

The magic begins to fail.

That's why the Gray works so hard to expel us.

So when the Council discovered that Mom had the audacity to marry a typic in secret, they did what they always do to traitors—they punished her. Which is a nice way of saying: they murdered him. They'd have murdered me, too, if Mom hadn't run while their binding spell was still sapping her veins of magic. If she hadn't spent every last coin she had changing her name and glamouring her face in order to escape their trackers, to keep them from discovering that she was with child.

I don't approach the monastery in plain view—even on a moonless night, at the forgotten end of the city, that act of reformist loyalty might draw attention. Instead, I jump the crumbling wall to the surrounding cemetery and phase into the Gray. Burial grounds provide a permanent In-Between, a spatial bridge between life and death that allows for unlimited access to the shadows, no matter the time of day. Sanctuaries, we call them. And this sanctuary allows me to phase out of view and enter through the door without fear.

But not without guilt.

Mom's face shames a path through my mind. She worries when I'm out past midnight—because she's sick, not clueless, and she knows exactly what kind of *work* I've been doing to make ends meet. Even if she doesn't know I've been doing it in the shadows.

I'll only stay a few minutes, I vow as I slip into the building and out of the Gray. *Ten minutes then home.* Though the moment I enter the magically embellished ruin, I know that's a lie. Ever since Mom fell ill, it's been my refuge, the one place that unsticks my shoulders from around my ears and releases the tension crackling between my nerves. There's just something so comforting about the hex-lights Novi hung like stars across the vaulted ceiling, the mismatched furniture

Ezzo scavenged from a retiring merchant, and the vivid jungle of wildflowers Eve painted along the walls. It's our home away from home. Not a sanctuary in the magical sense of the word, but every bit a sanctuary all the same. A necessary escape.

"How'd the lift go?" Novi's eyes find me the instant I step inside, the intensity of her gaze sending a maddening flush to my cheeks. Of the four of us, she's the only one resisting the Church-driven pressure to blend in. To make herself smaller. Duller. Invisible. Her hair is spelled an impossible white, shaved close on the sides, but long and mussed in the center, a stark contrast to her flint-black irises, ebony skin, and the silver vines tattooed into her scalp. The glamours that alter appearance aren't illegal on this side of the city—not yet, anyhow—and they're available to any Hue, Shade, or typic who has the coin to pay. But marking yourself as *faithless* in any way is a dangerous game in this age of zealous reform. Akin to wearing a target.

Novi doesn't care. If I'm the fist that stops an inch shy of your nose, then she's the punch that breaks it bloody, and she'll only hide the parts of herself that actually garner a death sentence.

It's what I love most about her.

That, and the fact that she doesn't make me speak my failures aloud; she's known me long enough to read the answer in my expression.

"Shit, Cemmy. I knew this job was too good to be true. Bastard tried to sell you out, didn't he?"

"Nothing quite so dramatic." I shrug out of my hooded cowl. If Vargas wanted me caught, he'd have stationed guards at every corner of the Governor's manse—and they'd have definitely spotted me when I phased out of the Gray in my reckless panic. No, this feels more like a case of greed eclipsing power. A man making a promise he didn't have the gall to keep. "He neglected to unlock the study door like he was supposed to. Probably got cold feet."

"That still makes him a bastard, Cem," Ezzo calls from across the nave, where he and Eve are sitting intertwined on the battered daybed, her head in his lap and his hands absently weaving her long hair into a braid.

"And a coward." Eve flashes me her dimples. "I'm sensing some serious cowardly cleric vibes."

None of them press me for details—or ask why I didn't pick my way through the lock. They never do when a job goes sideward, because we all know I'd be out celebrating right now if only I wasn't afraid of the shadows, or if I'd taken a single one of them up on the offer to help run the lift. And before you think it, no, I wasn't trying to avoid sharing the coin. I might be the reigning champion of bad decisions, but I'm not a self-serving scrooge. It's just that the last time I talked a friend into *helping*, I made it out of the Gray and Magdalena didn't.

And I won't have another shattered Shade on my conscience.

I won't survive it.

"You going to try again?" Eve asks, making space for me among the threadbare cushions. "Because if you are, then my offer still stands: I can buy you as much time as you need." Where my skin is white and pale, hers is all gold and umber. Black hair to my blond, soft brown eyes to my icy blue, a face as innocent as she is sweet. Eve is also an Emerald, which makes forging In-Betweens her gift in the Gray. The spell comes more instinctively to her; she can hold it much longer than the average Hue, tether it to smaller anchors across larger distances—even bolster it enough to survive in sleep. And unlike the rest of us, she can also project it to shield another half *without* the aid of physical contact. An obvious choice for a job like this—if not for the fact that forging an In-Between around others is the one thing that puts her at greater risk of shattering herself.

"I don't know—maybe." I rock back and forth on my heels, clinging hard to the belief that I'm *not* staying that long. "The coin might be worth it."

"Not if it exposes you." Ezzo fixes me his most disapproving look, the warmth leeching out of his brown complexion. He doesn't much like it when I drag Eve into my plans, and he downright hates it when a lift forces us over to the reformed side of Isitar, doesn't think it's worth the risk now that the Council's on high alert for anything—or *anyone*—that might set a spark to the rising tensions. Because the only thing worse than waging battle against a Church that's hells-bent on wiping you out, is having a bunch of illegal Hues running amok around the city, thoughtlessly stoking the flames.

"I'm careful, Ez. You know I am," I say.

Unless I panic, I'm as careful as it gets.

"Then be extra careful." Novi steals up behind me, dipping a hand into my back pocket. When I leave, I'll find a few scattered coins in there. Nowhere near as many as I need—she can't spare that much help, and I'd never accept it—but enough to buy me a day or two. Keep my head above water.

That is why I came here, isn't it?

Because when I'm in trouble, Novi's the one who pulls me out.

And that's never changed even though everything else between us has.

Dawn is breaking by the time I make it home—tense, tired, and thoroughly ticked off—the ghost of my failure drumming a tattoo inside my skull. On my way in, I slip Novi's gift under Madam Berska's door, to keep her off my case a little longer. As much as it pains me to admit it, she's not actually a villain; I've just pushed my luck with her one too many times. I need to make more of an effort to prove I'm trying.

Mom's labored breaths greet me as I sneak into the apartment, announcing my final failure of the night: I stayed out too late again. Left her worrying into an uneasy sleep. Quiet as I can manage, I tiptoe over to the washroom and seal myself inside, running the tub full and the contents piping. Scrubbing raw the shame.

When I break down, it's under the surface, where my tears won't infect Mom's dreams.

But once the water grows cold, my eyes are dry and my mind is made up.

Tomorrow, I go back to finish the job.

CHAPTER
Two

Finishing the job is, of course, easier said than done, since without Vargas, I've no hope of getting near the Governor's safe. No plan for convincing him to try again, either, now that the resolve from last night's anger has evaporated away.

If only you had Novi's charm. My whole body warms beneath the bed sheets, a wild heat flooding my veins as I remember all those times she's turned it on me. How dangerous her smile gets when we stay up late, drinking. How careful we have to be not to get too drunk to remember that we've been there, done that, vowed to *stop* doing it. That *I* vowed to stop doing it. Because I'd rather lose the heady bliss of her touch, and her scent, and her kiss, if it means not facing up to the truth that would cost me everything.

Why won't you tell me what's wrong, Cem? When did you stop trusting me?

It's amazing how much damage a single lie can wreak.

Even when it's designed to do the opposite.

"Cemilla?" Mom's worry gruffs through the paper-thin walls, rousing me back to the present and out of bed, to begin my morning routine of getting her fed and comfortable.

"Coming, Mom." I slip into the nearest pair of loose pants and an oversized woolen shirt, the morning chill biting at my fingers. *Mired veins*, the doctors called her condition, a degenerative illness that turns the blood thick, making it harder to move and eat, and eventually, breathe. On a good day, she can still manage all the basics herself—our apartment is small enough for her to get around, and

I've long since rearranged the kitchen to accommodate her failing strength. But if she overexerts herself on a good day, then a bad day is sure to follow. And a bad day costs us both more than we're able to pay. I've all but run out of ways to afford the good ones.

"You were out so late, I wasn't sure you came home," she says as I step into the living room, each breath a labor and every syllable a strain, the pain in her eyes dulling their blue of its luster. The two of us used to look alike, back before the sickness hollowed her frail. Same heart-shaped face and delicate features. Same high-cut cheekbones and pointed curve to the chin. But now the blond in her hair has been stripped to frayed wire, and when she smiles, her skin pulls tight with unease, as though her bones are trying to escape their wrappings.

"I know, I'm sorry. I lost track of time." I set to making our breakfast, a sour mix of guilt and hunger churning in my gut. In a perfect world, I'd get Mom a scry to wear and then she wouldn't have to worry; she'd be able to check in on my whereabouts and send me messages at will. Which is, coincidentally, the exact reason I can't risk giving her a scry. Because if Mom so much as glimpsed the true depth of my desperation—or realized that I've not only stooped to robbing the clergy, but that I'm doing it in the Gray—she'd never let me out of her sight again. She'd stop eating, and sleeping, and taking her medications, until she withered to a lifeless husk in her splintering armchair. So while I might not be able to keep the paint on our walls from peeling or the threat of eviction from our door, I can feign enough hope to keep her light from dimming. Ever since I watched Magdalena shatter, I've found myself feigning more hope than most.

"And you still have your ring?" Though *that* question agitates me a little more each time she asks it, the relentless reminder cutting short my fuse.

"It's right here, Mom." I hold my hand up for her to inspect. "I never take it off." Even though fencing it would solve all our problems. The delicate gold band is inlaid with a dozen diamonds, a treasure that would fill our coffers and Mom's tincture bottle for years. But as far as she's concerned, the ring is a priceless heirloom. A gift from the father I never got to know.

He made this ring to conceal your magic, she told me, over and over so that the message would stick. *No matter what happens, it must remain with you.* Why she picked such a fanciful lie, I don't know. It's not as if anyone can tell what I am just by looking, and when you cut us, we all bleed red—full and half Shades alike. Our colors are more akin to an essence that lives in the blood. An aura. A Shade can see it radiating off another Shade, but we Hues are trickier to identify. Not quite *enough* color in the blood, you see. We can only be exposed by getting caught in the act of phasing. But since there's no convincing Mom that her life is worth more than a sentimental trinket, I wear the ring. The perfectly ordinary, perfectly powerless ring that could buy our way out of poverty, because the one time I suggested selling it, her anger grew too frightening to behold.

"You're a good girl, Cemilla," she says when I place a tray of honeyed oatmeal and ginger tea across her lap. "I wish you didn't have to do so much."

"Then let me take you to see a Green." The plea escapes before I can stop it. Before I can remind myself that we've already exhausted every last version of this fight. "I'll find a way to get the coin." *Somehow.* "Enough to buy the healing *and* the Shade's silence. Then once you're better, everything would go back to—" The thunder in Mom's expression cuts my appeal off at the pass, her voice shaking around the same four words she utters every time I make this request.

"No Shades, no healing. We've been through this, Cemilla. I will not endanger your life."

You're endangering it now. I tamp down the objection with a scalding sip of my tea. *And for no damn reason.* It's been twenty years since the Council bound Mom's power, and in all that time, not a single tracker has ever picked up our trail—the only threat to our lives has been her blood-borne illness, and that's a problem with a clearer-cut fix. We are far enough removed from those who might remember her crimes to indulge in one singular spell. The casting Shade wouldn't even have to know she has a daughter; I could pay a sympathetic typic to make the arrangements in my stead. But whether it's guilt, or shame, or her own lingering fear of the Council, Mom's made it plenty clear that she'd rather die than risk exposing me—and I might well die trying to keep that from happening.

I guess that's why they call love the deadliest shade of all.

"You're right, I'm sorry." After last night's failure, I can't bring myself to prolong the argument in another futile effort to change her mind. "I'll go back to the apothecary today, see if they managed to get any new bottles of Green label." This lie I've told so often, it barely even stings my tongue. Though Mom can survive on her regime of magicless tonics, the spell-infused tincture is the only remedy that would come close to fully restoring her health. But it also happens to be so ludicrously expensive, that even if Isitar weren't in the midst of a shortage, there's no way I could foot the bill. You can add that to the long list of grievances I have with the Church: it's systematically depleting the city's contingent of Shades, driving them to seek greener pastures—wherever those might be. So now a tincture that used to cost more coin than I could steal in a week costs enough to keep me thieving for months. And while Novi could help me charm a healing from one of the Green Shades that's yet to leave the city, the apothecary owners aren't quite so forgiving. Not while I'm still deep in debt to every single one.

"We'll make do if they don't," Mom says, and when her eyes find mine again, their gaze is both ardent and clear. "I know you're doing your best, Cemilla. All that matters is that you're staying safe."

Safe.

The word plagues the rest of my morning, the naïve weight of it bearing down on my spine. I can't exactly blame Mom for being so oblivious—the reason she doesn't realize how bad things have gotten is because I won't let her see. But some days it hurts to be reminded of just how good I've gotten at lying. How the mask I wear at home is the only version of her daughter she wants me to be.

That version won't do you any good here. I pull my hood over my hair as I approach my meet with Vargas, steeling myself for a conversation I have to swing my way. I need him to agree to help me run the lift again. And since I'm woefully inept at Novi's charm-based brands of persuasion, I'll have to play the one card that never fails to win. Good old-fashioned greed. The only thing that flows more readily than ale at the Hidden Son tavern.

Where the faithless and the reformed unite in sin, reads the sign above the door. An accurate indictment of the crowd awaiting me inside. As one of the seedier establishments to sit along Isitar's outermost ring, this place is an oasis for those who claim to hate magic but enjoy the convenience and luxury a Shade can bring.

Before the Conclave decided to put the screws to blood color, the upper echelons of the Church were able to afford a magical solution to all their ills. When their bodies broke, a Green could heal them. If their homes needed protecting, an Orange enchantment could fortify their bones. Why spend years pouring over tedious texts when that knowledge is easily imparted by a Violet? Why preen when you can pay a Red for a glamour, or labor needlessly when unpleasant tasks can be accelerated to great speeds by a Blue? And why worry yourself sick when, with enough coin, an Indigo's taste of the future can be glimpsed and traded, your rags turned to riches by a Yellow's thrall.

Then there's the less visible—but equally useful—magics: the spell-infused tinctures, the amulets, the pre-made talismans and charms; all the hex-lights, and mood stones, and scrys. Shade-made but market-sold. Able to be used by anyone. And while the faithful were happy enough to renounce those spells for power, actually giving up the magic proved harder. So now they come to places like this, where the floors are sticky, and the seats are worn, the mead stale and watered-down, but the evils plenty. Where the Church would never think to look for its esteemed clerics.

Or their treacherous little aides.

I arrive at the fourth bell as Vargas instructed, striding in to find him waiting for me at the forgotten end of the bar, his cloak pulled low to hide his face, his hands nursing a near-empty tankard. Had my lift gone as planned, we'd be meeting here to split the bounty; he trusted me enough to honor that tenuous agreement. Largely—I suspect—because of the authority he commands as the Governor's aide. Had I double-crossed him, I've no doubt he'd have used his considerable resources to find me, and since he knew how badly I need the coin, I'd venture he knew *why* I need it, and that I couldn't just flee the city with the contents of the Governor's safe. He'd have had Mom rounded up and used her against me.

He still might.

Tread lightly here, Cemmy. I will my anger to stay at a soft whimper as I perch atop the neighboring stool. Vargas might make for a terrible ally, but he'd be downright dangerous as an enemy, and I can't afford to kindle his ire.

"The study door wasn't open; I couldn't make the lift." My words are the tip of a carefully considered iceberg, only betraying the barest hint of accusation.

"The Governor chose to dismiss me early." Vargas's eyes stay glued to the amber liquid staining his cup. "Why didn't you pick the lock?"

Because that wasn't the deal, you bastard. The muscles in my jaw clench tight. "Not enough time."

"Did you even try?"

I shouldn't have had to try. If I grind my teeth any harder, they're going to splinter and crack. Taking care of the locks was his job. It was the only reason I agreed to carry out this monumentally dangerous lift in the first place, and the one obstacle I didn't account for beating. The single promise Vargas had to keep.

And now he's making it my fault. I want nothing more than to rip back his hood and expose the coward underneath. Let the whole tavern see the ugly truth of Isitar's self-proclaimed elite. How they're no better than the rest of us. Instead, I bite the irritation down and say, "You should have found a way to warn me if you couldn't make good on your part of the plan." Saved us both from taking an unnecessary risk.

"Remember yourself, *Cemilla.*" Vargas wields my name in threat. A reminder that he knew who I was long before I had the audacity to try and pick his pockets. Knew what I could do—and what I *would* do if he drew my eye to his alluring abundance of wealth. Ensured I was the right kind of desperate to accept the job. "I won't hesitate to expose you for what you are." A note of steel creeps into his voice, the spear of his nose cutting in my direction. And though I know he means *thief*, not *Hue*, the words are still an anvil to the gut.

I am treading some deep, deep water here.

And in a fight with the clergy, the faithless aren't wont to win.

"But as luck would have it, I need that coin as much as you do," Vargas continues, absolving me of the need to sway his hand. "Which is why tonight, you'll be trying again." He slides a heavy key across the bar top.

Unbelievable.

"You couldn't have given this to me before?"

"I shouldn't be giving it to you now." The gold in his irises glows bright despite the hooded shadows. It's not a natural color—not for the pious, or for those with blasphemy in their blood—but rather a mark of the Church. A pigment they feed those who renounce the lure of magic that settles in the eyes and skin. "If you're caught, I'll swear on the holy sacraments that you stole this from me," he says.

And they'll believe him. My fingers twitch as they close around the cold metal. It's not just the risk I'm taking—again—that's gnawing at my insides. It's not even the capital nature of the crime we're committing, or the fact that in a game of he said/she said, Vargas would easily claim the win. It's just that something about his demeanor unnerves me down to the core. He was as jittery as a captive squirrel when he first proposed this endeavor, but now that edge has grown downright infectious. His hands grip his tankard too tightly, his shoulders tense in their hunch, his head hanging too suspiciously low and damp with sweat, as though he's finally realized what this treason might cost him.

Bastard wants the payday but none of the danger that comes with it.

None of the betrayal.

If this lift goes south, he wants to keep his damn job, not just avoid the blade.

"You'll have to clear the coast of guards again for me," I say. Because I shouldn't be the only one risking my neck for this coin, and because—as far as Vargas knows—I won't be creeping through the house in the Gray.

"I am perfectly aware of my obligations, Cemilla. And you'd do well to meet yours." With a final mouthful of ale, he pushes away from the bar, and it's only once he's swept out of the tavern that I realize he never bothered to confirm the particulars of our next meet.

It's not a sign, Cemmy. I try to shake loose the doubts. He probably assumed I'd know to head back here tomorrow. Considered "same time, same place" a message not worthy of repeat.

Still, no matter how much I push down the worry, my skin continues to prickle with unease.

Like I'm missing a crucial piece of the puzzle.

Like I'm being watched.

Like I'm being hunted.

Not that it makes a difference, since I'll be carrying out the lift either way.

That's the problem with desperation; the grip it has on you leaves little room for sense.

CHAPTER

Three

By the time night falls over Isitar, my desperation has turned from a stubborn whisper to an adamant scream. Which is why—despite the dread—I once again find myself scaling the gentle incline towards the holy quarter, weaving through the city's backstreets ring by ever-more affluent ring.

It's not like you have much of a choice. The key Vargas gave me sits heavy in my hand, like an unmade decision. I've spent the entire evening taking my suspicions to task, working to silence the voices telling me to cut my losses and find a different way to make ends meet. A safer way. Preferably one that doesn't involve robbing the highest-ranking member of the clergy.

But I can't do that.

I can't turn my back on such a windfall when I haven't been able to pinpoint a single reason for *why* Vargas would lie. I mean, one lowly thief is hardly worth this level of production. He could have easily had me arrested for simply possessing the key he'd slid across the bar. No questions asked. And unless I walk away clean tonight, he'll be down half the bounty—maybe even his whole head—so what could possibly compel him to set me up? In this deception, our interests are aligned.

Then why are you still hesitating? The voice in my mind sounds suspiciously like Novi. Had I shared my concerns with her and Ezzo, they'd have long since talked me out of this misguided lift. Mom would have, too, if I'd had the sense to return to the apartment. She would have taken one look at my face and realized I was planning to do something reckless in her name. That's why I've been avoiding her for hours—and why I've been ignoring Eve's increasingly frequent scrys. *You don't need to do this on your own, Cem,* she's been sending over and over. *You know full well that my gift can hold an In-Between around us both, so if you need me, say the word and I'm there, okay? Asking for help never killed anyone.*

Except it did kill someone.

It killed Magdalena.

But since I never found the guts to confess the full truth of *how* she died, my friends keep mistaking my fear for pride. And I can't bring myself to correct them because if I do, I'll lose them as well.

Then suck it up and get this done already. I try to relegate the thought of Eve from my mind. She means well when she pushes—and ultimately, she'll always respect my decisions, even when she doesn't understand them, or when they leave her feeling hurt and confused. Wondering why I'm no longer willing to place my trust in her gift the way I used to, when in truth, it's myself I don't trust anymore. My ability to protect her.

Focus, Cemmy, or you'll miss the temporal bridge. I force my attention back to the problem at hand. Around me, the houses have grown rich and menacing, oppressive in their uniform of flint, onyx, and bone. Even outside the reformed sectors, the buildings in Isitar have always favored this subdued masonry palette, creating the illusion of a city carved right into the cliff, beautiful in its symmetry, understated in its grace. Though up close, there's nothing *understated* about the houses built by the Church. They're bigger than their counterparts in the faithless quarter, their roofs spike taller, the accents around their doors and windows gleaming white against their ashen frames. But without a Shade's power to protect them, they're not any harder to rob. Especially if your accomplice busies the guards elsewhere and gives you a key to the door.

I arrive at the Governor's manse right as the twelfth bell rings out across the city, heralding the start of the midnight sanctuary and a disconcerting sense of déjà vu.

Here I go again. With a cautious glance over my shoulder, I set my time-keeper cuff ticking and phase into the Gray, turning the world to smoke, and ink, and shadows, an echo of a life lived in a color-filled haze.

Ten long strides and I'm across the yard.

Fifteen short seconds and I'm safely through the front door.

Five more and I'm to the neck of the corridor, Vargas's gift in my hand, ready to unlock the study so I can finish this job right.

The key slides through the pins without trouble, the mechanism giving way like butter melting beneath a hot blade. It may have taken him more than one attempt, but Vargas made good on his promise.

He got me in.

With thirty whole clicks left on my In-Between.

Maybe if I had moved a little slower, I wouldn't have had time to dally in the shadows, to scoff at the absurd excess of lavishly appointed furniture, or wander over to the enormous mahogany bookcase that dominates the back wall, or turn my nose up at the Governor's decision to hang a giant portrait of himself above the safe.

Maybe I would have phased right out of the Gray.

Too late.

My mistake shimmers across the study, smirking with all the arrogance of a predator that knows it's cornered its prey. That's the thing about full-blooded Shades: they don't just command the shadows; they *are* the shadows. The Gray doesn't threaten them; it sets their power free. They can winnow through it like snakes slithering through tall grass, near invisible among the dearth of color until they choose to prism into full blaze. And this Shade doesn't deign to do that until *after* he creeps close enough to slap an iron shackle around my wrist.

"No!" I claw at my metal prison, scraping my nails bloody against the fetter. But it's no use; the clasp's been spelled shut with magic, binding it to my arm. "Take it off!" I yell at my captor. "Take it off *now*!" The command in my voice is no match for the fear, not least of all because he's the meanest-looking Shade I've ever seen. Deathly thin with slicked tar for hair and sharp points to his nose, cheeks, and chin. Like a man made of knives. Or perhaps a knife made of flesh. Definitely not a Council Shade, this one—they don't let their eyes burn black to the edges, that upsets the typics too much, lends more credence to the conspiracies spun by the Church. But what scares me more than this rogue Shade is his method of execution.

Iron.

More commonly known as the Council's bane.

In the physical realm, the metal is a poison to full-bloods, sapping them of their magic and strength. Forcing them to shimmer back into the shadows before they weaken enough to lose that privilege as well. That is, in part, how the Church was able to assert such dominance over Isitar: by using it to contaminate the city's bones. Installing spokes of it along the streets and buildings in order to drive the Shades back from the holy quarter, keep them from peddling their magic on the clergy's watch. But since we Hues have no outward magic for the iron to target, we remain largely immune. Across both worlds. Unless a deliberate mass of it is bound against our skin. Then the metal works to suppress the one common power we all enjoy: our ability to phase. With only seconds left on my In-Between, this Shade's gone and tethered me to the Gray.

"Please take it off," I beg. "I'll stop stealing, I swear. Just please, let me go." *Let me go, let me go, let me go.*

"No." His voice is dry gravel. Steel to my hollow glass. "Now give me your scrys."

"Wh—What? I don't know what you—"

"The lies are costing you time, little half Shade. And time is not a luxury you have." He points to the ticking cuff at my wrist.

Twelve clicks remaining.

Crap. Shit. Damn. Fuck. If I surrender my scrys, he'll be able to track the others—the connection is bonded between crystals, not people; that's why these pre-made talismans run so much cheaper than a purpose-bought spell: they're only tailored for use. Discretion costs extra. Though that assumes this rogue means to find them, when it's far more likely he's simply looking to cut me off from my friends.

"Okay, fine—here." I rip the scrys from around my neck with a treacherous snap, betraying them in the moment so that I might live long enough to rectify this mistake.

I can't do that if the Gray shatters me.

And he'll get the scrys anyway once they're lying atop my splintered remains.

In order to protect them, I have to make it out of here.

I have to make it out for Mom.

"Now . . . please . . . let me go." My plea is a broken echo, the sum of all my fears reduced to a desperate whisper levied at a vindictive rogue.

"Better concentrate, little half Shade." Instead of granting my freedom, he shimmers over to the other side of the study and hangs an Orange talisman on the door. "Your salvation is only an In-Between away." Then with that, the full-blood phases out of the Gray, leaving me trapped, alone, and five seconds from death.

Move first, think later. I spring to action, making not for the talisman but for the tiny crevice between the antique bookcase and the wall. The two closest—and most solid—anchors I can reach.

"I am in between the bookcase and the wall." The magic explodes out of me in a rush, rising up to fortify the air against the shadows. *Just stay calm and don't lose your head. Holding this spell isn't as hard as you—argh!* I feel the exact moment the midnight In-Between collapses, the Gray sucking in around me like a wave lapping back towards the sea.

"I am in between the bookcase and the wall." I force it out again, throwing every last ounce of strength I have behind the shield.

I will not die in the Governor of Isitar's study.

Not today.

Not like this.

Not the way Magdalena di—

Stop it. I will the thought of her away, drowning it beneath another round of incantations.

"I am in between the bookcase and the wall. The bookcase and the wall."

Magdalena lost her life because she trusted me to do too much. To pick, *and* chant, *and* not succumb to a fit of cowardly panic.

I won't make that same mistake.

I'm going to stay put and keep myself alive until my captor returns.

And when I don't rise to his bait, he *will* return. I'm sure of it.

Because no matter which way you bend the numbers, they don't add up to: *rogue Shade randomly stakes out Governor's manse to steal scrys from a nineteen-year-old Hue.* That's not a thing that happens. In fact, the more I think on it, the more I realize that nothing about my current predicament is *random.*

"I am in between the bookcase and the wall."

No. Vargas didn't *randomly* show up at the Hidden Son tavern one day in search of a thief. He didn't offer me this bounty on account of my pickpocketing skills, or fail to leave the study door unlocked thanks to the Governor's interference.

He set me up.

He's working *with* my captor—though for the life of me, I can't figure out why.

What could a rogue Shade possibly gain by binding me to the shadows? *So he can catch me in the act* seems like too simple an explanation. He'd earn far more spelling open the Governor's safe himself, and those menacing black eyes tell me he's not doing it on behalf of the Council, nor is he looking to endear himself to the Church.

He wants something else from me. Wants it so bad he was willing to risk weakening himself with iron. While the metal can only affect him in the Gray when it's encircling skin, in the physical realm, procuring it would have placed him in danger—and in not an insignificant amount of pain. Which is quite the length to go to when there's nothing a full-blood would ever want that badly from a Hue.

"I am in between the bookcase and the wall. The bookcase and the wall."

I suppose he could just be looking to kill me; when you're a child born of typical flesh and blood color, that's always a worry. Whether that be the Council trying to eradicate the illegal scourge leeching power from the Gray, the clergy who think us unholy, or an opportunistic citizen looking to cash in on the price on our heads, there are ample ways for a half Shade to meet an early grave. Though if that were the case, why would he have bothered luring me here, specifically? Or taking my scrys?

If there's a logic to this madness, then he's buried it deep.

"I am in between the bookcase and the wall."

And colors help me, how did he even know what I am? How did *Vargas*? How did a cleric and a rogue Shade come together to trap a Bronze?

Better yet, how godsdamned long are they planning to leave me here? I start weighing my options as the shadows turn downright mean. The next temporal In-Between isn't until midday, and I know my limits; I can't hold the magic for a full twelve hours. If I'm to stay trapped in the Gray, then my best bet is a sanctuary—like the cemetery that rings our monastery, or a rooftop, or a beach. But even if the closest of those wasn't a whole house away, getting to it would require me to keep a stable shield on the move, and if I'm going to do that, then there's an infinitely easier solution awaiting me by the door.

The Orange talisman.

A pre-cast spell with which I can unseal the cuff.

He's testing you. All at once, the Shade's strangely specific actions begin to take shape. He didn't place my freedom across the room by accident, he did it to ensure I'd have no choice but to prove my worth. Took my scrys to stop me calling for help.

Your salvation is only an In-Between away.

As much as I'm loath to play into his machinations, his twisted game forces me to re-examine the conviction that he'll return. And if he's not coming back, then I have maybe another hour left to my name. Already, the sweat is soaking clean through my clothes, my whole body shaking with the effort of beating back the Gray. Either I do this now, or I might lose the strength to do it at all.

My captor laid his trap well.

Better to give him what he wants than die. I keep the magic flowing as I climb back to my feet, urging the In-Between to rise up with me.

The door is only a few steps away; you can make it. You can make it, you can make it—you will.

Committing to the decision is half the battle.

"I am in between the bookcase and the wall," I whisper, then with a giant leap, I change the story. "I am in between the bookcase and the desk. The bookcase and the desk." My shield ripples for a tense moment before accepting its new form. Since I'm now standing further away from both my anchors, it takes a more sustained effort for the magic to seize hold, but a grunt and a wish later, it stabilizes around their edges.

So far so good . . . I exhale through my teeth, steeling for the next exertion. "I am in between the desk and the chair." Another solid jump brings me one step closer to the door, though it also upsets my equilibrium, allowing the shadows to rush back and splinter my resolve. *Crack, clink, crunch, shatter.* My ears ring with the melodic memory of breaking glass, Magdalena's ghost wavering my shield.

No, no, no, no—I can't do this. Instead of moving to stand between the chair and the cabinet, I dive to cower beneath the desk, reining in the magic so that it sits as near and snug as possible.

"I am in between the desk and the floor." The tight proximity to my anchors immediately relieves the strain, leaving me unscathed—and unshattered—but no closer to the Orange talisman.

Damn it, Cemmy, you were almost to the door. I bang my head against the wood, cursing my inability to overcome this fear. I used to be able to control my In-Betweens. Not easily—traversing the shadows outside a sanctuary has always posed a challenge—but at least I had the competence to cross an amply furnished room. Whereas now, I can barely even manage a few measly steps.

Well then, you'd better think of something, because you can't stay here. I force in a breath and swallow down the panic. The shadows have a knack for sensing weakness, and my exhaustion is plenty evident by the salt glistening across my cheeks. Talisman or no talisman, I have to get this godsforsaken cuff off my wrist.

Okay . . . but how? No matter how much I twist, and beg, and tease the metal, the iron won't yield, and as the minutes speed fast towards the first bell of the morning, it gets harder to concentrate on anything but the words keeping me from shattering.

"I am in between the desk and the floor. The desk and the floor."

Until at last, the frantic delirium sparks an idea. My hand may not press small enough to squeeze through the fetter, but it would if my thumb were to fold inward against its will. An unpleasant solution, sure, but a dislocated thumb is likely to prove less painful than trying to chew through sinew and skin—which I doubt I'd have the stomach to do even if it *were* my only option.

Once a coward, always a coward, I guess.

Magdalena learned that lesson the dead way.

Guess it's my lucky day . . . I thank my colors that as a Bronze, I enjoy the gift of physicality in the Gray. For it means that I can interact with the furniture. Bend my thumb to its breaking point against the wood then use my foot to kick it out of place.

Simple.

I don't stop to overthink this endeavor, because if I do, I'll die here. The pain will almost certainly destroy my concentration, so I'll only have one shot—and a heartbeat—to get this escape right.

"I am in between the desk and the floor."

I twist my body into position, gathering my strength, and my courage, and my will to leave this wretched room alive.

"The desk and the floor."

My thumb twitches in protest, my stomach clawing acid at my insides.

"I am in between the desk and the floor."

A curse and a bang later, oak meets leather meets bone, popping the joint free of its moorings with a sickening crunch.

Three things happen in the eternal moment that follows: a grunt rips from my throat, the iron cuff clatters to the ground, and I phase back into the real world, threading light through the hungry shadows. The pressure instantly gives way to pain, a cruel and feral throb that brings my chest flush with my knees.

Son of a—

I cradle my screaming hand close as I draw in breath after ragged breath, urging the bile to stay down and my heart to cease racing.

Not dead, Cemmy. You're out of the Gray and not dead.

"That was quite the unexpected performance, little half Shade." The gravelly voice freezes me in place, chilling in both threat and malice. "I must admit myself rather . . . *underwhelmed* by the inelegant choice you made, but it will do." Despite the fact that I butchered his test, it seems my captor isn't done with me yet. And not just me, either. The air catches in my lungs as I spring back to my feet—to do what, I don't know, and it doesn't much matter seeing how the scene that greets me douses my fight down to embers.

This rogue Shade was busy while I was trapped in the Gray. Busy rounding up my friends, that is. Because that's Novi, Ezzo, and Eve he has neatly gagged and shackled on the Governor's chaise.

CHAPTER

Four

The Shade doesn't give me time to react. With a cruel twist of his hand, his magic seizes hold of the dislocated bone in mine, sending me crashing back to my knees.

"Now, now, little half Shade, no use picking a fight you can't win."

My answering groan of pain is met by muffled cries from my friends.

The friends I so selfishly gave up when I relinquished my scrys.

I may not have known what this rogue meant to do with them, but I knew full well what he *could* do. That he'd be able to use the crystals to pinpoint their location.

I all but led him to their door.

But what does he even want with us? I can't quite bring myself to meet the worry in their eyes. Why would anyone go to such lengths to test me? To capture them? To gather us all in the Governor's manse, with nothing but an unlocked door shielding us from the typics?

"You'd also do well to stay quiet," the Shade says, as though reading my mind. "Your friends are in no position to flee this room." He releases my hand with another flourish of fingers, the warning in his words ringing clear. If my protests rouse the guards, he can blink into the Gray and they can't. Not tied up and gagged; they couldn't properly control their magic. And I'd hardly fare much better myself, thanks to the state of exhaustion his trial by iron wrought me. Every single one of us would shatter.

"What do you want?" My question is part whisper, part growl.

"To right a wrong," he says. Which doesn't help at all.

"We've never *wronged* you," I spit. Hells, I've never so much as *glimpsed* this Shade before—and I never forget a face. It pays not to when you make your living as a thief, since hitting the same mark twice is the fastest way to get intimately acquainted with a cell. As is trying to rob any mark as sharp and menacing as this one, even if my sticky fingers would have instantly gravitated towards the glittering diamonds embedded in his ears.

"And yet, you've not done anything *right*." His features darken, searing stark against his chalk-white skin. "You Hues are a vile perversion of good power. It's time to earn your colors."

"Earn *this*." My good hand flashes him a crude gesture. Hardly the smartest response given my current predicament, but I'm far too tired—and in far too much pain—to mind my sense or my temper, or to let a rogue Shade, of all people, lecture me with that Council rhetoric. Been there, heard that, don't need another reminder that by sheer virtue of existing, we halves pose a clear and present danger to the Gray. That we're a blight that needs eradicating. As though spending our lives in hiding isn't punishment enough.

"Save the theatrics, Savian. You can force them to help you, but you can't force them to like it." The words come from the deepest corner of the room, belonging to a second Shade I hadn't noticed before. Not a full-blood, this one; his eyes are too pale a color for that, and he doesn't have the tell-tale spiked rim around his iris the way he would if he'd kept them from burning black to the edge.

Must be another half then, since a typic is unlikely to have broken into the Governor's study unseen—and they certainly can't accompany a Shade through the shadows. Not even the most reckless of rogues would risk phasing a typic into the Gray. They'd shatter instantly, for one thing. But more importantly, their presence would serve to destabilize the realm. That's why the Council forbids it.

"The Hue in the middle's the Sapphire," Pale Eyes tells his accomplice, pointing his chin Ezzo's way. How he puzzled that out, I don't know, but before any of us have the chance to deny it—or to try and stop what happens next—the full-blood, Savian, grabs hold of Ezzo's shoulders and blinks them both into the Gray.

"No—!"

In a heartbeat, a calloused hand is pressed to my mouth, cutting off my horror mid-scream. "Relax, he won't let him shatter. That would defeat the point."

The point? I claw at the half Shade's arm, adding my muffled curses to the ones escaping Novi and Eve, a chorus that only turns shriller as I upset the pain in my thumb.

"You've made a right mess of yourself," he mutters, moving his other hand to cup my wrist. "This'll hurt far less if you hold still." His words land too slow to prepare me. "But it's still going to hurt."

I mute another scream into his palm as he pops the bone back into place with a snap.

Motherf—

"I did warn you."

My stomach roils, the grisly sensation of sinew settling beneath flesh bringing a sour taste to my lips. But before I can double over and retch, a cloying warmth engulfs my fingers, the sudden—and inexplicable—kiss of magic soothing the throb in blissful waves. Fading, fading, fading it. As if it was never there.

Impossible.

"If I let you go, you have to promise not to scream again," Pale Eyes says once the feat is done. "If you scream, the guards come running, we all die, then Savian kills your friend." The threat is enough to keep me docile as his grip on me slackens.

"How did you do that?" The question slips out unbidden, my curiosity getting the better of my need to rebel.

"Magic." He shrugs, as if to say, *obviously*. Now that he's stepped out of the shadows, I can see the shape of him more clearly. The high cut of his cheekbones and the chiseled line of his jaw. How much younger he is than the full-blood—of a similar age to us, I would say, no older than nineteen or twenty. How up close, his eyes aren't just pale in color, they're a burnished silver. A perfect complement to the bronzed tan of his skin and the gold of his hair. Like a boy made of precious metals. Beautiful in a way that's oddly familiar, as though our lives have intersected before. Or perhaps that's just a trick of the light.

"But you're a *half*," I say, gritting the term in accusation.

"And you're perceptive." His head cocks lazily to the side. "Though I fail to see how that's relevant."

"It's *relevant* because half Shades can't heal." Only full-bloods can, and even then, that power lies exclusively with Greens. Seven different Shades, seven different specializations, each as set in stone as the gifts we Hues enjoy in the Gray. But while the full-bloods can exercise their magics across both worlds, ours are constrained to the shadows; in the physical realm, we're limited to pre-made spells like the typics.

Except Pale Eyes didn't feed me a tincture, and there's no charm or talisman that would have allowed him to heal an injury on command. No matter how smug his smirk is or how pretty his smile, what he did was impossible.

"Based on your performance these past two days, I'd venture you don't think half Shades can do much of anything." He sneers, appraising me with open disdain. "You could have saved yourself a lot of pain by picking your way through that door the first night. It's really not that hard."

"Then do it yourself next time." I bristle as he confirms my suspicions.

Vargas did set me up on their behalf.

He deliberately left the study locked so they could test me.

"We all have our roles to play, and that's not mine," Pale Eyes says, as though my life is some kind of sick game he's playing. "I am curious though; why dislocate your thumb instead of using the talisman Savian left you? Were you trying to make a point?"

"No, I was—" *Too afraid of shattering.* The second his partner slapped that iron cuff around my wrist, I fell apart. Forgot everything but the fear. "I couldn't reach it."

"Did you even try?" His reprimand echoes the one I got from Vargas. He even lends it the same cadence and pitch.

"Yes, actually." I mimic his derisive tone. "But it was too far away, so I decided not to die." Since he seems more interested in mocking me than keeping me from helping my friends, I stagger back to my feet.

"Gods, no wonder you gave up your scrys so willingly." His contempt follows me over to the chaise. "You're terrified of the Gray."

Yes, and for good reason. I lock eyes with Novi and Eve, begging them to understand that I never meant to put them in danger. That I thought I'd have time to warn them. That when faced with the same fate as falling glass, I panicked.

"I'm sorry," I breathe the words over and over, hands shaking as I battle the knots keeping them silent. "I shouldn't have given them to him. I swear I had no idea what he meant to do."

"He'd have taken them anyway—your scrys and your friends." At least Pale Eyes has the grace to admit it. "We've been watching you for a while now. All of you. Though you're far easier to track than they are," he says. "Reckless."

The implication sets a flame to my cheeks.

Because, clearly—*shamefully*—I've not been anywhere near as careful as I thought.

"Why?" Novi snarls the second I wrench her gag loose. "What in the nine hells do you want with us? Why bring us *here*?"

"You'll see."

"How about you show me now?" Despite the heavy chains constricting her ankles and wrists, she lurches up from the chaise to try and make him.

"Don't." He flexes his hand, and for a brief second, the rims of his irises spike red, the command in his voice oozing magic, forcing Novi to freeze in place.

Compulsion. He just ordered her still with compulsion. Every part of me tenses, the shock chilling me to the bone. I don't care what this traitorous Hue thinks of my skills, his are downright impossible. No half Shade should be able to master a full-blood's specialization, let alone two. Not unless he's a—

Gold.

I spot the moment Novi and Eve get it, the realization bleeding their color dull. It's little wonder he's so unconcerned with keeping us bound and helpless; his gift is far more effective than some flimsy gag and a length of chain. The ability to steal magic. From a Hue, or a full-blood, or—in this case—a Red. The Shade that specializes in control: spells that allow them to both command the body and trick the mind. With this kind of power flowing through his veins, Pale Eyes can demand our obedience with nothing but a word or a gesture, and if the guards do come running, he can simply compel them away. With this kind of power, he doesn't have to be afraid.

"And don't think about trying to escape, either." The angry twitch in his jaw tells me that he gets it, too. That he knows we've guessed the truth of his gift. "You can't overpower me, and you won't get very far without phasing into the Gray." *Which you won't do.* Is what Pale Eyes doesn't bother adding as he slinks back to brood in his corner. I've already proven my skills to be severely lacking in that department.

"How is this possible?" Novi whispers, straining to ungag Eve. "There hasn't been a Gold in Isitar for decades."

"That we know of," I say. Because if half Shades suffer from a case of low life expectancy, then Golds are the Hue bringing down that average age. That's the unfortunate side-effect of a gift that allows for stealing magics: it adds a layer of fear to the hate. Makes you dangerous and valuable in equal measure. Prone to being exploited by both sides. Which is probably why every story I've ever heard about a Gold ends tragically—and prematurely—in betrayal. Most meet their death long before they learn to properly wield their power.

"No." Novi's head shakes and shakes and shakes. "If there was a Gold following us around town, Ez would have noticed."

"Do you think that's why the full-blood took him? To remove the threat?" Eve's cheeks glisten with worry, the consequence in her question rending pieces from my soul. As a Sapphire, Ezzo's ability in the shadows is to track the presence of other Shades. Identify their color. That's how he found Eve the day the Council killed her parents, hiding in a derelict tannery in the Gray, too afraid to phase back into the world that robbed her of a family. The two of them stumbled across Novi a few months later, but owing to her speed in the shadows, it took them over a week to catch up to her, and a damn sight longer to win her trust. Though by the time they found me, I was so desperate for news of other halves in the city, my trust came far easier. That's what happens when you grow up entirely alone, with a mother who only gives you the most basic information about your magic. If not for Ezzo, I might have gone through life without ever meeting another Hue.

His power *saved* me.

And today, it may just be the thing that saves him.

"I don't think they're afraid of him, Vee," I say, sounding the idea out. His gift isn't passive enough to cause a problem; he has to engage it. Nor does it work unless the Shade he's tracking is in the Gray. So if Pale Eyes knew that—which I suspect he did—he could have easily moved through the city unnoticed, and if killing Ezzo was the goal, then Savian could have done that the second he traced my scrys. Instead, he brought Ezzo here and dragged him into the Gray. Why do that unless—

"They want something." Novi's quick to follow the same logic I do.

"Or *someone*." Eve then takes the puzzle piece and rotates it to fit. "Grabbing Ez must mean they're looking for another Shade."

"Or another Hue." My declaration elicits a soft clap from the corner of the room.

"Not bad," Pale Eyes says. "You got there faster than I expected." His irritation from before has melted back into arrogance, an air of unearned superiority winking in the raise of his brow.

Metallic bastard.

"No, but . . . Ez would never do that," Eve tells him, the fear in her voice changing pitch. "He'd never lead a Shade to another Hue. Please, you can't hurt him—you have to understand that *he'd never do that.*"

Unless, of course, that Shade threatened *her*. Another piece of the puzzle drops into place. Because Eve's right: Ezzo would never willingly endanger another Hue—not to save his own life, anyhow—whereas he'd gladly set a torch to the city to save Eve. He wouldn't even hesitate. And Pale Eyes will have only had to watch the two of them together for five minutes to know that. To see the way they orbit each other, like twin moons traveling together across the sky.

If they have Eve, they can control Ezzo.

She's the only leverage they require to force his hand.

"Who are you looking for?" I ask, more out of indignation than because I think he'll tell us. "What other unsuspecting Hue are you planning to *test*?"

The Gold remains silent, a tiny hardening of his shoulders the only sign he even heard me.

"Does it feel good to betray your kind?" Once I start pushing, the urge to provoke a reaction turns into a physical need. "Does it make you feel powerful?"

"Cem—" A warning creeps into Novi's voice, trying to rein in my fury, to keep me from wading into trouble too deep. But I don't want to stay in the shallows, and as much as I should be afraid of this half Shade, I can't seem to muster the will. Because if his accomplice went to all this trouble to test me, then I must play some sort of role in his plans, too. Enough to keep his Gold from harming me. To keep me pestering him for answers—my accusations taunting his silence—until we're barely an inch apart, close enough to feel the stolen power radiating off his skin.

"Not everything is simple, Cemilla." Pale Eyes finally breaks, his intractable mask slipping. But before I can push the advantage and demand to know what that means, a dull swish of fabric announces Savian's return.

"Ez!" Novi, Eve, and I all whip around at once, desperate to confirm that he's also arrived safely back in the study.

Well, thank my colors for that. The knot in my chest loosens as I take in the warm browns of his eyes, hair, and skin, the fact that he escaped the Gray unharmed and unshattered. Even if he was forced to help Savian capture another Hue.

Alabaster pale, a shock of red curls, green eyes wide with a silent scream. This girl is no older than we are, and judging by the fear staining her expression, every bit as in over her head.

"Excellent." Savian's grin is a flash of menace in the dark. "Now that we're all here, it's time to get to work."

CHAPTER

Five

Get to work? Is this—? He can't be serious. Our protests fill the study as one, a communal riot of anger that Savian silences with a lazy flex of Red magic.

"You will speak when I permit it."

A second wave of power ripples the walls, enveloping the room in a shimmering cage of magic that'll keep the guards out and our voices in.

A privacy spell.

Another strength-based magic like the Orange talisman still hanging on the door.

So is he an Orange or a Red? I glance over at Ezzo, asking the question with my eyes.

Green, he mouths, though that doesn't make a lick of sense. Yes, Shades grow more powerful outside of Council control—it's what makes rogues more dangerous; why they're more hunted than we are—but that doesn't mean they can cast across color. If Savian is a Green, then his specialization is healing, not fortifying rooms or asserting his will on others. He shouldn't be able to cycle through a rainbow of magics like his—

Gold.

The realization is as chilling as it is perverse. If the magic Pale Eyes steals can be passed on to his master, then that would endow Savian with more power than any ordinary rogue, make him an even more formidable threat. A venomous snake that's also poisonous.

And the girl? I tilt my chin towards the redhead at Savian's feet, curious as to how she fits into this baffling picture. Her gaze is darting wildly between me, Novi, and Eve, her pupils blown black, her hands caught in a dance of deliberate gestures.

Signs.

Though I don't understand the words, I recognize the language.

This girl might be deaf.

And she's most definitely a Hue. An Amethyst, according to Ezzo. Which—if I'm remembering the rumors correctly—means her gift is to communicate with the shadows. Understand them. Influence their might.

What in the hells is this rogue Shade playing at? Dread threads a tapestry through my bones. The collection of Hues Savian's amassed in this room isn't just novel—or wildly illegal—it's downright suspicious.

A Bronze who can interact with objects in the Gray.

A Cobalt who can traverse the shadows at speed.

An Amethyst who can speak to them.

An Emerald who can sustain an In-Between with ease.

A Gold who can steal power.

And a Sapphire who can identify it in others.

Even if Savian did only drag Eve into this mess to motivate Ezzo, and even if his Gold was only here to keep the rest of us under control while Ezzo completed his task—and those are two very big *ifs*—that still leaves three separate Hues he brought together for a reason. I just can't wrap my head around *what* that reason might be.

"Cemilla." Savian snaps me back to attention, the malice in his eyes burning bright. "Be a good little half Shade and open the safe."

"What?" The request is so unnecessary, it catches me off-guard.

"Was I in some way unclear?"

"No, it's just—wouldn't you get the job done faster?" I ask. I mean . . . hells, a rogue Shade wielding such a potent mix of stolen magics could probably melt the steel clean off the door.

"Yes, but I'd like to see *you* do it."

"Why?" No amount of fear could eclipse my confusion. Because it *doesn't make any sense.*

"Consider it an audition." The danger in Savian's voice turns savage. "And assume I won't ask you again." With a cruel twist of smile, he commands an invisible rope around my friends' necks, choking them to their knees.

"Stop it!" I spring forward to help them, only to find that my legs have been paralyzed by a spell of their own.

"Savian—" Pale Eyes starts, but a second flourish of fingers muzzles him as well.

"Do not mistake my mercy for grace." Savian's warning is an admonishment to us both. "Disobedience comes at a price."

Too high. The moment his hold on me weakens, I stumble over to the safe. No question or curiosity is worth exacting this high a price on my friends. I need to shut my mouth and do as he instructs.

"Work fast, little half Shade. They'll soon be turning blue."

"Please, I—I'm doing it." I press a hand to the door, imploring Savian to relax his grip on their air. The Governor's safe is a model I've encountered before, a squat but solid construction that favors size over stealth—and ease of use over impenetrability.

It's a simple combination lock, Cemmy. You can crack those in your sleep. My fingers settle against the dial, my nerves pulsing in frantic sync with my heart. There's nothing magical about cracking a safe; it's all touch, sense, and years' worth of hard-earned practice. Novi taught me that. She was ten when she lost her mother to a heinous act of random violence, eleven when the Council came for her dad—a Blue who abused his knack for accelerating time in order to exact his own brand of justice. So then he incurred theirs, leaving her alone in a world that isn't much kinder to orphans than it is to those whose blood sings with color. Learning to break through a lock is how Novi stayed alive. Then when Mom took ill, she passed those skills on to me, so that we could stay alive together.

Well then, stay *alive.*

The second I calm myself enough to think, my instincts take over. I press my ear to the metal, focusing on nothing but the rhythmic tension escaping the dial, listening for that invisible moment when the cam connects to the wheel.

Three and a half turns to the left.

Click.

One and a quarter turn to the right.

Click.

Another two full turns then four fifths of a turn back.

Click.

Click, clang, clunk.

The lock disengages with a satisfying slide of gears, the breath I've been holding escaping me in a gust. Unlike Savian's first test, stealing presents a challenge I understand. A risk that doesn't scare me.

"Very good, Cemilla." As the door to the safe swings open, he finally releases my friends. "Now fetch me the contents. You'll find that you know what it is I'm after."

He's right; I do know. Not because it's an obvious bounty, like a bag full of coin or a prized collection of gems, but because—as it turns out—the Governor of Isitar isn't all that averse to magic when it comes to protecting his treasures.

I feel the hidden partition the instant I slip my hand inside, a violent bloom of magic that pushes back against my arm.

It's warded? I suddenly realize why Savian needed me to retrieve the contents on his behalf. The Governor has had his safe charmed to repel Shades, a rare and costly spell that can only be overcome by an overwhelming amount of power—or fooled by the presence of typical blood. Make that another reason why both the Church and the Council hate having us pesky Hues around: we can beat the wards. Not enough color to trigger the magic, you see, or—when the spell's cast the other way—too much color to trigger it. So while they can hunt us, and shun us, and purge their cities of our kind, they can't keep us out of their stuff.

And the Governor will have paid a lot *to ensure no Shade could do* this . . . With a grunt and a touch of brute force, my hand penetrates the magic, searching for whatever riches Savian believes to be inside.

Except . . . no—this can't be right. "You went to all this trouble for a *note*?" My temper flares as instead, I'm met with a yellowing scrap of paper. A book I'd understand—some priceless tome or incriminating ledger, maybe even a journal of great merit and worth. But a scrap of ink-stained paper? Inscribed with nothing more than a single line of indecipherable text?

"Cassiel."

At Savian's behest, Pale Eyes slinks to my side. Cassiel, I guess his name is, though something about that moniker doesn't quite seem to fit, the stiff formality of it catching on his sharp edges.

"You're wasting your time," I say as he relieves me of the Governor's useless scrawl. "It's not legible."

"Have a little faith, Cemilla. I got you into this study, didn't I?"

"*Vargas* got me into the study," I hiss. And if I could go back and refuse the key, I would.

"Are you sure about that?" He flashes me his teeth. "Seems rather an odd thing for such a devout man to do. Someone must have gotten into him," he says, and for the briefest of moments, his irises flash red, the shape of his face flickering.

A glamour. The realization dawns fast and cold. Vargas was not Vargas at all; it was Cassiel under that hood. A ruse as plausible as it is foul. When he stole the Red's power to compel, he'd have also assumed their ability to glamour. To show people any reality he needed them to see. And what better reality to assume than that of the Governor's most trusted aide? A man with access to every locked door and closely held secret, who can order the staff away unnoticed and vanish a key at will. Who could make a lift like this possible.

"So . . . Vargas—? The bar—? That was *you*?" I ask, thinking back to our two encounters, the strange nervousness of his behavior taking on a brand-new shape.

"It's easier to steal a man's face than change his allegiance," Cassiel says, turning his attention to the portrait hanging above the safe. "And sometimes, a man's face isn't a face at all." The Governor's likeness flashes with the words, and it takes me a second to fully grasp what new illusion I'm seeing.

Gods, is anything in this room not *hidden behind a spell?* My gasp of shock is echoed by Novi, Ezzo, and Eve—as well as the Amethyst I have no name for. We all watch as the Governor's eyes dissolve to form a pattern of swirled black ink, his pompous frame yawning wide to reveal an etching of waves, and roads, and buildings. A city trapped between the mountains and the sea, draped in shadow and shaped like a waning gibbous. And though it's very obviously a map of Isitar—same encompassing wall and concentric maze of circular streets—it's unlike any map I've ever seen. It's not written in the common tongue, for one thing, but rather in some intricate language that screams of power and age. *And magic.* A glittering nebula of silver sparkles across its surface, tiny pinpricks of light that seem to flutter between blinks, as though straddling two states of existence. There, but not.

"It's a map of the Gray." Novi's voice splinters the stunned silence.

"Of the *Gray*?" I parrot, turning to meet her eyes. "I don't—how could you possibly know that?"

"Because she just told me." Novi points to the Amethyst. "I mean, I'm a little rusty, but I think I'm following her correctly. She says the shadows inside it are begging to be let out."

"Let out of the map?" I trade a look of confusion with Eve and Ezzo. "Is that even—?"

Wait. Go back.

"You can—" *Understand her?* The question sticks in my throat, a slow heat pinking my cheeks as the answer makes itself abundantly clear.

Novi can sign.

Which isn't an impossibility in itself—Novi's always been a fast learner, observant and endlessly curious, a jack of any trade she sets her mind to. It's just that after seven years of friendship—and two years of something more . . . *intense*—I thought I knew everything there was to know about her. The meaning behind every gesture and smile. Every tantalizing trick she can play with her hands. And for some reason, learning she kept such a secret feels like a betrayal. Even if it was *my* secret that ultimately drove us apart.

"What is the Governor of Isitar doing with a map of the Gray?" I ask instead, shoving the feeling down. I didn't even realize the Gray *could* be mapped, let alone mapped then hidden behind a glamour—by the very man who's hells-bent on ridding the city of magic, no less. So perhaps the better question is: how did the Governor get it? And *why*? It's not as if he can take a stroll through the shadows to brighten up his day. The Gray would shatter him faster than it would me.

"Where else would a hypocrite hide all those things he claims to despise?" Savian's answering growl is all venom. "Now get to it, Cassiel. My patience is wearing thin."

With an obedient nod, his Gold takes the scrap of paper I liberated in hand, closing his eyes as if in prayer. When he finally speaks, the words sound from some deep part of his chest, musical in their cadence, but alien on his tongue.

A wisdom spell, then. The hairs on my neck prickle with unease. Didactic magic stolen from a Violet Shade, made to grant those who wield it whatever knowledge they seek.

How much power can one half take? The entire room thrums in anticipation as he completes the casting, lending voice to the incantation the Governor keeps locked away.

Whoa.

Once again, we're all staring at the map, transfixed, watching the shadows remake themselves around a single building—the single most important building to those whose faith lies with the Church.

The Dominion.

Home to the Conclave and the holy sacraments.

A mammoth marvel of engineering that sits atop Isitar's centermost crest, its gilded spires shining like an ominous crown.

"The shadows call it *the cursed palace*," Novi breathes, interpreting the Amethyst's increasingly urgent signs. "They say it's . . . sorry . . . can you repeat that for me? A little slower this time?" Her hands struggle around the ask, clumsy with the lack of practice. "They say that . . . the end of everything lives inside," she continues as the Amethyst cycles through the signs again. "They're warning us to stay away."

They don't have to tell me twice. I shudder at the very thought. Even outside the Gray, we grant the Dominion a wide berth. Too many members of the clergy milling around that pious edifice. Too many prying eyes. The distinct stench of hate. Whatever sins the Governor is hiding in there are *his* to shoulder, a penance to be decided between him and the fates.

"I'm afraid that won't be an option." The silk in Savian's voice masks a dangerous bite. "You see, Isitar's esteemed Governor is keeping an important . . . *artefact* hidden in the Gray inside those walls. Something I need."

"Well, then go get it." Ezzo's anger is the first to peak, his body moving instinctively to protect Eve's. "You don't need *us* for that. Just like you didn't need us, or her"—he juts his chin at the Amethyst—"for any of this. You already knew this map existed, and your Gold could have gotten you through the warding in the safe."

"If it were that simple, do you really think I'd surround myself with filthy halves?" Savian's contempt cuts through us all, catching on his own Hue in the process—though Cassiel is quick to wipe the insult from his scowl. "The whole building has been warded against Shades, and the artefact is protected by magics that span both the physical realm and the Gray, with locks and traps across both worlds."

So he can't go get it. Dread pools in my stomach, suspicion setting a flame to my bones. If the Dominion is warded, then Savian is unable to step foot inside, no matter how much he might want or try to. Though if he's also right about the artefact being hidden in the Gray, then the Governor can't reach it, either. His protections would serve to bar them both—even without the extra magics.

"I'm sorry, but that doesn't make any sense." While Eve's objection is leagues more polite than mine would have been, the conclusion she's drawn is the same. "Why would the Governor hide anything in the Gray and then ward against the only people who could get it back?"

"To prevent it from being *gotten back*, of course." Savian's smile reeks of feigned sincerity. "Now—" He turns to address the Amethyst, ensuring she has a clear view of his lips. "Kindly ask the shadows to remake the image. We're going to want a better look."

We. The suspicion burns hotter. Savian might not have needed a crew of *filthy halves* to break into the Governor's study, but only an Amethyst can affect this map the way he requires, just as only a Sapphire could have led him to her through the Gray. And if this niggling suspicion of mine holds true, then I'm pretty sure I know why he needs a Bronze, as well.

"I suggest you all memorize the layout of this building." Savian wastes no time before confirming my fear. "Because you're going to rob it."

CHAPTER

Six

I was five when Mom first told me about my color. She didn't *want* to tell me about it—she's always been at her happiest when I was at my least informed, and my ability to phase wouldn't yet manifest for a few more years—but there are only so many truths you can keep from your daughter, especially when she grows old enough to realize that living in hiding isn't the norm.

That day, I could hear a group of kids playing outside the window, a vicious little game called *Hunt the Hue*—though at the time, their petty squabbles over who would be the Hue and who would be the tracker didn't strike me as callous or odd. Back then, I didn't know what a tracker *was*, nor what became of a Hue once they were hauled before the Council. The swift and brutal death they would meet. All I knew was that those kids were running, and giggling, and squealing with delight, and that I desperately wanted to be down in the streets with them, hunting the Hue.

"I'll be the Hue!" I'd shouted, hoping my willingness to assume the role none of them wanted would earn me an invite to their game. "Up here! I'm it! I'm the Hue!"

"Cemilla—no!" In the space of a heartbeat, Mom had run into the room to slam the window shut and pull me back from the sill. "You can never say that again!" she told me, her eyes panicked and her voice low. "If they find out you're a Bronze, they'll kill you. Do you understand what I'm saying, Cemilla?" It would soon become apparent that she'd only lent voice to that word out of fear. *"Do you understand?"*

I didn't understand.

Not in any real sense, anyhow, but I could see that it upset her, and so I pretended I did.

That was the day she finally revealed to me the true "significance" of Dad's ring—the reason she always checked, and checked, and checked that I was wearing it; on a chain around my neck at the time, until I grew old enough for it to fit my finger—and gave me the barest hint of an explanation for what being a Bronze means. And while the color in my blood is certainly no gift, in her effort to scare me silent, Mom made it sound like a curse. So much so that I'd turned to her and asked if I could simply . . . give the magic back. Return to being a typic.

"I'm sorry, Cemilla, but that's impossible."

That word quickly came to define my life.

It was impossible for me to play with the neighboring children; it was impossible for me to go to school. It was *absolutely* impossible for me to seek out other Hues, and when Mom took ill, it became downright impossible for me to keep us afloat.

If there's one thing I've learned, it's how to ignore the impossible.

Because when you live in a constant state of desperation, that's just what you do. You find ways to bend it. Evade it. Delay its inevitable bite. Eke out the life you were told you cannot have as an act of protest. But even I know when impossible is hard, and when it's actually *impossible.* And what Savian wants us to do is so far out of the realm of possibility, it borders on obscene.

I'm afraid your participation in this endeavor isn't optional, he'd said when we collectively voiced our refusal, flexing his stolen power once more. *The way I see it, you either do as I bid, or the Council finds out there's a whole palette of illegal Hues running riot around their city. I doubt they'd be pleased to hear their purges missed so many.*

You're a rogue; you can't go to the Council any more than we can, Novi had clipped in return. Only for Savian to remind her that, between the Council and the Church, there are plenty of ways for a half Shade to meet a sticky end—and that trying to flee the city would likely leave us even worse for wear.

The hate you experience inside these walls pales in comparison to the bigotry that exists beyond them.

It's hard to argue with a threat you know to be true. Isitar became a *walled* city for good reason: it's where the Shades went to escape the ugly prejudice rising among the continent's elite. They say the fear came off a ship from the west—an emissary of a world that sits beyond the Infinite Ocean. Before that, Shades and typics had coexisted for thousands of years, their roots growing intertwined, their history proud and deep. But then came the boats, and the clerics, and their faith—the belief that magic was an affront to the Gods, not a gift they bestowed upon their children—and city by city, the fear spread among those whose blood wasn't *cursed* with color, sweeping through the populace like a vicious plague. Because the pious don't much like it when there's a wealth of power they cannot reach, and they really don't like it when there's an entire realm they can neither claim nor access. They'd rather spurn the shadows than see them thriving in a Shade's hand. Or as Mom likes to say: a wise man will happily live in a house built with magic; a jealous one would rather light a match and burn it to the ground.

And so, with the tide of favor turning against them—and an insidious new trend for mixing iron with stone—the Shades fled in search of a sanctuary. That's how they came to find Isitar, a city perched atop a cliff at the forgotten end of the world, large enough to hold their number, but perfectly placed to create a stronghold they could defend with magic and fortify behind a wall. It was here, in an effort to assimilate peacefully, that the Council of Shades was formed. A way to assure the city's existing inhabitants that this sudden influx of power would be carefully controlled.

But like all good things, the peace only lasted until it didn't.

Until the Church found a way to sink its claws into this last bastion of heresy, and the Council started losing Shades to the continent and spending more time than ever policing its own. Trying to stem the rise of hardline sects within its ranks—those who seek to wage a full-blown war against *every* typic—and playing the grown-up version of Hunt the Hue.

So what choice did we have other than to agree to Savian's absurd demands? To study the Dominion map until we could draw its glimmering lines from memory and let him bind a scry around our necks so that there would be no evading his grasp.

At least he also agreed to return mine. The new crystal sits hot among the others, similar in weight to those I wear for Novi, Ezzo, and Eve, yet somehow heavier, the bonded connection charmed to convey only in his direction, the chain spelled shut with magic to prevent me taking it off.

Cassiel will be keeping me advised of your progress, Savian had said before unceremoniously shimmering us out of the Governor's manse. *You have until the cleansing moon to prepare.*

The cleansing moon. A violent chill shudders my spine. The one night of the year where every Shade in the city makes themselves well and truly scarce—even on the faithless side of Isitar—while the Church celebrates its campaign to rid the world of blood color.

Barely a week away. The chill turns to an outright frost. A week to put in place a plan for robbing a *cursed palace* and living to tell the tale. For traversing the shadows intact.

It's not enough time. My hands fist in my hair, my pulse thrumming like a trapped bird beneath my ribs. Even the familiar safety of our monastery can't seem to quiet my nerves, not when we know nothing of the artefact we're stealing, or the protections around it, or where in the Dominion it's being held. The Governor's map detailed twelve distinct floors and a thousand-odd rooms; more if we count the servant quarters. It would take us a week solid to search the place from dungeon to spire. There's just *not enough time.*

"By my colors, Cem, would you please stop pacing?" Novi slinks up behind me, a bottle of honey wine in her hand and a lingering note of anger in her voice. "You're making me nervous."

She should be nervous.

And the anger, well . . . yeah, I deserve that, too.

I'm the one who fell for Cassiel's ruse.

Who let a rogue Shade bind me to the shadows and abscond with my scrys.

Who gave up my friends without blinking.

Neither Ezzo or Eve were in any mood to talk things out as we made our way back to the faithless quarter, and when we reached the choice between home and our monastery, they slunk away together, wrapped in each other's arms. In all honesty, I was half expecting Novi to avoid me as well, but she likes to drink when a job goes sideward, and she made a pretty convincing argument for why it would be in poor taste to make her do it alone.

"Gods, how are you not *more* nervous?" I reach for the bottle, taking a large swig of wine before the contents are all gone. Savian tied a crystal noose around her neck, too, citing her speed in the Gray as integral to our success. Not our survival, our *success*; his choice of words felt deliberate. A sobering reminder that to him, our lives are just a means to an end. Collateral damage.

"Because I have no intention of breaking into the Dominion." Novi's defiance echoes bluntly off the bare stone walls.

"They have us by the throat, En." *Quite literally*. "We don't have a choice."

"There's always a choice, Cem." Her hands snake around my midriff. "Tonight, you made some bad ones. Tomorrow, we get to try again. Change the story." She smells of wine and cypress and juniper, heady nights and sweet mistakes.

"How?"

"By playing nice." Novi says it so simply, like Savian is nothing more than a blustering enforcer we need to placate. "We'll plan, and practice, and make him *think* that he's cowed us, then when he least expects it, we'll make a move of our own."

"Like what?" I want so badly to believe her. To believe that there's a way out of this mess that doesn't lead to the Dominion's door.

"I don't know yet," she breathes, dropping her forehead to mine. "But we'll figure it out. You just have to stay alive until we do."

"That's not a small 'just', En." It's a big fucking problem. Especially since Savian's test made it plenty clear that my ability to hold an In-Between would play a role.

The artefact is protected by magics that span both the physical realm and the Gray, with locks and traps across both worlds.

Both worlds. The enormity of his ask squirms my marrow. Novi and the others can help me move through the shadows faster, better, and with more deliberate aim, but only I can remove the prize Savian's after, and something tells me there'll be no sanctuaries to count on, no permanent In-Betweens to lend us aid.

And there isn't enough time.

Not to get over a fear that borders on hysteria; that rendered me so scared and flustered, I chose to dislocate my thumb instead of crossing a room.

If Savian forces me into the Gray, I will shatter. I won't be able to *stay alive.*

"The shadows are your birthright, Cem," Novi says, as though anticipating my doubt. "You can't let one bad lift define you. You are *not* responsible for what happened to Magdalena."

Except I am responsible. *I am responsible, I am responsible—I* am.

And if Novi knew the truth—the real reason Magdalena shattered—she'd blame me every bit as much as I blame myself.

"You can hold your nerve in there until we figure out what to do about Savian, I know you can," she continues, digging her heels in hard. "You'll have Eve to help you with the In-Betweens, and we have Lyria now, too, to appease the shadows."

Lyria. The Amethyst's name is a spear to the heart, a staunch reminder that Novi's been keeping a few secrets of her own.

Our reluctant new friend vanished home the second Savian released us from the study. Didn't yet trust us enough to reveal where that home was, but the scry he sealed around her neck ensured that the *wheres* and *how fars* wouldn't matter. He can now locate her any time, any place. Though something tells me we'd have seen her again even if disappearing were an option. I recognized the glint in her eyes when she realized she was surrounded by other Hues.

The relief of learning she wasn't alone. The hunger. But more than that, I recognized the way she looked to Novi even when there was nothing left to interpret, her gaze lingering longer than strictly necessary, sparking a jealous ache inside my bones.

"You never told me you knew how to sign." My whisper lands with all the subtlety of an accusation, startling Novi stiff.

"You never asked."

"I've never *had* to ask." I catch hold of her hand before she can pull away. "We've always told each other everything."

Ezzo may have been the one to find me, but it was Novi who made me feel like I belonged. Even at twelve years old, she knew how to command my attention. Not just with the glamours she chose to wear, but with the comfort she felt in her own skin, her unapologetic air of confidence. We were sixteen when we first turned our friendship into something more, then seventeen when that childish flirtation grew more serious. Eighteen when my guilt started causing her enough pain to set me loose.

And when she did, I let her.

Though every so often, I let her take me back, too.

"Not lately, we haven't," Novi says, as if in reminder. "But that was your choice, Cem, not mine."

"En—"

"No. No more talking." In an instant, she's shaken off the mood and drawn me close again, her fingers tracing slow circles around the bone at my hip. "Unless you're finally going to tell me what happened, we don't need to talk."

I know exactly what she's suggesting we do instead. Known it from the moment she invited me here to drink. *This is a bad idea.* I drain the last of the bottle as she leads me over to the daybed, savoring the distraction and the heat. It was a bad idea the last time we let the wine seduce us, and with Savian's threat hanging over our heads, this ill-advised dalliance is only likely to make things worse.

Go home, Cemmy. You need to go home.

I kiss her.

With a desperation I haven't felt since the night she broke things off.

Because I'm weak, and Novi's scared, and we might only have a few days left in which to hurt. Because her scent is intoxicating, and her touch is addictive, and the fire in her eyes is blazing hot. And because right now, I don't want to talk, or go home, or act sensible.

I want to burn.

CHAPTER

Seven

The problem with a burn is that it's wont to blister. And when it inevitably does, the pain only screams worse.

Stupid, stupid, stupid.

In the harsh light of day, my slip back into Novi's arms is an ache that tugs at my conscience, a churn in the pit of my stomach that has nothing to do with an empty bottle of drink. She was still sleeping when I crept away from the daybed, the white of her hair lying mussed across her pillowed hands, the vines tattooed into her scalp gleaming bright in the morning sunshine. And though the right thing would have been to wake her, doing that would've forced us to acknowledge the mistake we'd both made. So instead, I quietly reached for my clothes and left a note in my place.

Went to check on Mom, C.

A truth she'll believe even if it does reek of convenience, because it keeps us from having to address the real problem in the room.

Me.

Or to be more precise, my inability to give her the one thing she truly wants.

An explanation.

Unless you're finally going to tell me what happened, we don't need to talk. Though Novi has never been possessive, or insecure, or jealous, the one thing she's always insisted on is honesty, and ever since Magdalena shattered, that's been the one thing I couldn't give. It only took a few weeks for her to realize that I wasn't just withdrawing out of grief, I was keeping secrets—and a couple more weeks after that, she gave up on asking for my confidence and called us quits.

If I can't have all of you, Cem, then I can't have you at all.

And while I've thought about trying to fix it, close to a year on, I'm not sure the trust I broke could ever be fully healed. Because even if I were to come clean, and even if Novi did forgive me, the fact that I chose to lie would never cease to plague her. Like a bridge built on sandy foundations, we'd be destined to wash out to sea.

Which is exactly why I need to stop fanning this flame we've smothered, or else I risk losing the parts of Novi I got to keep. It's only in the last six months that our relationship has settled back into a natural rhythm, and I won't survive another stretch of overly polite conversation and trying to pretend the absence of her doesn't sting.

I need to stop falling into bed with her.

From the monastery, it doesn't take me long to snake back to the apartment, where—at this late hour of the morning—Mom's worry is sure to greet me the moment I step through the door.

Or not.

Her laugh is echoing down the corridor when I reach the third-floor landing. Not her cough, or her wheeze, her *laugh.* A sound she hasn't made in longer than I care to admit.

Who is she talking to? My strides lengthen in urgency and speed. Madam Berska isn't one for chit-chatting with her tenants, and Mom started keeping the world at bay long before she grew debilitatingly sick.

She doesn't have any friends.

These last few years, she hasn't had the strength to make any.

"Mom?" The hitch in my voice is pure panic as I fumble with my key. "Is there someone there with you? Are you—is everything all ri—?" I freeze at the sight awaiting me in the living room. Not only does Mom look better than she has in weeks, she's up and fussing over the boy who's commandeered her place in the armchair. A boy with gold hair, bronzed skin, and silver eyes blown wide with a sneer. A face as pretty as it is enraging.

"Hello, Cemilla." Cassiel flashes me a smile that's all teeth. "Your mother's brewing us some tea. Would you like to join us?"

Would I like to join *them*? My nails bite deep into my thighs. What the hells does he think he's playing at, showing up at my home unannounced? Demanding tea and a hospitable welcome? Looking around my life as though it's his to judge?

"Get out." I step between him and Mom, shielding her fragile frame with the outrage in mine. As far as I can tell, he's not carrying a weapon, but a Gold could just as soon stop her heart with an idle flex of power, wrap an invisible hand around her neck and command it to squeeze. Without knowing what magics Cassiel has siphoned into his veins, I can't predict how much damage he could wreak. What brand of violence he might choose to inflict.

"Cemilla, where are your manners?" Mom skirts around me to pass him a steaming hot cup of lemon and ginger. The good blend we save for when she's suffering through a particularly bad stint.

"Erm . . . I—" Am entirely dumbstruck by how strong her voice is. How much color there is in her cheeks. I'm so used to watching her stoically endure her illness that I'd almost forgotten what she looks like when the lines in her face are pain-free. "Mom . . . I—you shouldn't be on your feet." I try to steer her down to the couch.

Only for her to tut and bat me away.

"There's no need to fuss, Cemilla, I'm perfectly fine. This young man is from the apothecary. Since you didn't see fit to come home last night, he was kind enough to deliver my medicine." Though her admonishment is tempered for polite company, I don't miss the note of disappointment in her words, nor the way Cassiel's lips quirk up in amusement, as though he took one look at my bedraggled state and guessed exactly where I've been. And what I've been doing.

"Is that right?" My breath catches as I spot the glass vial sitting on the table. A Green label. The remedy I told Mom I'd try to buy her but never did, because no amount of lifts could cover the extortionate price it fetches—let alone arrange for a home delivery. "That is *unbelievably* kind of you," I say, searching his eyes for the catch.

Because there will be a *catch.*

There always is.

Savian's Gold isn't here out of the goodness of his heart, and a gift this expensive never comes cheap. There'll be strings attached to this bottle. A cost I'm expected to pay.

"Mom, would you please give us a second?"

"Always so afraid I'll embarrass her." She aims a wink in Cassiel's direction, flooding my face with heat. "But don't worry, I'll leave the two of you alone. I've been wanting to visit the market for weeks."

Which she's not been able to do, since the tinctures I *can* afford keep her alive but not living. I don't actually remember the last time she was strong enough to leave the apartment. Months, probably. Though the days have been running together of late, so it could well be longer still.

And I'm not even the one who made it possible.

"What are you doing here, Cassiel?" I hiss the second the door clicks shut behind her. "What do you want?"

"Chase," he says. As though that's somehow an answer.

"What?"

"My name is Chase. I don't like people calling me Cassiel." He's studying the pictures Mom keeps on the mantle. One of me and her from before she took ill, and one of her and Dad from before their love got him murdered, two tender moments frozen in time by an Indigo charm. A shrine to the family she chose in place of her magic.

"You let Savian do it," I hiss, sharpening my glare to a scowl.

"Yeah, well, he's the only one."

"And my mom's the only one who calls me Cemilla, but that hasn't stopped you." My eyes drift over to the tiny kitchen, to the sink full of dirty dishes and the pile of laundry that teeters as it grows. This whole apartment's a mess, if I'm honest. Peeling paint, broken shutters, more clutter than we have space to store.

But it is home. I square my shoulders and hold my head high. I will not apologize for the life Mom built us. Our apartment might be small and dust-bitten at the edges, but until her blood sickened, I never wanted for anything. There was always food on the table, clothes in my closet, and a dry and warm place for me to sleep. No amount of mess can change that. And if *Chase* has a problem with it, then he can take it up with someone who cares.

"Then what would you prefer?" he asks, raising a perfectly arched brow.

"That you get out of my house and leave us alone."

"Bit of a mouthful, don't you think?"

Colors help me. The arrogance on this half . . . "My mom is off limits, *Cassiel*." Anger strips my voice raw. "So if this tincture is some kind of threat—"

"Relax, would you?" he says, the muscles in his jaw clenching tight. "Savian's a fan of the stick, but I've always preferred the carrot. Which is why, until this job is done, your rent will be paid, your bills taken care of, and your mother will be provided with as much Green label as she needs."

"I—" *Oh no. No, no, no, no.* "How *dare* you?" It takes everything I have not to beat his smug face bloody.

First, he tricks me. Then, he lets a rogue Shade trap me in the Gray, abduct my friends, and blackmail me into accepting a death sentence. Now, he's trying to *save* me? There aren't enough expletives in the world.

"I don't need your charity." I seize hold of the expensive bottle and aim it at his head.

"This isn't charity." Chase catches it mid-air with infuriating ease. "Nor is it a favor, or a bribe. Think of it as an advance payment for your services," he says. "Because if you're distracted when we do this, we all die."

"We're all going to die anyway," I spit. "That's what happens when you try to rob the Dominion. You die."

"Then why not take the help? Leave something behind for your mother?" He's quick to turn the words against me, file their edges sharp and make a mockery of my fear.

"My mother is not your problem to solve, Cassiel. And if you actually gave a damn about *helping*, you'd use the power you stole to heal her properly, not try to buy me off with a temporary fix."

"That's not how it works." My derision spurs him to his feet. "The magic I take has a limit; once I use it up, it's gone. So you can thank your performance in the Gray for that *temporary fix*." The implication in his words rings clear. If I hadn't panicked last night—if I had used the talisman Savian left me instead of dislocating my thumb—Chase would still have enough power to heal Mom, though I'm not naïve enough to believe he'd have actually done me that kindness. *He probably wouldn't have revealed his stolen power at all.* While the thought is barbed, the sentiment fits. *Not until there was something in it for him.*

"Well, if I'm such a liability, then why not just take my Gray gift? Do the robbing yourself."

"Yeah . . . you really don't want me to do that."

"And why not?"

"Because it would kill you." The frank way he says it curbs my ire in its tracks. There's no hitch, no hesitation, no hint of a lie. *No reason to lie, either.* I follow the logic down the obvious path. If Chase could take my magic, he would; that's not even a question. But if the magic he takes comes with limits, then killing me would create a *single shot* situation. If anything were to go wrong, he and Savian would be back at square one and down a Bronze.

"So . . . when you steal power—does it always . . . kill?" I can't help it; I have to ask. Golds are rare enough that I know nothing of how Chase's gift works beyond that it's a dilution of Yellow magic. In a full-blood, that color confers the Shade with the ability to alter: to take an element and turn it into something new, change its composition, state, or meaning. Whereas in a half, that translates to the ability to *take*; that much I've learned from all the whispered rumors and exaggerated tales. But how he does the taking—and how he then dispenses that magic to another Shade—remains a mystery since the full intricacies of a Hue's power rarely make it into the telling, and it's not as if the Council keeps a comprehensive list. Or if they do, they definitely aren't sharing.

"No. Only if I take from a half." Chase speaks the words at the ground. "Not enough color to survive the drain."

"Oh." I don't press him for details of how he learned *that* horror. I don't think I can stomach the story. "But you do realize I won't survive *this*, either?" I say, throwing my arms out wide. "What Savian wants is not—it's impossible."

"Hard and impossible aren't the same thing, Cemilla." The tension in his eyes gives an inch. "You just have to let me help you get over this fear."

Right. *Just.* "I didn't realize it was that simple."

"I didn't say it was *simple*. I said I was here to help." Chase sighs, then with a whoosh and a whisper of wind, he phases into the Gray.

Despite the fact that we're hours away from a temporal In-Between.

And nowhere near a sanctuary.

"Erm . . . Cass—Chase—?"

With another rustle of air, he reappears in the kitchen, entirely unruffled and unharmed. "Look, I won't pretend that breaking into the Dominion will be easy. But it's only a death sentence if our Bronze shatters at the first hurdle." He blinks out of existence again, flaunting the casual ease with which he taunts the shadows.

"Gods. Would you please stop doing that." My teeth grind to a fine dust. I don't need yet another reminder of the myriad ways I'm failing to live up to my potential, or that every other Hue in this city is better equipped to survive this folly than me.

"Whether you like it or not, this lift hinges on your ability to navigate the Gray." When Chase pops back into being, he's standing right behind me, the words a gruff missive in my ear. "So if you want to survive it—if you want your *friends* to survive it—then let me help you. And everything else, well . . . consider it the very least I can do, because in case you haven't noticed, you're being used.

"*I* am using you, Cemilla," he says as I spin around to face him, his eyes blazing with a challenge forged in iron and steel. "So use me back."

CHAPTER
Eight

"Are you really not going to tell me where we're going?" I ask as Chase leads me away from the apartment, not inward through the city's rings like I expected—in search of the taverns and the gambling halls where I usually conduct my lifts—but outward to trace the encompassing wall that separates Isitar from the sea, with no hint as to how he plans to *help* me other than a wry smile and an instruction to dress for the wind.

"If I tell you where we're going, you won't want to come," he says, running a hand along the spell-rich stone.

"Yes, because telling me *that* makes it much more appealing."

Though Chase stands a head taller than me in stature, we're both dwarfed by the stark construction of magic and gray rock. Once upon a time, it used to be impossible to walk this close to its base without suffering through a haze of Orange power, but it's been years since the Council worried itself with the need to top up the spell. There's little point, I guess, now that the threat to its number is no longer coming from the world at large, but from the pious rot festering within.

"Will you at least tell me why we're leaving the faithless quarter?" I bristle, less than enthused about the prospect of following him into another Church-owned den.

"Too much wall on this side, don't you think?" When Chase smiles, his right cheek dimples, but not the left, a quirk I'd probably find attractive on someone less hells-bent on getting me killed. "You can't see the world."

"I'm not interested in seeing the world, Cassiel," I hiss. What I want is for him to stop playing games.

"Really?" My answer seems to catch him off-guard. "So you've never even thought about it? Leaving Isitar?"

That wasn't actually what I meant, but . . . "And going where, exactly?" I ask. "The rest of the continent is worse."

"I wouldn't say worse so much as *different*." Chase's eyes turn thoughtful as the streets around us shed their last vestige of magic. There'll be no more hex-lights from here on out. No more market stalls laden with talismans, or taverns that cater to both typic and Shade. In the holy quarter, it's all coal-powered lamps, effigies of the Gods, and protective spokes of iron to dampen the danger flowing through a full-blood's veins. Zealous reform in all its hateful glory.

"Different how?"

"It's kind of hard to explain, but once Isitar became a refuge for magic, the Church outside these walls got . . . complacent, you could call it," he says. "Found more pressing things to worry about."

"More pressing than wiping us off the map?" The disbelief in my voice is pure bite. "Have the Gods started smiting them down or something?"

"Smiting, no." His lips quirk with a smile. "But there's a false prophet vying for power in Sarotuza, and the czar of Nivengard is trying to do away with religion altogether, and in Heresse, the assembly is demanding a formal separation between the Cabinet and the Church, so fighting that dissent is keeping their clerics busy. Even in Astraya—where the clergy still reign king—the typics have started looking for ways to buy magic. They're not welcoming Shades into the city with open arms, or anything—the faithless quarter here truly is unique in that regard—but things are slowly changing out there. It's becoming easier for a careful Shade to go unnoticed."

"I don't suppose it's becoming easier for a careful *Hue* to go unnoticed?" I ask, at a loss for what elaborate point he's belaboring.

"No such luck, I'm afraid; it's the Council driving that vendetta. And their trackers are everywhere."

Which means there is no safer place on the continent for us to go.

There will always be a reason to look over our shoulder.

A phantom lurking in the shadows, trained by the Council to sniff out those who break their rules.

That's why we refer to their trackers as the curse of the Hue. Because we always lose something to them in the end, whether it be our lives or our families. Eventually, they come for us all.

"Then why is any of this relevant?" I snap. *What does it have to do with where he's taking me? How is knowing about the greater world going to prevent me from shattering?*

"It's . . . not," Chase says, as though that answer's a given. "I was just trying to make conversation. But we can walk in silence, if you prefer."

"I prefer." The word grits through my teeth. Though with the wall beside us dipping lower with every step—leaving nothing to distract from the cruel chill coming off the water and the maddening howl of the wind—it doesn't take long for my curiosity to get the better of me.

"How do you know so much about those places?" I ask, since on a good day, I can barely remember their location. Sarotuza lies to the . . . west? I think. Nivengard to the north, with Heresse and Astraya dotting the path between them. Each feasibly reached with enough time, will, and coin—none of which I have to spare. Even before Mom got sick they were little more than fanciful names on a map, places I never truly thought I'd see on account that Isitar is the devil I know. The devil I've learned to survive.

"That's the life of a Gold." Chase shrugs, stealing a glance at the ominous blanket of rain clouds creeping across the sky. "If I want to keep using my gift, I have to keep moving, otherwise, I start drawing attention."

Right. Of course.

Because his gift is to steal power and that's not an easy crime to miss.

"You could . . . *stop* using it," I point out, seeing how that particular problem has a fairly obvious fix.

"Could you stop using yours?" Chase counters. Then when my jaw clenches tight around the answer, he claims the victory and says, "I didn't think so." As if I *like* spending my nights risking my neck in the Gray. As if I have a choice. But since I do need his help to beat the shadows, I choke down the irritation and steer us back towards safer ground.

"So . . . does that mean you've been to Isitar before?" I ask.

"No." A shadow crosses Chase's expression, so quick and fleeting, I might have imagined it. "Can't say I ever saw the appeal of living this close to the Council's seat of power. Though my sister used to love it here."

Used to? There's no mistaking the melancholy in his voice. The tragic implication of tense. But before I can wrap my head around his inadvertent revelation, Chase brings the subject to an abrupt close by looking out over the cliffs to say, "Almost there now. We might even beat the storm down."

Beat the storm down where? I follow his gaze past a particularly derelict stretch of wall. In this part of the city, the once impenetrable barrier has been reduced to little more than a weather-beaten guardrail, stripped of both its magic and height. That was one of the first changes the Church enacted upon seizing control. Unlike the Council, the clerics saw no reason to keep shutting the world out; they were only too happy to invite the hate in.

No . . . I blanch as I realize what Chase means for us to do. *Absolutely, positively not.* The thin strip of sand at the cliff's base is shrouded in mist and shadow, the jagged outcropping of rock all but erasing the tiny beach from view. It's a hundred-and-fifty-foot drop to the bottom, at least, with nothing but a roughly hewn set of stairs carved straight into the rock.

"This is a joke . . . right? You can't possibly expect us to—"

"Climb down to the beach?" Chase hops the wall with a practiced indifference, the challenge in his eyes grinning wide. "That's the plan."

"Then make a new plan," I say, crossing my arms. Because if I had known that this was what his idea of helping me looked like, I would have just cussed him out of my apartment and stayed home.

"And why would I do that?" he asks, motioning for me to jump over and join him on the ledge. "We need a place to practice that's both out of sight and close to a sanctuary for when you panic"—I prickle at his use of *when*, not *if*—"and it doesn't get much more perfect than this."

I mean, yes, a beach is *technically* a good idea—a permanent spatial bridge between land and sea where I could phase without fear. But not only does this particular beach lie at the foot of a treacherous cliff, it also happens to be on the reformed side of Isitar, where our existence is both illegal and likely to garner a painful death.

"Are you actually stupid or are you trying to get us seen?" My stomach churns with acid, clenching my insides tight. I should have never agreed to follow him out of the faithless quarter, not without first ensuring that he had a plan that made sense. Some secluded cave or a secret hideaway, complete with boarded-up windows and a triple-locked fence. Nothing this . . . *exposed.*

"Relax, no one's going to see us—and they're definitely not going to follow us down these stairs," Chase says, pointing to the frayed length of rope that serves as a makeshift railing. "Now are you coming or not?"

Not is what I want to say. It's what I *should* say—and probably what I *would* have said if I hadn't witnessed him blinking into the Gray over and over again without effort.

For Mom. You're doing this for Mom. The memory of her up and healthy spurs me towards the deadly decline. The stairs are uneven and slick with salt, worn so badly in places we have no choice but to rely on the rope to hold our weight as we navigate the steeply cut steps, to keep from slipping on a loose piece of rock and falling. An ice-cold wind pounds us flat against the cliff-face, the ocean spitting a hungry spray at our heels. But even despite the chill, and the danger, and the thundering crash of waves, when we finally reach the sand, Chase is beaming.

"See? Perfect." His smugness is a dance of teeth. Though I am forced to admit that he was right about the beach; we really do feel invisible. A casual onlooker would never spot us without straining, and with the clouds hanging thick and pregnant with rain, it's unlikely anyone would think to bother.

Which does solve the obvious problem.

Just not the one that'll kill me.

"There are no anchors," I say, scouring the shoreline for anything I could conceivably use. The walls of the cliff converge to form a crescent, but they're over a hundred feet apart, and even before Magdalena shattered, I'd never anchored an In-Between across anything larger than a modestly sized room. The ocean is an option, of course, though not for a Hue of my skill since it's a moving target, and the pebbles strewn along the water's edge are far too slight to support the spell. Which means the only thing we achieved by coming down here is gaining access to a sanctuary. But I can't practice creating my own In-Between in one of those.

"Look again, Cemilla, there are anchors all around." With another grin and an overblown flourish, Chase phases into the Gray.

By my colors. I wish he'd stop doing that.

"Okay, so this is where the sanctuary kicks in," he says when he blinks back into being, etching a line in the sand with the toe of his boot. "You can start on the water side, but by the time we're done, you'll be"—off he goes again—"all the way over here." He reappears by the rocks, a whole universe away from safety.

"Yeah, I wouldn't hold your breath."

"I don't need to hold my breath; that's kind of the point." His taunt is as senseless as it is mean.

"I thought the point was to help me."

"Sure, that too," Chase says. Then, when I fix him the sharpest look in my arsenal, he adds, "If you don't at least try, we *will* all die doing this."

Why are we doing it at all? I want to scream the words at him. To grab hold of his shoulders and demand to know what stake he has in this plan. Whether Savian tied a noose around his neck, too, or if the two of them are in it together.

Does it really matter? The questions die a quick death on my tongue. Asking them won't change anything. It won't keep the tide from rising or the fear from taking root inside my heart. And hells, maybe if Chase sees for himself how hopeless my In-Betweens are, he'll be forced to reconsider the viability of this crime. Relay the disappointing news to his master. Maybe even set us free.

So instead of indulging my anger, I step back into the sanctuary and draw a breath deep. When Chase blinks into the Gray, I follow him.

A silhouette swallows the headland, draping stone in darkness and color with a smokey veil. The dull roar of the waves disappears, usurped by the seductive crash of ash meeting ink. And though I can't understand the obscenities the shadows are muttering to the wind—I'm not Lyria—I swear I hear them calling my name, trying to lure me out of the permanent In-Between so they can oust me. Shatter me. Devour me whole.

Rid both worlds of an unwanted half.

Beyond the sanctuary line, Chase walks the beach with an impossible ease, hands tucked into his pockets, hair ruffling with the salt breeze. He's not speaking an In-Between into being; he's not straining to hold the shield. In fact, he barely seems to be doing much of anything—except staring in judgement at me.

"How are you so *calm*?" The whine slips out unbidden, my disbelief ringing louder than the sea. Eve's the only other half I've seen look this comfortable in the Gray, but as an Emerald, forging In-Betweens is her gift. And he can't take another Hue's gift without—

Oh Gods.

"Please tell me you didn't," I whisper. "Eve—is she—?"

"Your friend is perfectly fine, Cemilla, but I'm glad you're finally starting to worry about the right things." Chase's eyes narrow with danger, the threat in them shining clear.

Our only value lies in our magics.

In our ability to service Savian's needs.

Fail to do that and his trusty Gold will take our gifts into his own hands.

He'll kill us himself.

"Then how are you doing this?" I ask, refusing to betray fear. "What are you anchoring to?"

"The sea, the sky, the rocks, the beach . . ." His warning gives way to a cold sneer. "Didn't anyone ever tell you? We're always in between something."

Great. Now he's spouting useless philosophy.

"Not everything around us can be anchored, Cassiel."

"Says who?" he asks. "The three halves you've crossed paths with? You don't think it's possible that there's a theory of magic out there they've missed?" He makes it sound as though Hues actually spend their time looking, when in truth, most of us aren't interested in learning to better survive the Gray, we're too busy learning to survive, period. Learning to stay clear of a tracker's blade.

I mean, I didn't even know the Gray *existed* until years after Mom first told me I was a Bronze, since she didn't want to share that part of my birthright until I was old enough to understand the risks—and not a second before my magic matured enough to sense the shadows. I had no name for that feeling back then, but when I started dreaming of a world stripped of color, Mom recognized the urge building in my blood, and knew that eventually, I would succumb to the need to phase with or without her blessing, instinctively discover how to push my body between realms. That's when she finally told me about my power, and even then, she made me promise never to heed the shadow's call outside a sanctuary; she gave me just enough information to satisfy the itch.

It was Eve who taught me how to create my own In-Betweens, though I never did take to that ability quite as readily as the others. While Ezzo and Novi could go a full quarter bell in the Gray without faltering, I would reach my limit after four or five minutes, tops. Never quite managed to hold the spell with their level of ease. Maybe I would have, in time—I was certainly growing more confident at it—working bigger, more complex lifts. But then I grew *too* comfortable, and Magdalena shattered, and whatever will I had to *practice* disappeared. Not that any amount of practice could have proffered me Chase's skill; his command of the shadows is downright unsettling.

"No. We wouldn't have missed a trick this important," I tell him. Because how could we have? Eve, Novi, and Ezzo were all taught how to cast a shield by their full-blooded parent, long before the Council made an example of their fates. That's three separate Shades passing down the same teaching. If there was a better way to cast an In-Between, one of them would have shared it.

"What makes you so sure?" Chase keeps right on pushing. "It's not like anyone writes this stuff down—and when they do, the Council finds it, destroys it, kills the scribe for good measure, and poof, it's like the truth never existed. We only see the version of it they allow us to see. So instead of anchoring your magic the way you *should*, you anchor it the only way you know how—and I guarantee you, if you trace that theory back, it'll lead you straight to one of their lies. They have a vested interest in making it as hard as possible for us to access the Gray; they don't want us experimenting with a spell that might make it easier."

Much as I hate to admit it, there's a kernel of truth to his rant; the Council does go out of its way to keep us in the dark. We don't get to attend the elite academy it built in the shadows, with its resplendent libraries, and endless archives, and rainbow of specialized instructors. Everything we learn about our gifts is through trial and error, mistakes and guesswork, rinse and repeat. It never even occurred to me that the physicality I enjoyed in the Gray was unique to my Hue until the day Ezzo found me, when, in his effort to "get back" and "stay away" as I demanded, I watched him step through a solid brick wall. Only then did I understand the true breadth of our gifts. That we each experience the shadows differently.

"Tell me what you picture when you create an In-Between," Chase says, as though reading my doubt. "How are you directing your power?"

"Erm . . . I don't know . . ." The question catches me by surprise. "By imagining a bubble, I guess? Kind of like a net that stretches between anchors."

"I had a feeling." He continues to prance around the shadowed beach as though it's nothing. As though the magic isn't exacting a devastating toll. "If you treat the spell like it's got fixed boundaries, you'll never be able to hold it for more than a few minutes at a time.

It takes too much energy. You have to think of it more like a liquid that's rushing to fill the gap. That way, you only have to focus on projecting your power."

"Yeah . . . that's not a thing." I roll my eyes. Not even Eve describes it in such an esoteric manner—and of the four of us, she's the one who could have feasibly found a better technique, though I suppose the nature of her gift would have negated the need for trying. But still. Pitching my magic around a fixed point was the very first lesson she taught me, because that's the most reliable way to inure your In-Between for maximum stability and reach.

It's how we all do it.

It's how every generation of Hues before us did it.

It's the only way to get the job done.

"Would you at least *try* it my way before declaring it won't work," Chase says, offering me his hand. "So long as we stay in contact, I can keep an In-Between around us both, ease it back when you're ready. You'll be totally safe."

"No. No way. It's too dangerous." I cling stubbornly to my place in the sanctuary. I made a similar promise myself not too long ago. Overestimated my own strength. And Magdalena paid the price. "You're not an Emerald—shields aren't—that isn't your gift."

"Forget everything you know about our magics, Cemilla. It's time to learn some new tricks." The challenge in his voice is pure steel. Around us, the waves curl like smoke and crash like cinder, the headland beckoning me near with a tormenting sigh.

He hasn't shattered yet . . . I steal a fleeting glance at the safety line at my feet. *Maybe it's not impossible.*

Maybe a year on from Magdalena's death, it's time to start conquering this fear.

"Cemmy," I say, sliding my hand into his. "If you're going to kill me, at least stop using my full name."

"No one is dying today." His conviction sears a brand against my skin. "Savian would have me flayed and quartered."

So they're not equal partners in this . . . I pick over the tiny sliver of information Chase just let slip. But as much as I want to ask the follow-up question—*then why are you helping him?*—I'm too busy holding my breath as step by quivering step, he leads me out of the sanctuary.

Only three steps to go now.

Two steps.

One.

Brace.

Every part of me tenses, my nails drawing blood and a soft wince.

"Breathe, Cemmy." His whisper is a peal of laughter in my ear, infuriating and bizarre in equal measure.

He shouldn't be laughing.

Hells, he shouldn't be *talking.*

With anchors this unstable, he should be entirely consumed by the spell.

Argh. "How are you making this look so easy?"

"The shadows can't swallow an ocean," Chase says, moving to stand behind me. "That's how you need to picture the magic, like a wave that's molding around you."

"And if I can't do that?"

"Then I'll be right here." His hands ease off my shoulders, leaving me no choice but to stop stalling and take over the cast.

"I am in between the cliffs and the sea." Speaking the words aloud is a force of habit, even if the feat I'm attempting is anything but. *My shield is a wall of water, not a net. A downpour, not a bubble. It flows with me, washing the shadows away.*

If only wishing made it true.

My whole body tenses as the Gray pushes back against my hubris, issuing a swift and stern reminder that the sea is too volatile a creature to catch. Pressure turns to pain turns to peril turns to panic, until all at once, I'm pressed flush to Chase's chest, his warmth a balm to my frigid failure, his hands gently circling my wrists.

"I've got you." His In-Between explodes out around me, cutting through the danger with an effort I can feel.

"Back. I want to go back." The terror pulses hard beneath my ribs. I don't care how calm and in control he seems, or how low and comforting his voice is. This was a mistake—and a colossal one at that.

The shadows don't want us here.

They're warning us to get the hells out.

"You can do this, Cemmy." Chase's grip is an iron shackle, keeping me in harm's way.

"No, I *can't*."

"Yes, you can. You don't even have to fight the Gray if that's too daunting; you can fight me, instead. Try to replace my In-Between with your own."

"Is that even possible?" I hiss. Because, seriously, how many new theories of magic is he going to just . . . *invent*?

"Try it and see." The smile in Chase's voice sets a fire to my fuse.

Fine. Let him have his fun.

At least if I die, I'll take his arrogant face with me.

Since his spell is currently counteracting the uselessness of mine, I close my eyes and will myself to focus. To unclench my fists, and swallow the bile, and keep the frantic beat of my heart from failing.

You're doing this for Mom, remember? I draw a quiet strength from my ring, twisting the metal band around my finger. She needs me to survive this endeavor and come home.

"I am in between the cliffs and the sea."

I picture a river overflowing its banks. Water filling a bathtub. The persistent rains that haunt Isitar during spring.

"The cliffs and the sea."

I picture a tidal wave hurtling towards the city. Ice melting to form crystal puddles. The fine mist of salt clinging to Chase's eyelashes and skin.

"I am in between the cliffs and the sea."

And inch by devastating inch, the magic begins to take, my In-Between holding its own against the shadows. Prompting Chase to pull away.

"No, don't—!" I grab for his arm, the confidence crumbling every bit as fast as it appeared. A second later, I'm not just back behind the sanctuary line, I'm back on the physical beach, with blood pounding in my ears and the bitter taste of adrenaline on my tongue.

"What happened?" Chase blinks out of the Gray after me. "The spell was working. I could feel it."

"It's not *sustainable.*" I gasp at the air, the cold wind whipping my hair into a frenzy. I barely held the shield for a few seconds, and it's left me as drained as though I'd run the city mountain to cliff. That's the problem with conjuring a tidal wave. It might be strong, and fast, and a marvel of nature, but in the end, it washes everything out to sea. "I need a solid anchor or the In-Between is impossible to maintain."

"What you *need* is to keep trying. Now let's go again." Without waiting for me to catch my breath, Chase drags me back into the Gray.

The second time, I manage to drive his magic back a couple of feet.

The third, I allow him to let go of me completely—if only for a brief moment.

By the fourth, the storm has engulfed the beach proper and the word 'again' becomes a nail I'd like to rake across his cheeks.

"You're too afraid." Chase is relentless, placing me at the shadows' mercy over and over and *again,* as though that might somehow eradicate my fear.

"That tends to be my default state when it comes to things that can kill me." I grit my teeth and try again.

And again.

And a-fucking-gain.

Popping in and out of existence until the tide is nipping at our heels, driving us ever closer to the looming cliff-face, our sanctuary diminishing along with it.

"*Again,*" Chase barks when I finally drop to the sand, drenched to the bone with sweat, and rain, and tears born of frustration.

"No, I'm done," I say, scrubbing at the tired wetness.

"We only have six days left until the cleansing moon. You don't get to be *done.*"

"And yet, here we are." I refuse to let him goad me back into the shadows. If I've learned anything these past few hours, it's that Chase will play whatever role best suits his needs. He's cold and critical one minute, soft and encouraging the next. When he's not taunting me, he's treating me as kindly as one would a friend—a villain and a saint in equal measure, all in the service of getting the reaction he wants.

Which I am done giving.

"You know, for someone who's so afraid to die, you're willing to do very little to stop it," he clips. And perhaps I'm imagining it, but a desperate edge creeps into his anger. Like he needs me to perfect the magic far more than he's prepared to admit.

"That's funny, because for someone who's doing a madman's bidding, you're giving way too much of a shit."

"Gods, you still don't get it, do you?" Chase looks up towards the city, the muscles in his jaw pulling tight. "If you don't master this spell, then Savian will make me—"

"Make you what, Cassiel?" *Kill me? Take my gift for yourself?* "Go on, say it, you coward." *At least have the decency to threaten me to my face.*

But he doesn't.

And it's only when I follow his eyes that I realize what new problem distracted him mid-rage.

At the top of the cliffs—despite the cold, and the mist, and how hard they'd have had to squint through the rain—a crowd has amassed beyond the derelict wall, stern and livid. Someone must have seen us phasing. Raised the alarm. On the reformed side of Isitar, where those with magic in their blood aren't allowed to exist.

They know what we are. The realization bleeds the fight right out of me. *They know what we are and they have us trapped on this beach.*

CHAPTER

Nine

"You arrogant, irresponsible, *reckless* piece of—"

"Yeah, I don't think insulting me right now is going to help." Chase paces what's left of the tiny beach, the coolness of his mask cracking. With every moment that passes, the crowd of spectators grows larger and more dangerously skilled, a contingent of armed enforcers having joined the vigil. Their taunts pierce the air in broken fragments, a chorus of jeers and hate that threatens to out-crash the wind. *Half breeds. Abominations. Ungodly.* All those ugly names I've bristled at my entire life.

"You said this was the perfect place to practice!" I seethe. "You said no one would see us!"

"I didn't think they would." Chase is clawing at his hair as though possessed—as though *surprised* the world's worst fucking idea went bad.

So perfectly, predictably bad. Anger bleeds my eyes red. I should have never followed him down here; I should have trusted my gut and told him exactly where to shove his *help*, worked through the problem with Novi until we had a plan for ridding ourselves of him and Savian.

"Come on, I can't think through all this yelling." Chase grabs my hand and blinks us back into the Gray, turning light to shadow and the ocean to a foaming abyss. Rain to stardust.

"You do realize we can't wait them out in here," I say as he recommences his march. Not because what's left of the sanctuary is fast getting swallowed up by the sea—he's proven his magic plenty capable of protecting us both, for a seemingly endless amount of time—but because the tide will soon be swallowing up the beach along with it. And no amount of magic can keep us from drowning. Not in the real world, or the Gray.

"Yes, I'm aware of that, thank you." More than anything, it's Chase's fear that rattles me, the pained clench of his fists and the way his eyes can't seem to focus their gaze. He's as lost in this moment as I am. Staring down the barrel of a problem he can't fix.

"I don't understand, how could they even know we're halves?"

"I don't think they *know* much of anything." Chase steals another glance up the cliff. Though the typics have no tangible form in the Gray, they do leave a trace in the ether, impressions that buzz like fireflies fluttering through ink. Echoes, we call them. And while echoes make no sound, the volume now gathered is a wild shriek. "They probably just figured no full-blood would be careless enough to get caught."

Nor would getting caught pose a threat to a full-blood. No In-Betweens to worry about, for one thing, and when they shimmer through the shadows, they can control their corporeality at will. Walk through walls when it suits them; affect their surroundings when they need, no matter their color or specialization. Freedoms Chase and I don't enjoy, and regardless of how the mob arrived at their conclusion, their guess has created the perfect predicament. A way of intertwining our fates.

"You can't climb the cliff in the Gray," I say, and it isn't a question. Unlike me, Chase is only able to interact with other Shades and natural objects—the sand, the stone, the surf, the sea—and when it comes to structures erected by man or magic, nothing more than the floor or ground that stands beneath his feet. So while the shadows would, theoretically, allow him to scale this roughly cut staircase, the rock is far too uneven and slick with rain to scale unaided, and Chase doesn't have the physicality with which to grab the rope. If he did, he wouldn't be panicking.

"Neither can you," he counters, arching a brow deep. "You're nowhere near ready to hold that kind of In-Between on your own. You'd shatter without me."

Yes, I would. There's no sense in pretending otherwise.

We either make this climb together, or we die.

I am using you, Cemilla. His words from this morning whisper an opportunity in my mind. *So use me back.* The idea forms quickly, and when it does, I don't waste time agonizing over its sharp edges—or allowing some misguided sense of guilt to smother it dead.

"If I do this, then at the end of the job, you steal more of Savian's power and heal my mom. Permanently," I say, making my price clear.

"Why would I ever agree to that?" The request stuns Chase still.

"Because you're the one who dragged us down here, so you owe me."

"And you're choosing to collect by swearing me to a promise I could break the second we're off the cliff?"

"Trust goes both ways, Cassiel." I ignore the condescending curl of his lip. And since I've got him trapped between a literal rock and the ocean, Chase huffs, rolls his eyes, and says, "Deal—but only if you stop calling me Cassiel."

"I can agree to that." My flare of victory is hollow and short-lived. I may have wrung an additional life out of this bargain, but I'm still a hundred-and-fifty-feet of devastating climb from reaping my reward. Not to mention an impossible trip through the Dominion.

"You'll have to take my waist; I'm going to need both hands," I tell him, staring up at the formidable wall of rock. The cliff may have cast an intimidating shadow in the physical realm, but in the Gray, it's downright chilling, an onyx titan of vertical knives and jagged maws. Far more daunting from the bottom than it looked on the way down.

"You sure you're up to this?" Chase asks as we leave the safety of the sanctuary behind, the soothing rush of his magic enveloping me with heat.

"Are you?" I snatch hold of the rope and take a tentative step upward. "Just . . . don't slip, okay? I'd rather not have to do this twice."

Or at all, to be honest. But that decision has long since washed away.

With his breath tickling my neck and his hands locked tight around my midriff, I tackle the ascent one steep stair at a time, my fingers hugging the rope so tightly my palms begin to blister.

Step—pull—step—wobble.

Step—pull—step—breathe out.

Ignore the pain, ignore the cold, ignore the hard press of Gold at my back, the ardent ripple of lean muscle and the cloying warmth of wet skin. The fact that both our lives are hanging by this frayed length of salt-licked hemp.

The first part of the climb passes without incident, our bodies moving in tandem, Chase following me up the slippery staircase with careful strides and a resolute effort to support his own weight. But as we creep across the half way mark, the strength in my arms begins to fail. Each step suddenly feels heavier than the last, every hard-won inch more painful. And while I may not be fighting to keep an In-Between around us, Chase's reliance on my gift is its own kind of anchor, a burden of responsibility I'm fast growing unable to bear.

Step—pull—step—grumble.

Step—pull—step—don't trip.

"Will you at least *try* to be careful?" I snap as Chase stumbles for the umpteenth time, driving us dangerously close to the edge.

"Sorry, I'm—I think we need to stop." The tremble in his voice immediately sets my heart racing. I've been so consumed by the need to keep putting one foot in front of the other, I didn't notice how labored his breaths have become, or the violent shake of his hands against my navel. How the pressure building around us is threatening to buckle his shield.

"Erm . . . Chase, what's wrong with your spell?" The panic in my question is shrill.

"I don't know—the magic, it's . . . I'm losing my grip."

"What?" His revelation is a match to kindling, a magnifying glass to dry wood. We're over a hundred feet up this godsforsaken cliff; high enough that a fall would kill us, and too close to the top to abandon the anonymity of the Gray. If we phase back now, the mob will see our faces, so even if we did manage to escape them—and that's a pretty big *if*—we'd never be safe again. On either side of Isitar.

"No, you . . . you have to pull it together!" My terror rises in pitch. "We're way past the point of no return!"

"Then help me hold the In-Between." Chase's plea sparks a shameful ache inside my soul, gnawing at a memory that's best left forgotten. Of another disastrous failure of gift.

"I *can't.* You know I can't." He said it himself: I'm nowhere near ready to cast a spell of this magnitude, not least of all while shouldering his weight.

"You have to." He shudders, straining to keep the shadows at bay. "Please, Cemmy. If you shatter, I shatter."

No, he won't. The darkest of possibilities steals through my mind. If the Gray shatters me, then yes, Chase would lose his footing on the stairs and tumble down the cliff, break bloody against the eager rocks below. But that's assuming he doesn't drain my magic long before that happens. Saves his own skin.

Which he will.

It's only a matter of time before he yields to that temptation, regardless of how thoroughly it might upset Savian. In the pursuit of survival, he'll act first, beg forgiveness later. I'd be a fool to believe he'd spare my life.

"You're a real son of a bitch, Cassiel." I force my magic outward, fortifying his shield with a curse and a desperate growl.

I am in between the shoreline and the city.

And my power is an ocean, endless and vast.

A waterfall, swift and unrelenting.

A flood that compels the shadows to surrender to my might.

The toll is unlike anything I've ever felt before. My vision blurs black with the effort, the fire in my veins making molten magma of my insides.

"Don't overthink this, Cemmy. Your magic knows what to do." Chase's whisper is a soft caress in my ear, an affirmation I do not want—or need—from the overconfident half who landed us in this mess to begin with.

"Shut up and help me climb." I tune out everything but the rope in my hand and the tithe of the incantation, operating on pure instinct, leaving my mind no room to question the stability of my anchors, or calculate the impossible distance they cover, or envisage what would happen if my boots or my concentration were to slip.

I am in between the shoreline and the city.

Scaling the treacherous incline as hastily as I dare, even as my head begins to pound in protest and the magic saps me of my balance and breath.

"Keep doing what you're doing, Cemmy. We're almost there." At least Chase has had the decency to start sharing the load of his own heft. A mercy seeing how with every step, the cost of the spell seems to double. Demanding more sweat. More power. More tears.

I am in between the shoreline and the city.

I set my jaw and grit my pain loud.

We're only twenty stairs from the clifftop now.

Fifteen.

Ten.

But my hands have shredded ribbons against the rope and fatigue is tugging at my marrow. And though we're inching closer and closer to safety—five stairs, four stairs, three—I feel my power stutter and wane, the color in my blood running empty.

"Close enough." With a strength he claims to have lost, Chase tightens his grip on my waist and blinks us out of the Gray, launching us to a rolling stop atop the windswept cliff-face, his body pinning me flat against the sodden grass.

"What are you doing?" Through the haze of exhaustion, a new wave of panic seizes hold. "We have to phase back or they'll see us! Chase—they're going to see!"

"Relax, there's no one here. Look." Though his words are soft, their meaning strikes an axe to timber.

Because there's no one here. I try to blink away the bewildering stretch of nothing. No enforcers. No violent chorus. No pitchforks. No hate. The only sound drifting across the wall to greet us is the regular bustle of the city, the resolute indifference of a crowd that's entirely oblivious to our escape.

"But I saw them." My head shakes of its own accord. Not just in the physical realm, but as echoes in the Gray, a righteous swarm of fireflies awaiting us beyond the shadows. "I don't understand, they were *right there.* Why would they leave—?"

They wouldn't.

The truth is stubborn and slow to land, but when it finally hits, it cleaves my chest wide open.

Chase did it again.

He used a glamour to trick me.

There was never an angry mob watching us through the rain.

They never raised the alarm or inexplicably deduced we were halves.

We were never in any danger save for the danger he put us in himself.

Nothing wrong with his damn magic . . .

"Oh, you unbelievable *ass.*" I throw a sharp knee to his stomach, shoving him off to the side in a furious fit of rage. "You set me up!"

"You needed a push," he says, lurching clear of my wrath.

"I should push you off the cliff."

Gods, I can't believe I fell for such a clumsy, obvious lie. If I had stopped to think, even for a second, I'd have realized how convenient it was for the mob to have appeared at the exact moment I gave up the ghost. How strange it was that we hadn't noticed them gather. How their presence—and the sudden waver of Chase's shield—created the exact set of circumstances he needed in order to spur me to act. Like he'd planned this entire lesson around my failure.

"We could have *died,*" I hiss, staggering back to my feet.

"But we didn't." Chase shrugs, unrepentant. "And in case you still don't think it was worth the risk, you should know that I didn't just pull back my In-Between; I let go of it completely. You held that spell by yourself."

"Is that supposed to make me feel better?" Fear screams a crucible through my blood, as though reacting to the past threat anew. It's little wonder the magic exacted such an excruciating toll. In a decade spent dipping in and out of the Gray, I've never secured an In-Between around such volatile anchors—let alone around another Hue. And I couldn't care less how *well* this twisted plan of his worked. Chase had no right to force that decision on me. No right at all.

"It is, actually," he says, following me back across the wall. "You want to know why?"

"Not really, no." What I *want* is to introduce my fist to his perfectly straight nose. Wipe the smug look off that pretty face for good.

"You think too much, Cemmy." He forges on undeterred. "That's what stopped you picking the lock to the Governor's study, and what hindered your progress today. Every time you came close to cracking the spell, you got in your own head and talked yourself out of it. Backing you into a corner was the only way to shut those voices up. Keep you focused on the magic."

It's the iron cuff around my wrist all over again.

The assumption that I won't fall apart when it matters.

"And how exactly do you plan to keep me *focused on the magic* next time?" If Chase had bothered to learn the first thing about me, he'd know that assumption is a crock of shit; my panic is just as likely to end deadly. "Because the only thing you taught me today is to never believe a single word you say." That's the problem with cycling through masks with a manipulative ease: you teach your prey that the mask and your true face are identical. That you can't be trusted.

"It'll be easier from here, you'll see," Chase says, strolling back towards the street.

No, I won't. I cinch my hood tight and storm off in the opposite direction, the fury burning hot beneath my skin.

Fool me once, shame on you.

Fool me twice, shame on me.

But I'll be damned if I let there be a third time.

CHAPTER

Ten

"He's *impossible.*" I echo the word around the stillness of our monastery. "Infuriating, rash, reckless, and *impossible.*"

"Sounds a lot like someone else I know," Novi clips, wrestling my hands back down to the table. "Now would you please hold still? Every time you flail around, I have to start again."

"Sorry." I settle back in my chair, wincing as she douses the broken skin with a sharp-smelling tonic. I used to think I'd lucked into one of the better Gray gifts, a way of using the shadows as more than just an invisible cut-through or an untraceable place to hide. But ever since Chase slithered into my life, the ability to touch and steal has fast become the ability to collect injuries. And since he's already exhausted his supply of healing magic, I'm stuck with the bloodied mess the rope made of my palms—and the stinging pain of tending to them. "Gods, En—what is this stuff? Lye?"

"Nothing quite so corrosive." She rolls her eyes, gently dabbing away the excess heat. "I'd say this serves you right for sneaking out on me this morning, but that seems a little mean."

"A little, yeah." A warm flush prickles my neck, the memory of last night's dalliance searing through my veins like wildfire. "And just for the record, I didn't *sneak out,* I had to— "

"Check on your mom." Novi sighs as she repeats the excuse I left in my stead. "Don't worry, Cem, we're not going to make this a thing." Whether she means a fight over my cowardly exit or our drunken slip into bed, I don't know, but I guess I should be grateful either way. Novi has every last right to be mad at me; she deserved better than a flimsy note and a hastily scribbled lie. I owe her better.

"Were you at least able to get anything useful out of Mr. Impossible while he had you trapped down on that beach?" she asks, letting me off the hook. "Like what Savian's looking for in the Dominion?"

Or not.

"No, I—" The thought didn't even occur to me. "I was too distracted to try." The flush spreads up into my cheeks—a perfect match to the sudden flare of irritation pinking Novi's. She doesn't blame me for landing us in this predicament; she made that much clear to me last night, when we were lying spent in a tangle of arms and sheets. *Cassiel was watching us all, remember?* she'd said when that worry finally voiced itself aloud. *They'd have rounded us up eventually.*

But it was me he tricked.

My scrys he used to track them.

My desperation that opened the door to this threat.

The least I can do is help slam it shut again.

"Okay, but do you think he'd tell you anything if you did try?" Novi's quick to temper the frustration.

"Maybe," I say. Because as much as I can accuse Chase of being enraging, and obstinate, and vague, tight-lipped is the one charge that doesn't quite fit him. He actually told me a lot of things while we were stuck at the base of that cliff. Some at my apartment, too—about the deadly cost of a Gold's magic—and there was also that inadvertent slip about his sister as we were making our way towards the beach.

When I goad him, Chase loves nothing more than to speak.

If only to emphasize how wrong I am.

"But he's a liar, En. How are we supposed to trust him?" I ask. For all we know, even the "truths" he's provided might well have been lies—the angry mob certainly was, and he had nothing to gain by revealing the limitations of his magic. Hells, he might have *invented* those limitations in order to avoid healing Mom, so that he could continue to hold her health hostage.

"By getting him to trust *you*," Novi says, binding my cuts with a generous length of gauze. "Turning you into the person he confides in."

"Can you please be serious?" I fix her a sharp look.

"I am serious, Cem—think about it. You're the one they need for the actual stealing, so Cassiel is bound to take more of an interest in getting *you* ready for the lift. He's already proven that, hasn't he? By trying to win you over with that expensive tincture and paying your bills. It is quite literally in his best interest to do whatever it takes to keep you onside, and that gives you the perfect opportunity to work him for information."

Her declaration chills me cold.

"What exactly are you suggesting here, En? That I *seduce* him?"

"*Hey*." Novi's eyes flash with danger. "You know me better than that—and I know you better than that." She softens. "You're more likely to break his nose than bed him. But if you can control that temper of yours for a few days and play nice, then maybe you'll learn something we can use to leverage our freedom. That's what the rest of us have spent the day trying to do," she says, laying the accusation on thick. "I've been working to dig up anything I can on Savian, and Eve's been helping Ezzo scour the Gray for where he might be hiding, but so far, we've all come up empty—even Ez. Which means Savian's found a way to cover his tracks."

"Is that even possible?" I flinch as she ties off the last of the bandages. I've never heard of a Shade escaping Ezzo's gift; that's what makes it so useful. An infallible way to track blood color across the city, stop the Council from uncovering the illegal Hues in their midst, warn us if it feels as though their trackers are getting too close to our palette. It's how he keeps us safe.

"Ez thinks it must be." The despondence in Novi's voice is bone deep. "When he went looking for the trails from last night, Cassiel's was there but not Savian's—even though we know for a fact that he shimmered through the Gray more than once. So then I paid a Violet to try and trace him through his scry, but she couldn't break the spell he'd used to keep the magic locked in our direction, and asking around about him got me absolutely nowhere, as well." Novi runs both hands hard through her hair. "There's not a single whisper on the street about a new Shade coming to Isitar—if anything, my contacts were more worried about the rate at which the Council Shades are continuing to leave. They've lost a dozen more in the last few weeks, apparently. It's almost as if they're running from something bigger than the Church, but no one seems to know *what*, and no one I talked to in the faithless quarter has heard of a Shade matching Savian's description, Green, rogue, Council, or otherwise. The man's a ghost," she says, and I can tell by the bite of her lip how much that admission costs her.

There's rarely a secret in Isitar Novi can't steal. She slinks through this city's underbelly the way a cat would a feast, wearing her glamours like a shield, wielding her smile like a weapon, her charm mimicking a Red's ability to compel. So to have failed at something this important . . . well, it sure explains the thorny edge to her mood.

"We can't track him, Cem." The black flint of her irises locks sight with my icy blue. "And unless that changes, getting answers from Cassiel is our best bet."

My best bet, she means, even if she doesn't say it.

Our ability to escape Savian lives or dies with me.

*

It isn't long before an opportunity presents itself—during our first official assignment from Savian: a trip to the reformed side of Isitar to determine how much security stands between us and successfully breaching the Dominion gate.

The High Commander will vacate his office at four bells to midnight, said the missive he sent through our scrys. *You'll have an hour.* To do what, he didn't make clear, but between us, we took an educated guess.

The High Commander is Isitar's top-ranking General, responsible for both the safety of the city and the smooth running of the cleansing moon parade. His office is likely to contain everything we need to orchestrate this lift. Problem is, it's located at the very heart of the military barracks, behind an army of trained enforcers and a lock that can't be picked. According to Chase, the Commander had it made special.

"You do realize this is a terrible idea," I tell him, stealing a glance at the tavern door. The Sacred Hearts Inn is a damn sight nicer than the last bar he conned me into, a place where Isitar's finest make a point of being seen. There's no magic changing hands in this establishment. No Council business taking place. No flagrant blasphemy. Maybe that's why it strikes me as infinitely duller than the Hidden Son. Everyone here is just so . . . *righteous*. The enforcers' uniforms are too crisp, their drinks too soft, and their conversations bordering on zealous. Those not sporting the military's crimson regalia are dressed in a grayscale of rich, embroidered fabrics, their colors muted as a mark of respect for the Church. And though I'm sat across from the only Gold Isitar's seen in decades, the opulent shine of gold is evident all around, embedded in the patrons' eyes and skin. Marking them as faithful.

Marking *us* as faithful, too, thanks to another of Chase's glamours. Since our part of tonight's plan is to *not* draw attention, he's charmed us both to look as flecked and glittery as the city's elite, dressed for the part in a uniform of heavy blacks that accentuates his chiseled edges, makes stark the razor-sharp cut of his cheeks.

"You say that about all my ideas." He leans back in his chair, looking altogether too relaxed given the ludicrous feat we're about to attempt.

"That's because all your ideas are bad," I grit. Novi had barely finished tending to my hands when he'd appeared at the monastery, all smug smiles, impossible asks, and a stubborn refusal to apologize for the hell he put me through on that beach. He's the one who supplied the *wheres* and *whats* of tonight's endeavor, though he left the finer details of the *hows* up to us. Because—and I quote—*stealing is your area of expertise.*

"Got us through the door though, didn't I?" Chase says, flashing me his teeth.

"Yes, it sure is convenient how you have endless access to Red magic, but almost none to Green."

"It's not convenient at all, actually." The glare he fixes me is puzzled. "Especially since I don't have endless access to Red magic."

"Oh, spare me." I dip my voice low. "This is the third time I've seen you cast a glamour, and you told me you can only use your stolen power once."

"I didn't say *once*. I said until *I use it up*."

"Sounds an awful lot like the same thing to me."

"Then maybe you should learn to listen better." I'm coming to recognize the agitated twitch in Chase's jaw. The one that tells me he's about to refute my assumptions with fact.

"Healing is the hardest specialization, even for full-bloods—"

Yup, there he goes.

"—so as a Hue, it's even harder for me. I have to take twice as much to heal half as many."

"Right." Because that definitely doesn't sound like an excuse.

"You don't believe me?"

"You've lied to me before, *Cassiel*." I wield the name he hates like a weapon, laying my bandaged hands flat on the table for him to see. "And this is where it got me."

"It also got you a better way to anchor your In-Betweens." The ice in his expression hardens. "And besides, I wouldn't call it a lie so much as it was a . . . trick."

"A fine distinction." I crane my neck for another fleeting glance at the door. If Savian was right, then the Commander will have left his office ten minutes ago, at the ringing of the eighth bell, and ventured this way soon thereafter for his daily debrief with his heads of guard, a meeting he always holds in the back room of this tavern.

Every part of tonight's plan rests on that single *if*.

"Look, I can't make you trust me, Cemmy." In the space of a heartbeat, Chase has assumed a mask of feigned sincerity, as though he's remembered that it's easier to get your way with soft words and a smoldering eye. "No amount of stolen magic will help me do that."

No, it won't. There isn't enough magic in the world.

But as much as I want to keep sniping at him, the echo of Novi's disappointment quickly quashes the urge, a reminder that I'm supposed to be feigning a little sincerity of my own.

By getting him to trust you, she'd said. *Turning you into the person he confides in.*

Sort of like he confided in me just now—with the bare minimum of prompting. Maybe I really could get him to reveal something useful if only I quit sulking and tried. Maybe all it would take is for me to start tricking *him.*

"No . . . but a little honesty might help," I say, affecting the lilt of Novi's charm.

"What kind of honesty?"

"Any kind you want." I shrug. "It doesn't have to be important—or about the Dominion, or Savian. Just something real." I don't push him towards the answers I need. For this ruse to work, he also has to trust *me,* and he'll never do that if the questions I ask arouse his suspicions.

"My sister's the reason I don't like being called Cassiel." The truth he offers me is so sudden and unexpected, it catches me by surprise. "When we were kids, it used to bother me that her name was longer—I couldn't tell you why, but it did—so I would never let her shorten mine. Then when I finally grew tired of that phase, she got her revenge by refusing to call me anything *except* Cassiel, and over the years, it became a type of . . . running joke between us. Something that was just ours. So I really would prefer it if you stopped throwing it in my face."

"Oh." The bile in my stomach turns to guilt, curdling my mouth sour.

But before I can think of some artful way to say: *sorry I kept taunting you with the memory of your dead sister,* the door to the tavern swings open and the High Commander of Isitar's military guard walks into the Sacred Hearts Inn.

Once upon a time, this city chose its protectors based on their stature and might, beholden to the belief that the more intimidating the man, the more intimidated the criminal. But Commander Aurelion

Rhodes is living proof that fear and size don't always correlate quite so neatly. He's a slight man—my height maybe—and excruciatingly thin, with tanned white skin, hooded features, and eyes so cold I'm amazed the gold in them hasn't frozen stiff. His regalia glints like a guillotine in the dim light, every accolade the Church has to offer gleaming proudly across his breastplate. And there, on a chain around his hip, the key to his office hangs low, barely visible under the flutter of his crimson cape.

"Like clockwork." Chase snaps straight in his chair, all thoughts of my pettiness forgotten. When he told us he's been *watching*, he didn't just mean watching *us*. Turns out, he's been watching every blurred edge of Savian's plan, for much longer than we had imagined. He knows everything there is to know about every rook, bishop, and pawn on the board. Not enough to win the game without our help, but enough to guide our hand in the right direction.

"You're up, Cemmy." He's quick to guide mine now. "Get them in here."

From brutal honestly to barking orders in five seconds flat; that has to be some kind of record.

"Sir, yes Sir," I mutter, sending the go-ahead down my scrys, along with an image of the Commander's face and his location, just to be safe.

We only get one shot at this crime; we can't afford to waste it on the wrong man.

May the colors give us strength . . .

Barely a minute passes before Lyria walks through the door, her chin held high and her skirts bobbing around her. Like us, she's dressed to blend in with the other patrons. Smart cloak, muted dress, a glamour of gold in her eyes, her red curls pulled back into a tidy bun.

The perfect picture of a pious lady.

The very model of an unassuming mark.

Though we've yet to learn much of anything about Lyria, she's so far proven to be less critical—and more obliging—than your average law-abiding citizen, quick to offer up suggestions and unafraid of lending a hand. When Chase summoned her back to the monastery, she came without argument. When we started floating ideas for how to break into the Commander's office, she didn't look scandalized by our knack for stealing, or repulsed by the fact that we've clearly conspired to rob a member of the clergy before. Mostly, she just seemed relieved that one of us could use the same sign language that she does—the form which evolved in Isitar, as opposed to the more dominant dialect favored in the West—and all she asked was that we turn to face her when speaking, say our words clearly enough for her to read our lips, and that we try not to talk over each other so that Novi can interpret our schemes into signs. Then when it became apparent that we'd need an extra body to play the distraction, she didn't even hesitate before volunteering for the job—but whether she's doing it to impress us, or to appease Savian, I don't know. She has made a couple of small allusions to her family. Which means that she does still *have* a family. Something to fight for. Something to lose.

Something she doesn't trust us enough to protect.

Not that I can blame her.

If it was Mom's life hanging in the balance, I wouldn't trust a bunch of strangers, either. I'd also be crossing this tavern in the hopes of removing the noose from around her neck.

With considered steps, Lyria approaches the bar, taking her place right next to the esteemed Commander. Not in any obvious fashion—getting noticed isn't her job—but with enough pomp to catch his eye then release it.

Holding it is up to Novi.

Who should be arriving in three . . . two . . . one . . .

She explodes into the Sacred Hearts Inn with all the subtlety of a loaded cannon, clothes bright, scowl deadly. Her shock of white hair has been glamoured a lurid pink for the occasion, the vines tattooed into her scalp altered to look like snakes, her face changed to allow for this memorable confrontation.

The point is for her to turn heads—which her entrance immediately does.

Including the head we want turning.

Rhodes's eyes practically burn with derision as she weaves between the bustling throng of patrons, making an exaggerated show of seeking out a pocket to pick, and an even bigger one of setting her sights on Lyria. Too obvious a show, in any other scenario. Drawing too much attention to her sticky fingers. But seeing how the reformed consider the faithless to be both careless and unwise, Novi's flagrant disregard is exactly what riles him to take the bait.

The second she sidles up to our Amethyst, the Commander pushes away from the bar, barking for Lyria to move so that he can apprehend the thief reaching for her coin.

"By order of Isitar's military guard, I am placing you under—"

Novi strikes before he can utter the word *arrest*, seizing hold of Lyria and shoving her hard against his breastplate, so that she can feign an exaggerated show of her own, gasping, and stumbling, and deliberately busying his arms while Novi completes her task.

"For pity's sake, woman—I told you to move!" By the time Rhodes manages to disentangle from Lyria's skirts, the deed is done.

"Oh, she's good," Chase mumbles as Novi breaks towards the door, using the timely appearance of Eve and Ezzo to facilitate her escape. With rehearsed malice, she pitches Eve into the curious crowd, turning heel to make a second obstacle of Ezzo, their practiced yells of surprise rousing a few kindly patrons to their aid, further blocking the Commander from capturing his culprit and leaving Novi free to disappear into the night.

"That's our cue." As soon as the commotion begins to settle, Chase and I rise to our feet, vacating the table we arrived early enough to secure. The one immediately outside the room reserved for Rhodes and his men. Which wouldn't usually allow for eavesdropping on their conversation—the tavern is too loud an establishment for that, and the door they meet behind too thick. Unless, of course, the Hues sitting outside it have been gifted an Orange talisman by their Gold. A pre-made strength spell they can use to enhance their hearing.

Chase and I follow a pair of the Commander's enforcers out of the bar, lingering just long enough to watch Ezzo and Eve recover from their altercation and claim their designated spot.

So far so good. The tension in my shoulders gives an inch, then another as Novi's would-be captors barrel straight past the alley where she lurks, hidden, a smile on her face and the key to Rhodes's office dangling from a satisfied finger.

"That lift was truly impressive." Chase's voice is thick with surprise. When Novi first suggested we simply *take* the key from right under the Commander's nose, he'd declared it to be impossible, offered up a hundred different ideas instead, each more ludicrous than the last. What he'd failed to learn in all those hours spent watching is that Novi's hands are the fastest in Isitar. While Rhodes was busy fussing over Lyria, she'd brushed past to relieve him of his property, a move so quick and flawless he'd never think to question it beyond checking to ensure the faithless pickpocket hadn't pilfered his bag of coin.

"Let's hope you're as impressive when it comes to doing your part." Novi glowers, offering us both a hand. "Can your In-Betweens really support three people?"

"I'm running out of ways to say this, but my In-Betweens are *stable.*" Chase's exasperation bristles loud. "So long as we maintain contact, the spell will hold firm." He blinks us into the Gray as if to prove the point, turning the sky to ink and the streets to sable, rending the color in our blood as brittle as glass. "Satisfied?" he asks as Novi lets out the breath she'd been holding, the realization that we are, in fact, not shattered escaping her in a rush.

"I'll be satisfied when you don't kill us at speed," she snaps, bracing for the danger yet to come. Novi's never used her gift to carry two before, and I know she'd have preferred to run this lift during a temporal In-Between to try and minimize the risk. But by midnight, the Commander will be firmly back in his office—rumor has it the bastard's so paranoid he sleeps in there—leaving us unable to phase back into the physical realm and search it for clues. With Chase's ability at our disposal, going in early made sense.

Even if he hasn't yet proven it at speed . . . For a brief moment, Novi's fear becomes my own, the clutch of her hand growing heavy. Stable or not, Chase has never experienced the shadows the way that she does, never moved so fast he's felt his skin cling like sinew to his bones.

To Novi, it's a state that's as natural as breathing, not a case of her feet moving faster, but rather, of the world turning slow, allowing her to cast her In-Betweens the same way she would otherwise. Which is to say, as sparingly and judiciously as the rest of us—and she's never risked speeding another half outside a sanctuary; she doesn't trust her shield enough to support the extra Hue. So it's by no means a given that Chase's magic will be able to adapt to the sudden burst of acceleration—especially since he and I won't be sharing in her experience so much as tagging along.

Only one way to find out. Despite the pain blooming beneath my bandages, I steel my nerve and grip Novi tighter, nodding as if to say, *let's show this arrogant Gold what a Cobalt can do.*

Then a *here goes nothing* and a curse later, Novi engages her gift.

CHAPTER

Eleven

The air catches in my lungs, the fear in my throat, the nausea in my gut. Novi's gift is like letting a storm rage wild in a bottle, packing a house full of tinder and pouring kerosene on the flames.

Our edges blur as we speed through the shadows, the night stretching to sharp wisps of onyx that twist, and shudder, and distort—and *shriek.* The sound is an all-consuming banshee, a hammer to my need to stay conscious. No matter how many trips I take through the Gray with Novi, the shock to my body remains the same. A thrill and an agony in equal measure.

"How's that spell faring, Cassiel?" She slams us to a stop at the top of the alley, affording Chase the chance to re-anchor and catch his breath.

"Like I said, my In-Betweens are stable." The snap in his voice is sardonic, though there's no hiding the sallow tinge to his skin, or how hard he's gripping the nearest wall for support.

Still doing better than I did . . . His mastery of the magic is truly a feat to behold. My first time out with Novi, I almost bit clean through my tongue then expelled the contents of my stomach the moment the world slowed its speeding—and that's without having to keep the Gray from shattering three interloping half Shades like glass.

"Yes, we're all very impressed." Novi's reply is a little less generous, though she does wait for Chase to right himself before setting us running again, smudging the world to black and the cobbles to shapeless smoke beneath our feet. If she were only herding him through the shadows, the lack of physicality would allow them to travel straight through any man-made structure, trace the path the crow flies instead of sticking to clear pathways and streets. But with me in hand, Novi can't just barrel through any building she wills. And while that does slow us down, her gift propels us through the holy quarter with such ferocity, we still make it to the barracks in a matter of seconds.

It's moving *through* the barracks that takes the best part of a quarter bell, seeing how my ability to touch comes with yet another drawback. When I affect my surroundings in the Gray, I affect them in the real world, too, so we have to check the coast for echoes at every doorway, ensure that the guards on duty won't notice anything amiss—least of all their Commander's office yawning open of its own accord.

The room we find ourselves in is the very model of a General's haunt. Smartly appointed, but not extravagant; spacious, but not excessively large; sparsely furnished, yet oppressive in its indulgence of blood-red crimsons and dark-stained wood, a utilitarian cot nestled in one corner which confirms that yes, he does in fact, sleep here. A man married to his duty and his duty alone.

"So what is it we're looking for, exactly?" Novi asks once we're safely ensconced and out of the Gray.

"Anything useful," Chase says, flicking on the lamp on the desk. "Guard numbers, peacekeeping measures, the route the procession will take through the city—if it concerns the Dominion or the cleansing moon, assume it's important. Memorize what you can, we'll take what won't be missed. I'll deal with the rest." He starts scouring the Commander's shelves, motioning for me and Novi to do the same.

So that's what we do.

And with the cleansing moon only six days away, we don't have to search hard. There are patrol schedules tacked to every wall, deep stacks of recruitment orders, lists that detail the number of enforcers the Commander has employed and where he means to station them. Not just on the reformed side of Isitar—to oversee the festivities—but on the east side in case of riots, as well, to quell the explosive anger at a Church that grows more formidable with each passing year.

"Does this seem like a lot of manpower to you?" Novi whispers, pointing me towards the third such list.

"Yeah, it does." I can't help but share her unease. If these enforcers are merely meant to safeguard the clergy, then why is the Commander stationing almost twice as many of them in the faithless quarter? Better yet, why is he planning to send them there hours ahead of the parade? And why is there a note to indicate that they'll be conducting their duties out of uniform and carrying weapons of iron instead of their usual steel? Bringing with them a supply of spokes with which to fortify their positions?

That's not really your concern right now . . . I force my attention back to the problem at hand, picking through an oversized rack of papers until I make my most valuable find.

Maps.

Lots of them.

Including the physical twin to the one the Governor keeps in his study.

Annotated—extensively—in the Commander's own hand.

"Erm . . . Chase . . . I'm going to need some help here." I balk at the exquisite wealth of detail. Committing it to memory seems like an impossible task, and there's no way we can take such an important document with us. If we do, then Rhodes will realize that someone was in here. Put the pieces of the night together.

"Whatever it is, leave it out, I'll get to it in a minute," Chase says, refusing to abandon his search of the Commander's drawers—though why he's chosen to focus his efforts there, I don't know. A man this meticulous would never keep time-sensitive papers buried in some forgotten corner of his desk. Chase is wasting his time.

"No . . . you'll get to it *now*," I grit, striding over to shove the map in his face. An annotated drawing of the Dominion is the very prize we came here to win, and at any moment, our scrys might warm with the call to turn tail and flee the barracks, forcing us to leave it behind. I refuse to let that happen just so he can indulge some curiosity. This ill-advised incursion was his idea; the least he can do is make good on his promise to *deal* with the documents we can't memorize or steal.

"By my colors, what's so important it couldn't wait—" His eyes widen as they settle on the bounty I uncovered, the irritation in his protest trailing down to naught. "Here, help me lay it flat," he says, spreading the map across the desk then pressing both palms to paper.

"What are you—?"

Oh.

I suddenly understand what he intends to do.

A deep hum builds around him, the map bleeding ink beneath his fingers, the rims of his irises spiking violet.

Another wisdom spell, then. Similar to the one he used in the Governor's study but designed to retain information instead of deciphering its gist.

"Can't you do that with the rest of it?" It takes every ounce of strength I have not to rake him upside the head. There are hundreds—if not thousands—of documents in this room, not to mention books, diaries, and ledgers; why not put a hand to each wall and make our lives easier? Exponentially increase the knowledge with which we'll return?

"The magic I take isn't endless, remember?" Chase shifts his attention back to the Commander's drawers. "So we need to prioritize."

By *we*, he obviously means me and Novi, since he's still concentrating his search in the entirely wrong place. *Or maybe he's looking for something different.* The thought strikes me unbidden. Something he and Savian don't want us to see.

Which makes it far more intriguing.

So imagine my disappointment when their secret proves to be nothing more than a tattered, leather-bound journal, the encircled seven-point star engraved across its cover the only real feature of note.

Huh.

That's the Council's mark.

Though it appears to have been deliberately etched upside down and blackened to emphasize a stern V among the points.

Not a variation I've ever seen before—which probably means it originated with one of their outlying sects—but since Chase is staring at it as though it's an undiscovered book of the sacraments, I find myself pleased that he only managed to locate it—tucked at the very bottom of the cabinet in the corner—after the last of his magic was gone.

And too little too late . . . The ninth bell peals out across the city, a strident warning that our time in the Commander's office has come to a close.

"That's Eve on the scry," Novi says, placing the heavy tome she was studying back on the shelves. "Rhodes is wrapping up his meeting; we need to go."

The man truly does live his life by the clock.

"Not yet." Chase continues flipping stubbornly through the journal, tearing through the moldy pages like an addict in need of a fix.

"That wasn't a suggestion, Cassiel. We are going. *Now.*"

"Not without me, you're not," he tells her, the threat in his voice ringing clear. Since Novi can't hold an In-Between around another Hue at speed, we're stuck waiting on him until he's good and ready. We don't have the luxury of leaving him behind.

"Chase, *please,*" I beg as the scrys around my neck warm for a second time, Ezzo joining Eve to say, *we can only delay him for so long.* "Whatever you're looking for, it isn't worth getting us all caught. I'm sure Savian would rather—"

"Gods—fine. We'll go," he cuts me off mid-plea, thrusting the journal into my hands. "But that's coming with us."

"Have you lost your mind?" Novi hisses. "If Rhodes notices that missing—"

"Then let's hope the two of you didn't make so much of a mess that he'll think to look." Chase struts up to Novi and offers her his hand, beckoning for me to do the same, as though I'm suddenly the one hindering our escape.

"He's not worth the fight, En," I whisper, tucking the musty book beneath my shirt. "We've got to get back to the others."

But though we speed through the shadows as fast as her gift can carry us, by the time we reach the Sacred Hearts Inn, it's too late. All nine hells have broken loose.

The yelling assaults us the moment we phase out of the Gray, thundering down the street with the wrath of a vengeful god. No—not a god, a Commander. A thoroughly pissed-off Commander.

What happened? The question burns hot against my scrys.

He knows the key's missing. Ezzo's reply comes almost instantly. *They're searching everyone.*

Well, that explains why there are two enforcers watching the door, and why the sounds drifting out of the open windows speak of upturned furniture and ire. Rhodes isn't going to let anyone enter or leave that tavern until he gets his key and someone to hang for stealing it.

Which is unlikely to happen since it's clasped in my fucking hand.

"This is all your fault, Cassiel," Novi snaps, shoving Chase against the alley wall. "If we had just left when Eve told us to instead of screwing around—"

"Yes, the seventeen seconds we spent arguing would have definitely made a difference."

They might have. His reply spurs me to action. A few seconds can easily mean the difference between life and death, success and failure, freedom and a cage; I learned that much the day Magdalena shattered, how the cruel whims of fate can easily turn on a cuff.

If the Commander scrutinizes Eve and Ezzo too closely, it will only take a few seconds for the glamours they're wearing to betray the lie. If he searches them, it will only take a few seconds to find their incriminating Orange talisman. And if he deduces what they are, it will only take a few seconds to drive a sword through their still-beating hearts.

We don't have a few more seconds to spend thinking.

So I don't think.

Nor do I take the time to let Chase and Novi in on my plan. In the space of a blink, I'm in the Gray and hurtling towards the tavern, fueled by a desperate determination, my shield blazing out of me like a burgeoning sun.

I am in between the alley and the street.

The street and the tavern.

The tavern and the sky.

And I will not shatter so long as I stay out of my own head.

Chase was right: the spell does come easier now that I've learned to trust it. It's as if my magic can anticipate my movements, surging from one anchor to the next like a river racing to overflow its banks.

I don't go in through the door—the guards would notice it opening—whereas the echoes buzzing around the windows shouldn't notice the glass swinging outward a crack. Just wide enough to allow me to squeeze through and steal inside.

I'm going to put the key by the bar, I send the harried missive down my scrys. *Right where Lyria was standing.* Will it strike Rhodes as suspicious that he didn't find it during his initial search? Probably. But since our Amethyst will have long since finished her drink and left the tavern, he'll have no reason to suspect that she was involved, nor any reason to link Ezzo or Eve to its sudden reappearance. They should be able to weather his scrutiny unharmed. Or at least, I have to hope they will, seeing how that's as much help as I can lend them from the shadows.

I am in between the window and the bar.

Fear and exhilaration.

Triumph and doubt.

I place the key behind the grimy foot rail, at a slightly awkward angle to make it look as though it fell from the Commander's keychain during his earlier fight.

I am in between the bar and the window.

Victory and ruin.

Elation and the night.

And holy shadows, I can't believe I just did that.

"Colors help me, Cem—what were you thinking?" The second I phase back into the alley, Novi's hands clamp around my shoulders, giving them a vicious shake. "Why didn't you take Cassiel with you?"

"I—"

"Because she didn't need to." Chase's smile is a snake that stretches from ear to ear.

And suddenly, I'm hot and cold and trembling all over, adrenaline vibrating my body like a violently plucked string.

What the hells *was* I thinking? A savage ache builds between my temples. Pulsing. Pounding. Piercing wild. I had no way of knowing the magic would work as well as it did on the cliff—nothing but the word of a liar who deals in half-truths and stolen glamours.

It'll be easier from here, you'll see.

The confidence Chase gave me could have just as soon gotten me killed.

It could have left Ezzo and Eve stranded.

"Cem?" Novi's voice is both a whisper and a hurricane in my mind. A muted thunder. "Cemmy—hey, you need to breathe, okay? Breathe."

But I can't breathe. *I can't breathe, I can't breathe—I can't.*

Not when the full weight of that reality is making splinters of my spine.

The last thing I hear before the darkness takes me is Chase's insistence that I'll be fine once the shock of the magic wears off.

The last thing I see is him reaching for the stolen journal.

CHAPTER

Twelve

The first time I ever blinked into the Gray, it didn't feel fraught or nerve-wracking, it felt like a relief. Like finally being allowed to glimpse the reason I'd spent my whole life hiding. I was eight years old, with enough loneliness and pent-up anger for a child of twice that many, plagued by dreams of a colorless world that seared so bright and so vivid, they could no longer go ignored.

That night, Mom waited until the sky was at its darkest—to ensure we wouldn't be seen—before leading me up to the roof of our apartment building, to the permanent spatial bridge that exists between the heavens above us and the ground beneath our feet. And though the Council's binding spell had taken her ability to phase into the shadows with me, she'd promised that the magic would come as naturally as air came to breathing.

"The Gray senses your color, Cemilla," she'd told me, "that's why it's been calling to you in dreams. All you have to do is heed the call."

It really was that simple.

With a shaky breath, I'd closed my eyes and surrendered to the insistent pull, following the magic in my blood across realms to where it wanted to be. There was a whisper of wind, the barest hint of pressure, then when I opened my eyes again, everything around me was the same but also different.

Everything around me was gray.

And it felt like *power*. Over a decade on, I can still remember the exhilarating swell of magic, the heady, intoxicating touch of it, the way it smelled like myrrh and tasted like lightning. Until then, all I knew of being a Bronze was that it made me illegal, but for no tangible reason I'd ever been able to fathom or see. Unlike the full-bloods, I couldn't *perform* my magic. I couldn't heal, or compel, or glimpse the future, yet both the Church and the Council hated me for existing, and I'd never understood *why*.

"The Church considers the Gray a blasphemy." Mom finally explained once I'd blinked back into the physical realm—another instinctive effort that only required me to picture a return to color. "But the Council is afraid of the damage too many half Shades could wreak. Every time you phase into the Gray, you draw power from the shadows, upset the natural balance of magic in the world. That's why you can only heed the call in a sanctuary. You must never—*ever*—heed it in another place," she'd said, with a fervor that bordered on frightening. "If you were to leave this roof, the shadows would turn against you. Do you understand me, Cemilla? They'll shatter you if you stray."

I can't begin to imagine what she'd say upon discovering how far I strayed tonight.

And with what reckless abandon.

"Would you please stop fussing, En—I'm fine." My face burns hot with embarrassment, the memory of my dramatic exit from the Sacred Hearts Inn setting my cheeks alight.

"You fainted," Novi says, forcing a steaming cup of chamomile tea into my hands. "That means you're *not* fine."

"Yes, but then I came round and walked all the way here, because I *am*." The dizziness had subsided almost as quickly as it had struck. Not a true sickness, but shock, an overabundance of fear in the blood. Just like Chase said. By the time Commander Rhodes had allowed the tavern to empty, I was already back on my feet, a little shaken and pale, but otherwise unscathed by my spontaneous trip through the Gray. Perfectly capable of hauling myself back to our monastery—and in no need of being coddled. "Now can we please focus on what's important? Ez, Vee—did you hear anything useful?" I ask, careful to ensure that Lyria has a clear view of my lips.

"I don't know if I'd call it useful, but it's certainly not good." Ezzo does the same, trading a meaningful glance with Eve. "Rhodes means to weaponize the cleansing moon parade against the Council. He's empowered his enforcers to incite a slew of riots in the faithless quarter, and to lace the streets with iron so as to weaken any retaliatory attack by their Shades. His hope is that Isitar will erupt into such disarray, it will enable the Governor to force through emergency measures to reform more ground. Maybe even take the city."

"Take the *city*?" Novi sputters, the shock delaying her accompanying signs by a staggered beat. "He's willing to start an all-out war with the Council? *Overnight?*"

I guess that explains the ludicrous number of enforcers he's drafted in for the task, and why he's made a point of ordering them to report for duty out of uniform. Can't have their actions traced back to the Church. For a ruse like this to work, the Governor's hands need to stay clean.

"Not just willing, he seems to think they can win." Ezzo lends voice to the part of the Commander's plan that reeks of naivety and hubris. The Church has spent decades chipping away at the Council's hold on Isitar one cobbled street at a time; why would a man as seasoned as Rhodes suddenly assume they can take the rest in an evening? How could he possibly expect to win?

"Thanks to what the Governor is keeping in the Dominion, they *will* win," Chase says, drawing every eye in the nave in his direction.

Fuck, I hate the way he looks in our monastery. Hate the way his hair honeys gold in the warm glow of the hex-lights, and the casual ease with which he's leaning back against the mural Eve painted across the wall, as though he deserves to be here. As though our sanctuary is his to steal.

"Oh good, the errand boy speaks." Novi's tone takes on a derisive edge. "Does this mean you've finally decided to let the rest of us in on that secret?"

"It was never a secret so much as I didn't think you'd believe me until you saw the signs for yourself." His shrug is entirely devoid of shame. "But there's a reason the Church's power has grown ten-fold this past year. You've probably felt it happening, even if you couldn't put a name to it."

"Put a name to what, Cassiel?" Novi says and signs. "Spit it out."

"The magic dying." His declaration is enough to make me choke on my tea.

"That's a bit dramatic, don't you think?"

"Is it? Or are spells getting more expensive for a reason?"

"Spells are more expensive because there are fewer Shades in the city." Ezzo's tongue clicks against his teeth. "It's a supply and demand problem, not the end of days."

"And what exactly do you think is driving the supply and demand problem?" Chase asks, arching a brow deep. "The Shades in Isitar have been losing their power for almost a year now; that's what's been prompting them to leave: they're trying to escape the drain. The Council's been blaming us, of course, for leeching too much magic from the Gray, but any Shade worth their salt will have realized that there are nowhere near enough of us left to affect much of anything. There's not been since the first time the Church got hold of a siphon and triggered the Council's purges."

"Erm . . . I'm sorry, but are we supposed to know what a siphon is?" Given the tension in the room, Eve's question is astonishingly polite—a stark contrast to the irritation creeping red up Ezzo's neck and the violent hostility radiating off Novi, the frustration pinking Lyria's cheeks now that the conversation has sped off in an exclusionary way.

"Sorry." Novi rubs a fist against her chest in a circular motion, apologizing for our lack of courtesy with a reproachful glare. "They're either going to be more considerate or slow down their bickering so that my rusty interpretation skills can keep up."

Well . . . crap.

This really would be much easier if more than one of us could sign.

"Think of it as an infinite container that consumes magic," Chase says, speaking the words more clearly at Lyria's behest. "Place it in the Gray and bit by bit, it sucks up power. Keep it there long enough and the balance between worlds reaches a tipping point. The shadows start to collapse. Until there's no more Gray, and no more magic. No more Shades."

Wait. What?

The sweetness of the chamomile turns bitter in my mouth.

"Is that—" I force myself to stop and catch Lyria's eye before I continue. "Is that even possible?"

"It's more than just possible; we've come pretty damn close to it before—about four hundred years ago." A peculiar note of anger creeps into Chase's voice. "The Council was able to destroy that siphon in time to stabilize the shadows, but if the Governor gets his way, they won't succeed in neutralizing this one. And to answer your next question"—he quells my coming interjection with a hand—"the reason it's managed to go unnoticed for so long is because the siphon's effect is cumulative. It will have started off slowly: weakening a spell here, driving away a Shade there, nothing the Council would have deemed suspicious given the current climate. But then one weak spell will have turned to five, will have turned to a problem, and suddenly, it wasn't just the odd Shade leaving, it was an exodus, and by the time the Council realized they were dealing with a siphon, the Church had already pushed its advantage. That's how things got this bad."

"No, that's not—it can't—" The objection dies on my tongue. Because as much as I'd love to scoff and call him a liar, the calamity Chase is describing fits in both timing and shape. While Isitar has never been a true haven for blood color—not during our lifetime, anyway—it wasn't all that long ago that the trade in magics still reigned king. Growing up, there were charm houses in every corner of the city, and the trend for *protecting* the streets with iron only truly spread wide in the last ten or so years. Before that, the Church was more insidious in its quest for reform. Less brazen. And though it had been systematically gaining ground in Isitar for decades, the recent spell shortages have served to galvanize the hate. It's easier to vilify the pleasure you cannot have than watch another man enjoy it, I suppose. With magic fast becoming the exclusive purview of the rich, the Church is all but assured the win.

"I think he's right." Lyria looks to Novi to speak her signs aloud. *"Or at least it explains why the shadows have been so angry of late. I've been sensing their fear for a few months now. They're panicked. Unstable. Pleading for help."*

"Do you mind if I—? Can I ask how that . . . works, exactly? Talking to the shadows, I mean." My curiosity gets the better of my want to avoid what might be a rude question. Because for some reason, Savian went out of his way to secure Lyria's gift. But if he and Chase already knew about this . . . *siphon*, then they didn't bring her here just to tell us that the shadows are scared. They need her to fulfil some other purpose.

"They don't sign, if that's what you're wondering." Her lips quirk at the idea, her expression betraying no hint of offense. *"It's a little hard to explain, but I don't talk to them the way you envision talking, so the fact that I'm Deaf makes no difference. There are no words or . . . sounds—obviously."* She keeps a gentle pace with her signs so that Novi can interpret them with greater ease. *"It's more akin to divine revelation. I think the question and then I sort of just . . . know the answer. Or if they're whispering among themselves when I'm near, I feel the same things that they do. And lately, all I've been feeling is fear."*

"Then why hasn't the Council stepped in?" Ezzo asks, rising from the daybed to pace his worry across the nave. "If this has been going on long enough for them to realize the Church has a siphon, then why aren't they doing everything in their power to destroy it?"

"Because they don't know where it is," Chase says, idly picking at the cuff of his sleeve. "The only reason they've been able to ascertain it's in Isitar at all is because until that tipping point is reached, the siphon's effects are localized, so the Shades here are bearing the brunt of the drain. But it's not a *beacon*," he stresses, as though that very thought is absurd. "It doesn't emit a visible signature they can trace, and the Dominion isn't the only holy building in Isitar that's warded, so it's not as if they can just guess where the Church put it. Not without inciting a full-blown war, anyway—which I'm sure they'll be panicked enough to do once the shadows actually start to collapse, but by then, it'll be too late."

"And how is it that *you* know what the Council doesn't?" Novi's eyes narrow in contempt, her signs sharpening with accusation.

"That's not important."

"Like hells it's not—if their trackers are out looking for this thing, we need to know how likely it is to put us in their way before we steal it."

"Not very." Chase's confidence is unnerving in its belief. "All that pesky iron the Church set in the streets is hindering their search, and Savian and I got our information from a source that can't be compromised, no matter how hard they try." The implication in his words rings clear.

The Council can't compromise their source because it doesn't exist anymore.

They ensured it took their secret to the grave.

"Then . . . I'm sorry, but . . . why doesn't Savian tell them where it is?" Eve asks, turning first to garner Lyria's attention, then back to address Chase. "If this siphon is as dangerous as you say, then they'd be sure to forgive whatever he did to get expelled from their ranks."

"What makes you think he was *expelled*?" Chase is quick to question her assumption. "Not every Shade wants to be beholden to the Council."

Not like Mom. The thought is as unfair as it is unkind. But I've never understood why she didn't just turn rogue when the Council discovered she'd married a typic. Why she let them bind her magic even though she had already resolved to run.

"Or maybe he has his own plans for that siphon." Novi's assertion yanks me back to the present, chilling the room cold. "What does Savian mean to do with it, Cassiel? What aren't you telling us?"

"Anything you don't need to know," he snaps.

"Do *you* even know?" Once Novi strikes a nerve, she'll keep hacking at it mercilessly. "Or is that what you were looking for in Rhodes's office? Is that why you—"

Stole that journal. I intuit what she's about to say a split-second before she says it—just in time to put my hand to my scry and send her a frantic plea to relent. *Don't, please. I have an idea.* I tilt my head enough for Chase to spot the message. To discern that I'm the reason she stopped half a sentence short of betraying his crime.

"It's not the *whys* that are important, it's the *hows*." He seizes the opportunity to change the subject. "We only have five days left to figure out a way into the Dominion and get this done, so I suggest you quit wasting time." Before any of us can get another word in, Chase turns on his heel and disappears into the Gray, the echo of his anger thundering loud.

Seems Novi didn't just strike a nerve, she flayed it raw.

And an exposed nerve makes for the perfect place to apply pressure.

"I'll be right back," I tell the others, racing out of the monastery after him. "What happened to preferring the carrot?" I yell the words into the shadows, trailing Chase across the cemetery as he barrels thoughtlessly through headstones and graves. "Because in case you haven't noticed, you're asking for a lot of grace here, but offering none in return."

"That's kind of how blackmail works, Cemilla," he calls back without slowing. "You do as I say, no grace required."

"Works both ways though, doesn't it?" I ask. "Unless you want Savian to find out about that journal you stole."

My threat stalls him in his tracks.

It was a gamble; I've no real reason to suspect he wasn't searching the Commander's office at Savian's request—other than the speed with which his mood had turned when I mentioned his master, how suddenly he'd thrust the journal into my hands and agreed to leave. I didn't think much of it at the time, but together with the way he then took that journal back as I fell unconscious, and how keen he was to avoid the subject just now . . . I think Chase is trying to hide it.

"I stole the journal *for* Savian," he says, though the fear rasping his voice suggests otherwise.

It tastes like a lie.

"See, I don't think you did." I hop up to sit atop a crumbling headstone, affecting an air of nonchalance I don't yet feel. "But I also don't think we need to tell him—*if* you do something for me." I may not have uncovered a secret large enough to buy our freedom, but I can use the one I have to make the coming days a little easier. Prevent a repeat of tonight's frustrations. Aggravate Chase as an added perk.

"I already promised to heal your mother once the job is done; I can't do it before that, whether you blackmail me or not." His hackles are instantly up and bristling. "Savian doesn't part with his magic lightly. He'll allow me to drain him in preparation for the lift—so that I can deal with any serious injuries we sustain on the day—but until then, there's no point in me asking."

"Then it's a good thing that's not the favor I had in mind," I say, relishing the ease with which he let slip that nugget of information. All the ways I might find to leverage it.

"Then what do you want?" Chase takes a step towards me, the irritation rolling off him in waves. Right now, he's a scared animal I've backed into a corner, and unless I play my cards right, he's either going to bolt or bite.

"Your help," I say, laying the pretense on thick. "That In-Between spell you taught me saved my friends tonight, and I won't forget that. But we both know this lift is going to require more than just a stable shield. Give us the skills we need to make an effective team—which we can't do while Novi's the only one who can freely communicate with our Amethyst." I ask for a type of magic I'm confident he can steal. Novi was able to solicit a Violet Shade just this morning, and the spell Chase used earlier is proof that he's had access to one before. What I want to know is how he'd go about draining another. That should shed light on the breadth of his and Savian's reach. Maybe even expose a weakness. And if doing that happens to break Lyria's dependance on Novi, well . . . I'll consider that a boon for me.

"You do realize there's no spell that will restore her hearing." Chase's eyes tighten at the corners, as though disgusted I even thought to ask.

Color me offended. "That is *not* what I meant." It's my turn to bristle. "Lyria's deafness isn't the problem here, our inability to sign is, and five days isn't long enough to learn. Help us with that."

"You want a wisdom spell." The judgement bleeds from his expression, the tension in his jaw dulling blunt.

"I mean, I'll take whatever other spells are going." I shrug, casually widening my request. "But yeah, that's a good place to start."

"And if I do this, the journal stays between us?" His hands fist at his sides, as though mad he's actually considering it.

But he is considering it . . . I can tell by the pensive crease of his brow and the way he's worrying at his bottom lip; he's mentally working through the problem. The *whens* and *hows* involved in achieving my ask.

"You have my word," I say in an effort to sway his mind. "I'll make sure the others honor it as well."

"Then you'll have your spell by morning." The second I sweeten the deal, Chase storms off towards the street, leaving me to stare after him in stunned silence.

By morning? But it's coming on midnight . . . How could he possibly get his hands on that magic by morning unless—

Oh.

A new theory strikes me as he speeds away from the sanctuary, a serendipitous sort of idea I never believed we'd be lucky enough to try.

Meet me in the cemetery. The moment he disappears from view, I call for Ezzo and Eve on the scrys. If Chase is planning to steal the magic I demanded tonight, then he must already have a Violet Shade in his sights.

And that means we're going hunting.

CHAPTER

Thirteen

Following Chase through the Gray isn't something I can do on my own. I'm not yet confident enough to trust that my In-Betweens won't falter, for one thing, and even if I were, I'd still remain too physical to pass through walls; I'd lose track of him at the first hurdle.

Ezzo, on the other hand, is uniquely built for this task.

The way the rest of us see the echoes typics leave in the shadows, he sees the echoes left by Shades, the ephemeral trails they cast as they shimmer through the smoke-clad darkness. And if he concentrates hard enough, he can search out a specific color or hue—even without a direct line of sight to his target, and from all the way across the city. That's the gift he enjoys as a Sapphire, though he's always thought of it as more of a responsibility. Because when Ezzo was nine, he learned exactly what could happen when he didn't pay enough attention to the invisible tracks in his head.

Unlike my mom, his mother—an Indigo Shade who could glimpse the future—taught him all about the Gray from the moment he was old enough to phase. She taught him how to blink between realms, and how to focus his power, and how to cast an In-Between to the best of her knowledge so that he could navigate the shadows without shattering like a fragile vase. The only thing she didn't teach him was how to avoid the one future she couldn't predict: her own death.

Looking back, Ezzo would remember noticing the trackers' trails, but at the time, he didn't know enough about the Council's Shade hunters to recognize their pattern. How they would observe their prey for hours beforehand, circling closer and closer while they documented their crimes and gathered for the raid. That's not a mistake he's ever made again, and from that day on, he's made it his mission to watch out for other Hues, as well. If not for that steadfast habit, he might have never found Eve, or Novi—and he most definitely would have never found me. Given how little time I used to spend in the shadows, it's actually a miracle he stumbled across my trail at all. I mean, hells, even now, Ezzo likes to poke fun at the way my Bronze barely registers unless he makes a point to look, as though even my trails are reluctant to linger in the Gray any longer than they have to.

"You sure this is a good idea, Cem?" he asks once I've caught him and Eve up to my plan. "Cassiel seemed particularly . . . *volatile* tonight. Maybe we shouldn't poke the bear." Though he aims the words at me, his eyes are fixed decidedly on Eve. He'd never forgive himself if anything were to happen to her while we were out chasing theories—just as he'd never forgive himself if anything were to happen to me, or Novi, or even to Lyria since he's the one who led Savian to her door. With the memory of that decision still weighing so heavily on his conscience, I'm not surprised he's playing it cautious. That's the downside of being the one who watches: there's no forgetting the horrors you see.

"I know it's a risk, Ez—but we might never get this chance again," I say, looking to Eve for help. "And if I'm right about where he's going, we might learn something important. Something we could use against Savian."

"Then I think it's worth doing," Eve says, and I can tell by the way she's holding Ezzo's gaze that the two of them are locked in a silent battle of wills. Him, urging her to think through the danger. Her, reminding him that she's not some fragile doll in need of protecting. That it's been a long time since she was the distraught girl he found crying in the Gray, too traumatized by the brutal loss of her family to move, or phase, or speak. I can only imagine the amount of patience it would have taken Ezzo to draw her out of that shell and win her trust, but sometimes, he forgets that even on that day—while Eve was at her very lowest—she was able to escape a whole team of trackers and hold her nerve in the Gray for *hours*, and Emerald or not, that was no easy feat. Of the four of us, sweet, soft-spoken Eve is probably the strongest. And the most adept at getting Ezzo on-side.

"We'll turn back at the first sign of trouble," she tells him, as though the decision's already been made. "Phase out if my shield starts to tire."

"Okay, fine." With a resigned nod and a protracted exhale, he blinks his eyes white, retreating into the depths of his gift. From the outside, it looks as though he's fallen into a trance, though Ezzo describes it as more of an enhanced state of vision, like flicking on the lights. Seeing in an extra color.

"Got him." Since Chase's trail is only a few minutes old, it barely takes him any time to trace. "He's heading towards the ruined quarter." The thin strip of land that stands between the Church's territory to the west, and the Council's domain to the east. As far away as one can get in Isitar from the seat of power of both.

"Are you sure you can hold the In-Between around the three of us all the way there?" Ezzo asks, shaking loose the haze. "It'll be faster to keep tracing him than cast my own, but if it's too much, we can—"

"Stop. Worrying." Eve puts a gentle hand to his cheek. "As long as we're careful, it shouldn't be a problem. And besides, it's been far too long since Cem and I ran a job together," she says, grinning her dimples wide.

Over a year, in fact. The reminder is a blade to my ribs. Until Magdalena shattered, I used to routinely draft them both into my lifts, though I saved the more complicated jobs for Magdalena. She may not have been an Emerald like Eve, but as an Amber, her gift was to mimic, and mimicking Eve's power granted her the ability to cast a stable shield. Not with quite as much flexibility or finesse—unlike Eve, Magdalena required physical contact in order to project her In-Betweens around another—but despite that limitation, running lifts was . . . *easier* with her. She had no overprotective Ezzo waiting for her at home, never seemed to exhaust her magic, and where I took the risks because I needed the coin, she took them for the thrill. Magdalena loved taunting the shadows. She loved phasing into the Gray between sanctuaries, and staying there longer than necessary just to prove that she could, so relying on her In-Betweens never felt like a risk. Until suddenly, one day, it did. Which is why, the second we cross out of the cemetery, I start testing the limits of my own power, unwilling to let that same faulty assumption endanger Eve—especially now that Chase has put the idea of the magic dying in my head. Made the threat feel bigger.

"You don't have to strain yourself, Cem," she says, pushing her spell outward to envelop mine. "I can hold you both."

"I know you can—but I could use the practice." I cast through it with a resolute grunt. As much as I'd rather not spend another second obsessing over anchors tonight, I refuse to let Eve shoulder this burden alone. Trailing Chase through the shadows was my idea, and that makes it my responsibility, and my fault if it goes wrong. It makes doing this myself important.

I am in between the cemetery and the street.

The magic takes even faster than it did outside the Sacred Hearts Inn, though I use it in a more considered way this time, thinking, and assessing, and ensuring my power has fully stabilized before renouncing my reliance on Eve.

Just move slow and breathe steady. No sudden movements, no reason to panic. The mistake I made with Magdalena was stressing the bounds of my In-Between until they splintered and snapped, promising her that I could both pick a lock and sustain the magic until *crack, clink, crunch, shatter.* The shadows took immense pleasure in proving their might.

"Easy, Cem—" Eve senses the abrupt waver in my shield, stepping in to relieve the pressure.

"No, it's okay, I've got it." I quickly heed Chase's advice and get out of my own head. There'll be plenty of time to lament the red in my ledger when I'm not actively placing another friend at risk. But first, we need to ascertain how he steals his magic and find a way to escape Savian.

With Eve safeguarding his passage through the shadows, Ezzo blinks back into his gift, following the golden trail of breadcrumbs Chase is leaving behind. Gray stone turns to graphite smoke turns to cindered ash, the buildings growing more decrepit as we head towards the very heart of the ruined quarter, home to the riots that sparked an uprising and cleaved Isitar in half.

The last time the Church tried to take the city, the faithless met the call to reform with blood, and steel, and magic, unleashing an inferno that blazed with the power of a thousand Shades. Both sides suffered heavy losses that night, and when the dust finally settled, neither was willing to feed more bodies to the flames. The ruined quarter has stood between them ever since. A no-man's land the Church can't claim without declaring war on the Council, which the Council refuses to restore so that it might serve as a reminder to the Church.

"Interesting choice of destination," Eve says as the trail leads us to a burned-out shell of a building. The remnants of a theater house, I'd say, judging by what's left of the eerie wooden masks hanging above the door.

"Interesting choice of company, too." Ezzo's eyes dart back and forth without blinking. "I'm counting . . . one, two, three, four . . . six other Shades in there. All full-bloods apart from our Gold. Every color except for Green."

So every color except Savian's.

"But that doesn't make any sense." Eve's brow furrows in confusion. "How could they be working with six other Shades without the Council catching wind of their plans?"

It's a good question.

And the only answer that makes sense is: they couldn't. Not while Isitar is in the midst of a historic dearth.

A plot this extensive would never go unnoticed, unless—

Oh Gods. It only takes me a second to put the pieces together.

"I don't think they're working with them, Vee," I say, almost choking on the words. When I threatened Chase in the cemetery, he promised me new magic by morning, like it was nothing to simply find a sacrificial Violet to drain. Like the whole damn rainbow was at his disposal. And now here that rainbow is, right inside this building. Not *apart* from our Gold—*for* him. "I think Savian's holding those Shades prisoner." Using the recent spate of migrations to hide their captivity.

"That would explain why their signatures are more solid than I'm used to." Ezzo snaps himself out of his gift. "And why they're not really trails so much as . . . blooms of color. Though for them to be this bright . . . he must have been holding them here for days."

Days. I appraise the theater house with a mounting sense of unease. As long as there's been a Council, there've been rogue Shades who chose to forsake its rules. Allow their magic to grow wilder. Stronger and less reserved. But even the strongest of rogues shouldn't have been able to overpower six of the Council's number and keep them trapped in the Gray for *days*. What Savian's done should be impossible.

Unless we're missing something . . . I scour the building for some way to see inside. The first floor is all boarded up—the city's doing, most likely, to keep the looters and vagrants at bay once the riots hollowed it to a ruin. The windows on the second floor, however, should be easy enough to pry open, and there's a broken awning I can use to get atop the shallow roof at the theater's side.

"Stay here—I'm going to take a look," I say, steeling my nerves for the climb.

"Cemmy, *no*." Ezzo reaches for my arm. "If your In-Between slips, even for a second—"

"Then the rest of you will be off the hook." I shrug. Because no Bronze means no physicality. And no physicality means no lift. Without me, Savian can't put the screws to my friends.

"That's not funny, Cem." The wince in Eve's expression makes me instantly regret the jibe.

"I'm sorry. I shouldn't have—I didn't mean that." I sigh, sheepish. "But we do need to know what he's doing in there, and this might be our only chance to find out. It's worth the risk."

In a perfect world, I'd take her with me, but Eve won't be able to make the climb, and as much as I'd love to just send her and Ezzo through the wall, we have no idea what's awaiting them on the other side, and we can't afford for them to get noticed. On the second floor, I'm less likely to be seen.

I take off before either of them can argue further, lending voice to my anchors out of habit more than need. "I am in between the theater house and the street." Even as I say the words, I know they're no longer necessary. The spell feels intuitive now, like breathing, as though learning to cast it properly was the key to keeping it stable. *Instead of anchoring your magic the way you* should, *you anchor it the only way you know how.* While it galls me to admit Chase was right, in this particular instance, his assertion rings true.

Two nights ago, I aborted a lift for fear of holding the magic for a few seconds—let alone some undetermined stretch of time—yet here I am tonight, anchoring it to nothing in particular and everything all at once. Living proof that a Hue's fear of the Gray is manufactured, not preordained.

That maybe the shadows don't hate us quite so much after all.

The first thing I notice as I near the theater house are the pained moans escaping from inside, the desperate pitch of a man's screams and his wild appeals for mercy.

Well, that's not concerning . . . I refuse to let the horror shake me. If anything, whatever torment is taking place behind these walls only spurs me to move faster, so that I can see the truth of it with my own eyes.

The broken awning is in better shape than it looked from afar—sturdy despite the flame damage—and once I'm up on the roof, it's only a few short steps to the window, where my picks make short work of a lock that groans heavy with rust. It practically disintegrates as I force my way inside.

"Hurry it up, Cassiel, I don't have all night to humor your requests." Savian's voice is a danger I'm not expecting.

Ezzo only counted six full-bloods inside the theater—none of them Green.

Which means he still can't track Savian . . . With exaggerated care, I lower myself down to the balcony. Even before the riots set a blaze to its glory, this theater house stood smaller than its counterparts in the reformed sector, boasting little more than a stage, a curtain, and an overhanging arrangement of seats. Now, those seats lay broken, the stage seared charcoal, and the velvet curtain reduced to a pile of ash and forgotten dreams. But despite the wreckage, it's not the theater's rotting carcass that commands my attention; it's the twisted torture unfolding in the cavity between its bones. The screams of anguish.

Colors help me.

Thick chains of iron snake down from the beam above the stage, each forging a prison around a different captive Shade. Not just Council Shades, either, I realize as I catch a glimpse of their eyes. Only a couple boast the customary spiked rim around their irises; in the others, the magic burns black to the edge.

Like Savian's.

Though how he managed to find and subdue so many others of his ilk is anybody's guess. In the Gray, the iron cuffs should only serve to keep them from phasing, not sap them of their color or cause them pain. So for all six to hang as limp and tortured as a pack of beaten dogs . . . the amount of power it must have taken Savian . . .

Or perhaps it's the power he's had his Gold take from them. Acid roils my stomach as I lean over the balcony for a better look. Before Chase blackmailed his way into our lives, a Gold's magic was the stuff of myth and legend—and none of those presumed to capture the true violence of his gift.

They didn't even come close . . . My teeth grind themselves brittle, my nails clawing blood across my palms. He's got both hands pressed to the screaming Shade's chest, skin on exposed skin, a purple glow pulsing beneath his fingers. Not a consensual exchange of color, a drain. A brutal, vicious drain that reduces his prey to a whimpering shake of limbs, all while Savian watches on with a bored expression.

I don't have all night to humor your requests.

I threatened Chase for some magic and he immediately ran to his master to acquire those spells. If nothing else, that tells me how badly he wants to keep the journal away from Savian—even if it doesn't tell me why. What could that dusty relic possibly contain that would prompt him to inflict so much pain? What kind of secret is dangerous enough to warrant . . . *this*?

"Please—no more. I beg you!" The Violet bucks beneath Chase's grip, the desperate pitch of his suffering shivering my blood cold. Not so long ago, while we were stuck on the cliff, those treacherous hands were wrapped around *me*, within draining reach of *my* magic, feigning weakness when the entire time—with a turn of his touch—he could have reduced me to a hollowed-out shell. Stripped me dead of both life and color.

And I want to look away. *I want to look away, I want to look away—I can't.* I can only stare, transfixed, with the sour smell of fear ripening the air and the bitter taste of agony stinging my tongue, until Chase finally breaks the connection.

The Violet Shade sags against his bindings, the strength in him bled clean, his breathing sharp and labored. It's in that moment, right before I'm able to force myself back from the balcony's edge, that Chase's eyes flick up, almost as if in prayer.

Their silver finds me instead.

No, no, no, no. Terror pins my feet to the ground, the shadows sensing a chink in my armor.

I am in between the railing and the wall. I catch the magic at the exact same moment Chase catches the surprise in his throat and locks it there, choosing not to betray my presence to Savian.

"Go." The word is almost imperceptible on his lips, a silent reprieve.

An inexplicable kindness.

So I go.

I don't try to intervene or save the pleading rainbow from their fate; I don't crouch to minimize my silhouette or slow to muffle my footsteps.

I just turn tail and flee.

Like a coward, and a traitor.

Allowing Chase to cover my retreat with a different color of pain.

CHAPTER

Fourteen

The screams stick with me all the way out of the theater house.

I hear their echo as I signal for Ezzo and Eve to leave the Gray.

I feel their agony as I scramble down the flame-bitten awning.

And I taste their rancor as I phase back into the physical realm and retch, the contents of my stomach protesting the brutality I witnessed.

For years, I've bristled at the Council's rhetoric, at their insistence that Hues are a dangerous blight on the Gray, when most of us spend our lives avoiding the shadows for fear of shattering.

I've never seen a Hue *take* the way Chase did.

Never imagined our gifts could pose such a threat.

But his does . . . The phantom kiss of his hands sears across my skin. A burning shiver. A close encounter with death.

Because it would kill you. That's what Chase told me would happen if he deigned to steal my color, and having watched what he did tonight, I believe him. If he can reduce a full-blooded rogue to a quivering mess, I've no doubt he could dispose of a half without issue. He probably wouldn't even break a sweat.

I'm glad you're finally starting to worry about the right things.

"Cemmy!" Eve's alarm is a whispered shout in the darkness, her eyes wide and her strides urgent as she runs towards me, Ezzo close at her heels. "What's wrong? What happened in there? What did you see?"

"The magic—I . . . I saw how he takes their magic." The story escapes me in broken fragments, the details uttered between a stitch of ragged breaths. *I saw the sickening effects of his power.* And somewhere, at the back of my mind, I realize that's important. That though it took an entirely different shape than I envisaged, I still managed to learn the truth we came here to find. The silver bullet we can use against Savian. But the *how* is blurred and elusive, and the more questions Eve and Ezzo throw at me, the fewer answers I have to offer, the crushing weight of the day tugging at every one of my muscles, tendons, and bones. I've barely slept since the night Savian trapped me in the Governor's study, and between the fear and the magic, the near death and Chase's show, I've got no more strength left to give. No more will to keep standing.

"Whoa—easy, Cem." Eve reaches out to steady me as I stagger on my feet. "Are you okay?"

"Yeah, I'm . . . fine," I say. Though I'm not fine. *I'm not fine, I'm not fine—I feel ill.* "But do you mind if we—can we finish this tomorrow?" I ask, trying to stay the tremble in my knees. "I think I pushed my shield too hard in there and I . . . I really need to get home, check on Mom." It's not a lie, exactly, and together with the crack in my voice, it makes for a compelling reason to table this discussion until morning.

And it will *keep until morning,* I tell myself, swallowing down the guilt. Nothing I discovered in that theater house is going to help us escape Savian tonight—not with my thoughts this muddled and exhaustion pulling me towards sleep. Quite the opposite, in fact; now that I've glimpsed the true wealth of power Chase's gift has placed at his disposal, I'm even more aware of how carefully we need to tread here. The noose he's tied around our necks has only grown more concrete.

Hells, I can't even avoid it at my apartment, where my rent is now paid, my bills taken care of, and my mother breathing peacefully instead of gasping for breath.

Savian's a fan of the stick, but I've always preferred the carrot.

If I weren't so damn desperate, I'd tell Chase exactly where to go stick his carrot.

But I am that damn desperate, and it's been months since I was able to creep by Madam Berska's door unafraid. Longer still since Mom slept so soundly, I didn't have to wince at the pain rasping through the walls. *I'm home safe,* I speak the words silently, as if they might improve her dreams. *And you don't have to worry, I'm still wearing my ring.*

A scalding bath and a heel of bread later, the shake in my limbs starts to fade. Since Chase placed no cap on his *generosity*, I use a few drops of Mom's tincture to rid my hands of the damage he inflicted on them on the cliff, then as soon as the cuts are done healing, I collapse onto my bed, desperate for the sweet respite of unconsciousness.

It's only when I turn to douse the hex-lights that I realize I'm not alone.

Move. Now. On instinct, I grab for the knife I keep in my nightstand.

Too late.

In a furious flash of gold, I'm pinned to the mattress, my assailant's knees straddling my hips, my wrists held flat above my head.

"Chase?" The sight of him rips his name from my tongue. His face is a picture of madness: hair wild, lips parted, eyes seared black to the edge. *Like a rogue.* I flinch away from the fire radiating off his skin. Despite the chill in the air, Chase is burning.

"You're afraid of me now," he says, anger snarling his voice deep.

"Look where you are—where *I* am." I push back against his grip. "How did you think I'd react?" Did he think I'd enjoy getting jumped in the middle of the night, while I'm wearing little more than a threadbare nightshirt, with my sick mother sleeping on the other side of a too thin wall? Was I supposed to like it?

"No, you're not afraid that I'm here—you're afraid of what I can do," Chase says, and we both know that he's not talking about what he could do in this moment. "What's the matter, Cemilla? Can't handle the pain you created?"

"*I* created?" The accusation is as sharp as the sculpted cut of his cheeks.

"You wanted a wisdom spell, didn't you? And—let me see if I can remember your exact words—*whatever other spells are going*?" He parrots the request I made in the cemetery. "Where did you think those spells would come from, Cemilla? Did you think they'd come for free?"

My wrists warm beneath his touch, a faint glow building around us. *Magic.*

I gasp as the heady rush of power arches me against him, driving my body into the scorching cradle of his arms.

He's pushing me his stolen magic.

"You never said your gift did that to Shades." My protest is feeble. Weak. An embarrassment of wanton breaths.

"And you never thought to ask." His answering growl is a taunt in my ear. "I told you it would kill a half Shade, but you didn't want to think about that. You wanted the magic you wanted when you wanted it, and you didn't care how it would affect anyone else. You didn't care how it would affect m—" he cuts off abruptly, too proud to lend voice to the word *me.*

That's when I realize that I'm not the one shaking, he is.

That there's sweat beading at his temples and a frenetic energy vibrating him from head to shin.

Delirium in his eyes.

"Chase, you need to stop." The magic he's sending me no longer feels heady; it feels wrong. Like we're committing a violation. "I don't—you need to stop this."

"No. I need to get the magic out," he says, though the weight pinning me to the bed grows lighter, his grasp on me turning from force to plea. "Please, Cemmy. He made me take too much. You have to help me get it out."

It's the fear in his voice that breaks me; the way the magic looks as if it's rending him soul from limb.

"Okay." I nod, rising up so that we're face to face. "Tell me what to do."

"Just let me give you some of this color." When Chase next starts the flow of magic, it's with my permission. A consensual exchange of power, not a drain. He trembles with relief, his lids fluttering shut, the scald of his skin slowly waning.

Fuck, that's intoxicating. My head falls back against the wall with a hiss, my nails biting deep into the strength of his arms. This must be what it feels like to command as much power as a full-blooded Shade. To have your magic feel vast and endless.

Except Chase's magic isn't endless; it's an ill-gotten collection of spells, and the second he's purged the excess of them from his blood, he passes out cold on my bed.

Well.

Shit.

I try to rouse him with a shake and a snap of my fingers, then when that fails to work, I gently wiggle out of his grip. Chase looks softer in sleep than he does upon waking, stripped bare of his secrets and the conspiring edge to his sneer. There's a delicate beauty to his hard-cut features, a captivating elegance that is both familiar and impossible to place.

Don't be ridiculous, Cemmy, you'd have remembered meeting this Gold. As I roll him onto his side, my hands slip under the folds of his jacket, brushing up against a book bound in leather and age.

The journal he took from the Commander's office.

The one he deemed more important than Ezzo and Eve.

It's not stealing if Chase stole it first. I tease the book out of his pocket and retreat into the living room, easing the door shut behind me and striking on the hex-lights.

What is with this bastardized symbol? The Council's seven-point star looks downright odd when it's etched upside down and burned to emphasize a V—as though it's been defiled, somehow. Perverted.

The private journal of Clayvern Versallis
A study of the modern witch epidemic

The name scrawled beneath the mark tugs at a memory, as though I've stumbled across its likeness somewhere before. In a tome of history, maybe? Or perhaps it was in an issue of the Council's papers.

Yes, that's it; I learned it from the Council. *Versallis* was the name of one of their elders, I think, from around the twenty-eighth cycle. *About four hundred years ago* . . . that date strikes a chord, too. According to Chase, that's when the Church first got hold of a siphon. It's when they first tried to destroy the Gray.

Well, that can't be a coincidence . . . The second part of the journal's title is easier to decipher. *Witch* isn't a word you hear that often anymore, but it used to be the most prevalent term for *Hue*, back before the masses got creative. And if Versallis is referring to us as an epidemic, then there must have been more of us during his time, since right now, we'd barely even class as a weak sniffle.

So then what did Chase want with this old relic? I sink down to the couch and flip through the musty pages, trying to ascertain which of these elaborate musings he refused to leave behind. There are whole essays on the myriad ways a Shade might make a witch—though why Versallis needed quite so many words to say: *by bedding a typic*, I don't know. Then there are the theses that discuss the dilution of a Shade's power, how a witch's Gray gift will vary depending on their parentage and Hue, but remains an offshoot of their base color's specialization. So again, nothing new there.

But this is new . . .

About halfway into the journal, I hit a spread of pages that detail, with unparalleled completeness, the variety of Hues and their gifts.

> *Having chronicled the birth of tens of thousands of witches, we have ascertained that certain Hues occur with greater frequency than others. Two distinct presentations of color have thus far been confirmed within the Red, Orange, Yellow, Blue, Indigo, and Violet dilutions, with a third recently observed within Green. Of which, one will prove to be the dominant presentation, and the rest, atypical and rare in their ability to manifest. And while the dominant Hues appear stable, their atypical counterparts are plagued by either a physical or psychological toll. It is hypothesized that their gifts are too powerful to be sustained by diluted blood.*

The list of known Hues is as follows:

Red (to control)
Ruby (dominant)—to mimic
Garnet (atypical)—to confuse

The more a Garnet witch uses their power, the more that magic begins to affect their own recollection of events, until such time as they lose all sense of who they are.

Orange (to strengthen)
Copper (dominant)—to hinder
Bronze (atypical)—to touch

The witch's ability to interact with objects in the Gray presents as a visible aura in the physical realm, evident to other Shades. It also renders them vulnerable to warding spells, tracking spells, and detection spells across both worlds, unless counteracted by a totem.

Yellow (to alter)
Gold (dominant)—to take from other persons
Amber (atypical)—to take from the world

This gift is as dangerous as it is rare. Once triggered, the witch is unable to control their ability, resulting in a catastrophic extraction of power.

Green (to heal)
Emerald (dominant)—to protect
Peridot (atypical)—to calm

A Peridot witch appears to bear the brunt of the anxieties they relieve, leading to extended bouts of hysteria.

Jade (atypical)—to kill

The ability to end life with a touch renders Jade witches incapable of skin-to-skin contact.

Blue (to hasten)
Cobalt (dominant)—to speed
Turquoise (atypical)—to reverse

A Turquoise witch is able to reverse the flow of time, but their body bears the cost of that reversal, aging in an equal measure. This acceleration of age appears to be permanent.

Indigo (to foresee)
Sapphire (dominant)—to sense
Lapis (atypical)—to revisit
The witch's ability to recount significant events with perfect clarity presents as an inability to form long term memories.
Violet (to know)
Amethyst (dominant)—to communicate
Tanzanite (atypical)—to remember
Though a Tanzanite witch is able to remember, without fail, everything they see or hear, the overwhelming wealth of information results in obsession and, ultimately, madness.

Versallis's breadth of knowledge is both a horror and a thrill. I've never seen so many of our gifts documented in one place before, never even heard of a few of these atypical presentations—or the idea that certain Hues are more dominant than others or plagued by a toll.

Shame he's wrong about some of them. It's a comfort to know that the Council's elite aren't infallible. Not only has Versallis listed my gift as having one of these physical tolls—which it very much doesn't; I'd have been caught and killed long ago if I were, in fact, trackable—but it also lists mimicry as a Ruby's gift when that's actually the purview of an Amber.

Like Magdalena.

The power he's attributed to her is plain wrong.

Though the elders originally thought to name these witches for precious metals and stones—so hopeful in their belief that they would prove equally valuable—it is fast becoming clear that their abilities are in actuality less a gift than they are a curse. The recent discovery of a third presentation of Green is proof that if the bloodlines continue to mix, new dilutions may yet come to pass, and when they do, it's impossible to know what dangers they might pose.

We cannot allow the events of this past year to repeat.

We must stop the spread of the witch.

The following two pages go on to outline a course of action with which I'm intimately familiar.

The purges.

The only thing the Church and the Council have ever managed to agree on: that both worlds would be better off without the scourge of us pesky Hues.

We will need to provide the full-bloods with a viable reason for the cull.

Versallis goes on to say.

Too many have chosen to make a home with the typics. Wed them. Procreate. They will not consent to this demand without anger. Nothing short of an immediate threat to our way of life will enable us to win their support. We must turn the witches' own mythos against them. It is already a fact well established that the presence of typical blood renders their magic brittle and prone to shattering; it would not be a stretch to posit that it also destabilizes the Gray the same way a typic's does. Place the blame for its near collapse at their feet.

Colors help me. My stomach sinks to my knees, the revelation paling me ashen.

He made it up.

Hues posing a threat to the Gray; draining the shadows of power; all of it.

He made it up because he was afraid of our gifts.

But appalling though that revelation is, it still doesn't explain why Chase would jeopardize our plan in search of some ancient history, or why he's so intent on keeping Savian from catching wind of his find.

What are you looking for here, Cassiel? I skim the subsequent pages for an answer. No amount of knowing the past will allow him to change it, and that's all this journal seems to contain: a glimpse into the Council's past. Observations Versallis made about the so-called witch epidemic; his ambitions to weaponize the full-bloods' fear against our kind; his intent to use the purges as a stepping stone to the ultimate rank of Chancellor. I'm yet to find a single mention of the siphon, or some detail that might prove useful to Chase—or serve to antagonize Savian.

If anything, Versallis's musings only grow less coherent and more extreme, the pitch of his entries rising as his increasingly radical proposals start encountering resistance.

Once again, the quorum has dismissed my calls for a bleeding as too drastic an action. So blinded are they by coin that they refuse to make use of the power at our disposal. To envision the world we might create if only they cease capitulating to the typics.

What will it take to make them realize that we need not bow to the sun?

The true purpose of the shadows is to grow long, and dark, and heavy.

To extinguish day with night.

A bleeding. The term instantly catches my eye. Though much to my dismay, the journal skips right over its meaning, choosing instead to indulge the ramblings of a man who is fast falling out of favor.

The quorum relieved me of my duties today—the arrogant fools. In my rightful place, they elect a man who seeks to make peace with the Church. The Church! Do they not understand that the clerics will never be content with peace? They wish us gone. Eradicated. And unless we act decisively now, their genocide will succeed. A bleeding is the only way to ensure the shadows are never threatened again. The purges—while just and necessary—will soon rob us of the means to turn this hateful tide. We must not allow this opportunity to slip through our fingers. And since they refuse to act, I must assume the responsibility myself. Already, I have amassed a loyal circle of followers who understand the urgency of this task. The Order of Versallis, I've termed them, and together, we will safeguard our way of life by bleeding that wretched w—

"Hasn't anyone ever told you that reading other people's journals is impolite?" The book is unceremoniously snatched from my hands.

Gods—Chase. I startle at his silent entrance. Since I didn't hear him leave my room, he must have done his moving in the Gray.

"So is breaking into their apartment in a delirious rage." I grab his arm and phase us back there, more willing to face the shadows' wrath than wake Mom's. "You want to tell me what that little performance was about?"

"I see someone's well and truly over their fear," he says, stepping clear of my grasp—as if to confirm the stability of my shield. "Welcome to the right side of your magic."

"Don't change the subject." His approval only serves to shorten my fuse. "You practically attacked me, Chase. I deserve an explanation." And the fact that I can now hold an In-Between without blinking—hells, without so much as *thinking* about it or having to obsess over my anchors in advance—doesn't absolve him of that. Even if it is remarkable.

"I'm sorry." His apology is entirely unexpected, a repentant whisper bleeding through the dark. "The delirium, it's called spell-shock, and I've never taken enough magic to experience it before."

"Is that true?" I'm not sure what prompts me to ask that question beyond the fact that sometimes, when I keep him talking, I feel like I can spot the lies.

"Yes." Chase suddenly looks as stripped and vulnerable as he did in sleep. "And I really am sorry for scaring you. I wasn't myself. Savian made me drain all six Shades in case we needed their magics and I could barely see through the haze of color."

Oh.

The depth of his honesty catches me off-guard.

"Is it always like that?" I ask. "Stealing power, is it always so—"

"Violent?" he finishes for me. "Yes. Our magic is a part of us; it's quite literally flowing through our blood. Extracting it is an act of violence."

"Then why do you do it?" There's no hiding the judgement in my voice, even if deep down, I'm not altogether sure I wouldn't do the same. The way it felt when Chase pushed that color into me . . .

the sheer, unadulterated high . . . the lingering buzz still bubbling in my veins . . . all those potential spells just waiting to be shaped and brandished. If that's how it feels to take power—to wield and possess it—I doubt I'd find the strength to resist the urge, either. To stop myself getting addicted.

"I am the violence the world made of me," is all Chase says in reply, though I get the impression that I'm skirting close to something bigger. Picking at the edge of a shameful truth he's trying to deny.

"And those Shades you took it from, are they—will they be okay?"

"They'll live, if that's what you're asking." His face hardens. "The extraction leaves them weak, not dead. I don't kill."

"Does Savian?"

"I am not Savian."

"But you do his bidding."

"I told you, Cemmy, not everything is simple."

"Oh really?" I tug at the scry his master bound around my neck. His way of keeping us compliant. "Because it looks pretty damn simple to me."

"Then maybe you should look again." Chase exhales through his teeth. And then he does about the last thing I expect: he starts unbuttoning his shirt.

The hells—? I lurch away from him, all too aware of the distinct lack of space between us, the bareness of my legs and the wealth of power still radiating off his skin. "What are you—?"

"Relax, I'm just making a point."

The air catches in my lungs as the fabric parts to reveal the point he's making. A slim shard of crystal protrudes from the center of his chest, not hanging off a chain, like mine, but crudely fused to the flesh.

No . . . surely it can't be . . . "Is that a *scry*?"

"This is what happens to a Gold who declines to cooperate," Chase says, covering the wound up fast. "So no, Cemmy, nothing about this is *simple*, and as much as you may not like him, Savian is right about one thing: if we don't get the siphon away from the

Church, they will use it to destroy all magic. And you saw what happened to that Violet I drained—we can't live without magic. If they succeed, we die. Every last one of us."

I can tell by the danger in his voice that he's trying to scare me. To stop me asking the very question Novi hurled at him in the monastery. The one that snapped him cold.

"And what will Savian do with it?"

Because there's no way a Shade goes rogue just to *save all magic* on the Council's behalf. If Savian's concern really was for the wellbeing of his fellow Shades, he wouldn't risk failure by keeping them in the dark. There has to be some reason he's operating in secret.

"You let me worry about that," Chase says, avoiding my question every bit as staunchly as he did hers.

"So . . . what—? I'm just supposed to trust you?"

"Maybe." He shrugs, rocking back and forth on his heels. "Or maybe we could agree to trust each other."

Trust each other. With those three little words, he offers me exactly the opportunity Novi's been begging me to exploit. A way of probing him for information.

"Trust is earned, Cassiel." This time, I don't wield his true name with malice, but as a reminder of the conversation we had at the Sacred Hearts Inn, when I convinced him to part with that raw kernel of honesty. "If you want my trust, you can't only show me the parts of yourself that are convenient," I say.

I need to see it all.

CHAPTER

Fifteen

"Alright. Ask me anything you want, and I'll tell you whatever I can." To my surprise, Chase agrees to my demand almost instantly—though I don't miss the subtle caveat he adds to the deal. "Oh, and since trust is *earned*, this game has to go both ways." The glimmer in his eyes is pure challenge.

"Fine. But I get to go first," I say, sinking down to enjoy the comfort of the couch and the warmth of Mom's crocheted blanket, both luxuries he can't partake in while the world around us continues to swirl gray. "How did you learn to cast your In-Betweens?" I ask as he settles on the ground in front of me, entirely unfazed by the slight. "If the Council destroyed all the records and every Hue has been taught the method wrong for four hundred years, then where did the theory come from?" I start the questioning with something easy, poking at the inner workings of a secret he's already shared.

"Another very old, very illegal book," Chase says, leaning back on his elbows. "My mother came from a long line of prominent Yellow Shades, stretching back generations before the purges. So when the Council decided to bury the truth of our magics, her ancestors were the ones tasked with altering the records, they couldn't burn. Which they did—for the most part. Except for the ones they didn't." His lips quirk with a smile. "They chose to keep a few of the more damning texts for . . . *posterity*, though I imagine leverage had something to do with that decision, too, in case the Council ever sought to turn on them. It really is amazing what you can learn from such illicit family heirlooms," he tells me, cocking his head to the side. "My turn. Why were you so afraid of the Gray?" There's no derision to his voice, no judgement or superior edge. He's asking out of genuine interest.

Which is a problem since Magdalena is the one sin I'm unwilling to confess.

"My mom." The answer I offer him instead is not so much a lie as it is an obfuscation. "She didn't want me in the Gray, so I didn't want to be there, either. Never got as good as the others at holding an In-Between." I close the subject with a purposefully detached shrug. "My turn—what's so important about Versallis's journal? Why risk the entire plan for some sordid history?"

"Because it's *our* history," Chase stresses, resolute and unabashed. "And the more we let the Council keep it from us, the easier we become to control." Despite the staunch note of conviction, his words sound every bit as carefully couched as mine, as though he's admitted to something real, but not the real reason.

"That's a fake answer," I say, crossing my arms tight. "Not in the spirit of the game."

"Right, and your answer was completely full and honest?" He meets my skepticism with a glare, making it plenty clear that he got the measure of me, too. Though when I set my jaw and raise a brow in retaliation, Chase grudgingly relents to add, "It's important to establish how much your enemies know about your power; it makes them easier to predict," he says, and this time, the words ring with truth.

But only a tiny sliver of it.

He's still holding something back.

"So then what's with all the secrecy?" I ask. "Why are you so desperate to keep it from Savian?"

"Uh-uh, you've had your turn—spirit of the game, remember?" He dodges the question with a satisfied smile, turning the interrogation back on me. "If you weren't confident casting an In-Between, why didn't you take the Emerald with you to rob the Governor? Do your friends not approve of you stealing?" He truly has an uncanny knack for sniffing around my secret. Coming at it from all different sides.

"Just because I'm a thief doesn't mean Eve has to be," I say, ducking the actual reason with another carefully concocted lie. "She'd help if I asked her to"—hells, she offers to help most every night, as do Ezzo and Novi—"but it doesn't seem fair to put her at risk."

"You do realize she could easily support an In-Between around you both?" Chase sits up to look at me properly, a penetrating mix of curiosity and confusion simmering in his eyes. "She could quite literally do it sleeping. That's the whole point of her gift."

Yes . . . except gifts can fail.

I watched it happen to Magdalena.

But since I refuse to have *that* conversation with this judgy Gold, I reach for a different excuse and say, "There are other dangers in the Gray besides shattering." We could be seen by a Shade, for instance, or found by one of the Council's trackers—both more likely to occur when we're ensconced in the shadows instead of hidden in plain sight. "And in case you've forgotten, robbing a member of the clergy is a capital crime. Hardly something I was dying to involve her in." Not when I'm the one who needed the coin. "It's my mom I do the stealing for; it shouldn't be Eve's problem."

"You seemed pretty happy to make it *my* problem," Chase says, alluding to the deal I forced him to accept on the beach. *If I do this, then at the end of the job, you steal more of Savian's power and heal my mom.*

"Yeah, well, *you* are currently blackmailing me, so I'm a little less precious."

"Fair enough." He lays back down on the shadowed floor, knotting his hands behind his head like a pillow. "Your turn."

"Erm . . . okay . . ." Though I mean to keep probing him about the journal, when I open my mouth again, an entirely different question winds up slipping my tongue. "Why us?" The words ring like thunder around the inky silence of the Gray, snapping his muscles taut. Was it simply our proximity to the siphon, or the convenience of having stumbled across a ready-made palette of Hues? Are our gifts the last of their kind on the continent? And how did they even learn what those gifts were, or where to find them, or which ones they'd need at all? Their choices to date have felt deliberate, but since they don't appear to know any more about the inner workings of Rhodes's plan than we do, what I can't understand is *how* they came to make each choice. How they decided *which* halves to enlist.

And for a long moment, it feels as though Chase might leave me to wonder, that I've inadvertently lent voice to the question that'll bring an end to this truce. But then with a sharp expulsion of air, the tension in his jaw slackens and he looks me dead in the eye to say, "A Cobalt, an Amethyst, and a Bronze; that's what our Indigo told us we'd need in order to retrieve the siphon."

Right . . . of course. They have an Indigo Shade. The answer is as obvious as it is unsettling. They have a way to predict the future.

"She couldn't divine the reason for why," Chase continues, "or tell us whether we'd actually succeed; only that it would need to happen on the cleansing moon, and that you, Novi, and Lyria would somehow be involved."

"Just me and Novi?" I ask, leaning forward with interest. "Not Ezzo or Eve?"

"Not specifically, no—but foresight is an imprecise specialization, and the future isn't fully knowable or set in stone; it's more like a glimpse into our unmade decisions. So it's possible her magic sensed that finding you would lead us to Eve and Ezzo, and that Ezzo could then lead us to Lyria, seeing how the visions weren't specific enough to take us to her door. They did, however, unearth a pattern to when she liked to visit the Gray. Always in the early hours, and never for more than a few minutes at a time. That's probably why Ezzo never happened across her trail before."

Huh.

Though I'm sure Chase doesn't mean it to, his answer sheds light on a few other truths, as well. Like how he and Savian have been able to amass such a glut of tightly held information, along with the endless bounds of wealth Chase seems to enjoy. When you have an unfettered supply of rainbow magics—and no aversion to iron slowing your accomplice down—there's almost nothing you can't achieve.

We continue that way for a while, firing questions at each other until our game stops taking the form of *turns* and settles more into a conversation. I learn that, like his movements, Chase's access to the captive Shades is carefully controlled by Savian, and that the two have been working together for several months now—though every time I try to coax him for more damning specifics, revisit my questions about the journal, or probe for the reason Savian embedded his scry, his answers grow clipped and restless and he changes the subject as fast as he feasibly can. But not before I'm able to deduce that he bears no more love for the Green rogue than we do, and that he has, on occasion, acted against his master's wishes—like when he bought the tincture for Mom.

In return, I let him quiz me about Isitar and the others, and though I don't really notice it happening, it isn't long before I've stopped courting his secrets and started telling him about my life.

"How does a Bronze who hates the Gray end up in a magically augmented monastery with three other Hues?" Chase's curiosity is so sincere, I don't hesitate to share the story. I tell him all about Mom's insistence that I only ever phase on our roof, and about the fateful night that Ezzo finally found me there, heeding the call of the shadows. How I'd blinked back into the physical realm at the very sight of him—because that's what Mom told me to do if I ever saw another Shade—only for my loneliness to get the better of me, as Ezzo instinctively knew it would.

"I'm not a Shade, I'm a Hue—a Sapphire," he'd said upon my return. "And if you'd rather not see me again, that's okay, I promise to leave you alone. But if you'd like to meet some other halves, then come back at the same time tomorrow."

Which of course, I did.

"That's when he introduced me to Novi and Eve," I say, glancing up at Chase through my lashes. About halfway through the tale, I'd decided to grant him a respite from the floor, blinking us out of the Gray so that he could join me on the couch, without stopping to consider the result of that kindness. How close we would have to sit to share the warmth of the blanket and continue our conversation in whispers that wouldn't wake Mom.

Too close. I can all but feel the rhythmic beat of his heart. See the light dusting of freckles sprinkled across his cheeks. The molten silver in his eyes.

Gods, he really is beautiful.

"And how long have the two Es been together?" Chase asks, already confident in his assessment that they're a couple.

"Since they were kids," I say, and it's impossible not to smile at his choice of phrasing. Because Eve and Ezzo have truly never been anything but *the two Es*. Even before they grew old enough to tangle romantically, their friendship was bonded in a way that felt inevitable, as though destiny itself had conspired to create the perfect pair. He gifted her the set of oils that sparked her passion for painting, and she taught him that there's more to life than the need to watch and make amends. When Eve smiles, Ezzo brightens, and when Ezzo's vigils in the Gray start bordering on obsessive, Eve's the one to pull him back from the edge.

Like the colors in their blood, they complement each other.

"And what about you and Novi?" Chase's follow-up question is a little less self-assured. A little more . . . *timid*. "How long have you two been a—"

"We're not," I cut him off, harsher than is strictly necessary. "Or at least, we haven't been for a while now," I add, instantly regretting the denial.

"Bad story?" Chase's voice is as soft as I've ever heard it, the gruff timbre of his sympathy sending a flush to my cheeks.

"No, just . . . sad," I say, and he must realize he's stepped into something painful, because instead of prying further, he affects a mask that's deadly serious and leans in to ask, "So . . . what do you think my odds are of getting her to stop calling me *Cassiel*?"

I have to muffle the sudden laugh that escapes me.

"Slim to non-existent, I'm afraid." I deliver the news with a grateful smile. "But I would really—*really*—like to be there when you ask."

"I'll keep that in mind." Chase rolls his eyes. And from that point on, he graciously steers the flow of our conversation towards the less emotionally charged.

He asks me where I learned to pick a lock, and whether I could pick one of iron. I tell him that the nature of the mechanism is far more pertinent than its housing metal—unless he means to trick me into running another lift so that his master can magically bind it to my arm.

"No immediate plans for that, no," he says, sheepish. Then in an effort to distract from his previous indiscretions, Chase regales me with stories about all those fanciful places he's lived. How the winter frosts in Nivengard turn the lakes to a sheet you can skate on—*I wouldn't recommend it though; when you fall, the ice bruises you for days*—and how the taverns in Heresse serve the sweetest honey wine he's ever tasted. He didn't find much to love about Astraya—*it's mostly warring gangs and crooked merchants*—but if there was one place he could choose to return, it would be Sarotuza.

"I think you'd like it there." By the time Chase is done with the telling, we've both sunk low against the couch cushions, the lateness of the hour pulling us towards the realm of dreams. "The sky there is just . . . endless. On a clear morning, it's so blue and so vibrant, it bleeds right into the sea."

"Maybe one day I'll get to see it." My lids are fast growing heavy, the words croaking out gravelly and thick.

"I hope you do." Chase pulls the blanket tight around us, shifting our bodies closer so that I can drop my head to his shoulder, his arm moving to rest idly against my ribs.

"Hey—Cemmy?" His whisper is a bated breath in the dark.

"Yeah?"

"What would you be if you weren't a Bronze?" he asks. And though the question is as strange as it is unexpected, I find that an answer immediately springs to my lips.

"Ordinary," I say, equal parts envious and sad.

"No. I don't think you could ever be ordinary." The heat of his hand—burning hot through my flimsy nightshirt—suddenly feels like an invitation, so chaste and subtle it practically borders on obscene.

"And you?" But I don't make to pull away, too afraid to break the spell of the moment, or open my eyes to see whether the exhaustion has led to me imagining this whole peculiar exchange. "What would you be if you weren't a Gold?"

"Free."

By the time he answers, I'm already partway to sleep.

By the time I wake, Chase is gone.

CHAPTER

Sixteen

Maybe we could agree to trust each other. In the cold light of day, I find myself conflicted. On the one hand, Chase's attempt to broker peace truly did seem in earnest, and he'd answered my questions with as much—if not more—honesty than I'd afforded him. But on the other sits the promise I made to Novi, to become the person he confides in so that we could get out from under Savian's thumb. And between what I witnessed at the theater house and our game of turns on the couch, Chase gave me everything we need to make that happen. The weaknesses we can exploit to banish both the Gold *and* the Green from our lives. Spare us the trip through the Dominion.

We need to talk. My first instinct is to reach for Novi on the scry, hoping I can catch her before she heads out to meet the others.

Too late.

The reply she sends me is both immediate and barbed. *Damn right we do. Cassiel's here and you still owe us an explanation.*

Son of a . . . Do Golds not have to sleep? I hurry to dress and get Mom settled—a feat that's become markedly easier now that her tincture is laced with a spell. Also his doing—and in direct contradiction to Savian's wishes. The guilt in my stomach is fast sharpening from a pang to an ache. In allowing Chase to show me his colors, I suddenly find myself at odds with my own interests.

True to Novi's word, he's already holding court in the monastery when I arrive, trying to convince my friends to let him push them the magic I demanded he thieve on their behalf. That it's only the extraction of power that leaves a Shade drained and screaming. That accepting that stolen power is safe.

Safe is one word for it. I flush with the memory of him hovered above me, the devastating rush of color scorching right through his skin. But much like the doubts I awoke with, the exchange feels different now that we're not alone. When Chase sidles up behind me in demonstration, the only thing I feel is confused.

"Once you have that raw magic, shaping it into a spell works like casting an In-Between," he says, giving Novi ample time to interpret for Lyria. "Except instead of imagining your anchors, you need to focus on the outcome you want. In the case of a wisdom spell, you're asking it to impart a certain type of knowledge, like how to use sign language. Just remember to be specific in your intentions, so that the spell doesn't have to guess. But as long as you have enough magic—and the right type of magic—the color should do the rest."

It really does prove to be that simple.

Or at least, *casting* the wisdom spell proves simple, *using* that newly acquired knowledge, on the other hand, is a whole different story. Because what I'd failed to realize when I sent Chase to steal us this shortcut is that there's so much more to sign language than merely learning to identify each sign. It follows a different set of grammar rules, for one thing, tends towards different sentence structures, and when Lyria signs, she's not just forming a series of static shapes with her hands, she's augmenting them with her posture, and her expression, and the position of her arms. So while the spell may have given me the ability to understand *her* signs without effort, when it comes time to sign *back*, I find I'm missing her years of hard-earned muscle memory. I have no instinct for doing it well.

"I'm sorry—I thought this would work better." It takes me far longer than I'd like to get the apology out, though when I do finally reach the last sign—a press of my fingertips to my lips then out to the right with a curl of my fist and my thumb pointing upward—Lyria is gracious enough to flash me a smile.

"The more you practice, the easier it'll come. Though for what it's worth, it means a lot that you're trying. Most people wouldn't bother—even if the magic

came free." She goes as far as to thank me, as though my decision to ask for the spell was driven by kindness instead of jealousy; the petty want for her to stop monopolizing Novi's eye.

Gods.

I really need to stop being such an ass.

But since my less-than-selfless motives *have* enabled us to communicate more freely, Chase shifts our attention to the second task of the morning, prompting the others to use the remainder of his stolen Violet to learn how to stabilize their In-Betweens, the magic sparing them the trial by fire he had me endure on the cliff.

"So do Hues not . . . always do it this way?" Lyria asks, refusing the spell when it's offered.

"No, they don't," Chase says, his accompanying signs forming slow. "Why, do you?"

"Yeah, it's . . . the way I was taught."

At that, even our know-it-all Gold looks surprised. "But that's not—how did your Shade parent learn the theory?"

A theory that the Council has systematically purged from the records.

A theory that only exists in a few very old, very illegal books.

"I don't have a Shade parent," Lyria signs, turning his surprise to outright shock. *"I mean, I do . . . obviously. But I wasn't raised by him; he was gone long before I was born, and he never saw fit to tell my mother what he was, so when she met my father a short while later, I guess they just . . . never figured out what happened. That I wasn't actually . . . his."* She pinks with the confession. And though I was able to follow her signs with a comfortable ease, it still takes me a few seconds to fully discern their meaning. To catch up to the other implication behind her blush.

"Wait, are you saying—do they not know you're a Hue?"

"Nobody knows." The red reaches the tips of Lyria's ears. *"My entire family are typics. Not particularly devout typics, but they're not quite faithless, either, so by the time my magic manifested, I'd heard enough about the 'evils' of blood color to keep it to myself."*

"Then how did you learn to cast an In-Between at all?" The confusion in Chase's eyes is verging on comical.

"The shadows." She shrugs, looking more and more eager to put this conversation to bed. *"They started calling to me around my eighth name day. Taught me how to phase without shattering."*

And how to do it properly, it seems. The version of the spell that wouldn't have required her to speak the words out loud the way the rest of us used to. That would have allowed her to exist in the Gray as effortlessly as Chase—even without doing the reading.

He leaves the monastery shortly after the magical exchange is complete, excusing himself to go report our progress to Savian, a not-so-subtle reminder of the axe still hanging over our heads and the pressing need to relay what I was able to tease from him last night, bar a few of the more . . . *compromising* details.

"How weak are we talking?" Novi asks once I'm done with the telling, focusing on the part of my story that best suits our scheme: the effect Chase's gift wrought on his master's captive rainbow.

"Not dead, but pretty close." I shiver with the memory of the Violet hanging limp against his bindings. "Definitely to the point of unconsciousness."

"Long enough to dump Savian's body on the Council's doorstep with a note that says he knows where to find their siphon?" The sign Novi uses to represent *siphon* is actually a modified version of *deplete*—a forward slide of one palm over the other, with the moving hand held at a ninety-degree angle until it breaks apart to form fists—since Lyria couldn't think of a distinct sign that fit the word and fingerspelling it became a nuisance.

"I didn't stick around to time it, but I'd bet a bag of coin on yes," I hedge, even as my mind starts mulling over all the reasons we can't do that. If we give Savian to the Council, he'd sell us out every bit as readily as we did him, ensure we meet the same sticky end at their lack of mercy. That much, he's already made clear. But with the very existence of magic on the line, we can't *not* alert them to the siphon's location, either. We have to find some way to thread a needle that's too narrow across the eye.

"And you're sure Cassiel is going to drain Savian ahead of the lift?" Novi asks, snapping me back to the sedition we're discussing.

"I think so." Or at least, I hope so. I need to believe that he means to make good on his promise to heal Mom. "He really doesn't want Savian to know about that journal, so I've got him by the throat on this one." And maybe—just maybe—I also swayed him with my trust.

"See, but that's the part I don't get." Though Eve's signs lack in speed and confidence like mine do, we've all resolved to both speak and sign our words at the same time, not only as a means of practice, but to take the burden of lip-reading off Lyria, since that's an imprecise science at best. "You said there was nothing in that journal other than ancient history. Why would Savian care that four hundred years ago, the Council lied about some Hues? How does him knowing that make a difference?"

"He wouldn't say." The admission leaves me frustrated—especially since I spent more than one of my *turns* trying to coax that answer from our game. "But I did get the impression that he's only loyal to Savian out of necessity. If it comes down to a choice, I don't think he'd choose him."

"You think the Gold that helped trap you in the Gray would choose *us* over Savian?" Ezzo raises a dubious brow. "Why?"

"Just a feeling." The image of the scry embedded in his chest flashes before my eyes. I'm not sure why I'm keeping this part of Chase's story a secret, other than it feels like too personal a secret to share. A revelation made to win my trust, not betray his.

"Well, until it's more than a feeling, Cassiel is staying firmly on the outside of this plan." Novi's foot drums a decisive staccato against the table. "So we need to keep pretending to run this lift."

Though of course, that doesn't come without risk.

Step one of *pretending* to run this lift was breaking into the Commander's office—and that almost ended with Ezzo and Eve in cuffs. The next steps are bound to be harder still. Last night's incursion yielded a bounty of information about Rhodes's plans for the cleansing moon parade, but nothing about the siphon, or the Dominion itself, and comparing the map Chase's magic enabled him to recreate from memory with the Governor's version has left us drawing a blank.

Those two replicas lay spread between us now, identical at first glance—as one would expect the overlying worlds to be—but radically different upon closer examination. The Commander has annotated his map with all manner of cryptic markings and signs, an idiosyncratic method of note designed to be understood by him alone. Three fruitless hours of guesswork later, we're still no nearer to discovering what protections are awaiting us inside.

"I don't suppose we could just . . . ask the shadows?" Novi turns to ask Lyria, her suggestions getting every bit as desperate as my own. "If they can teach you how to phase, surely they can answer a few questions."

"Questions . . . yes. These ones . . . I doubt it." Lyria's reply is half grimace, half regret. *"The shadows don't share a single mind; they don't know everything that's happening everywhere all at once. If I want a specific answer, I have to be close enough to the right shadows to get it, and even then, I can't force an answer they don't actually have. Do you remember how in the Governor's study they told me 'the end of everything' lives inside the Dominion?"* As much as Lyria doesn't need to look to Novi to interpret her signs anymore, I can't help but notice how her gaze still wanders there more than most, lingering longer than is strictly necessary.

Same way mine does, I suppose.

Though I've no reason to notice, nor any right to care.

"Well, I think they called it that instead of a siphon because they didn't know the word," Lyria continues. "*Probably because no one's ever said it in the Gray before, and I'd venture that's going to be true for whatever traps the Commander's set in the shadows. At a push, they could maybe tell us where those traps are."*

"Then we'll have to get the answers from Rhodes," I declare. Not because I've had some brilliant idea for how we might achieve that, but because I'm trying to reclaim Novi's attention. Because there's suddenly a new girl in our midst, with curls that burn like fire and lips that curve like a bow, and I'm not used to sharing the limelight. For the longest time, it's been just the four of us: Eve and Ezzo, Novi and me, the perfect partners in crime—and in other things, too.

Except Novi and I aren't together anymore.

We haven't been together for almost a year.

So it shouldn't make a difference if her eyes keep drifting back to Lyria.

It shouldn't make a difference that she was the only one who didn't need Chase's magic to learn to sign, or that I still don't know where she picked up the language, or that in the gaps between planning, I keep catching snippets of the conversation she and Lyria are having on their own.

It shouldn't make a difference.

Yet it does.

"And how exactly do you propose we do that?" Novi's all too happy to take the bait and call my bluff. She always could tell when I was just being obstinate.

"Erm . . . well . . . the Governor has a map of the Dominion in his study, right?" While I've never been particularly adept at thinking strategically, when it comes to saving face, I'm an expert. "Which means it's safe to assume that he's at least somewhat involved in the plan to collapse the Gray. So if he were to, say . . . get nervous about the Council upsetting that plan, he could go to Rhodes and demand reassurance. Get him to reiterate how the siphon's being protected." Connect the dots between the information we stole, and the specific trio of Hues an Indigo directed Savian to find. Give us the last piece of the puzzle.

"That's quite a few hypotheticals you've got there, Cem." Novi's answering objection is wry. "Especially since as far as we know, the Governor *isn't* worried about the Council upsetting their plan, and even if he was, him knowing the answers doesn't do us much good."

No, it doesn't. What we really need is for him to—

Holy shadows—that's it! The idea that strikes me is as reckless as it is bold, a veritable lunacy that might just get the job done—providing it doesn't get us all killed.

"Unless it's actually *us* that Rhodes tells," I say and sign, startling the others to my meaning.

We currently have at our disposal a Gold who is filled to the brim with magic.

Including Red magic.

The power to glamour and compel.

To become anyone we want him to be.

"Think Cassiel will go for it?" I certainly seem to have won Novi's attention now.

"He's the one who's insisting we do this—so unless he's got a better idea, he's going to have to." I shrug.

And just like that, we go from having nothing, to having a plan.

CHAPTER

Seventeen

"And you accuse *me* of having bad ideas?" Chase mutters as we snake our way towards the Church of Heavenly Thralls, an imposing behemoth of stained glass and looming bell towers where each morning, the Church elite go to, well, church. A daily call to faith that attracts the very cream of Isitar's clergy. Which also makes it the very last place any half Shade in the city would ever want to be caught.

Around us, an army of muted cloaks flutters by in an impatient rush, outnumbered only by the vast lines of armed enforcers and the overwhelming presence of gold-flecked eyes. We are—quite literally—at the heart of the Church's campaign for righteous reform. The mere act of walking these streets feels like climbing the gallows.

"In case you've forgotten, *my* idea was to glamour you to look like the Governor—not compel then kidnap him while he's observing mass," I hiss, keeping my hood low and my stride long.

"And in case *you've* forgotten, I told you that wouldn't work," Chase hisses back. "You only fell for my trick with Vargas because you'd never met him before. That won't fly with Rhodes. No glamour is convincing enough to survive familiarity."

Just as no amount of familiarity is enough to make him less of an ass, apparently. As much as I hadn't expected Chase to meet my suggestion with unbridled enthusiasm, I also didn't expect his rendezvous with Savian to chill his blood cold. Whatever had transpired between the two of them after he left the monastery had pitched him into enough of a mood to spend the rest of the day doing his utmost to pick apart my plan, until finally, he was forced to offer up this alternative. At which point, Chase grew determined to stop engaging with me at all. As though he suddenly couldn't handle the sight of me. As though he hadn't spent the previous night telling me his life story in an effort to win my trust.

I don't think you could ever be ordinary.

Perhaps that hushed confession really was just a product of an over-tired imagination and the fuzzy tendrils of sleep.

Or hells, maybe Savian just reminded him not to play with his food.

Either way, it serves to simplify my decision.

"But you're sure the compulsion will fool him?" I ask, stealing another glance at the pious monstrosity of gray rock.

"I guess we'll find out," Chase says, angling his head towards the esteemed delegation making its approach. "Since it looks like they're both here."

"Wonderful." My stomach gives a painful lurch. Our entire plan lived or died by this single detail: whether both men would choose to attend the same service on the same day at the same Church. In order to avoid suspicion, we need Rhodes to see the Governor out in public—engaged and protected—in a place where he would deem an attack to be impossible. And the Church of Heavenly Thralls makes attacks about as impossible as they come.

It's warded against Shades, for one thing, and there's no walking through these doors without an invitation or a Church-approved seal. Which is why Chase and I have no intention of crossing the threshold in the physical realm; we duck into an empty alley so that we can blink out of existence and do it in the Gray.

Whoa. Even stripped of its splendorous color, this cathedral is a marvel to behold. A triple-height ceiling looms high above the nave, a tapestry of ornate filigree spiraling up to meet the mural at its center. The myth of creation. As told by an artist who was happy to ignore the contradiction between magic and faith.

Behind the altar, each of the three Gods rests atop a marble plinth, their faces staring around the pews with an accusatory eye and a reproachful vengeance. *Perhaps they're searching for their fallen kin.* I blanch at the gravity in their expressions. Once upon a time, there used to be seven Gods in the pantheon, if the Council's word on the matter is to be believed.

Seven Gods, seven colors.

I suppose the Church found that symmetry unnerving.

"How close will you have to be to cast the spell?" I ask as Chase and I blink back into the physical realm, a shadowed corner of the transept allowing us to reappear without question.

"To fully take control? I'll need actual contact," he says.

"That might be a problem." Another rock drops heavy into my gut, the sheer scale of this misguided task pulling into vicious focus. In the time it took us to sneak inside, the Governor has already claimed his seat at the very front of the congregation, where, like moths to a flame, his advisors and aides have flocked to power, filling to the brim the pews around him on every side. There's no way we're infiltrating those ranks without drawing attention, and we can't risk doing that with the Commander sitting only a few rows away. If Rhodes so much as catches a glimpse of our faces, the jig is up. Step two of this plan will fall to pieces.

"Come on—we have until the end of the service to figure something out." Chase leads me towards the rear of the Church, into a quieter pew where we might go unnoticed.

It doesn't stay quiet for long.

Despite the early hour and the mid-week prayer call, by the time the Aralagio commences his sermon, the Church is packed full to the rafters, stuffing every pew with clerics and crushing Chase and me tight.

This is becoming quite the regular occurrence. My breath hitches as our limbs are forced to do battle for space. I shouldn't be spending so much time with this Gold pressed up against my side, or hovered above me, or sharing space beneath a blanket, or with his arms around my waist. Especially when he's proven so fickle.

"It has long been argued that magic is the will of the Gods." The words boom like thunder across the nave, magnified by a spell born not of a Shade, but of science. "Why else would they have wrought such a reckless sin unto the world? the faithless ask. Why else would they burden their children with the heady lure of temptation?"

Sin. Lure. Temptation. The Aralagio sure is laying the rhetoric on thick.

"But a wise man seeks not to question the Gods; he simply embraces the opportunity they lay at his feet. For there can be no strength without struggle. No joy without suffering. No absolution without faith."

"No paradise without order." The crowd chants back in unison, a chilling chorus of fervor that sinks me low in my seat.

"But how can there be order while the heathen blight continues to rage? How are we to return the world to its rightful glory if we turn a blind eye to this sweeping epidemic of Shades? For a hero to rise, there must first come a monster, and in their unerring wisdom, the Gods have infected our lands with an evil that defiles the blood of men. It is the job of the righteous to banish that evil back to the nine hells from whence it came. That is why we call the holiest of our days the cleansing moon. For we will cleanse this world of the disease rotting through its veins. We will hunt, and expel, and defeat the scourge known as magic. Bleed the demon of its color and strip the shadows of their Gray."

Beside me, Chase tenses, every muscle in his body snapping stiff, as though the Aralagio is addressing him alone.

"Not exactly subtle, are they?" I whisper, taken aback by the sudden ash of his face and the murderous set of his jaw. The fury vibrating off his skin. "Hey . . . this is just their normal brand of propaganda, okay?" I put a gentle hand to his arm. "Don't let it get to you." I'm actually amazed it still can.

"It's not me I'm worried about." Chase eyes the Governor the way a dying man would a reprieve, as though any second now, he might lurch to his feet and cast the compulsion spell in full view of the congregation. "You know what, screw subtlety. When he leaves, you're going to trip up in front of him. Stall the group." While the plan he proposes isn't quite as reckless as the one I envisioned, it still strikes me as too needless a risk.

"That's a little public, don't you think? What if Rhodes sees?"

"He won't." Chase sounds far more confident than I feel. "He's sat four rows back from the Governor, at the very end of the pew, and he's already checked his time-keeper five times. He'll be out that door the moment the Aralagio is done peddling his lies. We'll have a window."

Not a very big one. As the minutes tick by, I wrack my brain for some better solution. A way around the Governor's guards, maybe, or a reason to distract an aide from his side so that Chase can skirt near. Anything that won't turn every godsdamned head in this Church in my direction. But as the sermon draws to a close, I'm still coming up empty, and we can't afford to let this fleeting opportunity pass.

"Wait for my signal." Chase slips into the aisle before me, his heavy hood pulled low around his ears. Thanks to the departing crowd, the awkward maneuvering he does to get in place goes unnoticed, though that's mostly down to luck more than skill.

He's no thief, that's for sure.

At least not in the usual sense of the word.

Three . . . two . . . one . . . now, Chase mouths as the Governor sweeps past the neighboring pew, leaving me just enough time to stumble into his path.

"Gods above!" I gruff my voice an octave, keeping my face hidden as I make an elaborate show of tripping over my feet. "Oh Heavens, Governor Lazaar—" His name is a stain on my tongue, a disgust I have to swallow with venom. "I'm so sorry! Please forgive me for getting in your way." I clutch the rich fabric of his cloak in apology, bowing my head deep.

"Move away from the Governor." His guards are quick to shove me clear of their charge.

Too quick.

A pointed curse escapes from between my lips. They converged on the Governor too fast and too efficiently, before Chase could spring forward and brush a hand near.

Damn it. The panic in his eyes tells me he's not just inept, he's also out of ideas.

So I guess it's lucky that my reflexes aren't quite as slow as his.

Bad idea, Cemmy. This is a bad, bad idea.

"Erm . . . excuse me, Governor?" I go right ahead and do it anyway, since Chase hasn't left me much of a choice. "I think you may have dropped this." I produce the bag of coin I relieved from his pockets, a lift made more out of stubborn habit than good sense. And while it goes against every fiber of my being to reveal the sticky bent of my fingers, I'm trusting that the Governor won't suspect me of stealing the purse I'm attempting to return.

That's all the invitation Chase needs.

As one of the guards steps forward to retrieve my bounty, he shuffles past the delegation and reaches out to cast the spell, seizing control of the Governor's mind with a burst of magic that spikes his irises red.

Got him. He announces with a tiny nod of Lazaar's chin.

Which is why I'm not surprised when instead of marching out of the cathedral, the Governor turns to an aide I instantly recognize as Vargas and says, "Hurry after Commander Rhodes, if you will. I must see him at once."

CHAPTER

Eighteen

The typics have many reasons to fear a Shade—magic tends to do that; it swings every fight in its favor. But for the most part—as long as the full-bloods remain tightly governed by the Council—the typics find that magic to be more useful than it is a threat. For a price, a Shade can offer them a shortcut or a dream, a cure or a measure of comfort, a prophecy or a skill.

And so they forget the imbalance of power.

They forget that with a flex of their hand, an Orange could splinter their bones. Squeeze the air from their lungs. Tear down their homes. That with nary a thought, their wealth could be turned to ash by a Yellow, their thoughts broken by a crushing influx of knowledge from a Violet, their age accelerated towards death by a Blue.

They forget because it's easier to forget than to renounce their vices.

They forget because the Council makes a point of disciplining Shades who break their rules.

And in the faithless quarter, they forget because the Church isn't constantly assaulting them with hate.

But when they do remember their fear of blood color, they start with the Reds.

Full-mind compulsion.

The nightmare the clerics fuel to stoke the flames.

A total loss of control. Your body being driven like a puppet.

When the Council first resolved to seek an alliance with the Church, they even wrote it into the peace accords, promised to strictly regulate its use. Forbid it. Condemn it. Even in the faithless quarter, full-mind compulsion is one of the most harshly punished crimes, a death sentence for the Shade who offers it, and for any buyer who dares seek it out. But while the Council's trackers are trained to spot the signs of a Red's compulsion, the Church has grown complacent in its conceit. Their deliberate abuse of iron has done such an outstanding job keeping Shades out of their midst, they're no longer prepared for an attack of this manner. A few strange actions on the Governor's part shouldn't arouse suspicion.

What might prove a problem, on the other hand, is *keeping* him under Chase's control long enough to get the job done. No small feat considering that we're forced to hold our distance, to trail him through the streets from afar so as not to incite the ferocity of his guards.

"Please tell me the others are in position." The cost of the spell is evident in the sharpness of Chase's voice and the splintered gasp of his breaths. His hair is painted clammy with sweat, his jaw clenched tight, his limbs shaking. He may have stolen enough power to seize control of the Governor, but without renewed contact, that control is beginning to wane. We need to move faster.

"Novi says they're waiting in the next alley," I tell him, relaying the message she sent down my scry. "We should see them any second now."

And true to her word, the moment we inch around the corner, the sound of the fight they're staging fills the air with a chorus of angry snarls.

Draped in shadow and a uniform of black, Ezzo cuts a menacing figure as he terrorizes a convincing performance out of Lyria, who appears to be settling into her new life of crime with extraordinary ease.

There's this trick my brothers and I used to play, she'd signed as we were working to devise our distraction. *The three of them would fake a brawl in front of the sweets merchant, then when he'd hurry over to wrench them apart, I'd make off with a fistful of candies. My mother was livid when she found out.* The humor in her eyes had shone proud. And though she's been slowly getting more and more comfortable around us, letting slip more and more pieces of her life—especially since we resolved to both speak and sign in her presence—all I could think when she shared that was: three brothers. A mother *and* a father. Typics, sure, but still alive. Unlike the rest of us, Lyria had gone nineteen years without incurring the curse of the Hue. Which makes dragging her into this mess feel downright galling.

"Break that up," Chase commands through the Governor's lips, ordering his two guards to go and put an end to the violence.

"Sir—?" For a moment they look hesitant, as though surprised he'd direct them to intervene. But then Lyria lets out a bloodcurdling scream and they quell under the weight of his disapproval, unsheathing their sabers to stride off and deal with the ugly crime.

"Thank the colors for that." As soon as their backs are turned, Chase lurches forward, relieving the strain of the magic with a hand to the Governor's arm. "I was about to lose him."

Well, that's reassuring. "Can you hold him now?"

"So long as your friends take care of the problem," he says, dropping into an exhausted crouch. "We'll need to stay closer from here on."

Then it's a good thing problems are Novi's specialty.

She and Eve pop into existence right on cue behind the guards, startling them with an attack they couldn't possibly see coming. The Gray is nothing if not useful for gaining the element of surprise. Two sleeping spells later—Blue magic courtesy of our Gold—the Governor's men are slumped unconscious, their faces kissing the cobbles, their sabers lying abandoned at their feet.

"Not bad," Chase quips as we join the others in the shadowy depths of the alley. "I wasn't sure that would work."

"I could say the same for this." Ezzo waves a hand in front of the Governor's eyes, as though testing the fidelity of the magic. "Full-mind compulsion's not exactly something you see every day."

"It's not exactly easy, either." There's a barbed snipe to Chase's words and signs. "So let's please get this done."

It takes all four of us to strip the guards of their uniforms, which somehow proves more distasteful than spelling them unconscious in the first place, but it's the only way Chase and I will be able to follow the Governor into the barracks. And while masquerading as an enforcer is the true crime I'm committing, it's shrugging on the crimson tunic that feels like a betrayal. This color was not meant for those whose blood teems with magic, and wearing it—for any reason—makes my skin crawl.

"Breathe, Cem." Novi tucks a wayward strand of hair into my hood. "It doesn't look that bad."

"Liar."

She hates this wretched color more than I do. Hates every man and woman who opts to wear it, and every unpunished atrocity it represents. For while it may have been the Council who killed her father, her mother's death was far more mundane. Just another casualty of a man with a temper and a rank who didn't like hearing the word "no". Who felt entitled to the body of a woman he didn't know, and—because she was faithless—never expected to be held accountable. Kind of like he never expected to age sixty years overnight, or have his heart beat so fast it broke clean out of his ribcage.

But that's the risk you take when you murder the typic wife of a Blue.

The power to accelerate can make for some pretty creative justice.

It was that spell that brought Novi's father to the Council's attention, so I guess you could say it was the Church that killed them both. Or at least that's how Novi sees it. And if I were in her shoes, it's how I'd see it, too.

"If anything goes wrong in there, you phase and you run, okay?" she says, tightening the guard's saber around my hip. "I mean it, Cem—" Her voice drops to a whisper. "This charade isn't worth dying for."

Maybe not. But until we can dispose of Savian, it's the only thing keeping us alive.

And it's not all a charade. Out of the corner of my eye, I see Lyria watching us from between the others, and I'm suddenly struck by the realization that even if we do manage to escape his clutches, our lives will still remain changed.

She's a part of us now. Not in any formal way—as far as I'm aware, she's not yet asked to join our merry band of halves, nor have we agreed to fold her into our number.

But she will.

And so will we.

And sparing another Hue from a life of hungry longing—especially one who's never been able to confide her secret in another soul—is no bad thing, so I'm going to have to learn to deal with this incessant squirm. The feeling that she's trying to take something from me when that something is no longer mine to lose.

Chase and I don't linger in the alley. For this plan to work, we have to reach the Commander's office without delay—lest he begin to suspect that the Governor had time to be intercepted—though now that Chase is able to maintain contact, the trip through the barracks proves simple. And thanks to the message he asked Vargas to relay, Rhodes has forgone his morning duties and is keenly awaiting our arrival.

Or perhaps *keenly* is too strong a word. His expression could more accurately be described as inconvenienced, harried, or outright annoyed, with all the look of a man who doesn't appreciate having his routine disrupted. I can tell that much by the cold glint in his eyes and the veins pulsing at the side of his neck. The angry twitch in his brow.

"Governor Lazaar." Though he does manage to keep the irritation from his voice. "To what do I owe this unexpected visit?" he asks, beckoning his superior inside.

Moment of truth. My breath catches as Chase is forced to break contact so that we can take our places by the door, as is our duty.

"We need to talk about the Council." The Governor's declaration betrays no hint of coercion, Chase's grip on the magic holding firm. "My staff tells me they've flooded the city with trackers. They know the drain started here, Aurelion. They're doubling their efforts to locate the source." He keeps our concern as succinct and vague as possible, so as not to overplay our hand.

"As we assumed they would eventually," Rhodes replies, entirely unperturbed. "This close to the tipping point, the effects will be growing more pronounced. Easier to trace. But you need not trouble yourself; even if the Council were to attack the Dominion, there is no way for their trackers to breach it. The shadows will fall."

"Be that as it may, I would like you to run me through the protections you've put in place," Chase forces the Governor to say, "for my own peace of mind."

"We've been through them all before, Lazaar. I assure you, nothing's changed."

Damn. My hands fist at my sides, the air in my lungs growing thin. We feared this might happen; that the two men will have had this conversation before. That Rhodes would find the question suspicious.

"Then it shouldn't take you long to refresh my memory." Sweat begins to bead at Chase's temples, not just from maintaining the magic, but from the strain of having to steer this exchange. Trying to guess how far he can push our request. "And that is an order."

Too far. Every part of me tenses, my nerves readying for the rebuke that will surely come. We don't know enough about the Governor's relationship with Rhodes to predict how he'd react to such a brazen command. What if the two men are closer to equals than subordinate and superior? What if by pulling rank, Chase has inadvertently alerted him to our crime?

"Certainly, Sir." To my relief, Rhodes allows the disparagement to stand. With a click of his tongue, he fetches his map of the Dominion and spreads it flat across the desk, making ready to explain the wealth of annotations we were unable to decipher.

Relax, it worked. The glance Chase gifts me is smug.

Only because you got lucky, I tell him with my scowl. And the gambit working doesn't change the fact that we can't afford for him to be more reckless than he is wise. This plan is far too fragile to survive a misstep.

"As we originally discussed, a purpose-built cell of iron was erected here, at the top of the centermost spire." Rhodes taps a finger against the tallest of the Dominion's gilded towers. "The iron encircles that room without break, so it's entirely impossible for a Shade to phase in or out of it, though it's been secured with iron chains, as well, just to make certain. I hold the sole key to that spire, and the lock's been sealed shut by a spell in the Gray to stop any Shade from shimmering through it. Only I know the incantation to that spell, but believe me, it's all but redundant given the rest of my contingencies."

"Those being—if you'd be so kind as to remind me?" Chase has the Governor ask, even as the blood begins to pound in my ears. We're barely one layer of defense into the telling, and already, this lift feels like an untenable task. The epitome of a doomed folly.

"Well, the whole building is warded against Shades, for starters," the Commander says, drumming his impatience against the map. "But before those were cast, I had a rogue charm a dozen portals at intervals along the approaching corridor, so as to also deter a faithless incursion. In order to reach the cell, any prospective thief would have no choice but to walk through them, at which point, they would be sucked into a different place in the Gray and shattered.

"Then we have the additional redundancies, in case the wards should fail," he continues, blowing my pupils wide. "Alarms that will alert us if a Shade does breach the building, and arrows that will automatically trigger inside the portals, to prevent anyone from moving between them without injury. These discharge within a matter of seconds, and, as before, I alone possess the ability to turn them off. So I assure you, Sir, no one—Shade, faithless, or otherwise—will ever make it through that door. Myself included."

It's those final two words that break me, the realization that Rhodes has left no eventuality to chance. No recourse for saving the shadows.

"And what of Hues?" Chase barely manages to keep the shake out of the Governor's voice. "Have you put any additional defenses in effect to protect from them, since they would, theoretically, be able to get through the portals and the wards?"

"But not the arrows, the spell, or the lock," the Commander says, dismissing the prospect out of hand. "With all due respect, Governor, I am unconcerned with half breeds. My sources estimate that there are maybe a dozen left in the city—if that—and their abilities are far more limited than a full-blooded Shade's, so it would require a highly improbable assemblage to even attempt such a feat—here, let me show you." He walks over to the cabinet in the corner and starts rifling through the bottom-most drawer.

Oh, hells. A hundred livid curses die on my tongue.

He's looking for the journal.

And he's not going to find it because Chase made me steal it from this very office only two nights ago.

Like an arrogant fool.

What do we do? he mouths, face stricken with fear. The moment Rhodes discovers the journal missing, he'll know that someone has been in here. And once he grows wise to that reality, he'll start dissecting every possibility for *how*. He'll remember that two nights ago, his key briefly went missing. He'll ask himself why the Governor is suddenly taking such an interest in the siphon. Maybe even begin to suspect his motives for enquiring about Hues.

If anything goes wrong in there, you phase and you run, okay? Novi's voice rings through my mind. *This charade isn't worth dying for.*

She told me exactly what to do in this situation.

And it's exactly what we *should* do given that we're only seconds away from getting caught.

But then I think of Mom, and Savian's wrath, and the ramifications of burning this bridge down to charcoal, and instead of running, I meet Chase's panic with a foolishness of my own.

Do you have the journal? I mouth back, angling my head low.

Yes. He offers me a tiny nod in reply, motioning towards his breast pocket.

Then what's one more bad idea when I'm already drowning in a sea?

Without stopping to think through my actions, I draw my borrowed saber out of its sheath, loudly enough to demand Rhodes's attention.

"What is the meaning of this?" he bellows, the outrage bulging his eyes.

"A noise in the corridor, Sir. We must secure the Governor." I brush past Chase on my way out the door, slipping my hand into the folds of his stolen uniform.

He really is lucky I have sticky fingers.

Just drop the book and go. As soon as I'm out of the Commander's sight, I blink into the Gray and double back into the office, ignoring the fact that his echo is still stood directly in front of the cabinet, or that I don't have the faintest idea where in the order of documents this journal is meant to go. I have no way to communicate with Chase from the shadows, no time to question him anyhow, and if he isn't keeping the Commander distracted, then this endeavor is destined to fail no matter how carefully I work. So I place the journal between a couple of other ancient tomes and race away from the crime, sullying my lips dirty with a prayer I don't believe. A moment later, I'm back in the physical realm and engaged in a show of overt contrition, blaming the disruption on a lumbering guard that doesn't exist.

"Commander—the Hues?" Chase is quick to prompt the conversation back to the pertaining subject. To not allow Rhodes to spend any longer than necessary evaluating the strangeness of my act.

"Right, yes." He turns to resume his search of the drawer.

Please don't let him notice. Please don't let him notice. Please don't let him notice. Both Chase and I tense taut, our nerves flaying raw, our breaths stilling silent. Sweat shivers an icy trail down from the nape of my neck to the base of my spine, the stress in my limbs intensifying with every second that passes. Making ready to phase and fly.

"As I was saying, a half breed's abilities are far more limited than a full-blooded Shade's." With a dull thud, Rhodes sets the journal on the desk, exhaling the air through my teeth. "The dilution of power means that each is only able to perform one type of specialized action in the Gray, and my defenses would require the skills of no less than . . . let's see . . . three of them." He presents the Governor with the page that details our individual gifts. "They'd need a Cobalt's speed to beat the arrows . . . a Bronze to unlock the chains . . . and an Amethyst could maybe use their magic to circumvent the spell. *Maybe*," he says, coating my hands in a brand new texture of fear.

A Cobalt, an Amethyst, and a Bronze.

Just as the Indigo told Savian.

"But even if that combination of half breeds did exist in Isitar, and even if they did somehow learn that they could beat my protections, it's still unlikely that they'd be able to survive the Gray long enough to overcome them," Rhodes continues. "Of the half breeds we capture, most can only weather the shadows for a few minutes at a time, and only with tremendous difficulty. The unknown nature of the portals—the sudden change in setting that cannot be bypassed in either realm—would likely shatter them as readily as it would you or me. So no, Lazaar, I am not worried about an incursion. It is, for lack of a better word, impossible." His declaration chills me to the core.

Because he's right: it does sound impossible. He's gone to great—some would say *paranoid*—lengths to ensure that this time, the Church's attempt to destroy the Gray goes unchallenged.

"Yes, I see that now, thank you." In light of this troubling revelation, Chase's composure finally begins to crack, the magic visibly vibrating his fingers. "And I assume the drain is progressing on schedule?" Though he does manage to keep probing the Commander for the answers we need.

"Down to the day," Rhodes says with a satisfied smile. "The texts maintained that it would take a year of sustained exposure, and thus far, every milestone they foretold has held true. I expect us to reach the tipping point at midnight on the cleansing moon, just as predicted, so I'll have a contingent of rogues patrolling the shadows around the gates, as well, on the off-chance that the Council does attempt to mount an attack. But bar any trouble, the Gray should collapse entirely within the week."

Within the week*?* The blood escapes my veins in a rush.

No. That can't be—it's too soon. The tipping point is coming *too soon.*

What if we're forced to attempt this lift and fail?

What if we're not but the Council can't find a way to destroy the siphon?

What if we're putting too much stock in an Indigo's assertion to wait until the cleansing moon and cutting things too fine?

We need to get out of here. I catch Chase's eye and nod my head towards the door. We got the information we came for, and now, more than ever, it's imperative that we leave this office with our secrets intact. If Rhodes were to discover that a pair of *half breeds* had compelled the Governor to quiz him for answers, he'd quickly deduce the *whys*, change the rules of the game. Ensure that no matter what we do—no matter what the Council does—we'd never reach the siphon in time.

We can't let that happen.

So of course—*of fucking course*—Chase chooses this exact moment to keep pushing our luck.

"And how are you able to track this progress?" He forces the Governor to ask. "If the cell is as well protected as you say, then how is it you can see inside? Monitor the drain?"

What could that possibly matter? It takes every ounce of strength I have not to throw a fist to his arm. I mean . . . the damn thing's locked in an iron cell at the top of an impenetrable spire and it's still been driving Shades away from Isitar for a year; why would it even need monitoring? And why is Chase so willing to bend this brittle bond until it breaks to find out?

"A scry." The Commander, on the other hand, seems unfazed by the question. "You can rest assured, Lazaar, I am thorough in my work. Nothing short of an act of the Gods will upset our plans at this late hour."

"Then consider me assured, Aurelion. Thank you for taking the time." Before I can decipher the meaning of that last exchange, Chase finally compels the Governor to bid his goodbyes, forcing us to follow him out of the office in stony silence.

CHAPTER

Nineteen

I hold my nerve as we leave the barracks. I hold it as we lead the Governor back to his manse, and into his study, and as Chase uses the last of his strength to cast a tricky piece of Yellow magic that allows him to alter the Governor's mind. To make him believe that the trip to Rhodes's office was his idea. That the guards who escorted him there weren't in any way strange or unfamiliar. That nothing about this morning's excursion should cause him alarm. The same spell he'd gifted Ezzo so that the others could befuddle the guards whose uniforms we stole. So that—with a little luck—we'd walk away from this litany of crimes with our necks intact. Though why we're bothering to pretend that's still an option, I don't know. The sheer breadth of the Commander's defenses has all but ensured our demise.

By the time Chase is done with the magic, every part of him is trembling, the cost of wielding such an excess of power dimming the shine of his metals dull.

"In case you need to find me." Before he excuses himself to go rest, he presses a short length of chain into my palm.

Another scry to join my growing collection.

Another exchange during which I have to bite back the panic building on my tongue. Choke down the need to scream.

It's just not possible. The second Chase disappears around the corner, I relegate his scry to my pocket then reach for the one I wear for Novi, hoping to find her at home instead of at our monastery.

As much as I should share everything I've learned with the others, she's the person I run to when the pressure in my chest grows too tight to ignore, and right now, my lungs feel as though they're ripe for bursting.

The Gray should collapse entirely within the week. The Commander's words are a spear to the heart, angled directly at odds with the belief that we can simply close our eyes to the siphon. I'd love to leave this threat to the Council, I really would—I'd never willingly assume responsibility for such a gargantuan task, nor do I like the thought of burdening my friends with it. But with only a few days left until the shadows reach their tipping point, and a myriad of defenses designed to repel the Council's Shades at every turn, I don't know how to keep pretending that our role in this endeavor can remain just a charade.

Problem is, I also don't know how to convince the others of that.

Merely reminding them that Savian's Indigo foresaw our involvement likely wouldn't be enough; Chase said it himself: foresight is an imprecise specialization and the future isn't fully knowable or set in stone. When that Shade told Savian that he would need a Cobalt, an Amethyst, and a Bronze to retrieve the siphon, she could have quite literally meant that *he*, specifically, would need that combination of Hues to fulfil *his* specific vision for the future; the Council might have garnered a different answer altogether. A simpler answer, perhaps, something they could action with ease.

Except I don't actually believe that.

Having heard what I heard in Rhodes's office, I think this particular vision is absolute.

And if I'm going to convince the others of that, I need to start with Novi.

I *want* to start with Novi.

If only because she always knows what to say to make my fears feel less stark.

The boarding house she lives in sits on the outermost ring of Isitar, overlooking the bounding wall that—on this side of the city—still towers tall and complete. *So the view's terrible but it's cheap and you can smell the sea,* Novi likes to say. It's always been her dream to live by the beach. To live anywhere that feels like freedom, to be honest, though that's a steep ask for a Hue in a world this divided by fear. I don't care how different Chase claims things to be on the continent, there is no place we could go that the Council can't reach. No sanctuaries left now that the Church has infested this final haven. Turned freedom into a luxury reserved for the pious and the rich.

I'm as familiar with the quirks of Novi's building as I am with my own. The third stair creaks when you scale it, and the second floor reeks of tobacco, and the man who lives at the opposite end of the corridor is wont to argue with the Gods until night turns to dawn. *It may not be much, but it's home. Mine and yours,* Novi used to tell me, and that didn't change even after everything else between us had. These days, I rarely bother knocking.

Which isn't usually a problem since she makes a rule of not allowing her suitors to learn where she lives.

I guess that makes Lyria special . . . I freeze halfway through the door. The bedsit Novi rents is small enough to force proximity, but it's the way the two of them spring apart that tells me everything I need to know. And it doesn't much matter that they're both fully dressed, or perfectly kempt, or that the only thing I interrupted was an apparent cup of coffee on the threadbare loveseat. Because I recognize the cloying scent wafting off Novi's incense burner—it's the sweet blend of bergamot and vanilla she reserves for when she's trying to impress—and even if I didn't, the sudden rush of guilt to her cheeks immediately confirms that I've walked in on something private. Something that wasn't meant to include me.

"Gods, I'm sorry . . . I didn't—" *Realize how quickly the spark I'd noticed would kindle and catch.* "I should go." The moment I'm done fumbling with the signs, I turn on my heel.

"No, Cemmy—wait—!" Novi calls after me.

But I don't wait. I don't stay to watch her scramble for an explanation or force her to deny an attraction that's as clear as a bright summer's sky. I'm back through the door and down the stairs before she can follow, half-blinded by the angry heat stinging my eyes.

Stop it. I swipe at the tears with the flat of my hand. I have zero claim to Novi. *None.* That was the choice I made when I decided to keep the truth of Magdalena's death from her, and I made it long enough ago that this ache should have already rendered me numb. We've both dabbled in the months since she put an end to our relationship. With other girls, with other guys—*just never with another Hue.*

That reality is a lead pipe to the ribs. I've never felt the sharp sting of jealousy because our flings have always been hollow, transient things. Bedding a typic would prove too emotionally fraught otherwise; falling in love with one, too much of a risk.

Too much of a cruelty.

Whereas this has the potential to grow into something more tangible. And while I should want that for Novi—and for Lyria, who has thus far proven to be nothing but intelligent, resourceful, and kind—there's been too much upheaval these past few days. Too much change. Too much deceit.

I'm not strong enough to take it.

And I'm definitely not strong enough to deal with the storm of emotions raging inside me now. The confused mix of want, hurt, relief, and envy. I'm not even strong enough to understand it.

Maybe that's why I choose to ignore it, instead.

To reject the pain, and the fear, and the growing weight of responsibility, relegate Novi's scry to my pocket and go engage in a little frivolous behavior of my own.

The city blurs beneath my feet, the neglect of Isitar's outermost ring slowly turning into the bustle of the faithless quarter's innermost market. Here, the streets are packed to the brim with laden stalls and sun-bleached awnings, stubborn buyers and blusterous vendors, produce and wares. Silks from the sprawling continent to the west, fruit from the harbor cities to the south, talismans and charms from the Council Shades that still inhabit the city. There are heaped piles of breads that make my mouth water, glistening stacks of candies that fill my nose with rose and caramelized sugar, steaming vats of stew that growl the emptiness of my stomach loud. But it's the wealth of overstuffed typics that truly tempts my fancy. The dense press of bodies and the inviting lure of their coin.

An itch awakens in my fingers, the desperate need to take something from others, just so that it isn't only taken from me. Before I'm able to stop myself, I've hiked up my hood and blinked into the shadows, right in brazen view of the crowd.

Reckless.

Even in the faithless quarter, Shades tend to be more discreet.

The Council insists on it.

The Council can kiss my colors. I start picking the typics clean. A handful of coins from one echo, a bloated purse from another, the gold circlet from around the third one's wrist. It's never been this easy before—stealing from a moving target in the Gray seldom ever is—that's why I used to prefer brick-and-mortar lifts. Unlike property, a typic's echo is a fleeting, ephemeral glint. A flicker of light in the shadows. I can't interact with them directly, and it takes a feat of concentration to see their outlines at all, let alone clearly enough to unclip a jeweled broach instead of passing straight through a rib. And until today, I had to do it while also scrambling to maintain my In-Between. The midday sanctuary never afforded me enough protection.

What a difference it makes to finally be rid of that constraint.

I dance through the ink-clad shadows, relishing the freedom Chase's spell has unleashed, the speed with which I can fill my pockets when I'm not hindered by such an all-encompassing limitation. Maybe that's why I forget that it's only the typics who remain oblivious to my sin. Other Shades can follow me into the Gray without issue.

"Cemilla Constance."

It's not just the shock of my name that halts me in my tracks; it's the voice that utters it. The scandalized note of disbelief.

"Mom?" The sight of her is too unexpected a surprise, an iron cuff that tethers me to the shadows. "What are you—*how* are you—?" There are so many questions bubbling up in my throat, I can't seem to settle on a single one. Mom's magic is bound; the Council saw to

that the day they discovered she'd married a typic. She shouldn't be able to phase anymore. Even before she took ill, she swore it was impossible.

"Foolish girl. Have I taught you nothing?" The first thing she does is check my hand for Dad's ring, as though worried that if I'd break one of her rules, I'd break the cardinal. "You are a half Shade, Cemilla. You can't blink into the Gray outside a sanctuary—or in the middle of the street! You're lucky I'm the only one who saw you!"

At least on that, we agree.

In my misery, I'd acted without thinking. Took far too big of an unnecessary risk. I didn't need to steal this coin today, not when Chase has already taken care of all my bills. Hells, the tincture he provided is the very reason Mom was able to visit the market in the first place—which she always liked to do in the afternoons, because that's when her favorite butcher is more amenable to grant her a deal. It's been so long since she was last able to come and go as she pleases, it didn't even occur to me that she might be here.

And she saw *me.*

All those years of pretending I've renounced my color collapse around my ears.

"Mom, I—"

"We will talk about this at home." With a snap and a wary glance over her shoulder, she seizes hold of my wrists.

"Mom? What are you—?"

Whoa.

The force of her shimmer is akin to traveling at the speed of Novi's gift. My physicality ceases to matter, usurped by a burst of power she bends to her will, a haze of shape and shadow that doesn't abate until we're safely back in the apartment. Only then—once she's made certain we weren't followed—does Mom finally blink us out of the Gray.

"Sit down, Cemilla." Her face is a veritable crash of thunder, the anger and disappointment radiating off her in waves. Any other day, I'd be thankful for the strength in her voice and the fury painting her cheeks, how unaffected she seems by our impromptu trip through the shadows. But today, she saw her daughter flagrantly disregard the most absolute rule she'd ever set, and I doubt there's anything I could say to undo that damage. Telling her about Lyria or Novi wouldn't do me much good, and confessing that a rogue Shade has blackmailed me into helping him rob the Dominion is definitely a non-starter. The best thing I can do right now is sink down to the couch and keep my eyes on my feet. Try not to dig my grave deeper.

"I went to the apothecary this morning." Mom's reprimand doesn't begin the way I expect, though if this is where her grievance starts, then I'm in far more trouble than I imagined. She's not just mad about my reckless show in the Gray; she knows I've been lying. "I wanted to thank the nice young man who delivered my medicine," she continues, "but according to the owner, no one matching his description works there, and the shop has no record of you paying for this." She places her tincture bottle on the table, the calligraphy on the green label standing proud.

Right. Of course. It's a Green label. Her inexplicable ability to phase suddenly makes sense. This tincture is infused with a spell that targets the ills that ail you, and Mom's sickness is borne in the blood—where the Council's binding spell is also carried. It must be temporarily replenishing her color.

"Cemilla, are you listening to me?" She chides me back to attention. "They told me our account has been overdrawn for *months*. They've been refusing you service." One by one, she carves out my secrets, peeling back the failures I've been desperately fighting to conceal.

"You don't have to worry, Mom, I was taking care of it." The platitude feels empty on my tongue, uttered more out of habit than belief.

"Taking care of it *how*?"

"You know how," I whisper. Because Mom's not oblivious enough to believe that I could keep an honest job around her care schedule, and after the performance she witnessed today, there's no point in trying to maintain the pretense with a hastily concocted lie. Whether she wants to admit it or not, she's known I'm a thief for a very long time now—she just didn't realize I'd been doing my thieving in the Gray.

"Stealing." It still hurts to hear her speak the word aloud.

"Yes."

"From the shadows."

"Not exclusively—I do it in the physical realm, too, but . . . yes."

"And when did you learn to cast an In-Between?" she asks, her face growing paler with each reply.

"Years ago," I admit. "Though it took me a while to master the spell."

"Which was taught to you by . . . ?" Mom finally reaches the question I fear most. The one confession I'd hoped to never have to make. But unlike phasing into the Gray, there's nothing instinctive about casting an In-Between; you're either shown how to wield the magic, or you shatter. And since Mom never chose to share that teaching herself, the only logical conclusion is that someone else did. She just wants to hear that *who* from me.

"Another Hue," I say, my nails biting deep into the upholstery. "There's a small group of us in the city; we help each other stay safe in the Gray." I sugarcoat this particular truth a little. Mom doesn't need to know how close I've come to shattering in the past, or that I've watched the shadows make jagged shards of a friend. She doesn't need to know that until two days ago, I could hardly hold a shield without buckling, or that my fear of the Gray is what caused our finances to grow so stretched.

She doesn't need to know how close the water came to inching over our heads.

Or the real reason it receded.

"Of all the stupid, careless, irresponsible things—" She begins to pace the room, rousing from the rug a trail of angry dust motes. "I warned you to never reveal yourself to another Shade, Cemilla. What will it take for you to understand that it's too dangerous?"

"It wasn't like that, Mom." As much as I'm trying to keep my cool, I can feel the irritation bubbling beneath my skin. "They already knew I was a Bronze when they found me, and they're the only reason I've been able to pay our bills."

"Well, it ends today." My revelation only serves to rile her further. "We live this way to *protect* you. If the Council ever caught wind of what you are—"

"But we're not living!" I cut her off, springing back to my feet. "In case you haven't noticed, we've barely been *surviving*—all because you won't let me get you a real cure!" It's not fair of me to throw this sickness in her face. A disease of the blood couldn't have even affected her if not for me; her magic would have stopped it from taking root had it not been bound by the Council. A spell she only allowed them to cast in order to buy herself enough time to escape their trackers. Save her unborn half.

"How many times do I have to tell you this, Cemilla, I don't want a cure if it puts you at risk!"

"Not accepting a cure puts me at risk!" I explode, the words I've held on to, for *years*, finally forcing themselves out. Mom's staunch refusal to embrace our colors has made my life every bit as hard as her illness. If she hadn't forbidden me from using my magic, I wouldn't have had to keep my trips to the Gray a secret. If she had agreed to let me hire a Shade, I wouldn't have had to make them at all. And if she had only permitted me to sell this godsforsaken ring, I could have kept us afloat long enough to find a different solution.

But there are no different solutions to be had anymore.

Not with Savian pulling my strings and the Church working to cut them altogether.

Not with the shadows teetering on the edge of collapse.

"Did you know this tincture would restore your magic?" I drag a breath through my teeth, reducing the anger in my voice to a light simmer. "Is that why you won't agree to a healing?" I always knew that a Green label would soothe Mom's symptoms better than any typic-made tonic, but until I saw her phase, I never realized what else it might cure, so I never quite understood her refusal to see a full-blood—not when there were so many ways we could have ensured my safety. But if a bottled spell can temporarily replenish her color, then it would stand to reason that a healing could undo the Council's binding permanently, and the new squirm in my gut tells me that's what's been at the heart of Mom's reluctance to seek a Shade.

Actions deserve consequences, Cemilla. I made my choice when I knowingly broke their rules.

"Given the nature of my condition, I knew it was a possibility," she confirms, guiding me back down to the couch. "And yes, that's why I *can't* agree to a healing. I can't in good conscience counteract the Council's decree."

"Do you really hate your magic that much?" Her confession bleeds the fight right out of me, cowing my voice small. "Are you really so ashamed of falling in love with a typic"—*of having me*—"that you won't reclaim it even if it costs you your life?"

"Oh, Cemilla, this was never about your father," Mom says, taking both of my hands in hers. "I have never—*ever*—regretted marrying him, or having you, for that matter." She's quick to deduce my fear. "But if the binding spell is lifted, my color could be tracked again and the Council has a long memory. I doubt they'll have foreseen the unlikely confluence of events that would allow me to escape their punishment, but they will not be happy to learn that such a loophole exists. I can't take the risk that hunting me will lead them to you. I won't."

Though I can see in her eyes the absolute belief that she made that decision for my benefit, her stubborn refusal to put her health—which *is* failing—ahead of the chance that the Council might one day knock on our door only serves to make me angrier. And not just because that refusal has put me at an entirely different type of risk, but because all this time, she's been lying to me. Lying to protect me, sure, but lying nonetheless.

Like mother, like daughter, I guess.

Causing pain in an effort to avoid it.

Even when all that does is make things worse.

"I'm sorry I acted so recklessly today, Mom. That won't happen again," I promise. "But if you're not willing to reclaim your magic, then I have no choice but to keep using mine," I tell her, though the full and honest truth is: I wouldn't stop even if she did. Because whether she likes it or not, that magic is a part of me, and that would remain true even if Savian's threats disappeared, and the siphon was destroyed, and Chase cured her of this wretched illness. I would still be a child of typical flesh and blood color.

I can stop being a thief, but I can't stop being a half.

The shadows are my birthright.

"Now, I'm sorry, Mom, but I have to go," I say, before this fight spirals any deeper. Before either of us can inflict a wound that'll fester and refuse to heal.

"Cemilla Constance, don't you dare walk away from me." The warning in her voice grows flustered. "If you leave this house, then so help me, you will not be welcome back."

A wound like that.

I freeze halfway through the door, the ache in my heart growing heavy. And though I know she doesn't mean it—*she doesn't mean it, she doesn't mean it, she can't*—the sharp sting of her threat only serves to confirm what I've long since suspected: that on this, the two of us will never see eye to eye. She'll always be too cautious to accept the Hue I've become.

"I really am sorry, Mom." I don't look back as I walk away from the apartment, because if I do, I'll fall apart.

It's only once I'm out on the street that I realize there's no place I want to run.

For the first time since the others found me, all my sanctuaries feel hollow.

CHAPTER

Twenty

For the past few years, I've worn three scrys around my neck, and no matter what I was feeling, I could wrap a hand around them and know things would turn themselves right. There was always a kind word waiting for me on the other side, a bottle of honey wine, a touch that could set me on fire. The family I made for myself in the belly of a ruined monastery. I could go there to watch Eve paint her murals across the wall, poke fun at the way she'd splatter Ezzo with oils when he'd try to distract her, then drink my sorrows away with Novi once they'd disappeared into each other's arms. And in all that time, I've never hesitated to send any of them a message. Never wondered if I would rather weather the storm alone.

No, not alone.

Just not with someone who knows me inside and out.

Show me. My fingers close around my most recently gifted scry, igniting my connection to the Gold who took a flame to my life. *Gods, I must really be desperate.* I follow the crystal to an inn called the Sunken Anchor, a modest construction of gray brick that squats among the faithless quarter's glut of taverns and bars, my feet moving of their own volition. Past the dozing innkeeper, down the narrow corridor and up the stairs, towards the room I glimpsed through the shard of crystal.

"Chase—open up." I don't mean to bang on his door like a girl possessed, but when he doesn't materialize at first knock, my impatience gets the better of me. "Chase, come on—I know you're in there, so just open the damn—"

"Cemmy?" The door almost wrenches off its hinges, Chase appearing like a ghostly apparition on the other side. "What is it? What's wrong?"

Maybe I should be the one asking him that. He'd looked dead on his feet after relinquishing control of the Governor, but I guess I was too busy trying not to lose my nerve to realize the magic had hit him this hard. His face is bone pale, the gold of his hair ruffled, the shadows under his eyes so stark they're as bruised as a bloodied fist. The shirt he's wearing hangs open to the navel, revealing a fine latticework of rainbow-tinged veins that span shoulder to hip, as though the magics he stole have woven a spider's web beneath his skin. They glimmer like gems in the warm glow of the hex-lights, every bit as striking as the sharp cut of his stomach and the shard of crystal nestled at the heart of his chest. But though Chase is as big a mess as I've ever seen him, he's staring at *me* with a look of unfettered worry, as though I'm the one who's raked with exhaustion and barely able to stand.

"Wrong? No . . . what—? Nothing's wrong." *Other than the fact that I have no real reason to be here.* "I just wanted to—erm . . . we need to talk about the portals!" I grasp for the first explanation that fits.

Kind of.

"You want to talk about the portals?" Chase's brow furrows deep, my lie falling apart almost instantly.

"The cleansing moon is only three days away, isn't it?" I double down in an effort to salvage it. "It's not like we have time to waste."

"You're right, I'm sorry." His voice remains cautiously confused. "Why don't you call the others to the monastery and we can figure this all out."

Because that's the absolute opposite of what I want to do right now. I fix him my most withering glare. Why else would I have come here if not to avoid seeing my friends? In what world does Chase think he's anything other than my very last choice? "You know what, forget it," I say. "This was a mistake."

"Cemmy, wait—" He reaches out to stop me, the flush of his hand searing hot. "How about you come inside, instead, and we can . . . talk about the portals."

"Great idea." I push past him, full of a frenetic energy that threatens to kindle and burn. Until today, there have been exactly two constants in my life: Novi and my mom. So to have both called into question in one afternoon . . . I'm more rattled than I care to admit.

If the inn Chase has chosen is modest, then the room he occupies is downright plain. A bed. A closet. A washroom. A desk. With no outward sign of habitation save for the mussed sheets and a lonely picture stuck to the chipped paint. Of two kids—siblings, I'd venture, maybe even twins—running through a field of wild flowering lace and yarrow, their carefree smiles immortalized when Chase was young enough that I only recognize him thanks to the distinct combination of silver and gold.

"Is that your sister?" I regret the question the moment it passes my lips.

Chase lost his sister; I remember that much from the fractured details he's offhandedly let slip, the melancholy that gripped him as he spoke of her love for Isitar, and how adamantly he'd asked me to stop using the name he reserved for her alone. How both times, he was quick to move the subject back to less painful ground.

"That's from a long time ago." He's equally quick to change it now, snatching the picture off the wall before I can discern much of anything about the girl smiling beside him—bar that she was dark everywhere Chase is golden, draped in molten browns instead of his sun-kissed bronze, and also oddly familiar, though I can't, for the life of me, put my finger on why.

"Sorry, I didn't mean to—"

"You wanted to talk about the portals?" Chase clips, even though he's long since worked out that's not the real reason I'm here.

Fine. "Yeah." I, too, have no problem playing pretend. "The way I see it, Rhodes is right: it'll be the sudden change in setting that kills us," I say, reiterating the Commander's claim. "We can't predetermine our anchors if we don't know where each portal will lead." And if we can't predetermine our anchors, then it won't be like it was in my living room, or on the cliff-face, or during our ride-along with Novi through the streets. With no frame of reference for where we're going, or an existing picture we can hold in our minds, we won't be able to stabilize the magic fast enough to avoid the inevitable crack, clink, crunch, shatter. The shadows will break us like glass.

"Okay . . . but we have something Rhodes didn't account for: we have Eve," Chase reminds me, crossing his arms tight. "The instinctive nature of her gift should allow her to cast an In-Between even when she can't visualize her anchors."

"Not around the lot of us, it won't!" My objections are fast growing shrill. "Eve's never held more than two of us at once." She's never had to—hells, she's never even *tried* to—seeing how none of us would have ever dreamed of putting her at such great a risk.

"You're forgetting that Eve has been hindering her own power this whole time by casting her In-Betweens wrong," Chase says. "Now that she's learned the proper technique, I've no doubt she'll be able to hold us all. Easily. You're panicking for no reason."

No, I'm panicking because he's staying too calm.

"Then what about Novi, huh?" I counter. "She's never sped more than two of us, either." Taking both him and me the other night pushed at the limits of her gift. Which he'd have known if only he had bothered to ask. To not make an errant assumption.

"Then we'll practice until she can." Though Chase's eyes turn thoughtful, he still remains infuriatingly unconcerned.

"Gods, aren't you listening?" I jab a finger at his chest. "Your plan is broken. It's going to fail. *Savian* is going to fail, and I am not going to let you drag us down with him. I can't"—*no*—"I *won't* let another friend shatter." I don't mean to voice that last confession aloud, but now that I've created some reason to unleash my anger, I can't seem to keep the truth from tumbling out. I've already lost one half Shade to hubris, and even outside the Gray, I feel as though I'm losing Novi, and Mom, and the conviction that, somehow, this tangled mess will twist itself right.

I need to do something—to *hit* something—just to feel it smash.

I need to force Chase to see how much I'm hurting.

And then I need him to do up his damn shirt. I will myself to ignore the scry embedded in his flesh. Because what I *don't* need is a reminder that he's every bit as much a pawn in this as we are, or that beneath the indifferent façade, there's a whole universe of lean muscle and rainbow-flecked skin. That in a different life, a stubborn Bronze and an arrogant Gold might mix.

"No one is going to shatter. I promise." As though reading my mind, Chase reaches into his closet, fishing out a black linen that turns the metal in his eyes to flint. "Now come on, there's something I want you to see."

*

He refuses to say what as he leads me away from the inn, and by the time we've reached the northernmost tip of the city, I've stopped asking. Out here, Isitar's encompassing wall gives way to a border that seamlessly melds rock with hill, the ground beginning its ascent towards the Unpassed Mountains, the formidable barrier that separates us from the continent that curves like an outstretched talon around the sea.

Not a whole lot to *see* from this vantage point except the view.

Nothing that would improve our odds in the Dominion or keep my friends from shattering the way a wave would against the cliffs.

Nothing that would explain why Chase has brought me up to the top of the rickety observatory that overlooks the sprawling labyrinth of concentric rings.

"Is this a joke to you?" The last of my patience evaporates into the budding mist. I've been on edge the whole trip up this colossal waste of time, spoiling for a fight, an argument, any way to alleviate the pressure building beneath my ribs. I confided in Chase my biggest fear and instead of even *pretending* to reassure me, he hauled me to the vertigo-inducing brink of absolutely nothing for no reason I can glean.

I don't even know why I'm surprised.

"*This* is my first rule for surviving a new city: find the one place you can go where nobody can hear you scream," Chase says, stepping right up to the observatory's rim. Then before I can think to stop him, he lets out a thundering yell that echoes above the city, resonating like a menacing omen until it's carried off by the wind.

"Please tell me you did not drag me up here to *scream*." I grit the words through clenched teeth. Of all the pointless ways to waste an afternoon, this has to be the most inane—and the strangest. I mean . . . seriously. Not three bells ago, we learned exactly how well-protected the siphon is; how impossible to reach. Wouldn't our time be better spent figuring out how to counter the Commander's terrifying litany of defenses? Or doing literally . . . anything else.

"I dragged you up here because I've never seen anyone more in need of a release." With a hand to each of my shoulders, Chase shuffles me towards the platform's edge, his voice wry and his touch gentle. "So just try it."

"Can't I just push you to your death, instead?"

"You could, I suppose." His chuckle is a shiver against my skin. "But my way makes for less guilt."

"Bold of you to assume I'd feel guilty," I grumble, inching closer to the guardrail. The city shimmers like an apparition from this height, the circular maze of streets betraying no hint of the rot gnawing at its foundations. In the hazy autumn light, you can't even see the hate. Nor does the Dominion look as though it's harboring the demise of a hundred thousand Shades.

Here goes nothing. The first scream rips out of me timidly—hesitantly—as though it's whispering an apology for disturbing the peace. The second scream rings louder, with more confidence and a hint of impertinent relief. And by the third, I've collapsed to my knees, every frayed emotion of the past few days flaying itself raw against the mist.

Gods, it feels good to scream when everything is breaking.

Chase was right: it feels like a release.

I don't know how long we stay like that—me, yelling my lungs hoarse; him, lending his pain to the chorus of untamed grief—but when we're finally wrung clean, we're both lying on the moss-ridden deck of the observatory, our breaths coming sharp and heavy, a rosy flush staining our cheeks.

"So . . . you want to tell me what happened?" Chase finally asks, leaning up to rest his head on the cup of his wrist. "It can't have been good if it drove you to me."

At least he's honest with himself about what my coming to him means.

"I had a fight with my mom," I hedge, sticking to the parts that don't include Novi. "She found out I've been stealing in the Gray and gave me an ultimatum. No more magic, or no more home. I think you know which I had to choose."

"She'll come around," he says, confident in a way I wish I could believe.

"No, I'm not sure she will." That reality hits me with all the clarity of our widening rift. "She's obsessed with keeping me from the Council—to the point where she won't even consider a full healing of her disease. So I guess you're off the hook there," I tell him, though Chase is gracious enough not to acknowledge the win, to just listen as I free myself of this burden. "She's never told me the full story of how their trackers came to find Dad—only that he was already making plans for them to flee Isitar when they did—but I think something broke in her the day they killed him; I think that's why she couldn't leave the city. This was the last gift he ever gave her and I swear, she's convinced it's the only magic worth keeping." I claw at my diamond-encrusted ring.

And this magic doesn't even exist.

"She'll come around, Cemmy," Chase repeats, his eyes soft, the concern in them real. "Does she know you lost someone to the Gray?" he asks. "Have you ever—?"

"Talked about it? No," I say. Because if I told Mom that, she'd never let me out of her sight again. "I haven't actually talked about it to anyone." Haven't found the courage to confess the damning tale. The true reason Magdalena died.

"Maybe you should." Chase folds up to sit cross-legged on the deck. "I'm sure your friends would understand. They don't seem the type to assign blame."

"They would for this." My fingers bite deep into the woodgrain. Of my many secrets, this is the one that should follow me to the grave. A guilt so total and absolute the taste of it still makes my stomach retch. But right at this moment, I'm tired, and I'm hurting, and I've never felt more alone—and now that I've started talking, I can't seem to stop. I've been holding in this shame for a year, too afraid to confide it in anyone lest I lose the closest family I've ever known.

I need to commit this transgression to words.

Before it costs me more than just my relationship with Novi.

Before it eats me alive.

"I was the one who talked Lena into running the lift," I say, sitting up to wrap my arms around my knees. "The job was much riskier than usual—a paranoid spice merchant who'd spent a small fortune fortifying his home—but I overheard a member of his staff say that he'd be out of the city, and Mom's health was deteriorating so I needed the coin.

"We spent the whole day devising the details. How we'd get in, where we'd need to blink into the shadows, which anchors we'd use and how quickly we'd have to steal through the mansion and leave. And since Lena was confident enough to cast an In-Between around us both, I didn't have to worry about maintaining mine while I picked the lock to his study. All I had to do was get us through the door."

By far the easiest task of the lift.

Or at least it should have been.

"I have *never* broken a pick before." My voice cracks to a whisper, the heat in my eyes stinging with the sharp mountain breeze. "But it was as if the Gods had it out for us that night, because one by one, I snapped through every last one in my kit. *Every last one*. Almost like they had been sabotaged." Though in reality, that's far too kind of an explanation. A coward's way of absolving themselves of this sin.

"Then to top it all off, Lena started losing her grip on the shadows," I continue, fast approaching the shameful crux of my guilt. "She asked if I could take the reins for a bit, and despite all the rotten luck, I was so close to forcing open the lock that I couldn't bring myself to quit. I *promised* her that I could hold us both—and I was doing it, I really, truly believed that I was holding the shield. But then Lena screamed, and I panicked, and the magic slipped, and I—I thought I could catch it. I thought I *did* catch it."

I can even remember the weight of the spell as I fought to stabilize its reach.

Except I only caught it around *me*, and then the next second, I heard the tell-tale crack, clink, crunch, shatter.

That high-pitched collection of sounds haunts my dreams.

"You know what, it doesn't matter what I thought," I say, swiping at the ugly wetness on my cheeks. "Truth is, I got cocky, and Lena got dead, and by the time I turned around to help her, even the shards were gone."

That's how quickly the Gray can make memories of us all.

"It wasn't your fault, Cemmy." Chase shifts closer to me on the deck, wrapping a tender arm around my shoulders. "You can't blame yourself for losing grip of a spell you were conditioned to cast wrong—and I don't think your friends would ever blame you for what sounds like an accident."

I doubt he'd say that if he knew how many times they'd urged me to be careful. How many times Ezzo begged me to rely less on Eve, and how many times Novi offered me more help than I was willing to receive.

How many times they warned me not to let my idiot pride win.

They all knew that if I kept taking bigger and bigger risks, something like this would happen eventually—though had this strictly been an accident, I'm sure he's right and they would have forgiven me. But there is no way to confess to this sin without also confessing to my greed. Because Magdalena and I had ample time to abandon the lift once she'd told me about the waver in her shield. She died because I refused to heed the limits of mine. Because I put my need for coin ahead of her safety. And no amount of empty platitudes from Chase will change that.

"What the hells would you know about it?" I bat him away, meeting his undeserved kindness with rage. "You learned how to cast your In-Betweens from a secret book. Who have you ever shattered?"

"No one," he whispers, dropping the hand I spurned to his lap. "But when I was fourteen, I killed a Hue with my gift."

His admission is so unexpected, it halts my anger in its tracks.

"My sister's ability allowed her to absorb power from the Gray, so she always had an excess," Chase says, anticipating the storm of *hows* and *whys* brewing on my tongue. "Taking magic from her . . . it wasn't like taking it from anyone else. It didn't hurt her, for one thing—it was just something the two of us had always done. She'd take from the Gray, I'd take from her, and though we didn't realize it at the time, the reason it worked is because I wasn't actually taking her gift, I was taking the extra power. But since it was years before we crossed paths with another Hue, we had no way of knowing how rare that dynamic was. How uniquely balanced. So it never occurred to me that taking from a Copper would be different."

From a Copper. I think back to the list of Gray gifts I glimpsed in Versallis's journal. If I'm remembering the text correctly, then Copper is the dominant dilution of Orange magic—the ability *to hinder.* As in, the ability to hinder the malice of other Shades. Which is about as useful as Gray gifts come for a Gold who's spent his life on the run. I can see why Chase chose to steal it.

"I could tell something was wrong the second I started draining," he continues, looking out over the city instead of at me. "The magic felt too hot, and the Copper was screaming, but we needed his power to escape the Council's trackers and I had no reason to think that my gift would cause him any permanent harm. By the time I understood what was happening, it was too late. He was gone."

So that's how he knew the drain would kill me. The truth of Chase's threat suddenly takes on a whole new texture. Not from the musty pages of a book, but from his own experience. From the deepest, darkest recesses of his past.

"You couldn't have known." The words leave my mouth before I can stop them. Before I can recognize how perfectly they serve to prove his point.

"Just as you couldn't have known that your picks would break or that both of your shields would fail," Chase says, locking his eyes with mine. "Don't you see, Cemmy? Everything about us—the way we learn about our magics, the gaping holes in our knowledge, the risks we're forced to take in order to survive—it's all designed to ensure that we meet an early grave. So when it happens, I don't blame myself anymore; I blame the Council. They're the ones we should be angry at."

And I am angry at them.

I have been angry at them, day in, day out, since the moment Mom told me I was a Bronze—and that anger only grew more pronounced when I discovered that the purges were based on nothing but a lie and an order of bigots.

The Order of Versallis.

That name is a serrated blade to the ribs, a crime against those born of typical flesh and blood color.

"Why do they hate us so much?" I breathe, giving rise to the question that's taken root inside my heart. "Why demonize our gifts instead of using them? I know we're not as powerful as the full-bloods, but we're much more varied, and the Church can't ward us out—surely we'd make for the perfect soldiers?"

"A perfect soldier is a Shade they can predict and control," Chase says, jaw tense, voice bitter. "And when power is afraid, you can always trust it to make the most morally bankrupt choice."

Well . . . hells. That might just be the truest thing he's ever told me.

Because sitting atop this observatory, at the apex of a city that would rather crumble into the ocean than embrace us into its fold, I can see every morally corrupt decision that has led the Council to wipe out countless generations of Hues. How they allowed their fear to twist, and warp, and fuel this vendetta. Focused it against an enemy they could more easily destroy.

Where do you even begin *fighting that kind of logic?* All at once, every inch of me is dog-tired, overcome by the urge to channel this rage—and this pain—into a little moral bankruptcy of my own. And Chase is right here, and he's leaned in so close, and in the bright afternoon light, the conviction in his eyes is sparkling. And though it makes no sense to want this—to want *him*—the pull in my gut has turned into a wrench that's bordering on cruel. And I don't want to fight anymore. Not him, not the Council, not the Church. Not the voice in my head that's telling me to trace the rainbowed veins beneath his shirt with my fingers and spend a few stolen moments feeling less alone. And judging by the way his gaze keeps flicking down to my lips, I'd venture Chase is tired of feeling alone, too.

I don't think you could ever be ordinary.

So instead of doing the smart thing, I close the remaining gap between us on the deck, tilting my face up, and up, and up, until my palms connect with his chest and the hitch of his breath tingles my marrow. Until his heart pounds right through the fabric and the air between us crackles with all the unbridled energy of a storm.

"Cemmy, I—I'm not sure that's a good idea." At the very last second, his hands move to cup my wrists, the heat in them gentle but the rejection they deliver stinging hard.

"Right. No. Obviously." Gravity vanishes out from under me, the embarrassment flaming red into my cheeks. "I don't know what I was thinking. This is—I . . . just forget it, okay? You and I could never work." I'm back on my feet before the flush can reach my eyes, desperate to make my escape before the angry tears spill over. I can't believe the bastard waited until it was too late for me to save face before changing his mind. Or actually, yes, I can believe it. Humiliating me is Chase's favorite way to pass the time.

"Cemmy, wait—" Whatever he's planning to say, I don't want to hear it. I can't bear to see the quiet shape of his pity or taste the mortified sympathy building on his tongue.

So I phase into the Gray and I run.

And for all his protestations, Chase doesn't follow me.

CHAPTER

Twenty-one

But with the cleansing moon less than three days away, I can't avoid Chase for long. Because what he *does* do, just as soon as he's had time to climb down from the observatory and snake back to the faithless quarter, is summon us all back to the monastery to talk about the flaw I pointed out in his plan.

What about Novi, huh? She's never sped more than two of us.

I may not have gone to his room with the intention of highlighting a problem, but in my desperate attempt to explain why I was banging on his door like a lunatic, I ended up drawing his attention to a pretty damn big one. So now Chase wants to begin the process of practicing *until she can.* And while the only thing *I* want to do is ignore that summons—and him, and Novi, and Lyria, and the nauseating mix of hurt and rejection grinding my ribs to dust—the truth is, I don't have anywhere else to go. Not after Mom made it plenty clear that I'm no longer welcome at home.

"Did you get sick of the Gold already?" It's Eve who finds me sitting against the crumbling wall to the cemetery, too trapped by circumstance to leave, too stubborn to relent and go inside.

"You have no idea," I mutter, avoiding the real question in her eyes. "Did you finally get sick of Ezzo?"

"Not just yet, no—but it's bound to happen any day now." The smile she offers me is subdued. "Until then, I asked him to give us a minute. You looked like you might prefer . . . less company rather than more," she says, because even though it's Ezzo who watches, sometimes it's Eve who actually sees. "I take it the trick with Rhodes didn't go well?"

"That depends on your definition." I shrug as she folds down to join me in the grass. "We got the information we need, but it's only going to make Chase ask for something else we won't want to give."

Like my secrets.

Hells, he didn't even have to ask me for those, I volunteered them. I got angry, and then I got reckless, and then I bared my soul to the one person I should be keeping in the dark.

I gave him even more power.

"Look, Cem . . . I know you've had to bear the brunt of him these past few days, but did something happen between you?" This time, the concern in Eve's question is impossible to ignore.

"No, nothing happened," I tell her. Though I'm too ashamed to admit that the reason I'm sulking outside our monastery is because it didn't. "I'm just—I'm really sorry, Vee," I say instead. "For dragging you all into this. For what Savian forced Ez to do. For almost getting you caught at the Sacred Hearts Inn. For everything."

For always making things worse.

For not taking the time to apologize before.

"Colors help me, is *that* what's bothering you?" Eve's tongue clicks against her teeth. "You give yourself far too much credit, Cem. A man like Savian would never hinge his entire plan on you deciding to run a lift. If an Indigo told him he needed a Cobalt, an Amethyst, and a Bronze, he would have found a way to get at you and Novi eventually. And if Ezzo was his best chance of tracking Lyria, then he would have found a way to get at him, too. No matter what any of us did—we would have still ended up here."

Catering to the whims of a madman.

Trapped at the center of an age-old war between blood color and belief.

"But hey, if nothing else, that new In-Between spell Cassiel taught us will make our lives easier from here on out," she says, nudging her shoulder into mine. "So that's one good thing to have come from all this."

"You're assuming we'll live long enough to keep using it." I meet her optimism with a cynical raise of my brow. Because given what Chase and I learned this morning, that assumption feels laughably brittle.

"Argh, see, now you sound like Ez." Eve rolls her eyes, bouncing back to her feet. "Don't you ever get tired, worrying so much?"

"Don't you ever get bored, worrying so *little*?"

"I find plenty of ways to fill my time, thank you." She flashes me her fingers, freshly stained with color, as if she'd spent the afternoon respite distracting herself with her paints. Though as Eve grabs hold of my hand and starts leading me towards the monastery, her expression turns sharply from sardonic to grave.

"Don't let them take your hope, Cem," she says, and I can instantly tell that the plea in her voice stems from pain. "I know that right now, everything feels a bit pointless, but you need to remember that in some way or another, we've all faced the worst before. Worrying didn't stop it from killing your dad, or making your mom sick, and it sure didn't stop the Council's trackers from massacring my whole family." Even ten years on, that last truth winces her throat dry. "But say we had managed to escape the Council, and the Church, and the curse of the Hue, it's the things we didn't know to worry about that would have screwed us in the end. Just look at Lyria. She went her whole life without confiding her secret in *anyone* and Savian still found a way to suck her into his plan. No amount of worrying could have stopped that—and no amount of blaming yourself can change it, either."

The kindness in her words—the unerring show of grace—almost brings me to tears. It's a gentler sort of comfort than I'm used to getting from Novi, but every bit as healing and filled with love. A reminder that despite the Council's efforts, we've not only faced the worst before, we've *survived* it.

That maybe together, we'll find a way to survive this, too.

*

Though by the time night falls over Isitar, that hope begins to feel desperate and weak.

"I'm running out of ways to say this, Cassiel, but my gift can't support more than two." Novi throws some of Chase's words back at him for good measure—along with a crude gesture that is very much not a part of her accompanying signs. For the past few hours, he's been speeding her ragged across the nave, forcing her to push her power in an effort to prove that our trip through the Dominion isn't doomed. But no matter how tightly we crowd around her, or which formations of contact we try, Novi's gift stutters and stalls against our weight when we add a third—let alone a fourth—Hue into the mix. So as much as the Commander may not have designed his defenses with *half breeds* in mind, they'll be keeping us out just the same. He was right to assert that an incursion is impossible.

A view that—surprisingly enough—the others all shared once Chase had relayed the information he and I tricked from Rhodes.

But of course, *impossible* isn't a word Savian's inclined to hear.

Nor does his Gold believe that *no* qualifies as an answer.

"Can't isn't an option," he snaps, pacing the shadows with an irritation that borders on fear.

"Then I suggest you come up with a better idea, because the magic says no," Novi grits. "And if I can't control the speed, it makes no difference if Eve can hold an In-Between around us through the portals, we're still dead."

"Well, that's too bad, because dead isn't an option, either." Chase's mood makes itself plenty clear in both languages. The Gray ripples like spilled ink around him, alive with a tension that sizzles like stag beetles screaming in the summer sun.

Not that I've noticed.

Or at least, I've been doing my best not to notice.

To not look at him at all, for that matter, regardless of how ardently he keeps trying to catch my eye.

"Then what if we split up?" Though Lyria's question is meant for Novi, her gaze keeps flicking back to find mine, the way it has done since the moment I stepped foot in the monastery, as if worried that our earlier encounter will have turned me cold. *"You and Eve can ferry us through the portals one by one."*

"That's too many trips." Chase doesn't even pretend to consider it. "Rhodes has a scry in that cell, so we'll only have a short window to get in and out of it unseen. Sending them back and forth twelve times is too risky."

"Ten times." I can't help but correct his overdramatic slip. "But if you're so concerned about the number of trips, then how about we lose the dead weight, instead. You can stay back and help Ezzo." Which has always made more sense than dragging him through the Dominion when we don't require his gift. The only one who refuses to see that is Chase.

"No. I have to be there when you recover the siphon." He shakes his head, not bothering to provide us with an explanation.

"No . . . you *want* to be there. The rest of us don't, but for some reason, you do. So either tell us why or fuck off." It's not the lingering sting of rejection that sharpens my tongue—or how satisfying those last two words are to shape with my fingers—it's the bewildering lack of logic. Lyria, Novi, Eve and I have no choice but to venture into the darkest depths of the Dominion; this godsforsaken task requires each of our skills. Whereas Chase is *choosing* to involve himself for no reason, and I won't allow whatever game he's playing to trap my friends into a harder lift.

"I have to be there in case you need my magic." The excuse he musters is beyond weak.

"Then you'd better figure out how to stabilize an In-Between through the portals." Of the six of us, Ezzo's been struggling with his signing the most, so every now and then he'll still rely on Lyria to read his lips—especially when he's tense or frustrated. Much like he is now. "If you can all hold the spell, that would cut the total number of trips down to six." And shift the burden off Eve in the process; he seizes the first opportunity to lessen her risk. An opportunity I'd venture he's been searching for since the moment Chase insisted he stay behind to be our eyes and ears.

When the two of them had first had *that* conversation, Ezzo found more curses than I knew existed to express how categorically that would not be happening. Even after Chase made the annoyingly solid argument that in order to infiltrate the Dominion, we'd require a distraction on the street, Ezzo still refused on the basis that he wouldn't separate from Eve. *Not on something this dangerous*, he'd said. Which we all knew to mean, *not when there's a good chance I'll never see her again*. He would much rather die in there with her.

Chase's counter was to point out that by coming, Ezzo would only serve to increase the burden on her gift.

Ezzo's reply was to inform him that he'd happily relieve that burden by tossing our excess of Gold from the cliffs.

It was only after Eve had proven that using Chase's new spell, her power could comfortably hold the four of us—even when she was working with unseen anchors—that Ezzo finally relented. And regardless of the fact that he still believes we're not planning to run this lift for real, he can't help but look for ways to ensure her safety. That's just how he's built.

"Fine." Chase taps his thumb against his chest, harder than is strictly necessary. "Cemmy and I will go work on the spell, and the rest of you can keep chipping away at the plan for getting us in."

"And if I say no?" My answering growl is all spite and contempt, a stubborn resistance to being told what to do by the likes of him. Chase doesn't get to reject me, then nominate me for a crucible on a whim. I'm done feeding his god complex.

"You know perfectly well that—"

"No isn't an option." I do my best impression of his exasperating lilt. "Don't you find it exhausting, always being such a—"

"Erm . . . Cem . . . can I borrow you for a second?" Novi's quick to cut in. Then before I can rustle up an objection, she grabs me by the elbow and phases us out of the Gray. "What the hells, Cemmy?" she says once the monastery's blazed back to color. "I get that you're mad right now, but if you need to take it out on someone, take it out on me. Not on the Gold we're still trying to trick."

"What makes you think I'm mad?" I lean back against the daybed, staring resolutely at the floor, the table, the mural of wildflowers Eve painted to brighten up the brick. Anything that would keep me from having to look at Novi.

"Because I know you, Cem." She tilts my head up by the chin. "And I know you think you saw something earlier, but if you had just stuck around long enough to let me explain—or returned any of my scrys—I could have told you that there's nothing going on between me and Lyria."

Oh.

It's strange how little comfort those words bring.

"Why not?" The crystal I relegated to my pocket suddenly burns with guilt. "She sure seems to like you."

"And I like her, too."

There comes the vicious stab of jealous pain.

"And so would you—if you actually gave her the time of day instead of looking at her like she's *competition*," Novi says, far more kindly than I deserve. "We're the first halves she's ever met, Cemmy—and she's got no one at home she can talk to about this absolute mess. So she's been talking to me. Because you've been preoccupied with Cassiel, and Ez and Vee have been preoccupied with each other, and because sometimes, it's just easier for her to sign with someone who can sign back at the same speed. But even if none of that were true, I'd still hope that you'd give me the benefit of the doubt before jumping to the very worst conclusion. I'd still hope that you'd *know* I'd never start something that could jeopardize this"—she points between us—"without talking to you first. Especially not with another Hue."

Well, color me callous. Shame cuts through my chest like a knife. In my hurt, and my anger, I really did jump to the very worst conclusion, let my fear of losing Novi overwhelm what I know to be true in my gut: that the two of us are bonded in a way that's built to last. Tied at the soul, not the heart. Regardless of what we're doing in the bedroom.

"I'm sorry," I whisper, brushing the tips of my fingers against hers. "I'm not even mad at you—not really." *Not anymore.* "It's just been a hard few days."

I don't tell her about Mom yet.

I don't tell her about the almost kiss with Chase at the observatory, or how the looming threat to the shadows has been weighing heavily on my mind. How I'm leaning towards going through with this insanity.

Because if we *do* choose to retrieve the siphon, then that choice should be ours to make without threat or coercion from Savian, and the only way that can happen is if we also go through with our plan to get out from under his thumb.

Which means ensuring that Chase makes good on his promise to drain him of magic, and that when he does, we know the whens, wheres, and hows. And that means I have to put aside my pride and embarrassment and go practice my In-Betweens with him this one last time.

CHAPTER

Twenty-two

But it doesn't mean I have to like it. My scowl makes that abundantly clear as Chase lowers the blindfold over my eyes. I am only here, letting him lead me through the faithless quarter with one hand to my shoulder and the other to the small of my back, because I have to be. Because if we don't find a way to beat the portals, then all of our plans—real and pretend—will collapse.

"Are you ready to give this a try?" Chase asks once we've walked far enough for me to lose my bearings. Night has long since devoured Isitar, draping the city in a darkness that makes a labyrinth of the streets—even without the blindfold. My only clue as to where we are is the texture of the cobbles beneath my boots and the cacophony of sounds echoing in the distance.

A peal of laughter. An incessant howling. The drunken shuffle of feet.

Nothing I could pin my anchors to.

"Would it matter if I wasn't?" I bristle, wishing I could shed Chase's grip. But if I do that, I'll have no protection once we phase into the Gray. No fallback should I fail to stabilize my In-Between. This wretched task has placed me entirely at his mercy.

"Cemmy—"

No. He doesn't get to *Cemmy* me. Not here. Not now.

"Can we please just get this over with?" I cut him off, too keyed up to mind my temper or dampen the bark in my bite. It was a mistake to think that Chase could ever be anything more than a dangerous thorn in my side. Even if he hadn't pushed me away, I would have probably come to wish that he had. We're better off keeping things business.

"If you like," he says, a note of frustration winding his voice tight. Then the next second, I feel the air ripple as he blinks us into the shadows, the intensity of the light flickering behind my blindfold dimming to ash.

"On the count of three." With gentle fingers, Chase eases the fabric from around my eyes. "One . . . two . . . *three*."

I snap them open, quickly scanning our surroundings for the nearest landmarks in sight.

I am in between the gate to the market and the apothecary at its back.

The words set loose an ocean, a tidal wave of power that rushes out to bolster my shield.

Too late.

By the time the spell stabilizes, it has to push against the one from Chase, which means that without him, the Gray would have made short work of my efforts. I'd be nothing more than a pile of ruined shards.

"Not bad." He forces a light tone for my benefit. "It only took you a few seconds to adjust."

"It would take me less to shatter," I snap as we phase back into the physical realm. There are no prizes to be won for *almost* beating the shadows. I either get the magic right, or we die.

"Remember the beach?" Chase raises an eyebrow, returning the blindfold for me to tie. "All it takes is practice."

So we practice.

And we practice.

Then we practice some more.

Taking it in turns to both lead and to follow.

Chase steers me from the market to an abandoned masonry hut, an overgrown garden, a secluded patch of trees. I guide him towards the cliffside, the depths of the ruined quarter, the arches beneath the clocktower, the underside of a bridge. Anywhere we can find where our presence won't be noticed as we pop in and out of existence. At each new location, we rip off the blindfold and try to improvise our anchors unseen. And at each new location, our magic stabilizes a heartbeat later than we'd need it to in order to fully trust the shield. Even as we slowly start to improve our technique, I know that it'll ultimately prove futile. Our power isn't like Eve's: it's not instinctive. The shadows don't respect it.

"This isn't going to work," I say once Chase has failed to steady yet another fledgling In-Between. Several bells have passed since we first embarked on this endeavor, and we've both grown too tired—and too discouraged—to project our magic with any kind of speed. It's time to stop pretending this bad idea will save us.

"It has to work." Chase wipes away the sweat with the cuff of his sleeve, blinking us back to color. "We *need* it to work."

"Yeah, well, I hate to be the bearer, but *needing* something and *getting* it are two very different things." And in my experience, they're almost always mutually exclusive.

"Gods, could you please just—this isn't a joke, Cemmy." For the first time since I've known him, the crack in Chase's composure breaks right through the skin. I've aggravated him plenty before, seen him scared on occasion, witnessed the delirium that consumes him when he abuses his gift. But this isn't exasperation, or fleeting panic, or a color-born ill; it's a frenzied fear that has him wringing his hands and pacing circles around the empty alley. A manic edge that may yet turn infectious. "Savian doesn't take no for an answer, remember? And he's not keeping me around for the good of his health. If we don't figure the magic out, you know how this ends."

Right, of course. It always comes back to this threat. To the fact that Chase could run this lift by himself if only he were willing to murder four people.

"Then fucking end it already!" I explode. "If you're going to drain us, then *drain us*. Stop pretending you care."

"Stop pretending you *don't*." His eyes narrow to angry slits. "Or at least have the decency to admit what you're really mad about."

"I'm mad because you keep threatening to kill my friends."

"No, you're mad because I pushed you away."

The words send a mortifying flush to my cheeks. "Don't flatter yourself, Cassiel," I hiss, lacing his name with venom. "What happened at the observatory was a mistake."

"And that, right there, is exactly *why* I pushed you away." He bristles. "You'd just had a fight with your mom and you were very clearly upset. It wouldn't have been right to kiss you like that—and as much as I'm okay with being used for comfort, the one thing I won't be is anyone's regret."

"Oh please, if anyone was having regrets, it was you." After an entire night spent failing, I don't have the energy to try and save face. "We talked on my couch, Chase, for *hours*, then after five minutes with Savian you got cold, and you got mean, and you got—"

"Scared, Cemmy, I got *scared*." The air escapes him in a rush. "I don't make a habit of getting close to people, okay? That's not worked out so well for me before—so that game we played . . . the honesty . . . it's not something I usually do, and it's definitely not something I intended to share with Savian," he says, scrubbing back his hair with both hands. "Except he already knew. Not just that I came to your apartment—that much he could have gleaned from my scry—but he knew that we stayed up late talking, and he knew what we were talking about. In detail. Which isn't possible unless—"

"He was there." The breath in my lungs turns to ice, my truths feeling freshly exposed. "You think he followed you?"

"There's no other explanation; he must have shimmered in unnoticed while we were still in the Gray. So yes, Cemmy, I got scared," Chase says. "Because he could tell that I was starting to like talking to you, and practicing magic with you, and running these insane lifts with you, and so he reminded me what would happen if I were to start enjoying those things a little too much."

The implication in his words is impossible to miss.

"He wants you to drain us, doesn't he?" I guess at the reason Savian felt the need to embed his chest with a scry. *This is what happens to a Gold who declines to cooperate.*

"He's always wanted me to drain you." Chase takes a step towards me, the narrowness of the alley bringing him within striking distance of that now. "The only reason he hasn't forced me to do it yet is because I convinced him you'd be more useful to us alive than dead. That's why he tested your ability in the Gray: to prove that this wasn't a big waste of time."

"Hell of a risk, don't you think?" My answering step presses my back up against a wall of brick. "What would you have done if I'd shattered?"

"You were never going to shatter, Cemmy," Chase breathes, closing the gap further still. "Our Indigo was confident of that much; the only question was whether you'd free yourself from the Gray, or if Savian would have to send me in to save you. But we needed to get at the Governor's map anyway, so it was an opportunity to show him that it was worth keeping you around. That six Hues were better than one shot with a bunch of magics I don't fully understand. That way, if something were to happen to me, he could still reach the siphon."

"And you're just . . . okay with that?" My voice is little more than a shaken whisper, timid and stunned. "You're okay with giving such a powerful object to a man like Savian?"

"No, I'm not, actually." If Chase gets any closer, I'll be able to taste the magic in his blood. "I'm not okay with a lot of things, Cemmy, and I wish I could tell you the whole truth—I wish I could explain why I've had to align myself with someone like him—but I can't. I just need you to trust that it's important. I need you to believe that I know exactly what kind of monster he is, and that I'd never let him use the siphon to cause any more harm. And then I need you to remember how much is at stake here. What happens if we don't get that power away from the Church." His conviction is a sermon on the wind, a waver in my resolve to stay angry.

"You have every right to hate me, Cemmy," he continues. "*Every right.* But know that I mean to ensure we *all* make it out of the Dominion, and that I mean to keep the promise I made on the cliff. I will get you the magic you need to heal your mom." His hands sear a path from my shoulders down to my wrists, leaving my skin tingling in their wake. "Off the hook or not, you can have it in case she agrees."

"Why?" I can't help but ask him, searching his face for any hint of a lie. In the slither of light that penetrates the alley, it's easy to forget that we exist on opposite sides of an absolute divide. That he's the Gold spearheading Savian's bid for the siphon, and I'm the Bronze tasked with sabotaging their plan. That certain metals corrode when they mix. "You said it yourself: I have no way of holding you to this promise."

"Because I made the promise to *you*." The silver in his irises is a hundred liquid stars. "And because I'm hoping that, once this is all behind us, we can maybe . . . start over," he says, and I'm suddenly struck by just how vulnerable he looks when he drops the pretense, the sheer depth of pain he's been bottling inside.

He's lonely. I don't know how I didn't see it before, but I recognize the hungry yearn gleaming in his eyes. It's the same way I looked at Ezzo when he first found me haunting my sanctuary, and the same longing I saw in Lyria when Savian first shimmered her into our laps. It's the same urge that keeps pushing me and Novi together, even after my secret has long since broken us apart.

"We can start over right now," I tell him, brushing my fingers along the insides of his palms. Because impossible as though it might seem, I'm beginning to trust that on this, at least, Chase and I are perfectly aligned. That when he looks at me, he sees more than just a Gray gift Savian needs, or a means to persuade the others to his side.

He sees a color he likes.

"I'm not upset anymore," I say, turning the six inches of space between us to five.

Four.

Three.

And this time, when Chase cups his hands around my shoulders, it isn't to push me away, it's to pull me closer. To make clear that he, too, wants to take those remaining inches and erase them to none.

So we do it together, colliding with a desperation I can feel in his touch. His skin is fevered, burning, alive with the power that's sizzling inside, a stark contrast to the gentle heat of his breath and the careful path his fingers trace as they dance across my ribcage.

Too careful.

With a whispered word, I urge him to sate their curiosity, to shift his body so that mine can do the same along his hard-cut lines. And maybe it doesn't make sense for us to want this. To choose each other when the only thing that drew us together is a few days of forced proximity and the broken pieces of truth we've both felt compelled to entrust. The chinks we've forged in each other's armor.

But hells, maybe not everything has to make sense outside the moment.

Maybe sometimes it's okay to let the bad decision stand.

And Gods, that decision feels good. I gasp as Chase presses me harder against the bricks, flashing hot as his hands eschew the torturous hell of fabric, dipping beneath the hem of my shirt in their frenzied quest for bare skin.

Fuck. I hiss as he groans against me, the deepening timbre of his kiss making a jellied marrow of my bones. It should scare me to let him touch me like this, knowing how easily his gift could extract the color from my blood. How quickly it can turn deadly. But right at this moment, with his lips skimming my jaw and his fingers teasing along the edge of my waistband, I am not afraid of Chase's power.

Quite the opposite, in fact.

It feels as though his hands are melting away the fear, and the hate, and the anger.

As though his touch alone could keep me from shattering in the dark.

Holy shadows—that's it! The answer hits me all at once, shocking my body still.

Didn't anyone ever tell you? We're always in between something. When Chase said those words to me on the beach, I accused him of spouting useless philosophy, but since then, my abilities have improved leaps and bounds. He's the one who taught me that *anything* can be turned into an anchor, and that those anchors need only be as concrete as my self-belief. We both missed the stunningly obvious.

"What is it? What's wrong?" The moment Chase senses my distraction, he instantly pulls away, his pupils blown wide, his breaths panting heavy. "Was I moving too fast? I'm sorry—I shouldn't have—"

"No, it's not that." It actually pains me to disentangle our limbs. "It's just—I know how to beat the portals," I tell him, slipping the blindfold back over my eyes. "Lead me somewhere different."

"Okay . . ." Though I can feel his wealth of budding questions, Chase does as I ask. Then when we're finally in position, I kiss him again, harder this time, focusing on nothing but the way he feels against me—*around* me—and the space I occupy between the cage of his arms.

"Blink us into the Gray, now," I whisper, not bothering to restore my ability to see. If I'm right, I won't need to glimpse my surroundings; I already have everything I need to secure the spell tight.

Because *I am in between the cage of Chase's arms.*

And try as they might, the shadows can't break me.

CHAPTER

Twenty-three

People as anchors.

It seems so simple in retrospect, I'm honestly surprised Chase didn't come up with it himself. I mean, if anchors don't need to be solid, and they don't need to be fixed, then why would they need to be inanimate? Why couldn't a person perform the same function as a bookcase, or a table, or a tree? The magic doesn't seem to differentiate.

Chase and I spend another hour in the shadows, testing the boundaries of the spell until we're sure it'll work under pressure, even when the half Shades casting it aren't wrapped around each other like two giggling maidens nursing a crush.

This must be where the old myths come from, the tales of Hues traversing entire mountain ranges with nothing but the clothes on their backs. With this version of the spell, their shields would have moved through the Gray alongside them, no mess, no fuss, no need to re-anchor. Throw enough Hues together and they could have easily sustained it for weeks at a time—even without an Emerald—shared the burden of keeping the magic alive through periods of rest or sleep. Further proof that it's not the shadows that hate us—it's the Council that's been seeking to end our lives. They've been smothering us with ignorance.

"So . . . we should probably go back and tell the others," I say once our confidence in the spell has grown complete.

"Yeah, probably," Chase agrees, though he doesn't make to lead me away from the alcove in which we're hidden. Just as I don't make to message my friends on the scrys. Instead, I let him kiss me again, wondering when the offer to join him back at the inn will finally slip his tongue.

"But it could also keep until tomorrow," I hedge. "If we decided to go do . . . something else." The note in my voice is an invitation, though judging by the way Chase stills against me, not one that's particularly well received. "Or not, I guess." At least the darkness serves to hide the flame of my cheeks.

"It's not that I don't want to," he hurries to say, "because believe me, Cemmy, I *do*. But with Savian watching me so closely, spending the night together again . . . it's too much of a risk. I'd rather wait a couple more days than have him decide you're a problem."

"Just a couple more days, huh?" It's impossible for the hurt to bloom while his thumbs keep skimming this madness along my hip.

"Just a couple more days," Chase repeats. "We can finalize the plan tomorrow, then on the morning of the cleansing moon, he'll finally give me the Green magic you need. Once the parade's over, this will all be behind us. No more hiding, no more threat, no more fear."

No more conspiring to learn when he means to drain Savian.

"But until then, I think it's better for us to act as though this—"

"Didn't happen," I finish for him, since that solution actually provides us both with a mutual fix. When I last tried to convince the others he was on our side, their reaction was one part skepticism, a hundred parts disbelief. They won't take well to thinking I'm bedding the enemy.

So we agree to stay quiet, and we agree to separate for the night, and by the time morning comes and he returns to the monastery, I've already taught the others the spell we discovered in preparation for this final day of maintaining the charade. *He won't be draining Savian until tomorrow*, I told them, *so we need to keep pretending*. Solve the last few pieces of this puzzle so that after he does—and after I persuade them he can be trusted—we can all decide together whether to go through with this plan.

Though as it turns out, those last few pieces prove harder than anticipated to crack.

"The fence is going to be our biggest problem." Ezzo points to the spiked ring of iron surrounding the Dominion on the map, pausing to allow Lyria a brief look. "We were originally thinking Cemmy could pick the lock on one of the servant entrances, but they've all been chained shut ahead of the parade. The only way in or out tomorrow will be the main gate, and they'll definitely notice if we open that."

"Which is pretty much redundant if there'll be rogues patrolling the Gray," Novi adds, her accompanying signs growing clipped. "Even if we do get through the gate, they'll still be able to see us cross the plaza. And crossing it in the physical realm is clearly out of the question. We'd be seen by everyone else."

"Okay, so what we need is a distraction that works across both worlds." Chase wasn't taking no for an answer yesterday, and he isn't any more inclined to hear that word today. "Something bold enough to lure both the Shades and the enforcers away from their posts."

"Are all your solutions this vague or do you actually have a bright idea for how we might do that?" Novi's tongue clicks against her teeth.

"I have a bright idea," Eve says and signs, lurching up from the table. "En, can you—? Would you mind interpreting for a second? I need to grab something from my box of paints." She mouths a quick apology at Lyria before dashing across the nave.

"Erm . . . Vee?" I start, staring after her in confusion. "I don't think that's quite what—"

"Don't worry, I'm not suggesting we draw them a picture." She rolls her eyes, fishing out a set of multicolored dusts. "But imagine you're the Church, right? And you're putting on your yearly show of hate against magic, and you're pumping out that ridiculous gold pigment they like to spread, when suddenly, bam!" She tosses the pots into the air, unleashing a vivid cloud of powder that coats us all in a glittery rain. "Except we use a glamour, not paint, and make it bigger. Like, really big."

An overwhelming show of color on the Church's holiest of days.

An act of defiance that would serve to rile the crowd into a frenzy and distract Rhodes's enforcers, magical in nature so as to also mobilize his Shades.

"That could work." Chase's eyes turn thoughtful, the remnants of Eve's rainbow shimmering on his hair and hands. "I can get us enough Red magic to make a real impact. Orange magic, too, in case anything goes wrong and we need to make a quick escape, so that Ezzo can bring the gate down." Which isn't something we can do on our way in, or the Commander will suspect the true target of our attack. Whereas Eve's idea would serve to draw attention away from the Dominion instead of towards it. I'm just not sure it'll draw it away for long enough.

"We're putting a lot of stock in those Shades staying distracted while I pick the lock, *and* open the gate, *and* cross the plaza, *and* get through the main door." I raise the obvious objection, painfully aware of all the ways my physicality is complicating our lives.

"Actually . . . the plaza will be less of an issue once we've taken care of the Shades." Novi's quick to spot the opportunity I didn't. "As soon as they're gone, I could speed us across in groups. Even if I have to make two trips, it'll only take a couple of seconds."

Well, that's one problem down, I guess. "But you're still assuming that not a single Shade—or a single enforcer—will notice the gate swing open of its own accord." And if you ask me, that's a mighty big hope on which to hinge a plan.

"Then what if you didn't have to open the gate?" Lyria's brow lifts with the question. *"Or the main door, for that matter. Or any door in the Dominion?"*

"I mean, that would be ideal . . ." My answering signs are hesitant, less because I'm still grappling with the language than because I'm unclear as to where this wishful thought might land. "But I really am very physical in the Gray. It's not something I can just . . . turn off."

"The shadows probably could though. If I ask them to let you through, they might."

"Wait—that's a thing?" I gape at Lyria in surprise.

"Everything in the Gray is shadows." She shrugs. *"So theoretically, there's no reason they couldn't reform the gate around you. Though since I've not tried it before, we should maybe go test it out. Ideally before tomorrow."*

Yes, that's quite the important *ideally*, I'd say.

Before tomorrow would be wise.

Which is why, an hour later, the two of us are snaking a path towards the holy quarter, in search of a mansion with a similar iron gate we can appropriate for the task.

"So . . . I think I owe you an apology." It takes Lyria a good few minutes to work up to broaching the subject.

"An apology? For what?" I ask. If anything, the rest of us are about to owe her a debt of thank you.

"For yesterday," she signs, looking at me with wary eyes. *"I didn't mean to cause any trouble between you and Novi. If I had known about your history, I never would have—"*

"No, please—you didn't do anything wrong," I tell her, the vice around my ribs squeezing tight. "Novi and I haven't been together for a while now."

"Yeah, she . . . mentioned that too." Lyria's hands slow in their hesitance. *"But she also said that it was complicated, and messy, and hard, and that she would never do anything that might endanger your friendship. And I just want you to know that I have no intention of doing anything to endanger it, either. What the four of you have here . . . it's really special. I would never dream of ruining it."*

Too tight.

Her pledge only serves to sharpen my guilt.

Though Novi had told me that same thing herself, she was under no obligation to share that fact with Lyria. To shut the door on their possibility in an effort to spare me pain. *Meanwhile, you spent your night kissing Chase all over the city*. My guilt fast turns to shame. If I'm the one who broke us, then why am I allowing Novi to throw her own chance at happiness away, even as I skulk through the shadows doing the exact opposite? I don't have the right to let my jealousy dictate who she spends her time with, and as much as it hurts to admit it, that means letting her go. Trusting that if our friendship could survive a heartbreak, then it could also survive the arrival of a shiny new Hue. An Amethyst or a Gold.

"Novi isn't mine to give," I say and sign, working to smooth my expression. "And if we get out of this alive, the two of you have my blessing to be friends, or more than friends, or hells, you can be mortal enemies if you like. You'd still be welcome either way." To my surprise, the words come as a relief, like trimming a vine that had grown too dense and unruly to flourish.

Like admitting to a truth that's been rotting me from inside.

"So . . . now that we're both horribly uncomfortable, can I ask you something?" I decide to dispel the tension by meeting it head-on.

"Gods—please." When Lyria grins, I understand exactly what drew Novi's eye to her. The captivating mix of emerald, freckles, and fire.

"How did you manage to hide what you were for so long?" My question is a timid curiosity in the early afternoon light. Around us, the cobbled streets have grown wider, the bustle of the faithless quarter giving way to a more reserved commotion of solemn fabrics and gold-flecked eyes. The streets boasting their reform with iron.

"Three younger brothers who refuse to sit still and two utterly exhausted parents." Lyria's answering smile is fond. *"My father works as a tailor and my mother teaches at the local school, so it's not as if they're always watching, and they had their hands full with three screaming toddlers when my magic first manifested.*

"I did try to have the 'talk' with them a couple of times—once I understood what I was. By then, I knew enough about how the world treated Hues to wonder whether they were trying to pretend it wasn't happening. That maybe if they never told me about my color, it would simply go away. But it quickly became apparent that they really had no idea. And since neither of them is a Shade, well . . . it didn't take long for me to realize what that must mean, and then I realized how destructive my secret could be, and so I decided to keep it to myself. Did my phasing at night while everyone was asleep, and with so much going on all the time, they just . . . never noticed. Hard to believe, I know, but it's the truth."

"No, I believe it." I touch a finger to my forehead then clasp both hands. I've spent years hiding my own trips to the Gray from Mom. "But it sure does sound lonely."

"I mean, yes . . . but not as bad as you might think." Lyria remains upbeat. *"I was luckier than most Hues—I got to keep my family, and honestly, that made up for so many of the things I didn't get to have. Though I guess it helped that when I talked to the shadows, the shadows talked back."* This time, the smile she offers me is wry.

"Are you ever afraid of what they'd do if they . . . found out?" I ask, thinking of Mom's face when she caught me stealing in the market. When she realized I've been brazenly flouting her rules and utilizing my gift. Levelled her ultimatum.

If you leave this house, you will not be welcome back.

"A little, maybe?" The idea appears to take Lyria by surprise. *"But not because I'm worried about them disowning me, or turning me into the Council, if that's what you're asking. I was never afraid of that—and I've never been ashamed of being a Hue, either,"* she hurries to sign, as though worried I might have misconstrued her choice to lie. *"But I'm also not naïve, and I don't trust the Council's trackers to make the distinction between me and them, or to not hold them accountable for allowing me to exist. So in the end, keeping them oblivious felt like the best thing for all of us. The less they know, the less likely that secret is to get out."*

And the more inexplicable her disappearance would be if she were to die during this endeavor. The more devastating.

"Oh hey—this should work." Lyria's attention suddenly shifts towards the house at the head of the adjoining street, a proud-looking three-story mansion that sits behind a wrought-iron fence. Exactly the kind we need. *"Ready to put this theory to the test?"*

"No time like the present." I banish the gut-squirming thought as, with a cautious look over our shoulder, we blink the world gray, stripping the streets of color. In the physical realm, this amount of iron would weaken a full-blood in minutes, keep them from darkening the owner's door. Whereas to us halves, it's just a fence like any other—though to a Bronze, every fence presents the same ordeal. Across both worlds.

"Holy . . . wow." Lyria shakes an open hand in wonder as I brush my fingers along the metal. *"Sorry . . . I don't mean to stare, it's just—I've never seen a Hue do that."* Her cheeks flush as red as her curls.

Right, of course, she's never run a lift with me before. Never seen my gift in action.

What the four of you have here . . . it's really special. I sometimes forget how much we take each other for granted. How rare it is for a Hue to glimpse the Gray through another's lens.

"It has its downsides." I shrug, leaning my weight against the bars in demonstration. "The Gray is just another physical realm for me. No short cuts."

"Then let's see if we can fix that." Lyria stills in concentration, her silent exchange with the shadows taking place entirely behind closed eyes, making butterflies of her pale lashes. And though she's previously explained to me how her gift functions as a conversation in name only, it still comes as a shock when barely a few seconds later, she snaps them open to sign, *"Okay, you can walk through the gate now."*

"But . . . nothing's different," I argue, staring at the very solid-looking fence. I don't know what I expected to happen—that the bars would grow transparent, maybe? Or perhaps that they would flicker at the edge—but as far as I can tell, both me and the iron remain unchanged. Unyielding in an immutable way.

"You have to trust me, Cemmy," Lyria urges. *"The shadows say it's safe."*

Oh, well if the shadows say so . . . I wince as I take a step towards the rigid metal. I mean, it's not like the shadows have ever tried to kill me be—

Whoa.

I'm forced to eat my doubt as the iron wisps like smoke around me, ignoring my physicality as though the color in my blood isn't bronze.

I can't believe that actually worked. The sensation is thoroughly alien, like water shifting states from a liquid to a fog. I've never not been corporeal before—not unless I count the fleeting shimmer with

Mom, and during that blur of shadows, I was too distracted by the resurgence of her magic to marvel at the deadening of mine.

So this is how it feels to move without limit. As much as I've come to appreciate the bounds of my gift, I'm suddenly all too aware of how open the Gray becomes when you're unencumbered by walls. How free.

"Looks like we've found your way through the gate." Lyria's triumph is a satisfied flash of teeth. *"The main door, too. The shadows say they're happy to give us as much help as they can. I told them why we're doing this and they're angry . . . desperate. They've been pleading with the air for weeks now, but there's been no one around to listen."*

Ironic, really. When the Council turned against the Hues in their midst, they hunted to near extinction the ability to communicate with the dark, a gift that none of their full-blooded Shades have the power to exploit. If only they had chosen a different scapegoat, then maybe the shadows wouldn't need to be afraid. Maybe our way of life wouldn't be in danger. Maybe an entire world wouldn't live or die by the actions of six illegal half Shades.

Focus on one problem at a time, Cemmy. As the day draws on, we slowly work through the remaining question marks on our list. How we'll make our approach towards the Dominion, and through it, and what groups we'll need to split into, and when, and in which order Novi will ferry us across the plaza, and the portals, and whether there are other contingencies we should be prepared for, or additional protections we might choose to take with us inside. Chase bids me to bring a knife in case of emergency, Novi gifts Lyria a set of scrys—one to wear for each of us—and Eve and Ezzo make a trip to the market to gather the rest of our supplies. Come nightfall, all the pieces of our plan are placed and ready, and all that's left is for Chase to go and steal our magics, and for me to convince the others that we should stop thinking of this lift as a charade.

Soon, I tell myself, biting back the admissions I want to make to him—and to them. By tomorrow morning, we'll all be free of Savian. Free and able to approach that conversation with an open mind. Now that the others have seen exactly how impossible this lift would be for the Council, I have no doubt that they'll understand why we can't just toss Savian at their feet and take a step to the side. And Chase, well . . . he'll understand, too. Once he realizes I still mean to help him, he'll understand why I had no choice but to keep him in the dark.

Why I had to betray him.

I wish I could tell you the whole truth, he'd said to me last night. *I wish I could explain why I've had to align myself with someone like him. I just need you to trust that it's important.*

I wish I could tell him I do.

I wish I could tell him about my solution.

But the others need Savian gone before they'll consider acting, and without a firm commitment from the others, I doubt Chase will consider acting against Savian. On this, I'm better off playing both sides.

Though by the time Chase leaves to go report on our progress, the guilt is clawing acid at my insides. Because what if he tries to intervene? To protect Savian? Hurts himself—or one of us—in the process, all because I chose to let him walk into an ambush?

No. I can't tell him *nothing*.

So before he disappears from the monastery, I pull him into a shadowed corner and do the only thing I can without giving away our plan: I offer him the vaguest hint of a warning.

"After you drain Savian tomorrow, turn around and leave, okay? Don't look back, and please, don't worry, nothing else about the plan will change. I just need you to leave, then wait for me here. Can you do that?"

"Can you tell me why?" He raises a brow, searching my face for the reason behind the ask.

"No, I can't," I say, imploring him with my eyes. *I wish I could, but I can't.*

"Cemmy—"

"Please, Chase, I need you to trust that it's important." I repeat the request he made of me last night. *I need you to trust me.*

And though it takes him a long and excruciating moment—an entire lifetime of indecision and gut-wrenching doubt—with a nod, and a stolen brush of lips, Chase finally tells me he does.

He gives me his blessing.

CHAPTER
Twenty-four

So it feels like less of a betrayal when, the following morning, we make ready to enact the treachery we've been honing on the sly.

Chase will understand, I tell myself as we trail him from his inn to the ruined quarter, back to the burned-out theater house where he last committed this act. *He wants Savian gone as much as we do.* He may not have told me that in so many words, but I heard it in the ones he did say, and in the way he's spoken of their alliance, and Savian's cruelty, and his eagerness to leave the rogue Shade behind.

Once both sides of my plan come together, I'm certain he'll understand.

He'll understand and forgive me.

"What do you see, Ez?" I ask as the five of us appraise the building in preparation, watching his eyes dart back and forth beneath the haze of his gift.

"Our Gold . . . obviously, though I still can't find a trail for Savian." Frustration cocks his head to the side. "And as far as I can tell, there's no one else in there. So he's either moved the other Shades on or cut them loose."

Or he's disposed of them. That likelihood strikes me as equally probable. Chase has had ample time to extract from them the magics we need, so with the cleansing moon mere hours away, what other purpose could they possibly serve?

Then why would Savian have him do the draining here? The question is a niggling ache between my bones. Through force of habit, maybe?

Or perhaps because it's private and out of the way? A place where his screams would go unnoticed and his weakened state undisturbed, unthreatened by either Council or Church. It doesn't much matter, I suppose, since my role in today's coup remains the same regardless of the location: climb inside the way I did a few nights ago—our bag of purposefully picked supplies in hand—then let the others know once I've confirmed the deed is done. *And that Chase is gone.* That second part I keep to myself. They'll warm to him just as soon as he demonstrates that his loyalty never willingly lay with Savian. If he leaves him drained and unprotected, we'll know. I'll have all the proof I need to convince them.

The theater house stands quieter than it did the last time, the balcony greeting me with nothing but a soundless wafting of dust. No moans of pain escaping an imprisoned rainbow, no pleas for mercy, no desperate clatter of iron chains—those have actually been removed from the rafters, all evidence of them relegated to my memory of the past. In their wake, a sturdy chair occupies the center of the stage, high-backed with a cushioned seat and lavishly upholstered armrests. A comfortable place for Savian to recover once Chase's gift has bled his color dry.

That's where I find him sitting now, the knife of his features slicing through the inky darkness, the diamonds in his ears glittering like fallen stars. Above him, Chase cuts a menacing figure, his hands pressed to Savian's chest, a look of agonized concentration passing between them. Though unlike the captive Shades, Savian bears the drain in silence, the tense clench of his jaw the only palpable sign that he's in pain.

He's let Chase do this before.

And he's letting him do it now because it makes sense to equip his Gold with the ability to heal, in case anything goes wrong as we attempt to steal the siphon. Or at least that's how Chase will have sold him on the idea, when in reality, he's taking that magic in promise to me.

The green haze intensifies beneath his palms, Savian's color rushing to heed the siren song of his gift. It truly is astonishing how much power he'll entrust to a Gold—and I don't just mean the power he's willing to part with, but the power he relinquishes when the extraction leaves his body in such a vulnerable state. There must be some reason *why* he trusts Chase so implicitly, and it has to run deeper than the lowly scry embedded in his flesh.

But what could that reason be? For the first time since I slipped Chase my warning, I'm beginning to wonder whether I've risked our lives on a bad bet, let a few stolen kisses mess with my equilibrium. Savian could be threatening to expose him to the Council, I suppose. Dangling the threat of execution over his head—same way he did with the rest of us. *No . . . that feels too simple.* Dread fills my stomach with lead. If it was something so innocuous, Chase wouldn't have felt the need to lie about it. He wouldn't have bothered keeping it a secret.

I wish I could tell you the whole truth—but I can't. I just need you to trust that it's important.

Just as I need him to trust that leaving Savian weak and unprotected is important.

What happens next will hinge on whether we can trust each other.

The extraction only takes a few minutes to complete, and though it's Savian Chase is draining, it still turns my stomach to watch. To witness him reduce a full-blooded Shade to a quivering mess of limbs, his expression staying cold and unrepentant. Cruel. Almost as if he'd enjoyed it.

When he finally breaks the connection, Savian sags low in his chair, his eyes drooping shut, his breaths growing noticeably labored, even from my place on the balcony.

Moment of truth. The air catches in my lungs, my heart drumming a frantic tattoo against my ribcage. If I'm right about Chase, then he'll honor my request and leave the theater house, abandon Savian to recuperate without his help.

If I'm wrong, then he'll stay.

If I'm wrong, then the betrayal to come will prove harder.

We'll be going through with it either way, of course—since the others have no idea I made that request of him at all—but should he stay, it'll be my job to ensure he doesn't get in the way of our attack.

How I might do that, I don't know, and as he shakes his head clear of the magic, I'm praying to all three Gods that I won't have to figure it out.

Please go. Please go. Please go.

An eternity seems to pass before Chase moves, during which time, I swear he steals a glance in my direction, even though he has no real reason to suspect that I followed him to this crime.

Please go. I implore him with my hope, and my need, and my silence.

Please go. I implore him with the faith I placed in him last night.

Which Chase ultimately rewards by retreating towards the door at the edge of the stage, leaving Savian prone and at our mercy.

Well, thank my colors for that. A swell of warmth surges through my chest, the memory of his kiss tingling my lips ruddy. For the briefest of moments, I allowed myself to doubt what I knew deep in my gut: that Chase's loyalty to Savian is brittle. A marriage born of necessity, not regard. When push came to shove, he chose to ally himself with me.

Savian's down. I scry the message to the others, summoning them into the theater as I descend the stairs two at a time. A second later, the walls ripple as the four of them pass through the smoke-clad bricks the way a feather would through sand, like an army of vengeful apparitions.

Ready?

Their answering nods have me reaching for our bag of supplies.

A set of iron cuffs, chained in the middle, both to keep Savian from phasing and to constrict his hands should he rise. A length of rope with which to tie his legs. A wad of cloth with which to dull his protests. And to ensure we walk away from this coup with our freedom intact, a tiny vial of the most potent Yellow label memory tonic Novi could buy—not dissimilar to the spell we used on the Governor and his guards—so that once we dump him on the Council's doorstep, he won't be able to give them *us* in retaliation. At least not before they see fit to execute their justice. Their hate for rogue Shades means they'll act first, ask questions never; that's the Council's way when it comes to those who break their rules. They'll kill him just as happily as they did my dad, and Novi's father, and Eve's parents, and Ezzo's mom, and I don't feel the slightest bit of guilt about that because I'm sure Savian would do the same to us in a heartbeat. Hells, there was never any guarantee that he didn't mean to throw us to the wolves the second we delivered him his siphon. Dispose of us with the same apathy he did his rainbow of Shades.

I approach the stage slowly—cautiously—with the quiet grace of a thief's prowl, the cuffs held at the ready, my friends gathered in support at my back, our In-Betweens holding steady. At full strength, an iron chain and a length of rope wouldn't even come close to stopping a full-blood, but Savian's unconscious right now, and as soon as he's bound and addled, Novi will speed him through the shadows to face the Council's wrath. This entire nightmare could be over before the next bell is struck. I just have to get close enough to—

Savian's eyelids flutter and we all gasp in unison, freezing our advance in place.

Stay down. I will the drain to keep him incapacitated a little longer. For Chase's gift to grant us the time we need to finish the job right. We've spent the past week building up to this moment. We've planned, and we've practiced, and we've pretended, and we've *smiled,* all while putting ourselves in an ungodly amount of danger. We can't afford to fail at this final hurdle. We have to see this attack through and get out from under Savian's thumb.

So when he doesn't stir, we don't falter.

Step by painstaking step, we creep across the stage, fanning out to surround him on all four sides. Eve and Ezzo to my left, Novi and Lyria to my right. Five Hues united in purpose.

"On three . . ." Novi whispers as we inch within striking distance of the prize. While I'm the only one with the physicality to bind the cuffs around Savian's wrists, she and Ezzo can help maneuver his arms, hold him down on the off-chance he wakes and struggles. Make my life easier.

"One . . ."

It's already easy, I tell myself, steeling my nerves for the task. Savian is dead to the world, slowly sinking into a deeper slouch against the chair, his breaths rasping sharp and thready.

"Two . . ."

I lean over his prostrate form, my fingers trembling but determined, my heart beating an arresting line.

"Three." Savian's hand wraps around my throat with a speed I don't expect and a power I can't withstand, crushing the air from my windpipe.

Crap. Shit. Damn. Fuck. The shock rends my In-Between apart, leaving Eve to step in and reinforce the magic.

"Vee!" The moment she spurs to action, Ezzo does too. He lunges at Savian, his teeth bared in fury, a malevolent roar on his tongue.

But we're in the Gray, and in the Gray, full-blooded Shades *are* the shadows, their strength unrivalled, their color unleashed. In the split-second it takes Ezzo to spring forward, Savian's already shimmered across the stage, slamming my back into the wall, hard, my feet dangling as he pins me there by the neck—even as he paralyzes the others with a burst of Red magic that could have only come from his Gold.

"Be careful who you trust, little half Shade." My mouth tastes of metal, my lip blooming wet from where my teeth bit and drew blood. "If they'll double-cross *for* you, just imagine what they'll do *to* you. Isn't that right, Cassiel?" The meaning in his words is slow to land, and I don't fully comprehend it until Chase shuffles out from the shadows, his head hung low, his eyes fixed firmly on the ground.

That's when I get it.

That's when I realize that there's no shake in Savian's hand, no sweat on his brow, and the labor in his lungs is gone.

But Chase is still here. A vice squeezes the hope from my heart. He didn't leave like I asked him to or drain Savian of the magic he needs to heal Mom. It was an act. All of it. A performance designed to draw our sedition out. Perfect in every way, right down to the theatrical staging.

And suddenly, I can't breathe. *I can't breathe, I can't breathe—I can't.*

Because I was wrong.

I was wrong and Chase betrayed me.

He took my request and ran it straight to his master. Conspired to lead us here instead of allowing us to glimpse Savian's true hideout. Chose to remain on the enemy's side.

"Let this serve as a reminder to you all." Savian turns back to address the others, still held frozen in time. "Of how it only takes one weak link to bring down a rebellion." With a flick of his fingers, the four of them are forced to their knees, their groans of pain resonating through the theater.

"Your Bronze thought she was better at this game than I am." He states the charge clearly, so that Lyria can read his lips. "She thought she was capable enough to seduce my Gold into renouncing his loyalties, ask him to forsake me without consequence." He tosses me into their midst, ensuring that they understand exactly what happened here. That I'm the reason our plan went awry.

It's easier to steal a man's face than change his allegiance.

Chase told me that himself the very first night I met him, how futile it is to try and remake a man's trust.

But I didn't listen.

I convinced myself I'd remade his, when in reality, all I did was let him break mine.

"You've overestimated your capabilities before, haven't you, Cemilla?" Savian continues, the silk in his voice oozing danger. "Shall I tell your friends what other sordid secret you've been hiding? How you thought you could pick a lock and hold an In-Between around another half at the same time. Promised Lena you wouldn't let her shatter then abandoned her to save your own skin. Hardly what I'd call an *accident*." He screws the vice tighter, relishing the weight of eyes now furiously turned my way. Because, *Gods*, of course Chase told him that, too. Why would he merely break my trust when he could also expose my shame. Destroy me entirely.

"Is that true, Cemmy?" Novi's hurt cracks through Savian's spell.

"Yes." There's no point lying about it anymore, nor is she likely to believe any feeble attempt at denial. Not when the truth is so clearly etched into every line of my face, my biggest regret laid bare for them to witness. Chase took each piece of the soul I gave him and handed them—like sharpened weapons—to Savian. *And now the coward won't even look at me.* He's just standing idle at the side of the stage, gnashing his teeth and wringing his hands. Refusing to own the pain he inflicted.

"It's always a shock to learn that the truth exists at such odds with our beliefs," Savian says, stretching his grin wide. "For example, the five of you appear to be operating under the misguided belief that you can overpower me. Deliver me to the Council, I assume? Have their executioners do the killing for you?" He guesses at our plan. "So allow me to disabuse you of that notion." With another flourish of fingers, he sends a bolt of power rending through Novi, then Ezzo, then Lyria, then me, collapsing our In-Betweens in quick succession, his magic lingering to prevent us from recasting our shields. Though the true brutality . . . the cruel agony in Green . . . that he saves for Eve.

"Stop it, you'll—you're killing them!" she screams through the pain, forced to throw her arms out wide in an effort to keep the rest of us from shattering.

"And you'd do well to remember how easily I can," Savian says, watching his spell wage battle against her gift with a bored indifference. "A tedious business, isn't it? Dealing with the consequences of your own actions? Perhaps this will dissuade you from challenging my authority again, because make no mistake, you *will* retrieve the siphon for me, or you will die trying. There is no alternative that won't cost you your lives. I trust I've made myself clear?"

"Please!" Though we're all yelling for him to end Eve's torture, it's Ezzo's plea that seemingly changes his mind. "You have to stop hurting her! She can't fight you and hold this many shields at the same time!"

"Then perhaps I should relieve some of that strain." Savian finally relinquishes his grip on our ability to cast. "We wouldn't want our Emerald wasting her talents on a half that isn't *contributing*." The malice in his eyes grows sharp as he appraises our

Sapphire. The spare Hue who has already fulfilled the purpose with which he was tasked.

No.

We all realize what he means to do at the same time, the panic paling us to powder. We're instantly on the move, running towards Ezzo as though we might be able to save him from Savian's ire. And we're all begging, pleading, imploring Savian to stop. To show mercy. Hells, it even sounds as if Chase swallows his cowardice and calls for him to stay the flash of murder building in his palm.

Not every Green can kill with just a flex of their hand—it takes an astonishing amount of power, skill, and ruthless drive—but it is within the realm of their color.

For what is death if not the antidote to life?

A healer's magic can be used to both cure the body and effect its demise.

Time splinters into fragments, an inevitability I glimpse in scattered fits and shards. My boots pounding across the stage. Novi's cries echoing off the rafters. Eve lurching in front of Ezzo right as the spell meets its mark.

"Vee—no!"

The magic slams her backward with enough force to send her flying deep into the theater house, her small frame breaking against the grimy floorboards. And though I know, without a whisper of a doubt, that Eve's fate was sealed the moment Savian's curse struck her heart, I refuse to believe the horror unfolding before my eyes.

I refuse to let the Gray have her.

She's ours. I force my own magic outward, trying to project my shield the way Eve can project hers. But Eve's power is instinctive, whereas mine requires contact, and I'm still half an auditorium away from her side.

I'm too late.

The roar of the shadows is an unmistakable growl, incandescent and hungry. They might not hate us the way the Council has led us to believe, but there are still rules by which we must abide. An unwritten contract. And right now, Eve is lying in breach.

Oh Gods oh Gods oh Gods. The cracks appear as if in slow motion, like a porcelain doll splintering in a thoughtless child's grasp. Eve's lids flutter open, just in time to heed the pressure and feel Savian's spell extinguish the magic in her blood, robbing it of its color. Robbing her of her gift.

Please no. Inch by inch, the hairline cracks widen, howling with the shrill torment of a dying girl and rending glass. She desperately searches for Ezzo, her lips moving but making no sound, her last words passing between them in a silence only the two of them understand. A stolen goodbye.

Then with a sickening crack, clink, crunch, shatter, Eve bursts into a thousand pieces, leaving nothing behind but a memory and a jagged pile of emerald shards. Five anguished screams in a burned-out theater house.

"Idiot girl." Savian's epithet is a break to the heart, though he no longer needs to worry about keeping the rest of us docile. There's no fight left in me or Novi anymore, nothing but a shocked sickness gripping Lyria, and an excruciating agony escaping Ezzo's mouth.

With one spell, Savian taught us the true cost of insurrection.

He crushed our rebellion to dust.

"You have until the afternoon bell to learn how to do this without her, so I suggest you get to work," he says, as though Eve's death is nothing more than an inconvenience. A new logistical nightmare for us to plan around. That's when I know for certain we've lost. That Savian will stop at nothing until we place the siphon in his hand. He'll push, and taunt, and beat, and torture, hold a flame to our lives until we blister and burn to ash.

Until we shatter.

CHAPTER

Twenty-five

I lose track of how long we stay there, draped in ink and shadow, the somber silence broken only by the gut-wrenching sound of Ezzo's grief.

Because Eve is dead. I hug my knees tighter to my chest, rocking back and forth on the soot-covered floor of the theater house. Unlike Magdalena's shards, Eve's remains have lingered, her splinters glittering like broken emeralds in the early morning light. And though I *know* there was nothing we could do to save her—that if the Gray hadn't shattered her to pieces, Savian's spell would have continued to leach her blood of color until the magic stilled her heart—I can't help but feel like it didn't need to end this way.

It didn't need to end at all. My guilt is a creature I can see, and smell, and touch, a poison that turns my limbs heavy. Because *I* did this. I tipped our hand to Chase and he played those cards against me, told Savian every last secret I'd shared in order to bolster his grip on our lives.

He *used* me. Toyed with my emotions and beat me at my own game. And Gods, he did it so damn well I missed all the signs of his deception. How the only truths he ever let slip were the ones I couldn't turn against him. How he saved his gentle affirmations for when we were safely removed from the others, and urged me to keep our illicit coupling confined to the deepest depths of the dark. How every time I *tricked* him into confiding his secrets, he used the opportunity to poke at mine.

This game has to go both ways.

Well, it did go both ways. Right up until Chase won, and I lost, but it was Eve who paid the price for my naivety. And now the rest of them will suffer because I placed my trust in the wrong Hue.

"I know this isn't the best time"—so of course—*of fucking course*— that Hue is the first to speak—"but we should probably start—"

"*You* shouldn't do anything." Though Novi's hiss is whisper quiet, it reverberates through the theater house with enough malice to ignite a flame, her hands shaking so hard the accompanying signs falter. "*You* have done more than enough, and if I were in your position, I'd get the hells out of here before you lose the ability to breathe." Though she aims her anger at him, the words could just as soon apply to me. Every bit as relevant and deserved.

"You heard Savian; we only have a few hours left to amend our plan." Chase forges on despite the threat. "We can't afford to wait."

"You can afford to *care*." In the space between blinks, Novi speeds closed the gap between them. "You can afford to show some compassion and give us a minute to deal with the fact that your keeper just killed our friend." She spits the words in his face. "Eve was a person, Cassiel. Not a Gray gift for you to exploit, or a disposable means to an end. So yes, you can afford to wait. You can do us all a godsdamned favor, go back to the monastery, and fucking *wait*."

For a long moment, Chase looks to be on the cusp of arguing, his whole body vibrating with tension, the muscles in his jaw twitching wild. But maybe his *compassion* ultimately gets the better of him— or maybe it's the ferocity in Novi's eyes—because without another word, he blinks out of the shadows, leaving me to wish that I could shed my shield and do the same.

"Don't even think about it," Novi warns, as though reading my mind. Then with a terse apology, she bids Lyria to go, as well, preferring that only Ezzo remain to help her deal with my crime.

That's when he finally comes alive.

"How could you tell him?" For the second time in as many bells, a hand wraps around my throat, lifting me clean off the ground. "How could you be so—"

"Ez."

At Novi's insistence, he slackens his grip, sending me sputtering back to the floorboards.

"I'm sorry," I say between ragged breaths. "I didn't mean for this to happen. I thought Chase was—I was so sure he was on our side."

"Sure enough to *gamble* her life on?" Ezzo's pain echoes around the theater in vicious waves, the depth of the loss he's suffered flaying his composure raw. For all that Novi and I loved Eve, Ezzo was *in* love with her, and that's been true for longer than I can bear to admit. *The two Es*, Chase had called them. Inseparable right up until the moment my recklessness tore them apart.

"I'm so sorry," I say again, staggering back to my feet. "I just . . . I didn't know how he'd react if we surprised him, and I . . . I didn't want him becoming collateral damage."

So in his place, we lost Eve, our best line of defense against the shadows.

The kindest—most resilient—Hue any of us had ever met.

"By my colors, Cem, when I asked you to get close to him, I didn't mean for you to do *this*." Novi rakes both hands through her hair, her tone sharpening in pitch. "Please tell me this wasn't payback." The look she fixes me could sink a ship. "Tell me you didn't run to that Gold's bed to punish me for Lyria."

"I didn't *run to his bed* at all." I bristle, though in reality, that's exactly what I did; it's just that Chase stopped short of taking advantage. His act was better served by feigning chivalry, pushing me away so that he could lure me back in. Manipulate my feelings.

I'd rather wait a couple more days than have him decide you're a problem.

Gods. I suppose I should be grateful he drew the line at tricking me into sex.

"I went to Chase because I was upset," I say, swallowing the indignation down swift. "But I would never—*never*—"

"You'd never what, Cemmy?" Ezzo's quick to cut in. "Put us in danger? *Lie*? Like you've been lying to us about Magdalena?"

"I—" The objection dies in my throat, the need to defend myself stuttering itself silent. Because this time, I have nothing to offer them in way of an explanation. No possible excuse that could justify the choice I made out of fear. "I thought you would hate me," I whisper, going with the truth, instead. "I came so close to telling you so many times, but I—I didn't know where to start."

"And yet you told *him*." The hurt in Novi's face is my most egregious of sins. "You told a complete stranger the very thing I've been begging you to tell me for a *year*." It doesn't take her long to draw a line between the *whens* of my secret and the *whys* that drove us apart. "You broke my heart, Cemmy," she continues, the intensity of her pain searing a hole through my skin. "It damn near killed me to let you go, but since the four of us were a *family*, we got through it anyway. And we would have gotten through this, too, if only you'd trusted that we loved you enough to always—*always*—give you the benefit of the doubt."

I don't miss the way she relegates that assertion to the forgotten tense.

"The Gray was a risk we all took, Cemmy," she says, placing a steadying hand to Ezzo's arm. "We would have forgiven you for what happened to Lena. We would have *understood*. And if you'd only come to us first, we could have helped you find a safer way to get Cassiel out of the theater house, if you felt that strongly about it. We didn't need to lose Eve."

"I'm sorry." That useless word keeps slipping off my tongue, frail and empty. Novi's right: it wasn't just my fear that caused this, it was my lack of belief. In them. In us. In the bond we've forged through fire over the last seven years. Because, *Gods*, of course they wouldn't have blamed me for Magdalena; now that I've heard her speak that truth aloud, I can see every one of my mistakes. The exact moment at which I knocked our lives into a different orbit. I was so afraid of losing them, I forgot that love isn't a blaze you feed by only kindling your strengths. It demands your insecurities, too. It demands faith.

"Yeah, well, so are we," Novi says, and the snap in her voice tells me that this time, it's different. I've broken us for real.

She and Ezzo don't look at me as they gather up the remnants of Eve. They don't allow me to join in their mourning, and when Ezzo dissolves into another bout of heartrending sobs, Novi blinks him out of the Gray so that he can grieve her in peace, without my presence overhanging his sorrow.

Without any more of my too-late apologies to remind them of my betrayal.

"Cemmy?" My name echoes through the theater a short while after they disappear, uttered by the very last person I'd ever choose to see again.

"Don't you ever do as you're told?" I round on Chase with a violence in my gut and my hands clenched into tight fists. "Or is taking a victory lap part of your perverse game?"

"I had to make sure they didn't hurt you," he says, eyes skirting the grime at his feet.

Right. I scoff at the self-serving nature of his concern. An Indigo told his master that he'd need a Cobalt, an Amethyst, and a Bronze—not an Emerald or a Sapphire spare; the thought is comical in the most absurdly grotesque way. He gets to kill one of my friends but nothing changes because he happened to kill the *wrong* friend—a Hue that wasn't explicitly predestined. He gets to pretend we can still do this.

"That *they* didn't hurt me?" I gape at him. "They're not the ones who lied to me, Cassiel. They're not the ones responsible for killing Eve. *You are.*" Those last two words hang between us, dripping with my resent.

"Cemmy, I'm so—"

"Don't you dare tell me you're sorry." I cut him off before he can insult me with that toothless, two syllable refrain.

Of this, Chase doesn't get to absolve himself with *sorry*.

There aren't enough *sorry*s in either world to undo what he did.

"How could you tell him about Lena?" I seethe. "How could you take the one thing I shared in confidence, and let Savian use it to—"

Create a rift. The answer hits me unbidden, pulling Chase's cruel intentions into sharp relief.

If I don't have them, then I'm dependent on him.

It's no longer four against one, it's two against three.

The odds are better stacked in his favor.

Even more so now that he's robbed them of Eve.

"Cemmy, I *didn't* tell Savian about Lena," Chase says, taking a hesitant step towards me. "I swear I have no idea how he found out."

"*Liar,*" I hiss, raising both hands between us like a shield. "We were alone when I told you that story; there is no other way for him to know unless you did." No other place for him to have heard it. Because unlike the night we spent in my apartment, we didn't have this conversation in the Gray, we had it in the physical realm. At the top of a rickety observatory where Savian couldn't have gone unnoticed. "But here's what I really don't get, *Cassiel.* I've seen the way you look at Savian; I've heard the way you talk about him." And if that truly was all an act, then boy is he the best actor that's ever lived. "The man had to meld a scry to your chest just to keep you in line. You don't like doing his bidding any more than we do, and *I gave you an out.* Why didn't you take it?"

"I already told you why." Chase's exhale is bone-deep. "Savian may be a monster, but he's right to want to get the siphon back from the Church. Or did you forget what's at stake here, *Cemilla*? We're talking about the end of all magic. If that happens, *every* Shade dies."

Oh, for the love of blood color . . . "I was never going to let that happen!" I explode. "I was going to talk the others into running the lift regardless—I just needed you to prove you could be trusted first!"

"Then maybe you should have trusted *me*!" Chase reels back as though I'd struck him, as though he's suddenly realized how narrowly our ships had crossed. "You could have told me you'd made that decision—you could have warned me this was only about Savian!"

"I *did* warn you." I grit through my teeth. "I told you nothing about the plan would change!"

"Our plan? Or the plan you and your friends have been concocting behind my back?" If looks could kill, the one Chase levels me now would start a massacre. "I'm not an idiot, Cemmy. I know they've been searching for a way out of this since day one. You have, too—so don't pretend these misgivings were all in my head. Savian's threat was the only thing keeping you in line; without it, you could have gone straight to the Council, and that wasn't a risk I was willing to take."

"Then I guess I'm not the only one who's been pretending." Understanding cleaves my chest like an axe, the collision of our lies spurting bloody.

If I had told him what I was planning, would he have still decided to whisper his treachery in Savian's ear?

If he had been honest with us from the beginning, would we have still refused to help him steal the siphon without a blade pressed to our skin?

If we had trusted each other—allowed ourselves to embrace the possibility that the feelings stirring between us were real, not just part of some deceitful game—would Eve have still lost her life to our betrayals?

I suppose it doesn't much matter now, because those harmful decisions can never be unmade. And because—when given the chance—Chase didn't just choose to betray me; he chose to *destroy* me. Then he chose to lie about it, cling to the preposterous assertion that he didn't divulge my secret and lay the blame for Eve's shattering back at my feet.

He made damn sure I could never trust him again.

"I hope you rot in the deepest of hells, Cassiel." My wish thunders around the theater house with the wicked might of a spell, vengeful and proud.

"Cemmy, wait—" He makes to follow me as I break towards the door. "Please, just let me explain—"

But I'm not interested in his explanations. Or any more half-truths. Or anything else he has to say.

"Save it for the next Bronze whose life you wreck," I spit, turning heel to meet the plea in his eyes. "You may have backed us into a corner, but if we somehow manage to survive this lunacy without Eve, then you'd better disappear the moment we leave the Dominion," I tell him, spelling my threat clear. "Because if you don't, then I swear to all three Gods, Cassiel, I'll kill you myself."

CHAPTER

Twenty-six

We regroup at the monastery in near silence, rearranging the broken fragments of our plan around the absence of Eve. When he speaks, Ezzo's voice is a grunt of anger, Novi's is devoid of warmth, and Lyria's signs come fast and clipped.

Other than Chase, none of us truly believe that we can best the Commander's defenses without her. Other than Chase, none of us is truly expecting to escape the Dominion in one piece. For while we may have found a way to survive the portals, Eve's gift was the safety net we were counting on to fortify our In-Betweens, keep us from shattering in case of unexpected trouble—which we're almost certain to meet. Whether an Indigo predicted it or not. But hells, maybe if we're lucky, we'll manage to destroy the siphon before either Rhodes or the shadows are able to succeed, stop the Gray from collapsing, rob the Church of its win. Rob it of its genocide. So I guess I should be happy that both Chase and I got what we wanted. Though given the circumstances, happiness isn't what I'm inclined to feel.

By the midday bell, we're as prepped and ready as we're ever likely to be, too anxious to linger, too wounded to spend our remaining hours in the company of each other's grief. Or at least, I don't see fit to inflict myself on the others. Nor do I have any intention of squandering my last afternoon of life with the Gold responsible for our rift. So I leave the monastery, choosing instead to do the one thing I should have done back when Mom first got sick.

I sell Dad's ring.

And though I feel naked without it—and guilty, as though I've just committed another unforgivable sin—the diamond-laid band fetches enough coin to ensure that when I'm gone, Mom will want for nothing. I settle our account at the apothecary, purchase an ample supply of the Green label tincture, then pay Madam Berska enough rent upfront to see out the year. That should allow Mom to take care of the rest, and if the worst does happen and I don't come home, the note I arrange to have delivered a week from now will make her believe that I've left Isitar to find my own way. She can imagine a life for me outside the city. A life beyond these hate-filled walls and the Church's mission to eradicate us from their wake. And with no illegal daughter to keep from the Council's trackers, she'll have no reason not to seek the cure she needs from a full-blooded Shade.

She'll finally have that option.

It's not a perfect solution—dying rarely ever is—but neither is condemning her to a life of staring at the door, day after night after day, wondering when I might return. Because deep down, I know she had no intention of following through on her threat, that she would have welcomed me home the moment her anger had calmed enough to put the fight behind us and resume our fragile state of affairs.

Me, eking out a living in the Gray.

Her, pretending I don't pay our bills in the most criminal of ways.

Madam Berska, hammering on the door in search of the rent.

Hardly the life I wanted a few days ago, but with hindsight comes perspective, and an appreciation for all things lost to the fates. A few days ago, I worried only about losing Mom and the leaky roof over our heads. I bristled at her stubborn refusal to embrace my magic, swore that I'd know better than to behave in that same irrational way. I never imagined it would be my own shortsighted stupidity that cost me everything in the end. My own cowardly lies.

By the time the fourth bell echoes through Isitar, the last of my errands are run and the salt scrubbed clean from my face. I cross the city slowly, weaving through the crowds already amassed for the festivities that'll surge through the rings. Even in the faithless quarter, the Church's holiest of days casts a long shadow, enticing those who have yet to reform out of their homes and into the clerics' reach. The Aralagios toss coins to the gathered masses. They lavish them with wine, and pretty words, and freshly brewed hate, woo them with the promise of a world where they never have to feel inferior. No Shades means no power imbalance. Nothing to covet. No authority they cannot claim. And with the price of spells fast rising beyond what the average typic can pay, that prospect grows more and more attractive with each cleansing moon parade. For while a king might inspire adoration, it'll be jealousy that ultimately topples his reign. The second magic became the stuff of bitter envy, the Council started digging its own grave.

I pull my yellow cloak tight around me, sinking deeper into the hood as the Dominion's arched crown of spires appears at the mouth of the procession. During the festivities, it's customary for the crowd to wear color, the masses dressing for every prong of the rainbow the Church seeks to erase, a literal embodiment of the evil they're vowing to reject. To that end, it's only the clergy dressed in black today, a menacing throng of wraiths in crisp-pressed robes with crimson rosaries around their necks.

This early in the day, the celebrations remain peaceful, but in a few hours—once the wine has lowered inhibitions and the sky has darkened enough to obscure intent—the tensions building between the quarters will rapidly turn violent. Last year, it took efforts from both the Council and the Church to keep the burgeoning riots at bay, but given that a riot is what the Governor wants, tonight's forecast is wont to prove bloody. And if we don't rid him of the siphon, it's wont to prove deadly, as well.

I reach the square that rims the Dominion a few minutes ahead of the fifth bell, slipping out of the crowd to meet the others down one of the adjacent alleys. Despite the mild autumn breeze, a frost instantly chills the air between us, the ghost of all those things I've not yet found the words to say. If we make it through this alive, perhaps they'll give me the chance to find them, but until then, I keep my eyes down and my apologies to myself. I'm not owed their forgiveness any more than they deserved to lose my faith. I've done nothing to earn it.

"We go in, we get the siphon, and if, by some miracle, we get out, then we go our separate ways." Though Novi's looking at Chase, I get the impression that her words—and the harsh edge to her accompanying signs—are meant for me, a clear and resolute missive that there's no hope for reconciliation.

Okay, so perhaps not.

I guess that's just the reality I have to live with.

"Don't worry, I won't be sticking around." Chase's reply sends a second wave of needles lancing across my skin. It shouldn't hurt to hear that he means to do exactly as I bid him; I'm the one who ordered him away, after all. I threatened him with death.

And yet . . .

No. No "as yet". Get it the fuck together. I shake the errant thought from my head. This is just my fear my *loneliness*—talking, and Chase is the very reason I've lost all my friends, one of them forever.

There'll be no putting that behind us.

"Good. Then let's get this over with."

As the clock tower chimes with the fifth bell, we all raise our hoods, our colored cloaks mingling to form a rainbow. Since Rhodes has a contingent of rogues patrolling the Gray, we'll be approaching the Dominion in the physical realm, using the dense pack of the crowd to disguise our movements as we near the wrought-iron fence.

A gold smoke curls above the procession, the acrid scent escaping the clerics' thuribles stinging my nose. Spice, sandalwood, and sulfur—along with flecks of the pigment that marks the faithful as blessed. Those irksome flecks will linger in the streets for weeks after the parade, the wind scattering them around the city like a foul omen that threatens to devour Isitar whole.

Maybe today it will.

We weave through the press of bodies as discreetly as we can, staying within sight of each other even as we move alone. A group of five cloaks pushing against the direction of the festivities would draw too much attention, and we can't risk alerting the guards to our presence outside the gate. If they spot us, we're finished. This incursion will be over before it ever begins.

Up close, the Dominion is a stern goliath, an imposing monstrosity of gray brick and stained glass that was no doubt erected with magic, though—naturally—the Church claims it to be a feat of the Gods.

The Gods sure do lack subtlety. I've always hated this spiteful building, with its sweeping perron, and its menacing dart of gold spires, and the enormous, stone-carved entry arch that's inlaid with crimson marble and ornate molds. There must be a thousand-odd windows encircling the dozen floors, all depicting a different facet of Church doctrine. The war of the Gods; the unification of the pantheon; the rise of the shadows; the fall; every dark myth the clergy use to peddle their reform.

"Obnoxious, isn't it?" Lyria signs as I sidle up to her in the crowd.

"Yeah." I knock my fist twice in agreement. *And not the least bit impenetrable.* The very definition of a *cursed palace.* On the opposite side of the gate, I see Chase rendezvous with Novi, their cloaks only distinguishable thanks to the distinct fold we pressed into our hoods.

Everyone ready? Ezzo's question vibrates my scry, relieving one of the worries that's been gnawing at my nerves. With the grief barely a few hours old, I wasn't sure he'd still care enough to complete his part in today's task, or worse—that with Eve gone, he'd welcome the danger a little *too much.* That the moment he was left to his own devices, he'd try to follow her into the black.

I needn't have worried.

Because while Ezzo has always been Eve's, he's always been ours, too. And though he currently bears no love for me, there's no version of this story where he'd turn his back on Lyria or Novi. Hells, there's no version of this story where he'd turn his back on an entire *world.* Or on every other Shade and Hue who would lose their life if the Gray collapses and the color in their veins runs dry. That's just not who he is.

Ready. We all send at the same time, giving him the go-ahead to enact the plan Eve demonstrated with a grin and her pots of paint.

Then a moment later, a shrill howl detonates the air, our defiant show of glamour raining magic over the parade.

Go. The second the spell erupts we blink into the Gray, trusting the commotion to mask the brazenness of our blasphemy. Light turns to shadow and color to smoke, the masses to a bright swarm of echoes. Make that a *panicked* swarm of echoes; even in the dull silence of the Gray, their flare of fear is apparent. Plenty distracting enough to draw the full-bloods away.

So far so good. Novi and Chase are the first to cross through the bars, their lack of physicality allowing them easy access to the plaza. They're already speeding towards the Dominion by the time Lyria's efforts convince the shadows to grant me passage, as well, and by the time we've wisped through the iron, Novi's returned to speed the two of us across the cobbles and up the oversized staircase.

From phase to door, the entire run takes about fifteen seconds.

"Is anyone else feeling that?" The moment she slams us to a halt, I stagger backward, the blazing sear of the wards setting a flame to my bones. How many rogues would it have taken to erect a shield this powerful? How many Shades would have had to conspire against the Council? How much hypocrisy truly lives at the heart of this wretched Church?

"Get it together, Cemmy." Novi's in no mood to indulge my weakness. "This is hardly the first time you've experienced my gift."

"No, I don't mean your speed—I mean the wards," I clarify. "Gods, are you not—do none of you feel that?"

"You shouldn't be feeling it, either." When Chase looks at me, it's not irritation in his eyes, it's concern. "Is it different to what you felt in the Governor's safe?"

"I mean, it's kind of the same, I guess, but much . . . hotter. More noticeably there." As though the magic is asserting its might in warning.

"Could it be because we're in the Gray this time?" Lyria's brow furrows with the question. *"Maybe your physicality is affecting the spell?"*

"Well, let's hope it doesn't affect it too much." I grit my teeth and turn my attention back to the triple-width wood door. Ezzo's glamour will only keep the Shades on watch distracted another minute or two, tops, and we need to be inside by the time they resume their vigil. We have to keep moving.

"The shadows don't seem to think it's a problem, at least," Lyria signs. *"They've cleared your way."*

"Then let's take the win while we still can." With a roll of her shoulders, Novi vanishes through the door, making the leap from which there might be no returning. Not without the siphon.

Okay.

So we're doing this.

"Here's to winning." I steel my nerves as Lyria follows suit, my fingers grazing along the spell's periphery. Like with the hidden partition in the Governor's safe, I don't get the sense that it'll try to block me; it's more like a burning chafe of friction than an impenetrable seal, as though the wards have grown wise to my presence, but not declared me a threat.

And here goes nothing . . .

"No, wait—" Chase grabs for my arm. "Where's your ring, Cemmy?" His voice is pure panic. "You can't breach the wards without your—"

But it's too late.

I've already forced my weight through the blistering wall of power, and while the shadows seem content to let me pass without a fight, the magic says different.

The Dominion alarms begin to blare.

CHAPTER Twenty-seven

Even in the Gray, the wails are earsplitting, tearing through the shadows like the echo of a banshee's scream.

"Inside—*now*." Chase wisps me through the door, into the mouth of the Dominion where the Commander's rogues can't follow.

"I don't understand, what did we do wrong?" I ask as we join Novi and Lyria on the other side. The alarms are designed to warn against full-blooded Shades, not halves. There's not enough magic in our blood to trigger them—or at least, there shouldn't be. If there was, the wards would have barred us from entering.

"Your ring, Cemmy," Chase barks again, the rage in his voice twisted with fear. "Where the hells is your ring?"

"Gods, I sold it, okay?" I paw at the empty space on my finger. At the pale line that marks where the last remaining piece of my dad used to be.

"You *sold* your totem?"

"No . . . I sold my ring. I've never had a totem."

"Yes, you did—they're one and the same, remember? We talked about it!" Chase looks damn near ready to combust. "You said your mom's convinced it's the only magic worth keeping."

Colors help me. "She was being sentimental!" I hiss. "There was never any actual magic in that ring. It was a myth—a story. Her way of keeping my dad's memory alive."

"No, it was her way of keeping *you* alive!" He claws at his hair as if possessed. "And quite frankly, I'm amazed she managed it given how little you know about what you are." His words are a slap to the face, a callous missive that staggers me silent.

"Hey, idiot Gold—" Novi cuts between us, putting an end to the exclusionary argument we've been having. "Now's not the best time to be playing it cryptic, so either tell us what Cemmy's ring has to do with anything, or take that superior intellect of yours and shove it up your—"

"She's a *Bronze*," he grits the term with enough scorn to make the accompanying sign feel like an obscenity. "That's the atypical dilution of Orange magic; the less stable presentation that comes with a toll. In Cemmy's case, an aura that makes her visible to other Shades. Vulnerable to warding spells unless—"

"Counteracted by a totem." My stomach drops to my knees. Just like Versallis maintained in his writings. "So what I saw in that journal you stole . . . it was all true?"

"Everything in that journal is true." Chase's eyes bulge at the question. "I thought you understood that."

"How could I have possibly understood that?" I could just kill him—*I could kill him, I could kill him—I might.* It's not like he bothered to explain its significance before he collapsed on my bed, drunk on power, or when he plucked the book out of my hand and refused to give me a straight answer about it when I asked. So of course I dismissed that particular claim as mistaken. Why wouldn't I when, thanks to Mom, I'd never experienced the effects.

He made this ring to conceal your magic. No matter what happens, it must remain with you. All at once, her vehement obsession makes sense. The physical toll of my gift is the reason she had the band resized every year, and why she wouldn't let me sell it even at the cost of her life. Why she was so afraid of my color.

Mom escaped the Council's wrath only to bear a child they could track in her stead. But in her bid to protect me—from them, from the truth, from the Gray—she made it that much harder for me to protect myself.

"Would the two of you please stop speaking in *vague*?" With the alarms still blaring, Novi's impatience is fast turning mean. "What are you saying here, Cassiel? That Cemmy's ring was a totem?"

"Not the ring, no—the diamonds in it." His reply is both hostile and condescending. "It's the only substance that can obscure a Shade's visible trace."

Well, that certainly explains why Savian had a pair embedded in his ears.

What it doesn't explain is why his diamonds rendered him invisible to Ezzo when mine only served to diminish my trail. But now that we've tipped our hand to the Commander, that particular curiosity is going to have to wait.

"So what does that mean for us?" Lyria waves to get our attention. *"Do we run, or do we still make the lift?"*

"Running isn't an option—we need to stop wasting time," Chase mutters, less to us than to himself, as though annoyed he got sucked into this conversation. "Rhodes might know there's been a breach, but with the wards up, he can't send his Shades in to investigate, and even if he was willing to bring that spell down, there's no way he has enough rogues to do it right away. We have some rope to play with," he says and signs, talking through the plan as it pulls together in his head. "As long as we stay in the Gray until we reach the portals, he'll have no way of intercepting us. We just need to go fast enough to beat his enforcers there." The moment those last few words leave his mouth, Chase is urging us to move again, to ignore the incriminating wail of the wards, and the gathering army of echoes, and the danger which has all but ensured that this mission will be one-way.

It was always going to be one-way, *Cemmy*. My hand seeks the comfort of the knife he told me to bring. And as much as I hate to admit it, his logic is sound. There's no real reason our plan can't adapt to the presence of Rhodes's men.

"Quickly." Chase leads us through the flecked marble maze with a series of snaps and crudely signed gestures, the alarms lending a menacing note to his haste. Around us, the Dominion yawns as wide as the Infinite Ocean, draped in an obscene splendor that transcends the Gray's muted palette of slate. Twelve double-height floors. Dozens of winding stairways. Hundreds of lavishly appointed doors encircling the atrium's edge. There are over a thousand rooms in this exquisite labyrinth, but thanks to the directions Chase's spell absorbed—we know exactly how to reach the spire at its centermost crest.

Everywhere she can, Novi speeds us through the corridors in pairs, and at every obstacle we encounter, Lyria bargains with the shadows to take my physicality away. We run, we wisp, we climb, we do it over, until finally—with screaming lungs and sweat-soaked temples—we reach the X on the map Chase is following in his head.

"You're sure this is it?" Novi braces her arms against her knees, her breaths gasping fast and heavy.

"Even if I weren't, the echoes would confirm it." He nods, pointing to the excess of fireflies buzzing around the door.

Six stationary guards when the rest of this floor doesn't call for any.

Six stationary guards who haven't moved an inch despite the shrieking disruption to their day.

"Can the shadows get me through this one?" I ask Lyria, hoping to all three Gods that the answer is yes. Six guards tells me this door is never left unprotected. That no scale of distraction is likely to lure the entire squadron away. If the shadows can't bend the wood around me, I'll have to pick the lock the old-fashioned way. Visibly turn the handle. And if I do that, well . . . I don't like our odds of success.

"This one—yes." Lyria's signs appear hesitant. *"But after that, we're on our own. They call the magic beyond this threshold . . . wicked. Unholy. They want us to promise we'll kill the drain."*

"That's the plan," I assure the ether, even as the words bleed Chase pale.

"Cemmy—wait." His request is a bated whisper in my ear, a circle of pressure around my wrist to stop me following her and Novi through the door. "I need you to do something for me," he says, keeping his voice low.

"Well, that's too bad." I bristle, breaking out of his grip. "Because I don't do favors for lying Hues who kill my friends."

"Cemmy, please." Chase flinches. "I wouldn't ask if it weren't important." The desperation in his eyes is a weapon, sharp and honed. Silver and effective.

Gods. "What do you want, Cassiel?"

"Once you're through the portals, wait for me and Novi to arrive before you go into that cell," he says. "We all go in together."

"I don't suppose you're going to tell me why?" My answering sigh is a hiss.

"No. But if you do this for me, I'll keep my promise to you." Chase flashes his irises green. "I have the magic."

"You seriously expect me to believe Savian still let you take his magic?" I must strike him as the stupidest half Shade to ever walk the earth. That's probably another glamour he's showing me. Another manipulation designed to further his cause. Whatever that might be.

"Savian's trust came at the cost of yours, but once I had it, he agreed to let me make the drain." With a skim of his thumb, Chase heals the cut I bit through my lip, leaving the skin tingling with the magic. The *Green* magic. Not a glamour in Red. "So—do we have a deal?"

"I guess you'll find out." I push past him, refusing to sate my hunger on a whim. He's hardly asking me for much here, but just because I'm not seeing the downside doesn't mean one doesn't exist, and I'll be damned if I give him what he wants too easily. I'd rather leave him to squirm.

"You two sure took your time," Novi clips as we both wisp through the door, crossing into the final passageway that stands between us and the siphon.

"The echoes shifted. We waited to see if they would come inside." The lie slips like butter off Chase's tongue. It's a good one, too. A relevant concern. For while the Gray may have shielded us this far, the portals will be driving us in and out of the physical realm, into full view of any enforcer who ventures past the wood. And though they can't risk triggering the portals themselves, their weapons face no such constraint. A crossbow can kill a Hue as readily as any blade.

"Then it's a good thing you're staying behind to watch our backs." Novi reaches for my hand, prompting me to lace the other around Lyria's and form the prophesied chain of Cobalt, Amethyst, and Bronze. "If you want in that cell, you'll keep them away."

"How do I know you won't just leave me here?" Chase asks, returning her suspicion with a doubt of his own.

"It's called trust, Cassiel. Some of us don't squander it." And with that, Novi puts an end to his grumbling by blinking me and Lyria out of the Gray.

Color floods my senses, the corridor exploding into bright relief, a tapestry of Church-approved crimsons blooming red across the walls. Had we not tricked the Commander into telling us about the portals, we might never have known just how deadly this harmless-looking passageway could prove. The magic is entirely invisible, the spell giving off no sound, no smell, and no shimmer. A nasty surprise for any thief who dares to try and breach the spire. A death sentence for any unsuspecting typic or half.

"You ready, Cem?" Novi asks, careful to ensure that Lyria can read her lips.

"Yes." I infuse the word with a confidence I don't yet feel. Anchoring to another Hue felt so easy when I was wrapped in the heady thrall of Chase's arms, but in the harsh light of day—staring down the chasm his betrayal forged between us—my certainty turns brittle.

I am in between Novi and Lyria. I start chanting the words long before she shuffles our feet forward, their edges melding to form a whispered shield in my mind. Useless in the real world, but I can feel the magic bubbling beneath my skin, standing by to project at a moment's notice.

Which is all the notice I get.

I am in between Novi and Lyria.

One second we're inching across the marble tiles, then the next, I'm hurtling through a storm of smoke and ink, speeding through a room that Novi's gift blurs to shadows.

"So . . . that was unpleasant." She exhales as the portal spits us out of the Gray, returning us to the deadly corridor.

"I'd say." I lean an arm against the wall for support. "What just happened?" Though we've only moved a few steps away from the door, my insides feel as though they've been thrust through a metal grate, my tongue stinging with the taste of iron.

"It worked." Lyria's incredulity is written into every line of her face. *"We didn't shatter—or trigger the arrows."*

"Not yet, at least." Novi doesn't share her relief. "A ballroom," she mutters under her breath. "The first portal leads to a ballroom." Which she'll have to remember if she's to turn around and retrieve Chase, or else she won't be able to anchor her own In-Betweens on the trip back. An added risk she shouldn't have to take. That she *wouldn't* have to take if we still had Eve, or if Chase wasn't so stubbornly adamant about joining us in the cell.

I have to be there in case you need my magic.

Given the desperate bribe he just offered me, I'm beginning to think that he's expecting we will. *But why?* I'm forced to push the question aside as Novi resumes our campaign. *I am in between her and Lyria.* The second portal sucks us from the corridor, depositing us in a library, I think, though Novi's speed makes it almost impossible to tell. The third also rushes past too quickly, and by the fourth, I've stopped trying to guess altogether, concentrating on nothing but the escalating toll of the spell. My shield ripples, then retracts, then recasts, and remakes, my eyes blurring with the strain of the magic.

I am in between Novi and Lyria.

And my power is a downpour.

A tidal wave.

A torrent of floods during the monsoon rains.

It's the dam that breaks before the waters drown the village.

"You can let go now, Cemmy." Novi's whisper thunders through my brain, her fingers straining against my too tight grip.

Fuck. "Sorry." I quickly pull away as the world sharpens back into focus, not with a swell of color, but with a glint of charcoal and black jade.

The Gray.

We're still in the Gray.

But with solid anchors around us and Chase staring on, resentful, from the corridor's opposite end.

We've reached the door that'll lead to the siphon.

"Final hurdle." Novi lets out a low whistle, appraising the imposing slab of ornately carved wood. "Just a lock and a spell to go."

Right. *Just.*

None of us mentions the way out yet, or how—with the alarms still blaring—it'll be a miracle if we're able to do more than *just* reach the siphon's cell. How our head start won't protect us forever.

"I guess that means we're up." I fish my picks out of my pocket and shoot Lyria a small nod, setting her loose on the shadows while I tackle the lock and Novi speeds back to collect Chase. The metal is a gentle comfort in my hands, a dance to which I memorized the steps a long time ago. And though the pins to this particular mechanism are complex and stiff with disuse, breaking into places I shouldn't be is the one thing I know how to do. In every world.

In this one, it only takes me a few seconds.

And . . . I'm . . . done. With a twist and a pop, the pins fall into place, the door unlocking with a satisfying click. "Any luck with the spell—?" My brief swell of confidence instantly deflates as I notice how grim and pallid Lyria's become. How unsteady. "What is it? What's wrong?" I check the corridor for echoes, scanning to ensure that nothing terrible has befallen Novi.

"No, it's not that, it's . . . before they gave me the incantation, the shadows made me promise to kill the siphon again." Lyria emphasizes the sign for *kill. "They said she drains everything in her wake. 'She', Cemmy."* Her hands stutter as they shake. "*They used the word 'she'.*"

As though it's a person. A violent shiver races down my neck, the blood in my veins frosting icy. "And you're sure you didn't misunderstand them? Or misinterpret?" I ask, though I fear I already know the answer.

"That's not how it works, remember?" Lyria confirms. *"Their language is revelatory; it doesn't allow me to mis-anything."*

Whereas Chase has been deliberately mis-everything. All at once, the game he's been playing crystals as it clears. Every detail he misrepresented, and intention I misconstrued. Every lie he told to make me misjudge him. *I just need you to trust that it's important, and that I'd never let him use the siphon to cause any more harm.*

Or at all, for that matter. I don't think Chase means to let Savian use the siphon at all.

I think he knew, from the beginning, that the siphon is a person.

I think he knew that we'd never agree to do the killing for him, and so he tried to keep the truth from us long enough to be the first to step into this room. To be the first to reach her.

Wait for me and Novi to arrive before you go into that cell.

This whole time, Chase has been setting up the classic misdirect. Keeping us too worried about Savian to see the bigger picture. The more immediate threat.

And he used me to do it. My nails gouge deep into the flesh at my thighs. Chase played his hand perfectly. He found a way to distance me from the others, bait me into doing his bidding, assure that—once again—if it came down to a choice, my decision would serve to benefit him.

If you do this for me, I'll keep my promise to you. I have the magic.

But what good is having magic if you don't use it to protect the ones you love? The last time I chose to help Chase, Eve's shards wound up scattered across a theater-house floor. I won't make that mistake again. Even if the rift between us can't be mended, I owe it to Novi and Ezzo to put my trust in them instead of some duplicitous Gold. They have *earned* my loyalty. And loyalty is the choice you make even when there's nothing to be gained in return.

"Stay here, okay?" I sign once Lyria has relayed the incantation that will get me through the door. A stolen glance down the corridor shows that Chase is still waiting for Novi, though I doubt she's more than a portal or two away from ending his impatient watch. If I go now, I'll have a couple of extra minutes to determine our new approach. That's time I don't mean to squander.

"Cemmy—no!" he yells as I make my decision known, breaking through the last of the Commander's defenses. "Please—don't! You have to wait!"

But I don't wait. And there are a dozen-odd portals standing between Chase and the outcome he wants.

Good. A jolt of triumph tingles my bones. He deserves a taste of how it feels to be helpless. To have his faith shattered and his certainty rocked.

To get betrayed.

Since the cell stands at the very top of the Dominion's centermost spire, it's a circular stairway that awaits me behind the door, narrow and unrelenting.

They just had to put her in the tallest one . . . I attack the stairs at a furious run, forcing myself to keep climbing up and up and up until my breaths feel like glass and every muscle in my legs is screaming. Until finally—an eternity of stone steps later, with an angry stitch stabbing both my sides—I reach the iron hatch that marks the entrance to the cell.

Don't you dare stop now, Cemmy. You can rest later. You've still got to beat Chase inside.

A girl's life depends on it.

And I have absolutely no intention of letting her die.

The moment I pry the metal open, I'm assaulted by a wave of malevolent power, a tempest that rushes past me like a wildfire that seeks to cinder the world. My shield shudders, the drain plucking at my magic, my marrow, my mettle for keeping the Gray whole. Whoever this girl is, I'm starting to see why the shadows want her gone—though there must be a better way to end this than murder. Some ritual or method for turning her power off. *There has to be.*

The hatch slams shut behind me as I step into the cell proper, fortifying my In-Between with every ounce of strength I've still got. Commander Rhodes wasn't exaggerating when he said this room was entirely encircled with iron. Both the floor and the walls are lined with it, hefty sheets secured in place by a litany of intractable bolts. The effect is oppressive, transforming what's already a small and unsettling cage into a claustrophobic metal box.

I almost don't see the siphon-girl at first, draped as she is in darkness and the tattered ruins of a black robe. She's chained against the back wall, her arms pinned wide like a butterfly, her face hidden behind the heavy folds of a deep hood.

"Hello?" My voice is such a broken whisper, I'm not surprised the figure doesn't respond. Since a typic can't withstand the shadows, it must be a Shade wasting away in this lightless prison, some inexplicable corruption of power, maybe, or perhaps a *deliberate* perversion designed to destroy the Gray for good. Could the Church have actually created this weapon? Or is it just a peculiarity of nature they're happy to exploit? Another casualty in their war against magic?

Gods, what did they do to you? As I edge closer to the withered husk of a girl, the full scope of the Church's malice becomes sickeningly apparent. There are dozens of mottled scars running the length of her arms, as though before they left her to rot here, her captors took a serrated knife to her skin, indulged their lust for cruelty. And though my proximity to her power is threatening to disrupt the fidelity of my shield, I can't help but reach out and try to wake her. To catch a glimpse of the victim they entrapped beneath the hood.

"I'm not here to hurt you," I say, though in truth, I don't know what I'm here to do anymore.

Savian wants this Shade alive.

Chase and the shadows want her dead.

I just want her to stop draining the Gray of its power.

"Please, if you can hear me, tell me your—" The question dies in my throat as the fabric slips from around the girl's face and her eyes snap open.

Round eyes. Wide and familiar—even when they're burned black to the edge.

A face that should be impossible.

No, no, no, no. Shock roots me to the spot, my ears ringing with the echo of a half shattered. Because that's no full-blood the Church has locked up in this iron coffin.

It's a Hue.

It's Magdalena.

CHAPTER

Twenty-eight

The shock fast gives way to pain as my hand grazes Magdalena's skin, the force of the drain growing overwhelming.

"Lena, please. You have to stop this," I say, clinging to my In-Between by the very tip of my strength.

I am in between logic and madness.

Truth and impossibility.

A deadly half Shade and the ghost of a friend.

How is it Magdalena's here, and alive, when she's in no state to keep from shattering?

How is it Magdalena's here at all when I *watched* her shatter last year?

Not watched—heard. The thought is both slippery and barbed. Because what I saw were the remnants of Magdalena the shadows left behind. Remnants that didn't linger like Eve's. That disappeared like a glamour.

Like a glamour with a capital Red.

No. That doesn't make any sense. And even if it did, the drain would keep me from knitting the disparate threads together. It's making it hard to think of anything but the pain.

"Please, Lena," I whisper. "I need you to stop."

But it's no use. Magdalena's eyes might be open, but there's no recognition in them, no awareness, no light. Right now, she's not the girl I used to know, she's the siphon. The weapon the Church invoked to unmake the shadows' world.

And I'm fighting her power as hard as I can. *I'm fighting it, I'm fighting it—except I can't.* There's not enough color flowing through my blood to sacrifice this much to the ether. That's what Chase told me, isn't it? That Hues can't survive the loss of their magic. Hells, trapped in this suffocating iron box, I won't even survive the loss of my shield. I can't phase my way out of it.

"Cemmy—move!" The voice screaming in my head is neither Magdalena's nor my own.

"I'm *trying*," I tell it, though my feet are stubbornly refusing to listen, as though they've turned from flesh, bone, and sinew to lead. The cell begins to blur like tar around the edges, a web of hairline cracks appearing at the crest of my spell. I can practically feel them widen as they multiply, and split, and fracture. As they race to claim my life with the inevitable tragedy of a shattered pane.

"Mags—*stop*!" A pair of arms suddenly wrap around my waist, relieving the pressure on my In-Between. "Go. Get as far from her as you can." It's Chase issuing the command in my ear, *his* hands pressed flat against my navel. *"Now."*

I stumble away from him, thinking of nothing but restabilizing my shield; forgetting, for a moment, the real reason he's here.

No. "You can't kill her!" I rush back into the drain. "I don't care if she's the siphon, Chase, you can't kill her. Please, that's—"

Mags. The realization staggers me still. *He called her Mags.*

He didn't just know she was a person; he knew her by name.

I read his intentions wrong.

"You can stop this, Mags. You can control it," he murmurs, leaning his forehead into hers, the gold of his hair perfectly complementing the warmth of her chestnut, like two sides of the same honeyed coin. Two kids running through a field of yarrow. "I'm going to help you get it under control."

That's when I finally see it: the resemblance that first struck me as a familiarity too improbable to conceive. It's not the color of their eyes that's similar, it's their depth. It's the crooked quirk of their smiles. The razor cut of their cheeks.

My sister used to love it here, Chase had told me before our misadventure on the cliff, a sentiment I took to mean that his sister was gone, so I never thought to ask the follow-up question: what color was your sister's magic?

If I had, then maybe I'd have put the truth together much earlier. Come to suspect the coincidence of likeness and Hue.

An Amber and a Gold.

Two different dilutions of the same Shade.

Siblings.

"But you have to help me, Mags." The storm in the air changes as Chase starts drawing her power into himself, slowly lessening the lethal wrench of the shadows. "You have to fight it."

"What in the nine hells—*Lena*?" Novi's voice echoes around the cell, her face aghast with a bewildered thunder. "How is that *Magdalena*?"

"She's his sister." Out loud, the words sound every bit as right as they do insane. "That's why he was so desperate to break in here."

"That doesn't explain how she's alive!"

No, it doesn't. It also doesn't explain how he knew where the Church had imprisoned her, or why Magdalena tricked me into thinking she'd shattered all over that spice merchant's floor.

It doesn't explain why Novi's bleeding.

"What happened?" I'm instantly at her side. The left of her shirt is soaked through with crimson, Lyria's hand pressed tight to her shoulder to stem the hemorrhaging wound. To keep her standing. Steady her In-Between.

"Rhodes knows we're here." Novi grits through the pain. "Bastard caught me with a bolt between portals."

Colors help me. If he's got weapons in that corridor, then she's lucky to have made it through with only one wound to the shoulder—and the rest of us will be lucky to make it out of the Dominion at all. Though with Chase still trying to coax Magdalena out of a spell-shocked stupor, it's hard to think past anything but the impossibilities unfolding inside this cell.

"Come on, Mags, come back to me." The amber glow building around them pulses as he battles to help her regain control. *My sister's ability allowed her to absorb power from the Gray,* he'd told me. *Taking magic from her . . . it wasn't like taking it from anyone else. It didn't hurt her.*

Quite the opposite, in fact; the longer Chase holds the connection, the more the light begins to return to Magdalena's eyes, her assault on the Gray growing weaker.

"Cassiel?" When she finally gasps, it's as if a switch has been flicked to sooth the shadows, immediately halting the drain.

"Mags," he breathes, and there's so much love in that exclamation, it seems ridiculous that I ever thought he was racing in here to kill.

"Please tell me you found me in time." The chains holding her to the iron rattle as she panics against their grip. "Please tell me I didn't—"

"You *didn't,*" he assures her. "But we're still a long way off from escaping the Church. Cemmy—" His attention snaps abruptly back to me. "Get her free of these cuffs."

"I don't think so." Novi's good arm shoots out to keep me in place. "Not before you tell us what the fuck is going on."

"Cassiel . . . what did you do?" The second she spots us, Magdalena turns an even sicker shade of green. "Why are they—? They shouldn't be here."

I interpret her words for Lyria before offering up a complaint of my own. "That's a little rich coming from a dead girl." The charge rings harsher than I intend, cold and seething with anger. I've spent the last year terrified of the Gray on account of believing I'd killed her; I lied to my friends to hide the shame of it; lost Novi because of it, as well as the only family of Hues I'm ever likely to know. Yet here she is—a prisoner, sure—but perfectly alive.

"We don't have time for questions right now," Chase insists, though I can tell by the way his eyes dart between us and his sister that he's suddenly nursing a few of his own. That he's just realized the name for which *Lena* was short. Guessed at our shared connection. "I can explain everything once we're out."

"Awfully bold of you to assume we'll actually be *getting* out," Novi says, signing her derision one-handed. "Rhodes already has us surrounded, and we're currently in the only room in the Dominion his enforcers can't reach. So you can either spend five minutes explaining how *this* happened"—she points to Magdalena—"or you can spend it figuring out how to beat a lock you can't pick. Choice is yours."

"It's okay, Cassiel." Magdalena's voice takes on a big sisterly tone. "They deserve to understand."

"Mags . . ." For a long moment, it appears Chase might argue. He bounces nervously on the balls of his feet, his fingers drumming an impatient rhythm against his pant leg, as though he's trying to compose himself an excuse. But then with an effort I can feel, he forces his hesitation down to a simmer, his own curiosity enticing him to relent. "Okay, fine, just make it quick."

"No, make it thorough," Novi tells her. "And don't even think about skipping the whole *faked your own death* part."

"Oh—and try not to speak too quickly," I hurry to add. "I'm not the world's greatest interpreter." Though I am now practiced enough to spare Lyria from having to rely solely on the impreciseness of lips.

"Alright." Magdalena nods, studying our new addition with a curious eye. "Well, for starters, you've probably figured out that my power isn't to mimic."

Yeah . . . that much, I think we got. I keep my commentary to myself as I turn her words into signs.

"I *am* an Amber, and my Hue *is* a dilution of Yellow magic—like Cassiel's," she says, "but it's the atypical presentation, which makes it extremely rare. For every thousand Golds, you'd maybe get one Amber, so we're not particularly well documented. Nor does the Council want us to be given the danger our gift presents."

To take from the world. I think back to the list Versallis penned in his journal, reframing that information now that I know the siphon isn't an object, but a Hue.

Their abilities are in actuality less a gift than they are a curse.

We cannot allow the events of this past year to repeat.

We must stop the spread of the witch.

"You're the reason the Council started purging Hues!" All at once, the extreme nature of his proposal begins to fit.

"Yes," Magdalena confirms. "After the last Amber almost destroyed the shadows, they couldn't risk something like me happening again. So when one of their elders keenly pointed out that the more entangled Shades and typics become, the more likely it is another Amber would be born, they made it illegal to mix the bloodlines. But they couldn't admit to the real reason in case the Church used that knowledge to its advantage, so instead, they blamed us for the near collapse of the Gray. And it worked, for over four hundred years. Until I came along.

"Our mother was not a careful woman," Magdalena continues, the memory glinting her eyes sad. "She trusted too much and fell in love too thoughtlessly. Told the wrong man about her twin Hues and lost her life because of it."

The polar opposite of my mom, then, I can't help but think. Reckless in every way mine was stern and cautious. Though Savian was able to catch my scent just the same.

"We were thirteen when the Council killed her." Chase takes over the telling, granting me a brief respite since he can both speak and sign for himself. "Old enough to know that their trackers would never stop hunting us. An Amber and a Gold is not a combination of power they want loose, and after a while, it didn't make sense for us to stay together. We each drew less attention alone. So we split up, and we started searching the continent for a less hostile place to call home."

"That's how I came to reside in Isitar," Magdalena adds. "And how I eventually found all of you—or, I should say, how Ezzo found me." She aims that last refrain at her brother. "I'm sorry I didn't tell you, Cassiel, but I knew how you'd feel about me getting close to other Hues, and I couldn't face the prospect of moving on again so soon. Not when I was so—"

"Lonely." His exhale is a breath of understanding, the yearning in his face shining stark. "You don't have to apologize, Mags. I doubt

I'd have had the strength to leave, either." His eyes flutter in my direction, lingering long enough to flood my stomach with heat. Corrode my anger.

"If I'd have known what you'd all come to mean to me, I'd have done things differently," Magdalena says, turning her story back to the crux. "But Ezzo's gift made it impossible to lie about my Hue, and I panicked. Since I couldn't tell him about my true power, I had to get creative, assign myself a more innocuous ability. And since Cassiel and I had learned a better way to cast our In-Betweens, the ability to mimic seemed a sensible choice, so that I could pretend to mimic Eve.

"It was a bit of a stretch, as far as Yellow dilutions go, and I had to saddle this assumed power of mine with a few arbitrary constraints to stop you asking too many questions, as well—like why I *only* ever chose to mimic Eve—but on that, the Council's purges worked in my favor; they've controlled the flow of information so well that most of us only ever get familiar with our own magics, so you were content to take me at my word. Just as I expected most halves would be."

If nothing else, Magdalena has the right of that assertion. Because while it *had* occurred to me that mimicry was an odd manifestation of Yellow magic, it had never occurred to me to question the legitimacy of a fellow Hue's gift. Even when Versallis's journal attributed that exact power to a Ruby, I chalked it down to error, hardly gave it a second thought.

"Problem was, I'd trapped myself in my own lie." Magdalena shudders with the regret. "The minute I got to know you, I wanted to tell you everything—not least of all how to cast a more stable In-Between. But doing that would have meant coming clean about my power, and so I said nothing. I kept pretending. And I told myself it was because the truth was too much of a risk—both for me, and for you—when in reality, I was afraid of losing the new home I'd made. The new family.

"I still don't know how the Church came to discover I was here," she says, voice small, head shaking. "Maybe it *was* the risk I took by staying after Ezzo identified my Hue—though it could just as soon have been unrelated. Either way, a rumor reached Cassiel that they'd learned I was in Isitar. It was time for me to move on."

"So you *faked your own death*?" I barely beat Novi to the outrage, the indignation contorting our faces as one. "During my lift?"

"I am so sorry, Cemmy." Magdalena sags low against her chains, the bones in her wrists protruding sharply, the hollows in her cheeks jutting blunt, as though the shadows kept her alive but not sustained. "Coming to Isitar . . . meeting you, and Novi, and Ezzo, and Eve . . . it was the first time I'd experienced a family outside of Cassiel. The way you all cared for each other—the way you cared for *me*—I didn't think you'd accept it if I just . . . *disappeared*. You'd have tried to find me, and with Ezzo's gift, you might well have succeeded, and it would have put you in danger. I needed you to let me go, and without the truth, I didn't think that would happen unless you believed I was—"

"Dead," I finish for her, butchering that last sign so badly, I have to do it again. "So you . . . what? Set the whole thing up? Used a glamour to make me think I'd killed you?" *Left me to shoulder the blame?* That disastrous lift suddenly makes sense. The picks that broke for no reason. The Gray gift that inexplicably failed. The guilt that tore my life to pieces.

For absolutely no reason. The anger swells high in my chest.

Despite Magdalena's bid to protect us, we still wound up in this iron cell.

Surrounded by enemies.

And her brother's efforts cost us Eve.

"I'm so sorry," she says again, the words laden with misery. "I spent days trying to come up with a better idea, but strategy was always Cassiel's forte, and I was running out of time. So when you told me about that lift, I saw my chance and I had to take it. And I can only imagine what that did to you, Cem." Magdalena meets my gaze head-on, acknowledging the pain she'd inflicted. "If I could do things over, please believe me, I would. Especially since in the end, I couldn't escape the Church at all. I didn't even make it out of the city."

"Wait, so . . . they've had you locked up since the day you shattered?" That grim reality pulls me out of my own hurt. "This whole year?"

"A *year*?" In an instant, the sorrow in Magdalena's face turns to fear, her eyes desperately seeking her brother. "By my colors, Cassiel, how close did I come?" she asks. Then when Chase looks down at his feet to avoid replying, she laces her voice with steel and asks again. *"How close?"*

"Within hours," he finally admits, whisper quiet. "But all that matters is we stopped it, Mags. We stopped it in time."

"Why did you ever start it?" Though I'm the one who speaks the question, the want of it belongs to Lyria. To the shadows leveling accusations in her mind. *"Why would you agree to drain the Gray?"*

"That's *not* how it works." In spite of the perfectly reasonable ask, Chase's answering signs are furious. "Her gift—"

"My gift doesn't work the way yours do." Magdalena calms his indignation with a sigh, looking to me to interpret. "It's less an ability and more of a . . . *hunger*, really. As long as I spend enough time in the shadows—siphoning small amounts—I can keep the urge sated and my power at bay. But the full might of it can also be triggered against my will."

"Triggered?" Novi raises a brow. "Triggered how?"

"Magic lives in the blood." Magdalena points her chin towards the scars crisscrossing her skin. "Spill enough of mine in the Gray and I lose control. Begin taking too much. And once that frenzy starts, it's like a boulder rolling downhill. I forget who I am. Where I am. What I'm doing. Even after the bleeding stops, my gift continues to drain—we discovered that much the first time I phased into the Gray injured. If it hadn't been for Cassiel, I would have lost myself entirely that day. He might be the only one who can pull me back from the edge."

"So they—?" My insides tie themselves into a painful knot, the truth of her scars grinding them to offal. "All those cuts?"

"I fought them as long as I could." The ghost of that torture haunts Magdalena pale. "I thought that maybe, if I could keep my magic reined in, they'd give up eventually. Assume their histories had overestimated my gift. But no matter what I did, their Shade, he—he wouldn't stop cutting"—her voice cracks with the memory—"and he was careful enough to ensure that nothing I did to try and . . . *end* . . . things would accidentally drive the knife too deep. I think he—I got the sense he enjoyed it."

"That's enough." Beside her, Chase has grown equally pale, every part of him trembling with her confession. "You asked your questions; you got your pound of flesh. Now would you please get Mags out of these chains."

"No." Novi turns the full danger of her scowl on him. "Not until *you* answer a couple, too. Like how Savian fits into all this?"

"Savian was a means to an end." Chase bristles, and I don't miss the telling change in his tense.

"Was?"

"Yes, *was*. As in, Savian will no longer be a problem." He's being cagey. Trying to keep yet another secret from us, and—if I'm reading the twitch in his jaw correctly—from Magdalena, as well.

"Cassiel, what did you do?" She doesn't miss the squirm in his tone. These two may have spent the past few years separated, but they're clearly still as close as twin siblings can be, their love for each other etched into every line of their worry. Evident in the way Chase would have walked through all nine hells to free her of the Church's prison. In the unsavory alliances he chose to make.

"I tried for months to reach you, Mags," he hedges, a guilty flush climbing his neck. "But the Dominion was too well protected. I had no hope of getting inside without help."

"Help from who, exactly?" Magdalena snaps straight in her chains. "Because I never told you about Novi and Cem—and it's beginning to sound less and less like they are here voluntarily."

"Help from the Order of Versallis," he murmurs, fingerspelling the name.

"Cassiel." The reprimand in her voice is a tempest, tumultuous and brash. A mirror to the jolt of shock that grips me at that revelation. The sudden stab of disgust. "Have you lost your mind?"

"I lost my *sister*," he stresses, though the conviction is gone from his eyes. "I had to get you back."

"Would you please share what that means with the class?" Novi growls, her patience waning faster than her shoulder leaks blood.

"If you explain, I'll deal with the cuffs," I add before Chase can argue, sweetening her request. And though the grind of his teeth tells me he'd rather protect this most shameful of secrets with his life, he's not willing to risk Magdalena's. As I fish my picks out of my pocket, he scrubs both hands through his hair and begins.

"The journal I stole from Rhodes's office was written by a man called Clayvern Versallis, a Council elder who believed that Shades shouldn't have to capitulate to the Church. He was already petitioning for war when the Conclave last got hold of an Amber, and that Hue came so close to destroying the Gray, it served to turn him against the rest of us. He became convinced that we posed a danger to the shadows. Didn't like the random opportunity a half created, or how the more of us there were, the more chance a dangerous new gift would be born." He starts by recapping the truths I'd read for myself.

"But though he managed to convince the Council to sanction his purges, his other views were a little more . . . *extreme*," Chase continues, moving towards the ones I hadn't. "Even as he made it illegal for a full-blood to procreate with a typic, he petitioned for a law that would force Yellow Shades to bear halves until the Council got an Amber of its own, so that they could use it to destroy the physical realm."

Wait. What? My picks stall against the lock. "Is that possible?"

"Think of me as an infinite container," Magdalena answers in his stead, her breath tickling my cheek. "The power I take lives inside me—that's why it's so hard to control. Over time, it'll dissipate, feed back into the world, but if it was released all at once . . . in the physical realm . . ."

"Light turns to shadow and color to gray." Chase's jaw hardens as he presses his thumbs forward. "Permanently."

"And this Versallis guy actually wanted that?" Novi lends voice to Lyria's signs. *"Why? Wouldn't it—"*

"Shatter every typic? Yes," Chase confirms with a knock of his fist. "It was a fringe belief that eventually saw him expelled from the Council, but by then, he'd already amassed a small—but loyal—sect of followers who continued to pursue his ideals long after his death. Savian is a disciple of that sect."

"*Cassiel.* What possessed you to work with such a man?" Magdalena sounds downright appalled.

"I didn't have a choice, Mags. There was no other way to get to you." He springs to her side as the first of the cuffs falls away, holding her emaciated frame steady. "The Council would have never let you live if I had gone to them for help, and only a fanatic would risk breaking into the Dominion to save a Hue." With his hands busy, he turns to ensure that Lyria has a clear view of his lips. "So I pretended to want the same madness Savian did, and though he had no love for the fact I'm a Gold, I was able to offer him the one thing he couldn't get on his own: your location."

"Which you knew . . . how?" Novi repeats the question she'd first asked him at the monastery, what feels like a lifetime ago.

"Twin Hues are bonded." Though this time, he answers without equivocation or delay. "It's not as good as a scry, but we can always find each other on a map."

"Okay . . . and what happens now that you have found her?" she asks. "Do you really think Savian is going to *forget* you promised him your sister?"

"Savian doesn't know she's my sister." Chase rolls his eyes as if to add, *because I wasn't stupid enough to tell him.* "And when I made him aware of the coup you were planning, I may have broken *your* trust, but I cemented his in me. I ensured he'd stop watching me as closely, so that I could lace his flask with a memory spell and alert the Council to where he was hiding ahead of the lift. He won't be able to expose us anymore. Not before their trackers put an end to him for good. That's why I had to do it." His voice softens, his gaze intensifying at my back, as though speaking to me alone.

Would you have really done any differently? The unsaid words seem to demand. *Is there any line you wouldn't cross for your family?*

If there is, I'm yet to find it, and much to my dismay, Chase is harder to hate now that I know what he was trying to protect. Why he felt as though he had to betray us. Hells, his plan for ridding himself of Savian was almost exactly the same as ours; he just enacted it a few bells later.

Too late to spare Eve.

"You seem to have forgotten one thing, Cassiel." Novi's indulgence is much harder to earn. "You told us the siphon was an object, not a person, and Lena is hardly going to fit neatly in the palm of Cemmy's hand. We can't hide her, and that corridor is now flooded with guards who are never going to let an Amber walk out of here alive."

"Actually, they are." Chase smiles as the second cuff succumbs to my picks. "They're going to quietly step aside and clear our way."

"And why, in either world, would they ever agree to do that?"

His smile stretches to a self-satisfied grin. "Because we're going to threaten to do exactly what Savian wanted."

CHAPTER

Twenty-nine

A knife to his sister's throat; that's Chase's big idea for escaping the Dominion alive. My knife. The one he bid me to bring in case of emergency, as though he knew all along that we might be forced to threaten our way out. Or at least as though he'd feared it.

"And how does threatening to kill Lena help us?" The longer we remain in this iron prison, the more unsteady Novi looks on her feet, the wound to her shoulder leaching at her strength. Fast enough that it's beginning to pale her pallid, but too slowly for Chase to offer up a healing. Not when there's still a possibility that magic will be called on to heal something worse. Something fatal.

"We won't be threatening to kill her." His words are an impatient sigh, his accompanying signs growing clipped. "We'll be threatening to make her bleed."

"And that's better because . . ."

"Magic lives in the blood." Thanks to Versallis's journal, I'm the first to catch up to his thinking. *A bleeding is the only way to ensure the shadows are never threatened again.* Those words meant little when I read them inside those musty pages, but having learned the truth of Magdalena's gift, it's not a stretch to deduce why Versallis chose to use that term. "It works the same in the physical realm, doesn't it?" I ask. "Triggering the frenzy?"

"We've never put it to the test, but yeah." Magdalena picks nervously at her scars. "While my veins are ripe with this much power, I imagine it would trigger the same way."

"Thus leaving Rhodes no other choice but to let us go." Chase declares that outcome to be a given.

Which it's really—*really*—not.

"You're betting an awful lot on him knowing exactly what Lena can do, don't you think?" I can't bring myself to share his confidence. "What if he doesn't realize the bleeding works in both worlds?"

"Versallis's journal *proves* that he does." An annoyed flush reddens his cheeks. "That's why I was searching his office for anything bearing the Council's mark. I needed to see which writings he had consulted ahead of enacting his plans, so that we would know *exactly* what he believes Mags can do. Shape our own plans accordingly."

Right, yes. He'd told me something similar during the game we played on my couch: how it's important to establish what your enemies know about your power, so they'd be easier to predict.

So he could plan for every eventuality.

Well . . . Gods. He's certainly done that. He even planned for the one I inadvertently set in motion when I sold the totem I mistook for a ring. Assured we'd always have a bloodless exit.

"And what happens if Rhodes calls our bluff?" Novi asks, remaining thoroughly unconvinced.

"Then we'd be in no more trouble than we are now." Chase shrugs. "But if you ask me, he wouldn't have gone to such lengths to protect this cell if he didn't know how dangerous Mags could become. He's been watching her drain the Gray for a *year*. He's watched the Shades in Isitar lose their power, and flee the city, and he knows precisely where all that magic's been going—and what it could do if it were released into the wrong realm. This close to the tipping point, the threat of a bleeding should be more than enough to make him disable the arrows and stand his enforcers down. No arrows means we don't have to split up, so we can tackle that corridor as one, then as soon as we're through the portals, we'll make a run for it in the Gray," Chase says and signs, laying out the rest of his plan. "His Shades can't touch us until we're through the warding, and once we hit the plaza, we can make them think you've sped off with Mags"—he looks to Novi—"so that they'll focus their efforts on you while the rest of us phase back and lose ourselves in the crowd. Then once you've drawn them away, you can phase back, too. The iron in the holy quarter should keep them from following."

"That could work, you know—if you're up to speeding?" Unlike Chase, Lyria chooses to acknowledge that our Cobalt's injured. "*Magdalena and I are a similar height, so if we trade cloaks before the final portal, and keep our heads down, Rhodes probably won't notice the switch.*"

Should. Could. If. Probably.

There's an awful lot of wishful thinking happening in this plan.

"We've still got Ezzo out there, as well," Chase adds, as though reading my doubt. "In case we need a more drastic diversion. But with a little luck, the parade will do the hard work for us, then we can meet back up at the monastery. Go our separate ways from there," he concludes. And since none of us have a better idea to offer him, we all nod our assent. Including Novi, who maintains that she's fine—*so stop fussing*—and that "a measly scratch to the shoulder" shouldn't interfere with her gift.

The climb down the spiral staircase passes in near silence, the sound of haste on smoke-clad steps echoing loud around us, the taste of fear and nervous anticipation sitting heavy on our tongues.

"Everyone ready?" I ask when we reach the foot of the spire, ensuring that we're all in place before throwing the door to the corridor open wide, a deliberate action the Commander's guards aren't like to miss—even if they can't yet see us.

"Stay sharp." Chase is the first to cross the threshold and blink out of the Gray, Magdalena and I close at his heels, Lyria and Novi following at our back. "We have your Amber," he bellows, informing Rhodes that we've successfully liberated his prize. "Have your men put down their weapons or we'll bleed her like a stuck pig."

"Your brother's a real charmer," I whisper, clutching Magdalena tight, the blade held theatrically beneath her chin.

"Don't judge him too harshly, Cem." Her answering murmur is sad. "He's spent half his life trying to protect me. It's the only thing he knows how to do." The words wrap a hand around my heart and squeeze, the pain in them rending me brittle. We all grew up hunted—that's just the cost of being a Hue—but I can't imagine what it was like to fear both death and the possibility of being used. Of being forced to unmake a world. Destroy your own kind.

"You must realize that I cannot let the girl leave." The Commander's voice booms down the corridor, superior and proud.

So far so predictable . . . We shuffle out of the stairwell as one, Novi relaying his words to Lyria as we emerge into full view of his guard.

"Just as *you* must realize what will happen if you try to stop us." Chase levies the threat without fear. "We're willing to die to prevent the collapse of the Gray, but I doubt you're willing to die to ensure it. So I suggest you disable your fail-safes, because whether you like it or not, we *are* walking her out of here."

A terse silence descends upon the corridor, a soundless battle of opposing wills.

Come on, come on, come on . . . It takes everything I have to quell the shake in my hand, to steady my nerve and stay the flight of my feet. We have absolutely no recourse here, no alternate plan, nowhere to run if Rhodes decides to call our bluff as Novi envisaged.

Gods, please, just let this one thing go right.

"As you wish." A whole eternity seems to pass before he yields. With an annoyed suck of teeth, the Commander rips a talisman from around his neck and crushes it with the flat of his heel, destroying whatever spell used to live inside the Orange crystal. "You're free to go."

"Do you think he means it?" Novi asks, glancing between Chase, Lyria, and me.

"I don't know," I say with a shrug. Though if it's a trick, it's a damn risky one. He'd be gambling on his arrows leaving all of us too incapacitated to phase Magdalena back while she bleeds. And if he's wrong, it'll be power she's bleeding. And she'll be bleeding it all over his world.

"I guess we'll find out." At Chase's behest, we step into the portal together, bracing for a lethal storm of swift and sharpened sticks.

I am in between him and Magdalena. My magic rushes out to greet the shadows, the wine cellar around us pulling into stark relief, the air hanging cold and fusty.

Stale.

But devoid of death.

"Huh. Looks like he did mean it," Novi mutters as we weave through the deep stacks of barrels, signing the relief with one hand. "Color me surprised."

Color *me* suspicious. The moment we land back in the corridor, the hairs on my arms begin to prick. There's no way Rhodes is allowing us to go this easy. There's no way he looks this indifferent and nonplussed as portal by portal—chapel by bedchamber by crypt—we draw ever closer to escaping his clutches.

What are you missing, Cemmy? As Chase leads us through the penultimate library, I try to unravel the errant thread before it sticks. The Commander's enforcers have been watching us approach with murderous scowls and their hands glued to their sabers, but the door behind them remains open, and they do appear to be holding still.

Too still.

Too *calm.*

Rhodes's expression too impassive for a man who's about to lose his conclusive triumph in the war against Shades.

What is he hiding? I slow to a crawl as we traverse the last stretch of corridor, searching his army for the secret they don't want us to see. Their weapons are useless in the face of Magdalena's need to stay unbloodied, so an ambush is out of the question, but allowing us to abscond through the Gray seems an equally unlikely conceit. *So then what does that leave?* The question sears through my mind as the final portal sucks us into the shadows, depositing us in the ballroom I first glimpsed on our way in.

"Time to switch." Chase motions for Magdalena and Lyria to trade cloaks, leaving me free to grapple with the worry. *Can't attack . . . won't let us go . . . can't attack . . . won't let us go . . . can't attack . . . won't* have *to let us go if we're trapped here . . .*

That's it. He's going to trap us here. The answer hits me two seconds too late, as we're already hurtling back towards the corridor. *And if his guards aren't holding the* hows *in their hands, then the only other place it could be is—*

The moment our boots hit the tiles, I look up to see the iron-ringed threat.

"Phase! Now!" I yank us all back into the Gray, evading the falling net by a whisper, my strangled litany of curses echoing through smoke and ink.

Crap. Shit. Damn. Fuck him.

We should have realized Rhodes wouldn't waste the time we spent in Magdalena's cell standing idle. He's the most decorated military mind in the city, of course he'd find a way to rectify his mistake.

And to avoid making new ones . . . The blood turns to caustic acid in my veins, my gut bubbling with a sense of foreboding.

Because Rhodes didn't just drop a net, he shut the door.

Literally.

While we were conspiring to stage our plan in the ballroom, he enacted his to keep us put.

"Nice save, Cem." Magdalena's not noticed the problem yet; she's too busy admiring the ghost of the prison bunched harmlessly at our feet. "How did you know what he meant to do?"

"I didn't know, I guessed," I say. And as Lyria's face pales of color, I also guess at our next predicament—and at the one Novi uncovers as she makes a quick flit through the wood.

"He's had it barred from the outside," she tells me, scrubbing at the vines tattooed into her scalp. "You won't be able to pick it open." Which wouldn't have been an issue before—though Rhodes may not have known that; he may not have yet determined how I was able to steal inside. But now . . .

"Why does she need to pick it open if Lyria can just—" That's when Chase notices it, too. The shake in our Amethyst's signs.

"The shadows won't let Cemmy through," she confirms the reality I've begun to suspect, biting at the inside of her cheek. *"They're angry with us for lying."*

"When did we lie?" Chase rages at the swirling darkness. "We promised to stop the drain and that's exactly what we did!"

"Not stop, kill." There's no danger to my words, no ill intent or malice; I'm merely stating fact. "They made us promise to kill her."

Twice, in fact. And both times we agreed—in principle—by accepting their help.

"Well, we're definitely not going to do *that.*" Chase moves to shield Magdalena, as though he suddenly considers me a threat. "So Lyria needs to convince them otherwise."

"You think I haven't tried?" Her face tightens with frustration. *"I've been begging them to see reason—begging them to see that none of this was Magdalena's fault. But we lost their allegiance the moment we let her out of that cell. They believe leaving her alive poses too great a risk."*

And they're right, I realize. They might be callous but they're right. While Magdalena—or *any* Amber—lives, the Gray will never truly be safe; it'll always be at the mercy of those who seek to exploit her power. The shadows' fear isn't irrational; it's the truth. Nothing Lyria can say will change that.

"Take Lena and run," I tell the others, solving the problem the only way I see how. "I'll keep Rhodes distracted."

"No. Absolutely not." Magdalena's head shakes and shakes and shakes. "I won't let you trade yourself for me."

"Mags—"

"You don't have a choice." I beat Chase to the argument, since it would hurt a lot more coming from him. "The most important thing right now is to get you away from the Church. If we don't do that, then they'll use you to kill us all."

"But Cem—"

"No. No buts." I refuse to let her break my resolve. "I'm a Bronze Hue with no totem, Lena; you were always going to have to leave me behind." The truth of those words hits me at the same time it does them, illuminating the one glaring issue Chase couldn't foresee.

My visible trace.

The aura that'll identify me to other Shades.

Even in the physical realm.

And that's entirely my fault. Rhodes may be the reason I'm trapped here, but *I* gave rise to this possibility when I decided to sell Dad's ring. I'm the reason the alarms went off, and the reason there's an army of enforcers standing between us and the street. The reason we could too easily be followed.

I should be the one to fix it.

"Hide in the Gray as long as you can," Chase tells me, the intention in his eyes sincere. "We'll come back for you as soon as Mags is safe."

No, you won't. As much as I'd like to believe he means it, I think we both know it's a fantasy he's unlikely to commit. From the moment Chase stepped foot in Isitar, he's only had one Hue in mind—and it wasn't a Bronze.

He's not here for me.

He's never been here for me.

And breaking into the Dominion a second time would prove even more impossible than the first. Once they flee this cursed palace, I'm on my own.

Or perhaps not, as the case might be.

"Erm, En . . . what are you doing?" I ask when Novi opts to stay behind, watching the others wisp through the door.

"I know I'm mad at you, Cemmy, but I'll never be mad enough to let you martyr yourself like an idiot," she says. "Though just for the record, if we do make it out of this corridor alive, I reserve the right to *stay* mad at you, and you still have to make it up to me—to all of us. You have to earn that trust back, understand? You don't get to just . . . *die*."

"En—" My throat begins to sting, a wild mix of hope and relief prickling beneath the surface. "I don't know what to—"

"Later, Cem," she says, but the bite in her voice blunts an inch. "First, we figure our way out of here."

Right. Yes. I swallow down the longing, joining her in evaluating the gathered siege. "There's too many to fight"—I state the blindingly obvious—"so that's out of the question." Especially with her already injured and losing blood at an alarming rate.

"Maybe not . . ." Novi's eyes turn thoughtful as she considers the army awaiting us in the physical realm. "Rhodes is clearly banking on us all having to move together, or else he wouldn't have barred the door—probably thinks we're relying on an Emerald to hold our shields—so I doubt he'll have bothered accounting for my speed."

"And that helps us . . . how?" I ask.

"Well, thanks to the portals, they're as trapped by that door as we are. More trapped, actually, since if they get sucked into the Gray, they'll shatter. So that's what . . . ten enforcers in about fifteen feet worth of corridor?"

"I mean . . . yeah. Sure. Thereabouts."

"Okay, then what we need to do is make those fifteen feet feel really small. Panic them into wanting that door open. Hells, I bet we'll only have to spook half before the rest of them lose their mettle."

"I'm still not quite following you, En," I say, mentally trying to paint the same picture she's seeing. "How does your speed panic them?"

"Not just my speed—your physicality." She points to the sabers hanging off the enforcers' belts. "We're going to incapacitate them with their own swords."

"What do you—*oh.*" It takes a second for the full genius of her plan to sink in. For while I can't harm a typic from inside the Gray, what I *can* do is steal their stuff. And if their stuff is sharp and deadly, well . . . once we phase back into the real world, it'll harm them just fine. "That could work."

It will work. I force myself to think as she settles behind me, putting one hand to my shoulder and another at my hip. Or at the very least, it's better than any idea I had for escaping without her. Which isn't saying much, to be honest, since the sum total of my ideas came to naught.

"When the screaming starts, you ignore it." Novi's missive is a stern command in my ear, a preemptive pardon to both my conscience and her own. "They don't deserve our pity, you hear me? What they did to Lena they would happily do to us. They would *enjoy* it, Cemmy. Cut us to tiny ribbons just to watch us bleed." The absolution in her voice turns bitter. And though I'm instantly consumed by the memory of the pain they carved into Magdalena, I know that Novi's mind is with the man who killed her mother. How protected he felt by his religion and his crimson cloak. How little regard he deigned to show a fellow typic—never mind a filthy Hue.

I am the violence the world made of me. Chase had uttered those words the night I watched him inflict agony on a rogue. And while I've never relished the thought of hurting anyone, when push came to shove, he was right: it didn't stop me asking him to go back and steal us more. My hands are already stained bloody.

"Ready?" Novi asks, moving us to stand in front of the nearest guard.

"Ready." With a breath, I focus my power, prompting the edges of the man's echo to burn clear so that I can close my fingers around the hilt of his saber. "On three," I tell her, solidifying the might of my grip. "One . . . two . . ."

"Three."

We both move at the same time; me to wrench the sword from his grasp; her to speed us over to a different guard in the corridor.

And phase.

The world bursts into color, a rainbow of confusion I spatter with red. A surprise attack they couldn't see coming.

And phase.

I barely have time to liberate steel from flesh before Novi has us speeding again, or to wipe the warm kiss of blood from my face. Dampen the nausea.

When the screaming starts, you ignore it.

And phase.

The first guard has only just woken up to the pain when I bury the saber in the second one's leg, sending a formidable-looking woman crashing to her knees.

And phase.

Ink and shadow flood my vision, Novi setting a relentless pace as we reposition, reappear, then repeat.

And phase.

My efforts skewer an arm, a thigh, the hollow between two ribs, filling the corridor with a sickening chorus of wails and the tart tang of metal, my eyes with a sticky ruby rain. *They don't deserve our pity,* I remind myself over and over. *They would happily cut us to tiny ribbons. They would enjoy it.*

Just as they enjoyed torturing Magdalena.

I silence the guilt and continue to strike, though by the time we've maimed our sixth enforcer, the rest have grown wise to our tricks. They're pounding a savagery against the door now, imploring the guards on the other side to release the barricade and set them free.

And phase.

"It's the same two half breeds!" The Commander roars, his realization assaulting us in blink-broken waves. "They're trying to distract our attention from the Amber! Send word to the rogues at the gate!"

No, no, no, no. "We can't allow them to do that—the others may still be inside!"

"Way ahead of you, Cem." The moment the heavy wood swings open, Novi speeds us past the echoes fleeing our wake.

And phase.

One by one, we target them as methodically as we did their friends, until my hands are slick with crimson and my clothes are soaked bloody with sweat. Until the Dominion halls are lined with the resonant moans of the injured and Commander Rhodes is the only slippery opponent we've not yet managed to fell.

"We need to make this one count, Cem." Novi's whisper booms loud through my head. "We need to stop him for good, or we'll never be safe in Isitar again."

I know exactly what she's asking me to do—and how much she must hate herself for asking it—though she's as right about Rhodes as the summer rains. He's not the kind of man who would simply move on and let a grudge rest; if we show him mercy, he'll hunt us to the very ends of the earth.

Don't think about it, Cemmy, just aim a little higher on his chest.

There'll be plenty of time to indulge the shame once we've left this unholy mess behind us. Plenty of time to retch, and scream; scrub my skin raw of the violence and dream of horrors drenched in red.

But first, we have to survive those horrors.

Put an end to the man who came within hours of collapsing the Gray.

"I'm ready," I tell her, then with a final burst of speed, Novi brings us and the Commander within arm's length.

And phase.

I lunge my saber forward, aiming a killing blow to his heart instead of the kinder wounds I offered his brigade. But he's faster than they were, a better tactician and more prepared. He blocks my first attempt without effort, and then the second, and the third. By the fourth, Novi's no longer the only half Shade bleeding color all over the marble.

And phase.

"This isn't working, En," I hiss through the pain he nicked across my leg. He's too swift with a blade. Too good at predicting our movements, and the two of us are growing too lax with the fatigue. Skirting too close to ruin.

"Then let's try something different." Her hands slip away from my waist. "On three, you go right, I'll go left; divert his attention so that you can catch him unawares. Got it?"

Before I can think to argue, Novi's already muttered "one", "two", and "three" under her breath.

And phase.

But since it's a good plan, it goes off exactly as she intends.

With his back turned, Rhodes can't see his mistake, nor can he stop my saber piercing clean through the meat of his torso. A grunt of shock exhales with his air, the disbelief stumbling him like a cheap bottle. Though even as he falls to his knees—even as his jaw slackens and blood fountains spittle all over his chin—his eyes remain bright with victory.

Triumphant, even in defeat.

Oh Gods.

That's when I realize his own sword hasn't yet clattered to the floor in disgrace, nor is it still clutched between the cage of his fingers. Because—*oh Gods oh Gods oh Gods*—his last act was to meet my murder with a stroke of revenge.

He speared his saber through Novi.

CHAPTER

Thirty

No. I rush forward to catch Novi as she falls, phasing us into the Gray before a new crop of enforcers can arrive. "En—look at me," I beg, cradling her in my arms, my In-Between projecting out to shield us both. "You have to look at me, okay? You have to say something."

"That didn't go the way I planned." Her lids flutter open, the blood pricking garnets across her lips. "I think Rhodes saw it coming."

"Not well enough," I say. Then with a harried apology, I wrap my fingers around the saber's hilt and pull it out from between her ribs.

"Argh—*fuck,* Cem." The pain in Novi's cough is wet, the croak of her curse rough as gravel. "A little warning would have been nice."

"Wouldn't have made it hurt less." Without relinquishing contact, I bunch up the fabric of her cloak and press her uninjured hand to the wound. "You stay alive, I'll get us out of here."

"Cemmy—"

"And if you even *think* about telling me to leave you, I'll take that saber and shove it somewhere worse." We both grunt as I haul her back to her feet. "Chase stole some of Savian's magic, after all, so once we get you to the monastery, he can fix this. He *will* fix it." I speak the vow into the world. I will *make* him fix it, no matter what it might cost.

"Like he fixed my shoulder?" Even hurt and bleeding, Novi remains shrewd.

"That was different," I say, leading her towards the stairs. "He wasn't going to waste that magic on a *measly scratch*. He was saving it. For an injury like this."

"Cemmy, Cassiel's gone." This time, the pitch of Novi's voice is sad. "If he managed to get Lena out, they'll have fled the city."

"You're wrong—he'll be there," I insist, stubborn. "He promised me a healing." And so what if I had technically reneged on the deal he offered? So what if I hadn't waited before breaking into his sister's cell? Chase only swore me to that promise because he didn't know how we'd react to finding a fellow Hue in there, and besides, it was *his* idea to return to the monastery upon our escape, to reconvene one last time before separating forever. Surely Magdalena would never agree to up and leave again without saying goodbye? Surely Chase would want to bid a few goodbyes of his own, too? Or at least a couple of damn thank yous.

There's no surely about it. Salt prickles my eyes as I begin our descent. After the unmitigated disaster we'd encountered in that corridor, there's every chance that they decided to forgo that unnecessary risk. To flee Isitar before the Church could marshal its enforcers and haul Magdalena back into her iron hell.

Don't go. My fingers close around his scry, sending the plea down the bonded connection. *Novi's hurt, and without your magic, she'll die. Please, Chase, if you care about me at all—if you ever cared—come to the monastery and save her. Please.* But since my message garners no response, I'm forced to stake his agreement on faith. To pray that he still cares enough to listen.

We're going to need another distraction. I try Ezzo's scry next, turning my attention to the more immediate problem: getting Novi back to the monastery. *It's not for me, okay? It's for Novi; she's in really bad shape,* I add once a few seconds elapse without answer. *Please Ez—are you there?*

I'm here. I've got Lyria. Tell me what En needs.

A way out. I ignore the coldness of his reply, how he made a point of only offering his help to Novi. *You'll have to bring down the gate.*

The more drastic diversion for which we had prepared.

One last desperate show of magic on the Church's holiest of days.

I supply Ezzo with the rest of the details as I half drag, half carry Novi through the endless labyrinth of passageways and stairs, a full rundown of what transpired in the belly of this pious building. And though the plan we cobble together is both wishful and incredibly frail, with Novi injured and the Dominion on high alert, it's the best we can hope for—especially given the added complication I created when I sold my ring.

"Stay with me, En. In a couple of minutes, we're going to need a burst of speed." I pull our hoods up as we steal across the atrium, hiding our faces beneath the vibrant depths of our brightly colored cloaks. Mine yellow, hers red. The same colors Ezzo and Lyria will have hopefully acquired by the time we reach the entrance.

"Do I even want to know why?" Novi's question is a whimpered sigh, as though exhausted by the very idea.

"Probably not." I try to ignore the erratic hitch of her breaths, how her entire shirt is sodden with blood now, the rising burn of her skin. "But I promise to make it quick."

I'm not sure she'd be capable of it otherwise.

Ready when you are, Ez, I send the moment we're in position, hovering behind the crowd of echoes amassed around the door.

Then start running in five . . . four . . . three . . . two . . .

One.

The shadow of an explosion ripples through the Gray, turning ink to rain and smoke to stardust, the blast initiated by the wealth of Orange magic Chase provided Ezzo for the job. Yet another spell we were only too happy to extract from his gift, brutal though it is to brandish.

I am the violence the world made of me.

And our lives are the price it continues to inflict.

The commotion springs the guards to action, prompting them to wrench open the door and flood the plaza with haste.

And phase.

I tighten my grip on Novi as I blink us back into existence, ensuring that they get a nice, good look at the yellow-cloaked figure absconding with an accomplice in red.

"You there—stop this instant!" Our sudden appearance ignites a chorus of fury and fervent yells, immediately pointing the guards in our direction.

And phase.

The moment we're back among the shadows, I urge Novi to engage her gift. "You only need to get us as far as the gate, okay? That's all the help I need."

Which is lucky, seeing how a brief blur of stairs and cobbles is about as much exertion as she can manage. Just enough to speed us past the Commander's Shades as we leave the safety of the warding. Just enough to allow me to blink us back into the physical realm before they're able to shimmer and give chase.

And phase.

Thanks to the messages our scrys relay, Ezzo and I time the ruse perfectly. He and Lyria await my signal from beside the hole they blew in the wrought-iron fence, dressed in the same notable combination of red and yellow.

And then they phase.

Confirming that Novi and I are safely ensconced in the panicked crowd before making a show of blinking out of the Gray themselves, so that the guards will mistake them for the two intruders they're trying to apprehend. From here, they'll continue to lead our pursuers astray, buying us enough time to vanish among the chaos.

"See that, En? We made it. We're out." I allow myself a tiny exhale. This close to the site of the explosion, the procession has erupted into utter disarray, the drunk throng of revelers rushing to abscond the danger. It's exactly the kind of confusion we need in order to disappear without a trace, but the pandemonium makes for a slow and difficult journey, each shove and jostle drawing a pained moan from Novi and a winced apology from me.

I'm sorry. I'm sorry. I'm sorry. At least moaning in pain means that she's still breathing. That despite the blood loss, she's still alive.

But for how much longer? The second I'm certain our trail has cleared of enforcers, I steer us down a quieter alley, leaving our cloaks tucked behind an overflowing garbage pail. Owing to my distinct lack of totem, I can't risk leading us back to the monastery through the Gray, but as luck would have it, the Church's proclivity for lining the streets with iron works to safeguard our escape. To keep my visible aura from crossing paths with another Shade.

"Tell me a story, En." As Novi's pain begins to quiet, I try to lure her back from the edge. "Tell me something you've never told anyone else."

"You already know everything about me, Cem." Novi's voice is so weak, I can barely hear her over the fading roar of the parade. "I don't like secrets, remember? Wasn't that the rule we made?"

"Then why won't you tell me where you learned to sign?" I blurt the first objection that comes to my head. Not because I have any right to her confidence—not least of all after today—but because it might keep her talking. Keep her with me a little longer. Keep her alive.

"From my mom," Novi whispers, taking me by surprise.

"Your *mom*?" I sputter. "How did I not—? You never mentioned she was deaf."

"That's because she wasn't. But she had friends who were and she really loved the language, so she decided to teach me, as well. Said that more ways to communicate would always be better than less. And I wasn't keeping it a *secret*. It's just . . . I still find it hard to talk about her. You know that better than—" A violent cough robs her of the rest, filling the air with crimson.

"I'm so tired, Cem." The strength finally gives out in Novi's legs. "I think I'd like to stop now."

"Not yet," I say, doubling my efforts to support her weight, ignoring the piercing scream in my muscles and the sharp stitch wracking my chest. "But we're close, okay? We're almost there."

We're not almost there.

And by the time that feeble lie gains a grain of truth, Novi's lips are tinged with blue, her life hanging by a strained hiccup of rasping breaths.

"You have to hold on, En." I blink back the sharp sting of futility. This far into the faithless quarter, the streets stand almost deserted, the festivities concentrating around the square that will play host to the procession's end. As of yet, there's no sign of the riots the Commander had hoped to inflame—though dusk is only just beginning to fall proper, and it sure does feel as though his enforcers are stationed at every turn, waiting for the opportune moment to incite their hate. Adding another needless obstacle to a journey that Novi's body is too weak to make.

"You're still mad at me, remember?" I tell her. "You're not allowed to die mad."

You're not allowed to die at all.

I may not have actually killed Magdalena, but for a full year, I lived with the ache of believing I did, with the ghost of her shatter making a nightmare of my dreams.

I can't go through that again with Novi.

Not on the same day we already lost Eve.

I won't survive it.

I won't *want* to survive it when it was my stupidity that led her to the point of Rhodes's blade.

My decision to sell my totem.

When this hell of a night is over, I'll have to find a way to get that ring back, or else the Council will catch wind of my existence within a matter of days. Sooner even, if I'm not careful. Though at this particular moment, the only disaster I care about averting is Novi's death.

Please be here, please be here, please be here. When we finally—Gods, *finally*—reach the safety of our monastery, I search out the relief of Chase's face. The place still stands as messy as we'd left it this morning, the remnants of our planning littered across the table, the memory of Eve evident in the stains of multicolored dust that haunt the nave. But though I spot both Lyria and Ezzo—their borrowed cloaks lying discarded, their exhaustion glistening with sweat—I don't see Magdalena, and I don't see Chase.

I don't see a way to save Novi.

"Please tell me they're here." My fear cracks as Ezzo helps me lead her over to the daybed. *They have to be here, they have to be here—they must.*

"Are you sure Cassiel said they'd be coming?" The indictment in Ezzo's voice rings clear.

"Yes, I—" *No.* The words die on my tongue, the truth of them shaming me silent. When Chase left the Dominion, he technically owed me nothing, and whatever *feelings* I hoped would drive him to honor his promise were obviously just another in a long line of mistakes. A product of wishful thinking.

"It's okay, Cemmy," Novi murmurs as we lay her down, prying her eyes open an inch. "We did a lot of good today, setting Magdalena free. It's okay."

"But it's *not* okay." The tears spill hot against my cheeks. "I really thought he'd do this for us, En." *I really thought he'd save you for me.*

"You're an idiot, Cemilla Constance." Novi's hand is sticky with blood, the fight in her growing dim. "But I love you all the same. Always have, always will."

"Stop it. Stop saying goodbye." I rip Chase's scry from around my neck, gripping the crystal tight enough to shatter. *I don't care if I broke our deal, you hear me?* I infuse the sending with every ounce of my rage. *You get your ass to the monastery right now, Cassiel. You owe me this, you Gold bastard. You owe me* her, *you selfish, arrogant, treacherous piece of—*

You forgot "late". The crystal warms against my skin in reply. *I might be all of those things, but in this particular instance, I'm just late,* he says, then the following minute, the door to the monastery flies open and he and Magdalena burst inside.

"Where is she?" His eyes find me immediately, widening in alarm as they take in the full gravity of my bloodied state, a telling depiction of the scale of Novi's injury.

"Here. She's here." The swell of hope lurches me out of his way. "Please, save her."

"I promise to do as much as I can." His fingers graze mine for the briefest of seconds, the sincerity of his touch breaking my sobs loose in savage waves.

Do more. I try to tell him with my heart, and my guilt, and my terror, to impress on him the unparalleled importance of this singular feat of magic. *Do everything.*

And without delay, Chase puts his hands to the wound at Novi's ribs, his face screwing up in concentration, an effort far more pronounced than when he'd healed my thumb in the Governor's study a week ago.

Gods, has it really only been a week? My back crashes up against the wall, my body crumbling down to the paint-flecked flagstones. It feels as though a lifetime has passed between that first ill-advised lift and tonight's escape. A lifetime of lies, and loss, and betrayals—and enough revelations to rewrite the holy sacraments. So much so that it seems downright ludicrous that *any* of us survived to tell the tale. That we've somehow regained Magdalena, and learned the truth of our magics, and that beneath the green glow building around Chase, Novi's gradually beginning to stir, the blood returning to her cheeks and her breaths growing steady.

So ludicrous, in fact, that when the air around us explodes, my first thought is that I should have seen it coming. Because no story as fraught as this one could ever end in such a blissfully mundane way. No Hue since Clayvern Versallis instigated his purges has been that lucky.

The force of the blast pins my insides to my bones, the back of the monastery bursting apart in a furious hail of debris, filling my mouth with the bitter taste of metal.

"Novi! Chase!" I try to crawl towards them, only to find that the pressure holding me against the bricks is both immovable and absolute. Colorful in nature.

What in the hells . . . I buck against the impenetrable barrier, a flood of worst-case scenarios flitting through my head. Horrors doused in spite, and cruelty, and iron; visions of a death delivered by a Shade dressed in crimson or a noose spelled Orange around our necks. But when the dust finally settles, it isn't the Commander's rogues leering down at us from across the nave, or even a Council tracker come to rid the city of an illegal palette. No, somehow, the menace grinning out at us is both more predictable and infinitely worse.

It's Savian.

"Letting sentimentality get the better of you, Cassiel." He tuts, keeping us all trapped in place with his stolen supply of Red. Chase and Novi by the splintered daybed to my left; Lyria and Ezzo behind the upturned table to my right; Magdalena painfully out of reach of her brother. "Consider me disappointed—but not surprised. You always were too beholden to your emotions. It's what made you ripe for manipulation." Savian strides into the wreckage without a care or a doubt, as though Chase didn't betray him to the Council just a few short hours ago. As though it isn't impossible for him to be here.

"Did you really think you could dispose of me so readily?" He makes no effort to ensure that Lyria can read his lips, nor does it seem to bother him that the rest of us are in no position to interpret. "Or did you truly believe that one filthy half Shade could ruin my plans?" His fingers curl to form a tight fist, squeezing the breath from Chase's lungs.

"Cassiel—!"

"Quiet, girl, your time will come." With his other hand, Savian plucks Magdalena from the rubble, suspending her mid-air with her arms thrown out to the sides, her mouth frozen in a silent scream. A perfectly bloodless imprisonment.

"The slippery Gold and his Amber sister. You were a fool to think those rumors escaped me, Cassiel, and an even bigger fool to think that you could stop me from—what was it you promised the Bronze?—*using the siphon to cause any more harm.*" His declaration stuns both me and Chase cold.

Those were the exact words Chase used the night we learned to beat the portals.

While we were entirely alone.

Not in the Gray where Savian could have overheard our conversation unseen.

"No . . . that's not . . . how could you know that?" Chase grits through the spell constricting his windpipe. "You weren't there. You couldn't have been."

"Honestly, you halves know so little about magic, you're almost too easy to control." In a flash of Orange, Chase's shirt rips open from sternum to hip, revealing the crystal buried in his chest. "There's a reason scrys are usually worn instead of embedded, Cassiel," Savian tells him lazily—languidly—like a sated predator picking at his excess food. "Embedding a talisman in flesh amplifies its power. In this case, it works to enhance the bonded connection. Allows the subject of the spell to be monitored at will."

Oh Gods. I instantly snap to his meaning.

I didn't tell Savian about Lena. I have no idea how he found out. That's what Chase said when I accused him of divulging my secret, and in reply, I'd called him a liar. Threatened to kill him if he stayed in Isitar.

Except Chase wasn't lying, Savian has simply been playing him from day one. Listening in on every conversation. Every incriminating admission—including one of mine. And if he's been monitoring his movements, then he'll have seen Chase spell his flask and approach the Council. Removed himself from danger. Counted on us to fetch Magdalena for him because all along, he knew that the slippery Gold of rumor would never leave his Amber sister to die.

Just as he knew how to obscure his trail . . . I suddenly understand why the diamonds in his ears are embedded. With a Sapphire in the city, Savian must have realized how easily he could be tracked, took that extra precaution to ensure he'd stay invisible to Ezzo's gift. Safe from retaliation.

"Still, you served your purpose well enough, I suppose," he continues, appraising our ruined monastery with a disdainful eye. "And I dare say your chosen hideout will make for a fitting conclusion to the physical realm. What better place to end the Church's tyranny than the very house in which their Gods reside?" With a flick of his hand, Savian relegates the five of us to the furthest corner of the nave, uniting us in our horror behind a shimmery Orange wall.

Me, watching on helplessly as he floats Magdalena to his side.

Ezzo, paling white against the mural of flowers Eve painted while she was alive.

Novi, still unconscious but breathing steadily in Lyria's arms.

Chase, beating his fists bloody against a spell he can't hope to overcome, yelling obscenities at the devil circling his sister.

"You, my dear, will blot out their sun," Savian says, unsheathing a ceremonial dagger from the scabbard at his thigh, a waved-blade with a curved hilt that glints like rubies dipped in silver. "You will shatter their bones and turn day to perpetual night. You will usher in the age of shadows."

"No . . . please don't do this. I don't want to do this—I don't want to hurt anyone—*please.*" Magdalena's fear fast turns to anguish as with a flourish of steel, Savian begins to cut, a mirror to the desperate pleas escaping her brother.

"Mags—no! Leave her alone! Leave her alone, you sick—*fuck*!"

But no matter how hard they both scream, and beg, and struggle, they can't break free of the spells holding them captive, and their appeals do nothing to stay the violence of a madman's hand.

"Shallow cuts . . . shallow cuts." Savian runs the blade across Magdalena's wrists, her forearms, her palms, the elation in his grin turning manic. "We can't have you dying too quickly, now, can we?" he says as she starts bleeding shadows, a darkness so absolute it swirls around her like a gale of obsidian night.

"Please—you have to stop before I lose control." The tears in her voice are a spear to the gut, the desperation in her eyes growing feral. "You have to stop before I—"

Too late.

As Savian slashes a vicious wound across her hip, Magdalena's irises burn black to the edge, the outpouring of power bowing her body crescent. After a year spent siphoning magic in an iron cell, her veins have grown too rich with the darkness to fight his torture for long.

It would need to happen on the cleansing moon. Now that I'm watching Savian's true intentions unfold, I understand why his Indigo foresaw him sending us into the Dominion today. By allowing the drain to continue right up until the shadows reached their tipping point, he's ensured that Magdalena would be fit for bursting. Ready to devour the world whole.

With an agonized scream, her head snaps back, the sound turning from pain to thunder.

The air around her dulls Gray.

Literally.

Unleashing a deadly storm of shadows that billows as it expands.

Oh fuck.

"In-Betweens up, now!" I throw myself at Novi and Lyria, my shield rushing out to meet the churning tempest as I yell for Ezzo and Chase to cast their own. And if Savian cares that we've not yet shattered, he doesn't show it. Nor does he make to curb our magic or feed our lives to the insatiable hunger growling in the dark.

Because, why would he?

The bleeding his order has spent four hundred years pursuing is finally coming to pass.

He doesn't need to worry about a few hapless half Shades.

He's already won.

CHAPTER

Thirty-one

The shadows swirl, and swell, and spread, wringing out of Magdalena the way water would a sodden rag. Air turns to ink turns to smoke turns to darkness, the magic gaining in strength as Savian continues to slash mercilessly at his prize, unleashing her power.

Shallow cuts . . . shallow cuts.

The windows are the first casualty of his malevolence, exploding in a violent hail of soot-covered shards.

No, no, no, no. Lead fills my lungs as the marauding tendrils escape into the night, the ramifications of their freedom spinning dread around my bones. It's not just the typics Savian's condemning to death with this unholy bleeding, it's every half Shade who's managed to evade the purges and eke out some semblance of a life. The Council has spent four hundred years ensuring that we know the bare minimum about our magic, to keep us scared, and to keep us helpless, and to keep us from reaching our full potential in the Gray.

To keep us easy to kill.

There'll be no advance warning for those halves—no time to align with an Emerald, or reach a sanctuary, or prepare for a world that seeks to eradicate the typical tint of our blood. Between one moment and the next, day will become night and safety will breed danger. A death sentence for all but the tiny minority that's been able to see past the Council's rhetoric and learn to anchor their In-Betweens right.

Hundreds of Hues will shatter.

Hundreds of thousands of typics will die.

An entire realm will be lost to the whims of a zealot.

We can't just stand by and watch that happen. *We can't let this happen, we can't let this happen—I can't.*

There has to be a way to stop it.

"Lyria—" I command her attention with a frantic wave of my hand. "Is there any chance you can talk to the shadows? Get them to see how wrong this is?"

"I'm trying, but they won't listen to me," she signs, her eyes darting back and forth with unsettling speed, as though she's engaged in a silent battle of wills to which the rest of us are blind. *"As much as they hate that we allowed Magdalena to live, they understand the opportunity she's giving them. They want to be free."*

Yeah, well, so does everyone. I put my fists to Savian's impenetrable wall, joining Chase in his attempt to bring down the magic. If we could just get to Magdalena ourselves, then maybe we could find a way to stem the bleeding. Prevent the shadows spreading further. Limit the damage Savian's caused. But until we're free of his prison, we won't be able to do much of anything; I quit pounding on the shimmery Orange glass.

In order to save Magdalena, we first need to end Savian.

"Then what about turning the shadows against *him*, instead?" My signs are hesitant, unsure, racing three steps ahead of the seed that's taking root inside my mind. "Do you think you could make them believe that Savian's their enemy?" I ask. "Get them to attack him on our behalf?"

"How in the nine hells do you expect her to do that?" Even as Ezzo snipes at me, he settles beside Lyria to draw Novi into his lap, so that he can bear the cost of her In-Betweens, allow our Amethyst to focus on this more pressing of tasks.

"Gods, Ez, I don't know—but there has to be *something* she can say." I'm fast losing my ability to tolerate his doubts. Yes, Ezzo has every right to hate me—he has every right to never speak to me again, if he so chooses, let alone afford me his trust—but since he clearly understands the need to be helpful, then maybe he can save his anger for when the world isn't falling apart. Give me a second to think through the damn problem.

"Tell them that he's the one who put Magdalena in that cell to begin with." I reach for the lie that would incense the shadows the most. "Tell them that he deliberately gave her to the Church. That he's known where she was all year and chose to do nothing. That he wanted the shadows to grow weak. That once he tricks them into killing his enemies, he means to use her gift to draw them right back." The more this questionable idea of mine solidifies, the more hopeful I become that it's got legs. "Nothing you tell them has to be true—or even make that much sense. You just need to convince them that they'd be safer without Savian around. Freer."

"I can certainly try." Lyria sets her jaw as she begins to parley with the dark, her lids fluttering like autumn leaves with the effort.

Please let this work. I steal a glance over at Chase, still screaming himself hoarse at the spell separating us from his sister, his hands bruised stark against the magic, his cheeks wet with the fear that he won't reach Magdalena before Savian bleeds her dry.

Come on, come on, come on . . . this has to work. If the shadows can bend themselves to help a Hue, there's no reason they can't also be coaxed to do a rogue Shade harm. With their power growing stronger by the minute, I'd venture there's never been a better time to ask.

"By my colors, is that—? *Look.*" Ezzo's disbelief is a whisper in an ocean of howls, barely audible above the chaos. "I think it might be—she's actually doing it."

You don't have to sound so surprised. I ignore the barbed cut of his incredulity, following his gaze to where, at the core of the raging tempest, a few of the burgeoning wisps have begun to twist against the crowd.

They're listening. The kernel of hope I've been stoking crackles as it ignites. Tendril by tendril, they're beginning to turn against Savian.

Of the five of us still conscious, he's the last to notice what's happening. A full-blooded Shade is not accustomed to fearing the darkness. They *are* the shadows, able to winnow through the Gray the way a snake slithers through tall grass. They would never dream that the power they trust so implicitly might one day rear up and bite their hand. That possibility would have never even occurred to him.

"What is the meaning of this?"

But it sure is occurring to him now.

"How dare you presume to—" I spot the moment Savian gets it, the realization narrowing his eyes, their scrutiny immediately falling on Lyria. "Do not listen to the girl—she's lying!" he yells into the vengeful storm. "I am the one who set you free! Your fealty belongs with *me*—with the Order of Versallis—not with some filthy half!" He aims a Green bolt of magic directly at her heart.

No dice.

The shadows spring a dam between them, rushing to the aid of the Amethyst fueling their rage with lies, an alliance Savian can't hope to break because while Lyria is speaking their language, he's merely yelling self-serving protestations into the night. They're not going to believe his story.

Versallis was right to fear us.

The more Savian's terror intensifies, the more his grip on our magical prison begins to crack, his bloodied dagger clattering to the floor amid the panic. The full-bloods have spent so long vilifying our existence, they've forgotten the utility our gifts could provide, their unique breadth and value. In focusing solely on the danger we presented, they ensured that *danger* was all they would ever find. They robbed themselves of an opportunity.

We won't make that same mistake.

Nor will we stop to think, or question, or indulge the guilt when it comes.

Savian doesn't deserve our mercy.

With another urging from Lyria, the shadows turn savage in their attack, suffocating him with a violence that splinters his magic and finally brings the intractable wall of Orange down.

"Go—now!"

The second our cage springs open, Chase and I are on the move. Him, towards Magdalena; me, towards the knife Savian carelessly dropped to the ground.

Thank my colors I'm a Bronze. Though my physicality may have hindered us in the Dominion, right at this very moment, there's no other Gray gift I'd rather have. It allows me to bend low and scoop up the fallen blade in my hand. To clutch the curved hilt tight between my fingers and relish the cool bite of metal pressed against my palm.

When the screaming starts, you ignore it. As I charge into the merciless swarm of shadows, it's Novi's voice staying the shake in my arm. She almost died today thanks to Savian's madness. Eve *did* die because of it, and if we don't find a way to reverse the frenzy he's triggered, then an entire realm will die. And since stopping him is the first step to stopping that from happening, I find that—in the end—plunging the dagger into his heart isn't a difficult choice at all; it's a decision that's already been made.

This is for Eve. The steel guts effortlessly through his flesh, the waved blade finding its mark with a purpose. His eyes bulge with surprise, the shock grunting him silent as he staggers away from me, the rubied hilt protruding from his chest like a grotesquely shaped charm.

"This changes *nothing*, girl." When finally Savian does speak, his guttural growl is defiant, zealous and vindictive right down to his last. "I have set a flame to this world and extinguished day with night. I have fulfilled my destiny."

There's no denying the truth in his brag.

Magdalena is still bleeding shadows, a devastating rush that's fast escalating in speed and might. If it hasn't yet engulfed the cemetery, it won't be long before the Gray eclipses its bounds, and once it breaks out of the sanctuary and surges through the streets proper, hundreds—no, *thousands*—of typics will die.

"Maybe you have." A new sort of idea kindles inside my mind, born of the cruel need to enact a little vindictiveness of my own. "But you won't get to watch it burn. This is how it feels to fear the shadows," I tell him. Then with a couple of resolute signs to Lyria—a firm point followed by a snapping of fists—I arrange for Savian to meet the same twisted fate he was all too happy to inflict on this realm.

Shatter him.

How she convinces the Gray to do that, I don't know, but her eyes only close for the briefest of moments before the shadows are goaded to action, enveloping Savian in a blackness so deep it threatens to swallow the light whole. He shrieks, and the sound reverberates around the monastery like a promise, his fear souring the air in pungent clouds, his blood drip, drip, dripping down to the flagstones until finally with a crack, clink, crunch, shatter, Savian bursts into a thousand pieces of glass.

He dies like a half Shade.

He dies the way this entire city is soon wont to die.

Lena. The instant his shards hit the ground, I'm running towards the broken girl hanging limp in Chase's arms.

"I can't stop the bleeding." His voice is thick with despair. "There's too much, I—I can't make it stop." He's already stripped off his cloak and the remnants of his ruined shirt, wrapping them tight around as many of her wounds as he could manage.

But there are too many of them—and Savian did his job too well.

Shallow cuts . . . shallow cuts.

Just deep enough to prevent the skin from readily knitting shut.

Just deep enough that Magdalena bleeds through the fabric.

"Please, Mags, you have to fight this," Chase begs. "You have to fight because I can't heal you."

Not now that he's healed Novi. A vicious pang of guilt stabs through my chest. Chase did have enough stolen power to save his sister, but then I urged him to use it to save Novi, instead. Which he only had to do because I sold my ring and alerted Rhodes to our presence in the Dominion—and I might never have done *that* had we simply chosen to trust each other instead of plotting our betrayals. Led with our hearts rather than our heads.

Gods. In hindsight, it's so damn easy to spot the exact moment at which our plans went off the rails. The entirely avoidable cascade of mistakes that led to the decision Chase now has to make.

Because Savian was wrong, there is one way to stop the bleeding.

One Hue who can claw the shadows back to their rightful place.

Though he'd never think to do it.

"You need to take Lena's gift," I whisper, shuddering the appeal through Chase. Her *gift*, not her *power*; my words are chosen with care. "That's our only hope for ending this."

"I am not *killing* my sister, Cemilla." His face sears vibrant with rage. "There has to be another way."

But there isn't, and we both know that. We both know that with this much magic surging out of Magdalena, Chase can't just siphon off the excess like he did in the cell. He'd go into a spell-shocked stupor long before he made a dent in the shadows, then she'd keep right on bleeding until the frenzy exsanguinated her dead.

Her gift is the only option we have left.

"It might not kill her," I say, twisting the logic around a wishful prayer. "Think about it, Chase—after this past year, Lena's blood is *brimming* with power—so much more than any ordinary half Shade's. If you're careful, then maybe the extraction won't affect her as badly as it did that Copper you drained. If you only take as much as you need."

"No. I won't do it," he growls, redoubling his efforts to rouse Magdalena from the haze. "I only just got her back. You can't ask me to—"

"She didn't want this, Chase." But I have to ask him to. I have to ask him to because no one else will. "Remember how scared she was when we found her? She didn't want to be responsible for so many deaths."

"She is not *responsible*." His voice is little more than a pleading breath. "This was Savian's doing—and it would never have happened if the Church hadn't tortured her into losing control in the first place!"

"I know." I place my hand over his, the shadows curling lazy knots around our fingers. "But you need to think about what a world like this looks like, and I'm not just talking about all the typics it would shatter—but what it would mean for other Hues, as well. We're not built to spend our lives in the Gray," I tell him, pushing my magic against the edge of his shield, a reminder of the relentless toll we're constantly paying, no matter how adept we've grown at bearing that expense. "We'd never be able to let our guard down again, or sleep outside a sanctuary. We'd always be worrying about our anchors, or about what would happen if our In-Betweens were to fail. We were a dying breed long before the Church stuck its claws into Lena, and if we let this happen, it'll drive us extinct. You *know* she wouldn't want to be responsible for that," I say, and I'd believe that much even if I'd never met her. Because I doubt there's a single Hue in existence who would willingly shoulder that blame.

If I were in Magdalena's shoes, I'd be begging Chase to take my gift.

Even if it meant my life.

"Promise me you won't leave her." The nightmare I've painted spreads an agony across his face. "No matter what happens—promise me you won't let her shatter."

Not die, *shatter*; Chase chooses his words with equal care. Despite my hollow assurances, he's already guessed at where this story might end, and if it does, he's telling me what he's afraid of.

He doesn't want to lose his sister to the shadows the way we lost Eve.

"I promise." Carefully as I can manage, I tease Magdalena from his arms. "But you'll stop before it's too late. I know you will." I fill my voice with confidence, though this particular promise is not one I have the ability to make. I've no earthly idea whether he'll be able to control the drain, and Chase hasn't risked stealing magic from a Hue since that childhood extraction that left a Copper dead. This is one trick he'll have to perform on faith.

"Forgive me, Mags." A sob ripples his shoulders as he moves to place his hands gently—so heartbreakingly gently—against her collarbone, pressing skin to exposed skin and his will to the color in her veins. And though Magdalena's eyes remain vacant, her back arches as his power seizes hold of her gift, an amber glow pulsing between them. "Forgive me. Forgive me. Forgive me."

She gasps, and bucks, and convulses with the pain, the magic in her blood protesting the violation.

I am the violence the world made of me.

Chase had said those words in reply to my condemnation, yet here I am, only a few days later, working to hone him into a blade. Working to ensure that when the deed is done, my fingers will be in reach of another.

I guess this world makes a violence of us all.

"Don't stop—she'll be okay," I say as slowly—so excruciatingly slowly—the flood of shadows swirling around Magdalena gradually begins to ebb, quieting the ravenous storm. "She'll be okay, Chase. Don't stop, she'll be okay." That's the lie I use to keep him from breaking contact until her cuts bleed nothing but red.

That's the lie I use to keep his heart from shattering.

And when he finally does pull away—his breaths gruff and heavy, his irises burned black to the edge—I don't give him the chance to put those flimsy lies to the test. Because if Chase did take too much—if he did cause Magdalena's death—then I can't let the grief distract him from the most important task we have left.

Stopping the shadows isn't enough.

We still have to banish them back from whence they came.

My fingers close around the curved hilt of rubies, the desperate need to end this nightmare guiding my aim.

"I'm so sorry, Chase." With a flick of my wrist, I lurch up to run Savian's dagger across his chest, slashing a crimson trail down from the tip of his shoulder to the hard-cut cleft of his hip, a wound brutal enough to trigger a new kind of drain.

"Cemmy—what—?" The shock in his eyes is a spear to the soul, though the protest dies on his tongue long before he's able to fully register the pain, the raw rush of power pitching him high into the air. Unlike Magdalena, he's not spent his life learning to suppress the hunger. The moment he starts bleeding, the gift he's imbibed commences feeding on the Gray.

Chase's head snaps back, his spine arching, his arms spreading open like wings. With his shirt gone and his chest bloodied, he looks like an avenging angel, a herald sent by the Gods to recover their domain.

And the Gods have never been kind to half Shades.

"Take Novi to the sanctuary—now!" I yell for Ezzo to get her and Lyria clear of the threat, throwing myself around Magdalena. *Please don't be dead. Please don't be dead. Please don't be dead.* I pray for the solace of a stirring breath. For the rhythmic march of a heart that's still beating. To not have to witness her die again. *Please—he needs you to not be dead.*

Though what he needs from me is to keep the shadows at bay. To fight the pressure gnawing furiously at my shield and spare his sister from the splintering might of the drain.

I am in between Chase and Magdalena.

Victory and defeat.

The relief of a pulse and the fear that it'll fail.

"Stay with me, Lena." No matter how hard the darkness rails at me, I won't leave her to face its cold revenge.

I am in between the ceiling and the floor.

Hope and despair.

The urge to wash my hands of an infuriating Gold and the need to have him stay.

"Chase—hurry!" I howl the words into the rage-filled squall, though I very much doubt he can hear me. The shadows scream loud as they're dragged back into their given realm, seething, their talons vying to take a lying Bronze along with them, as though they know I'm the one who conspired to foil their escape. They maul at the edge of my In-Between, piercing, biting, clawing the magic until it's all I can do to stop them tearing clean through the spell.

I am in between typical flesh and blood color.

Consciousness and the ether.

The age-old war between the Church and the Council of Shades.

And even as my vision blurs to fog and my strength wanes to nothing, I refuse to let this story end with the death of the girl I swore to protect.

I won't let them take you, I won't let them take you—it's going to end different this time because I learned the spell.

When the dark finally turns to light, my arms are still clasped around Magdalena.

When that light flickers and turns to gold, I know it's safe for me to let go.

CHAPTER

Thirty-two

My head weighs too much—it weighs *way* too much—and my body's full of lead, my blood stinging through my veins like acid.

Dead. I think I might be . . . dead?

"No such luck, Cemmy." A voice vibrates through the haze, answering my unasked question. So either it can read my mind, or I said the words aloud.

"That second one, I'm afraid." This time, I recognize the voice as Novi's. Just as I recognize the spiced scent of her favorite incense, and the soft skim of her threadbare sheets. The salt air wafting in off the cliffs beyond her window. "It's like you're trying to narrate your own wake-up."

So just dead of embarrassment, then. I blink hard against the warm glow of the hex-lights, every part of me groaning as I force myself to sit up in the bed. To look at her properly. Take in the fact that Novi's here, and alive, and no longer losing life from an arrow wound to the shoulder and a saber stabbed through her chest.

She survived the toll of my failures.

Barely. Despite Chase's healing, there's still a pallid tint to her skin and an exhaustion simmering behind her eyes. A pain that speaks of loss, and sadness, and grief. A pain that speaks of heartbreak.

Oh Gods. "Lena—Chase—are they—? Did any of it work? Did we stop the Gray?" The memories assault me in a frenzied rush, the darkness swirling outside the window taking on a stark new shape. I remember the power bursting out of Magdalena. Savian shattering at the mercy of his own knife. Chase hanging suspended in mid-air as the shadows collapsed back into him. The world dulling of color and light.

"Easy, Cem—" Novi's hands clamp around my shoulders, keeping me from lurching upright and stumbling on dizzy legs. "They're fine. The Gray is back where it should be. The typics live to hate us another day."

Right.

Okay.

I force in a breath to sate the panic. If nothing else, I can instantly confirm those last two parts of her claim. Because Novi doesn't live in a sanctuary, nor could she have held an In-Between around me from her place on the loveseat while I was monopolizing the bed.

That's just a regular night rippling outside the window.

Impossible though it might seem, the city beyond it remains unchanged.

"So it . . . *worked?*" That hopeful idea feels way too far-fetched. "Did we really—?"

"Stop a zealous fanatic? Stem the Governor's bid for power? Save an entire world?" Novi raises an eyebrow. "Yeah, I guess we kind of did. Or at least, mostly." With a sigh and a brewing of tea, she launches into the tale, catching me up on everything I missed while I was sleeping.

How—using Magdalena's gift—Chase was able to banish the Gray back to its rightful place in the shadows.

How—as I'd wishfully predicted—the overabundance of magic in his sister's blood allowed her to survive the theft of that gift.

How—given my stubborn insistence to fulfil a promise—it was actually *me* who almost ended up losing her life to the drain. Who spent the best part of three days burning with a color-sick fever.

But the true crux of Novi's story only starts once my own recollections grow dim, with a cleansing moon parade turned to violence. The moment darkness fell over Isitar, the Commander's enforcers carried out their orders with a merciless glee, inciting a slew of riots that raged across the faithless quarter. But with him gone, Magdalena freed, and the shadows set loose upon the physical realm, the Church's attempt to take the city succeeded only in painting blood across the streets, equal parts faithless and reformed. Since the Gray never reached its tipping point, Isitar's remaining Shades were never fully stripped of their color—quite the opposite, in fact, their magics were fast restoring in strength—and since the Church had proven its willingness to break with the accords, the Council was only too happy to allow its own contingent of soldiers to slip the leash.

To remind the clerics that with a flex of their hand, a Red can seize control of their bodies, a Green can stop their hearts, a Blue can speed the rate at which they ripen and grow sick.

To remind them that iron alone is not enough to overcome the imbalance of power.

And once their Aralagios started dying, the Church put an end to its campaign for conquest pretty damn quick. Hells, in their subsequent show of contrition, they went so far as to offer the Council a couple of additional seats in the senate, as a way to calm the turbulent waters, which—owing to Savian's madness—were churning both angry and deep.

"It was bad, Cem," Novi says, idly running her fingers through the curls of steam escaping her cup. "The shadows had already spread across several streets before Cassiel was able to rein them in."

Several streets. As she continues the telling, the full weight of that implication wraps a cord around my ribs. The festivities may have drawn the majority of faithless out of their homes and away from the consequences of Magdalena's gift, but the stubborn minority who spurned the parade weren't so lucky.

Dozens of typics were shattered in the wake of the magic.

Hundreds more saw the darkness descend with a vengeance that'll haunt their dreams.

And though only a precious few in Isitar will ever know the truth of how that darkness came to exist—and none remaining know of our involvement—the unknown has always done more to stoke the flames of hatred than concrete answers ever did. This tenuous new alliance the Council has brokered is rooted in fear and loss rather than a real want for peace—with each side furious at the other for the part they played in the near destruction of the life we currently lead.

The Council blames the Church for seeking to exploit an Amber.

The Church blames the Council for losing track of a maniacal Shade.

And so this city still hangs on a precipice; the escalating war averted only because they both experienced the price of defeat.

"Gods, we're right back where we started," I mutter, my head shaking with the disbelief. "After everything that's happened"—*and everything we've been through; everything we've lost*—"absolutely nothing's changed."

Not for the better, anyhow.

The pain of Eve's death only stings sharper now that the danger's behind us, the distance lingering between me and Novi a stark reminder of the faith I'm yet to re-win. I might be in her bed—and she may have cared enough to bring me here to recover—but a week ago, Novi would have been pressed up against me, having this conversation shoulder to shoulder instead of from the loveseat across the room.

I've lost that part of her now.

Maybe just temporarily, or maybe for good.

Only time will answer that question.

"Change doesn't happen overnight, Cemmy." The conviction in Novi's voice rings more hopeful than sad. "And it rarely ever happens when one side is holding all the cards. That's what we took from them. We made sure the Church would think twice before triggering another Amber, and we drew the Council's attention to some pretty glaring holes in their ability to keep the Gray safe, empowered them to stop capitulating. That's not what I'd call *nothing*."

No, I guess it's not.

Neither is the health Chase's tincture gifted Mom or the fact that it'll have protected her when the shadows escaped their realm. Neither is the improved command we have on our magic and the parts of our history we've been able to reclaim. And neither is the knowledge that Magdalena is alive, and unshattered, and that the lies her brother fed me weren't told out of malice, but out of desperation and despair. That, much like me, he's just no good at weathering his decisions unscathed.

"They're gone, aren't they?" I ask, not yet willing to invoke their names.

"Yeah." Though Novi breaks the word gently, there is no gentle way to tell me they left. "Ezzo too."

"Ez too?" His name is an anvil to the chest, the loss I didn't see coming. As much as I'd already suspected that my friendship with Ezzo wouldn't survive my betrayal, I never imagined he would sever ties with Isitar, as well.

I never imagined we would lose our watcher.

"Can you really blame him, Cem?" Novi's answering grimace is pained. "Our monastery is now an *actual* ruin, and everywhere he looked, all he could see was Eve. It wouldn't have been fair to ask him to stay."

No, I guess it wouldn't.

Nor was I owed the chance to atone for my mistakes.

Not after the love I took from him.

"I don't suppose that—erm . . . did he happen to say where he was going?" I ask, though the real question I'm asking is, *did Chase?* Because despite all the lies—and in that regard, I'm hardly blameless—the inexplicable feelings he's awakened don't seem to have gone away.

I'm hoping that, once this is all behind us, we can maybe . . . start over.

I didn't even realize how much I was hoping for that myself, not until the chance was suddenly ripped away. And though I understand why he and Magdalena had to go—with both the Church and the Council out for Amber blood, Isitar's the last place they'd have been wise to stay—it still hurts to know that I didn't matter enough for them to linger. That the Gold who was willing to walk through all nine hells for his sister wouldn't even wait out a fever for me. That I really was just a means to an end.

"I'm sorry, Cemmy—Chase didn't," Novi says, instantly guessing at my meaning. "But he did leave you this." The velvet pouch she tosses me flashes black through the air, the note tucked inside rustling upon open.

Consider this my apology for all the lies, Cemilla.
You were never one of them.

The words are like cool water splashed on a sizzling burn, and I'm surprised to discover how much hurt so few of them can dispel so quickly. How much power there is in having your feelings returned.

More than just your feelings . . . When I spill out the contents of the pouch, the flutter in my gut intensifies, flooding my veins with a grateful heat.

My ring.

The totem that obscures the visible trace of my magic, returned before I had the inevitable misfortune of crossing paths with a Council Shade—or having to weather a very uncomfortable conversation with my mother.

Or at least, a *more* uncomfortable one. As I gather my wits and slink away from Novi's bedsit, the pit in my stomach pitches with nerves. Not enough time has passed for Mom to have received my note yet, and though our fight feels like little more than a smudge in the annals of history, when the cleansing moon festivities turned deadly, she must have worried herself sick wondering what became of my fate.

And that was three days ago. No matter how much I fear the hard truths hanging between us, it would be cruel not to go back and alleviate her dread. All this time, Mom was just trying to protect me. Her methods may have been flawed, but the intention behind them has always been rooted in the right place.

I suppose we have that in common . . . Once I've snaked my way back to the apartment, I hesitate in the hallway, wanting nothing more than to go inside, but afraid of what will happen when I do. The anger that's like to greet me.

"Cemilla—? Is that you?"

But it's not anger I hear in Mom's voice when I finally push open the door—it's a wishful hope, and a frantic longing, and a strangled cry of relief.

And it damn near breaks me.

"Hi, Mom." I rush straight into her arms, allowing her to hold me the way she used to before she took ill. "I'm sorry I didn't come home sooner."

"All that matters is that you're home now," she says, and I can tell by the pitch of her sobs that she won't be demanding any difficult answers today. That knowing I'm safe will be enough to soothe her qualms until tomorrow. That those trying conversations will keep.

Instead, she allows me to run myself a bath without question, and when I emerge from the washroom—scrubbed clean of the blood and grime that had stuck beneath my clothes and nails—she insists on fixing me something to eat, a tender act of mothering she's not been able to indulge in years.

Also Chase's doing . . . The mark he left on my life is everywhere I look.

In the diamonds glittering on my finger, and the green-labelled tincture that's restoring Mom's health.

In the bridges I'm yet to mend with Novi, and the red-headed Amethyst we've welcomed into our midst.

In the wreck of my friendship with Ezzo, and the hole in my heart left by Eve.

In the way Madam Berska hasn't knocked on our door in a full week.

Hells, when I finally retire for the night, I swear I can even sense his presence in my room, the air crackling with the scent of stolen magic.

Except.

Wait.

As a cold breeze gusts through the open window, I shiver with the possibility that the feeling may not exist entirely in my head—though

I'm loath to trust it. Loath to allow myself a hope that could turn crushing with the wind.

"Novi told me you'd left." I speak the words at the dark, too afraid to reach for the hex-lights and throw reality into sharp relief.

A second passes.

A whole lifetime of silence encompassed in a fractured beat.

But then . . .

"I did." The words are a gruff confession, a breathless whisper meant only for me. "Got as far as Heresse, actually, before I stole some new magic and ended up back here."

"Why?" I still can't bring myself to look at him, lest it upset whatever spell is orchestrating this dream.

"Why do you think?" All at once, Chase is standing behind me, the gentle graze of his fingers proving beyond doubt that he's real.

"I thought you didn't make a habit of getting close to people."

"It's not a habit, Cemmy," he says, phasing us clear of Mom's ears. "You're the first."

I am in between him and the bed.

Want and confusion.

Butterflies and relief.

"And Lena?" I ask. Because after everything that's happened, I find it hard to believe he'd ever leave her side again. "Didn't she need you in Heresse?"

"Mags is an Amber, remember? The power she takes heals her quick. Though when you start hearing rumors about her death at the hands of a pious mob, remember that I'm a Gold." As Chase turns me to face him, the silver in his irises flashes red. Two lone specks of color in an undulating ocean of gray.

Right, of course. Glamour magic. I can only imagine what elaborate performance he'll engineer next. It'll be something public, no doubt. Sensational enough for word of Magdalena's demise to reach both Council and Church, buy her a few years' respite. A few years of not being hunted before the rumors start up again and the cycle repeats. Before the curse of the Hue catches up with them.

"She was right not to tell me about the four of you," Chase says, the admission in his voice dipping low. "I would have definitely tried to talk her into leaving Isitar. I would have convinced her you weren't worth the risk. And I would have been *wrong*." There's a tremble to his hands as they seek the press of mine, an explicit call for permission to step closer than it's wise for us to be.

Which I grant him anyway.

"I was so sure we had to do it all again," he continues, tracing idle circles along my wrist. "The running, the hiding, the never staying in one place. But then we got to Heresse, and Mags got her strength back, and she reminded me that the one thing we can't do is stop the rain. We've been living this way half our lives for the sole purpose of keeping her away from the Council, and keeping her away from the Church. But then the Church went and found her anyway, and all that effort—all that *loneliness*—none of it made a damn bit of difference in the end. What made the difference was *you*, Cemmy." In the dim light of the mottled shadows, his eyes shine like iridescent gems. "It was the friends I'd have told her to leave. And I don't know if it was luck that brought you together, or if it was a deliberate act of fate, but I do know that you're the only reason I was able to save her. So since the worst has already happened, we both decided that maybe it was time to stop running and try something different. Like being happy."

Those words settle deep inside my chest, the tug of them inching us ever closer. For while it makes no sense to want him—to *trust* him—after so many lies and betrayals, it equally makes no sense for Chase to want or trust *me*.

Because I lied, too.

As did Magdalena, as did Mom.

We all made mistakes in our attempts to protect the ones we love.

We all have to hope those mistakes can be forgiven.

So when Chase leans his face towards mine, I let him. And when he wraps his arms around my waist, I let him do that, too. I let him kiss me. Not because it makes sense, and not because I trust him, and not because we've overcome any of those less-than-inconsequential doubts that still remain. I let Chase kiss me because right at this moment, I *want* him to kiss me. And because the only way we'll ever know for sure what we *could* be, is to allow ourselves to live that different life and hope the happiness might stick. To prove whether a stubborn Bronze and an arrogant Gold can mix.

And maybe that idea *is* reckless, and foolhardy, and naïve.

Maybe it does exist in that liminal space between faith and madness.

Love and loneliness.

Magic and belief.

But didn't anyone ever tell you? We're always in between something.

Bonus content

As a reader—and a massive shipper—I always loved it when authors would share snippets of my favorite scenes from the love interest's point of view, so when I was asked to provide some bonus content for this edition, I instantly knew that I wanted to write something in Chase's voice.

There were a few obvious scenes to choose from: his game of truth with Cemmy on the couch, their almost kiss at the observatory, the kiss kiss once they learned how to beat the portals, or even the last scene of the book when the two of them reconciled. But ultimately, I decided to go with a scene that wasn't technically romantic in nature, but is nonetheless one of the most emotionally charged in the novel—and my absolute favorite scene—the exchange of magic in chapter 14.

This scene takes place at the height of Cemmy and Chase's animosity, so there are a lot of big feelings flying around, and since Chase's ability to take power—both for himself and on behalf of others—lends rise to so many of the ethical questions surrounding magic in the book, I really enjoyed getting to explore his relationship with his gift in more detail.

And I really hope that you enjoy it, too.

Chase

She saw me.

The screams I'm extracting fade beneath the roar of blood pounding in my ears, the power searing through my veins like lightning.

She saw *this*.

The true face of my gift.

"That's enough, Cassiel." Savian's voice echoes sharply around the theater house, chiding me to break the connection before I accidentally take too much, leave the Red I'm draining too weak to replenish her magic so that I can take more. Give *him* more. Feed his vendetta.

Mags. You're doing it for Mags. I remind myself, trading the Red's screams for a nauseating chorus of Blue. I'm not inflicting this pain for no reason, it's a means to an end. Just as I am a means to an end for Savian, and Cemmy is a means to an end for me—no matter how interesting I find her or how effortlessly she prickles my ire. How I've never met anyone quite so uniquely obstinate.

Too reckless, too scared, and too proud—a combination that's both exasperating and impossible to predict. As much as I knew she'd react badly to my offer of help, I thought she'd jump at the chance to learn a better way to cast her In-Betweens, then when she didn't, I assumed she'd need a lot more coaxing to properly embrace the spell. I never imagined she'd trust it enough to follow me here and witness this horror. I didn't plan on having to deal with a stomach full of squirming shame.

You need her physicality, nothing more. I try to focus on the Blue I'm extracting instead of the blue of her eyes; on the way the magic feels as it floods my body instead of the way her waist felt beneath my fingers; on anything but the look on her face when she learned what it means to have your color run Gold. Once the cleansing moon is over, I'll never see her again, so it doesn't much matter if today she really *saw* me.

The violence I've become.

It doesn't matter because it *can't* matter. Because even if she didn't hate me, there's no future to be had here. No sense of indulging a curiosity that would make it harder for me to leave.

Which is why the only Hue you should *be thinking about is Mags.* As soon as the Blue loses consciousness, I move to replenish my supply of Orange and Yellow, taking more power in a single night than I've ever held in one go. So much magic, in fact, that even after Savian has commanded his fill, my blood feels fit to bursting. Not just hot, but scorched with acid. Not just wild, but brimming with rage. At Savian, at myself, at the maddening Bronze who insisted I commit this offense then had the nerve to look so appalled.

The fucking audacity of it. My hands clench and clench and clench.

One day.

That's how long it took for Cemmy to start exploiting my gift.

She got there even faster than Savian.

And the worst part is I can't blame her. I'm under no illusion that I'm the victim here, and I know exactly how it feels to be backed into a corner. How the unthinkable suddenly consumes your dreams. Savian's threat—his promise to betray her palette to the Council—I've lived at the mercy of that blade, too, though it wasn't a rogue Shade holding it to my throat; it was the man who supposedly loved my mother. He didn't much like the fact that she had a power he couldn't possess, and when she told him about us, he didn't see two kids, he saw an opportunity—and it wound up getting her killed.

My gift always winds up hurting someone.

Every time I take another's magic, I lose another piece of my soul.

And Cemmy should know that. The anger propels me through the streets as though accelerated by a Blue. For while I never intended to show any of them the full brutality of my gift, I suddenly *want* her to see the cost of the spells she demanded. The violence *and* the consequence. The burnt black eyes, and the sweltering skin, and the shaking, and the shaking and the—Gods, I need to make her *see* so that this incessant shaking might stop. And the shadows are a blur. The city is a blur. Her building is a blur, and a breach of trust, and a terrible idea. But I wisp through the door just the same, and into her room, and out of the Gray, until I'm surrounded by the dizzying scent of the girl who hasn't earned the right to infuriate me in such an absolute way.

And I shouldn't be here.

Not in the cold dead of night.

When she hasn't even made it home yet.

But she will. I pace the room from corner to corner, fighting the urge to rifle through the depths of her life and figure out what makes her tick. Cemmy always comes back home eventually. More often than not, she hides in that ruin of a monastery until the early hours, but in all the weeks that I've been watching, she only stayed out until morning on the one occasion. Last night. With the Cobalt. Which didn't bother me then, and the only reason it's bothering me now is because tonight, I need for her to come home and see.

That's the *only* reason.

It has to be the only reason.

I can't afford for it to be anything more.

So then where the colors is she? My boots wear a hole through the dusty floorboards, adding a grumble of creaks to the rhythmic breaths filtering through the paper-thin walls. Cemmy's mother. Fast asleep and no longer dying as quickly as she was this morning. Magic can do that. Heal instead of inflict. Soothe instead of torture. Hells, with one Green spell, it could even make Cemmy stop looking at me like I'm a monster.

The truth might do that, as well. The voice in my head has always been dangerously optimistic. If I tell her about Mags, then maybe she'd understand why I've had to align myself with Savian. If I tell her what he actually wants me to do with her palette, maybe she'd appreciate that a trip through the Dominion is better than having to watch me drain all her friends.

Or maybe she won't. I silence the voice with that spiked possibility. Because the real truth here—the only truth that matters—is that I can't risk telling her anything she could potentially use against me; her knowing about the journal is already complication enough. I've spent months working to ensure that Savian doesn't learn of my connection to Mags, I can't throw it all away now.

I have to keep being the monster.

And there's no version of this story that ends with Cemmy looking at me any other way—especially since I'm lurking in her room uninvited, with a whole delinquency of stolen power vibrating me like a snapped chain.

You really shouldn't be here. The moment she steals into the apartment, every nerve in my body stands to attention, my blood flooding with a frenzied mix of anticipation and dismay. *You should phase. Now. Phase now.*

But I don't phase.

I stay right where I am for what feels like an eternity, waiting, waiting, waiting for her to finish doing . . . *whatever* it is she's doing instead of coming into her room, the magic in my veins all but searing its way out of me. Too hot. It's suddenly burning too hot and too livid, turning the world crimson on every side.

I hear the door swing open.

Taste the fragrant cut of soap in the air.

Feel the sharp crack of tension as Cemmy senses my presence and lunges for the knife she keeps in the table beside her bed.

I don't think so. The spell-shocked frenzy reacts on my behalf, spurring me across the room until I'm no longer on my feet, but on the mattress, her hips pressed flush between my knees, her wrists pinned flat above her head, my hands forming solid shackles around them.

Oh shit.

"*Chase*?"

My name rips from Cemmy's throat, her pupils blowing wide at the sight of me, not just with surprise, but fear. Deep and incensing.

"You're afraid of me now." The question blunts to a jagged statement, my anger lending it a spiteful edge.

"Look where you are—where *I* am." She bucks beneath me, gritting the words through clenched teeth. "How did you think I'd react?"

Only then do I realize what she was doing while I was pacing restlessly around her room. Why her hair is damp around my fingers, and why she smells of lavender and rose scented shampoo. Why she's wearing little more than a threadbare nightshirt.

Double shit.

Cemmy was bathing.

I caught her getting ready for bed.

"No, you're not afraid that I'm here." Despite the bareness of her legs and the compromising distraction of too-thin fabric, I can tell she's not worried about *that.* This flavor of dread reeks of a wholly different fear. "You're afraid of what I can do," I say, and Gods, the hypocrisy of it only serves to heighten the red swimming across my vision. "What's the matter, Cemilla? Can't handle the pain you created?" I hiss. Not because I want to scare her, but because I'm on the verge of losing control of the magic and I can't stomach the way she's looking at me—like I'm every wicked word that's ever been hurled at a Gold. Dangerous. Untrustworthy. A threat. All those damning accusations people love to level at me even as they seek to exploit my power.

"*I* created?" Even now, she refuses to see it.

They always refuse to see it.

"You wanted a wisdom spell, didn't you?" Her eyes are two treacherous sapphires in the dark, the defiant warmth of her feeding an already rampant delirium. "And—let me see if I can remember your exact words—*whatever other spells are going*?" I parrot her request with as much vitriol as I can muster. "Where did you think those spells would come from, Cemilla? Did you think they'd come for free?"

Cemmy doesn't need to find her voice for me to glean the answer: she didn't think about it at all.

They never think about it.

Never spare a thought for what their twisted asks might cost *me.*

How hot the magic might burn.

Way too hot. Way too impossibly, viciously, overwhelmingly hot. To the point that I can no longer contain the whims of this furious tempest; it's spilling right out of me. Roaring, rushing, releasing, arching Cemmy's body into my touch. She gasps, and the sound is like putting a match to tinder, dousing the wood with kerosine and taunting the magic to ignite the flames.

"You never said your gift did that to Shades." Her reply is a breathless whisper, barely audible over the frenzied pounding of our hearts. Too close together. Too riled, and too frantic, and too ensnared by the heady press of flesh and color to recognize the wrongness of this moment and break apart.

"And you never thought to ask." My growl echoes through us both. "I told you it would kill a half Shade, but you didn't want to think about that." *They never think. They never think. They never think.* "You wanted the magic you wanted when you wanted it, and you didn't care how it would affect anyone else. You didn't care how it would affect m—" The shake in my limbs stays my tongue before it can break rank and solicit her sympathies.

I don't need Cemmy's pity.

I don't need some half-baked platitude, or an apology she doesn't really mean.

The only thing I need is for her to *see.*

And for her to rid me of this godsforsaken color. My grip on the magic continues to slip and slip and slip, the outpour crushing every part of us together. *Too hot. Too hot. Too hot.* The heat is threatening to rend right through my skin. Splinter my bones. Drive me insane.

"Chase, you need to stop. I don't—you need to stop this."

Her words send an acute pain shooting through my temples.

"No. I need to get the magic out," I say, though I force myself back from her just the same, the realization that I've crossed some invisible line turning my blood cold. "Please, Cemmy. He made me take too much. You have to help me get it out." My words are a broken plea. Because I was wrong: I don't need for her to *see*, I need for her to *understand.* I need for her to trust me.

"Okay." With a nod and a rustle of sheets, she rises up to meet my desperation head on, the fear in her eyes replaced entirely with worry, molten and warm. "Tell me what to do."

The relief trembles me from head to toe, the air between us crackling with power.

"Just let me give you some of this color." I press my hand to the nape of her neck, trying to ignore the sudden intimacy of the moment. How much closer she feels now that we're sitting face to face in the darkness. The alluring hiss that escapes her lips as her head falls back against the wall and the sharp cut of her nails as they bite deep into my forearms, the magic driving her hard against me.

Mags, you're here to save Mags, I remind myself. I can't afford to get distracted by an entirely different Hue—no matter how tempting that idea might be, or the relentless ache of longing it sparks inside my bones. *That's just the magic talking.* I focus on purging my veins of this indomitable blight. Once I get the color out, this . . . *pull* will go away. This haze will go away, too, and the feeling that I'm falling, falling, falling under her spell. That despite every reason I have not to, I *want* to fall.

Since when did want *have anything to do with it?* Even as my thoughts grow fuzzy and the room around me begins to dim, the starkness of my reality remains clear as crystal. A Gold doesn't get to want—we only get to take.

Take to survive.

Take to barter.

Take to live.

In some way or another, I have been taking from others since the day I manifested my gift. But right at this moment—as the darkness takes me—I can't help but marvel at how much better that magic feels to give.

Acknowledgements

I don't know how I've gotten to this point for the third time in three years . . . but somehow, it happened. I wrote another book. I didn't die doing it. My sister really is right: I'm just a drama queen who whines a lot.

You know who else is always right? My wonderful publishing team—who not only allowed me to keep writing books, but to make the transition from sci-fi to fantasy so seamlessly.

Thank you to my wonderful agent, Andrea Morrison at Writers House, who first saw this book back when it was still a contemporary fantasy set in New York (don't ask) and pushed me to leave my comfort zone and bring this second world heist to life. Thank you to my absolute wizard of an editor, Molly Powell at Hodderscape, who then took that book and helped make it fully realized. I often joke that if you love a scene, there's a 50/50 chance it didn't exist before Molly got her hands on the manuscript. Which is obviously a joke since that number is probably closer to 70/30.

I also need to thank my wider Writers house team—Alessandra Birch and Cecilia de la Campa—who have worked tirelessly to take this book places. And to my wider Hodderscape team: Kate Keehan, publicist extraordinaire, for making sure my books get to all the right places, Laura Bartholomew, for all the incredible work behind the scenes, Sophie Judge, for handling every tedious request and keeping me on schedule as the moving parts of this book started biting, and Calah Singleton, who is somehow always tasked with keeping me out of trouble when they let me out in the world. I appreciate you all more than I can say.

Then we have the invisible hands that make sure the book you get is the best book it can be on a technical level. My copy editor: Alyssa Ollivier-Tabukashvili, my proof reader: Sharona Selby, my authenticity editor: Philippa Willitts, and my typesetter: Claudette Morris.

Oh, and if you knew nothing about this book and only picked it up thanks to the cover, well that's the work of the unbelievably talented Jeff Langevin (illustration) and Natalie Chen (design). At every step of the design process, I experienced a total failure of imagination for what this cover should look like—so it's a good job I had you both to see the vision for me.

To the wonderful Illumicrate team: it's no secret that being in a monthly box has been a long-time dream of mine, so thank you for making it come true—and for a truly stunning special edition. It's an honour to be able to call myself an Illumicrate author.

And now we get to the people who kept me sane while writing this book. I'll start with Saara, who is both an incredible friend and a relentless champion of my work. You make me better. In every way. I couldn't have written this book (let alone on time) without you. To Tasha: I owe you both a thank you and an apology. Thank you for always shipping the wrong characters and making me 'update' the plot accordingly. Sorry for ruining the big twist 35 seconds before you got to it. That was a special kind of special, even for me. Thank you to Sam, who'll happily confirm that I'm using words in all the wrong ways—while at the same time staunchly defending my right to do so. To Alice for being my partner in all Hodderscape related crime. To Hannah for all the D&Ms on my couch—and for teaching me not to touch the fly tape. Lesson most definitely learned (lol as if, I will definitely touch the fly tape again). To Cherae, Tori, Meg, Jesse, and Daphne—you are all a delight and I'm so grateful to have you in my corner. To all my friends in London, I'm so lucky to have so many of you to lean on (and write with, and cry with, and try new cafes with). And to my online friends (you know who you are), I really couldn't have done this without the community we've built together—with a special thanks going out to Anna Sortino, who helped me brainstorm a few key parts of this book, and to Chandra and LC for dropping everything to read and tell me if the twist worked.

To all the booksellers and book creators who've supported me throughout this journey—Laura Dodd at Forbidden Planet, Harveen Khailany at Goldsboro books, Victoria Alyesa at Alyesasworld, Hannah Kingsley at Kingdom book designs, and every wonderful indie and Waterstones bookseller I've been fortunate enough to meet so far—thank you so much for all your ongoing support, it truly means the world.

A huge thank you, as always, goes out to my family, who have remained my number one fans no matter how surly I get around deadlines (and these days I am always on deadline and surly).

And to every reader who's made it this far: whether you stumbled upon my work during my pink era, my blue era, or this new fantasy era, I thank you from the bottom of my heart for every read, shout out, DM, review, kind word, and hello. You are the reason I do this—and the reason I get to keep doing this. I hope we get to *keep* doing it together for many more years to come.

WANT MORE?

If you enjoyed this and would like to find out about similar books we publish, we'd love you to join our online Sci-Fi, Fantasy and Horror community, Hodderscape.

Visit hodderscape.co.uk for exclusive content from our authors, news, competitions and general musings, and feel free to comment, contribute or just keep an eye on what we are up to.

See you there!

@HODDERSCAPE HODDERSCAPE.CO.UK